Hearts of Gold

BY THE SAME AUTHOR
Without Trace (under the name Katherine John)

HEARTS OF GOLD

Catrin Collier

CENTURY

LONDON SYDNEY AUCKLAND JOHANNESBURG

First published in Great Britain in 1992 by
Random Century Group
20 Vauxhall Bridge Road, London SW1V 2SA

Century Hutchinson South Africa (Pty) Ltd
PO Box 337, Bergvlei 2012, South Africa

Random Century Australia Pty Ltd
20 Alfred Street, Milsons Point, Sydney, NSW 2061
Australia

Random Century New Zealand Ltd
PO Box 40–086, Glenfield, Auckland 10
New Zealand

The catalogue data record for this
book is available from the British Library

Phototypeset by Intype, London

Printed in Great Britain by
Mackays of Chatham Plc, Chatham, Kent

ISBN 0 7126 4606 X

For the people who lived in Pontypridd and on the Graig during the depression. Especially my grandmother Nurse Katherine (Kitty) Jones, *née* Johns, who worked in the Graig Hospital during those difficult years, and my father Glyn Jones, who did so much to guide me back into her world.

Acknowledgements

I apologise in advance for the length of this acknowledgement, but I owe a great debt to those survivors of the depression in Pontypridd who gave me their time, and generously shared with me their most personal and precious possessions – their memories.

My father Glyn Jones, who spent a year talking to everyone he knew in Pontypridd (and a few he didn't) in an effort to track down those who lived and worked there during the thirties. Not to mention the days and weeks he drove around with me, noting and explaining all the changes that have taken place since the depression. (And not only in the pubs.)

My mother Gerda Jones, for providing bed and board, and for listening patiently while my father and I tried to recreate a world that disappeared long before she came to Wales.

My aunt and uncle, Grace and Evan Williams, who still live on the Graig, in the house where I grew up.

My father's oldest friends, Cyril and Nellie Mahoney, who helped me from the outset, when this book was no more than a single scribbled idea in a notebook. It was their rich fund of stories that inspired me to take the project further.

All the staff of Pontypridd Library, especially Mrs Penny Pughe, who came in on her days off to help me with my research. They were working under incredible pressure and appalling conditions during the reorganisation of the library which took place when I was in the throes of trying to do my research. Without their heroic endeavours I would not have amassed anything like the material I now have to draw on.

Mrs Pat Evans, the librarian at East Glamorgan Hospital, for her time, help and unfailing sense of humour, and for putting me in touch with so many people.

Councillor Des Wood, a former Administrator of the Central Homes on the Graig, who drew up a detailed map and notes of the Homes as they were before they were rebuilt in the sixties (practically a book in its own right) and without whose assistance

I would never have finally tracked down the records of the old Graig Hospital.

Mr Colin Davies, who used to work in the Homes and who was kind enough to send me a booklet on the closing of the old Homes and the opening of the new Dewi Sant Hospital that stands in its place.

My family, old friends and neighbours from the Graig. Principally my cousin Marion who married into the fine Graig family of the Goodwins, and others whom I have not seen for many years. I always was an inveterate listener, even when they didn't know I was eavesdropping.

Marge Davies, the cousin my father rediscovered after more than half a lifetime, and who had so many stories to tell.

Jennifer Price for her unstinting, unselfish friendship and incredible generosity of spirit, and Margaret Bloomfield for her help in so many practical ways.

The best boss I've ever had, Jack Priestland, who doesn't mind me writing at work during the *quiet*? times.

My husband John and my children Ralph, Sophie and Ross, for their love, support and the time they gave me to write this book, and for not moaning, even when we drove around the Graig 'Again'.

And above all my editor Rosie Cheetham, who suggested that I write a book on my home town and steered it on course from the very beginning, and my agent Michael Thomas for his encouragement and many kindnesses.

Thank you.

I have taken the liberty of mixing real 'characters' such as 'Cast Iron Dean' who was well known in Pontypridd in the thirties with my fictional ones. The actual events involving the 'Forty Thieves' happened, and some women were sentenced to terms of hard labour for their involvement with the gang. However I would like to *stress* that all the main characters in this book, including those involved with the thieves, are fictitious, and creations of my imagination. If any reader mistakenly believes that they recognise themselves or a member of their family in any person depicted in this book, I can only say that I have tried to make my people representative of both the times and the place they lived in.

And while I wish to fully acknowledge the help I have received, I would also like to state that any errors in *Hearts of Gold* are entirely mine. I have tried to get at the truth wherever possible, but unfortunately many records have disappeared from the face of the earth, and the gaps have been filled in as far as possible by using newspaper accounts, and people's memories.

My hope is that the readers of this book enjoy this small glimpse of Pontypridd's past, as much as I enjoyed writing and researching it.

Catrin Collier, September 1991

Chapter One

'Bethan! Bethan!' Elizabeth rapped hard on the door of the bedroom that her daughters shared.

'Coming, Mam,' Bethan murmured sleepily. She listened as her mother retreated back to her own bedroom then, keeping her eyes firmly closed, she reluctantly forced her hand out of the warm cocoon of sheets and blankets to test the air. It was icy after the warm snugness of the bed, and she quickly pulled her arm back beneath the bedclothes for a few seconds more of blissful warmth.

'Bethan.' Once again Elizabeth's voice cut stridently through the frosty air.

'I'm up, Mam,' Bethan lied.

'I hardly think so.' Elizabeth opened the door and pushed the switch down on the round black box. Bethan screwed her eyes against the sudden glare of yellow light. It wasn't enough. Eyelids burning, she burrowed into the bed and pulled the blanket over her head.

'Breakfast in ten minutes, Bethan,' her mother's voice intruded into the warm darkness.

'Yes, Mam.'

She waited until she heard the fierce click of the iron latch falling on the bar. The third stair from the top creaked, then the seventh as her mother descended to the ground floor. Keeping her nose hidden beneath the blankets, she opened her eyes and peered sleepily at the room around her. Apart from a change of wallpaper, it hadn't altered since her grandmother had left it fourteen years before. The thick red plush curtains that had been hers hung, faded but well brushed and straight, at the windows. The old-fashioned Victorian mahogany bedroom furniture Caterina had inherited as a bride gleamed darkly against the heavily patterned red and gold walls. Her favourite Rossetti prints hung on the wall next to the wardrobe, and the pink glass ring holder, candlesticks and hair tidy that had been a present from her sons

1

stood on the dressing table. The room might now belong to Bethan and her sister Maud, but it was also an encapsulation of Bethan's earliest childhood memories.

She had toddled in here when she was barely high enough to reach the washstand. Crouching behind the bed, she had watched her grandmother wash and dress, and afterwards sit on the stool in front of the dressing-table mirror to brush out her hair. Rich, black, it was scarcely touched with grey on the day she'd died. Once Caterina had finished, she'd turn and smile. A warm, welcoming, special smile that Bethan knew she kept just for her. And then came the excitement of *the tin*. The old Huntley and Palmer biscuit tin in which Caterina kept her prized collection of foreign coins. Bethan had spent hours as a child, sitting on the cold, oilcloth-covered floor at Caterina's feet; playing with them, grouping them into armies, fighting strange and wondrous battles that she'd heard the grown-ups talking about – Mons, Amiens, the Somme . . .

Not only Bethan's, but also her sister's and brothers' happiest childhood memories stemmed from the time when Mam Powell had lived with them.

Evan Powell's mother, Caterina, had been a large, warm-hearted, old-fashioned Welsh widow who'd spent her life working, caring and cuddling (or *cwtching*, as they say in Wales) her family. True happiness for her had ended along with her husband's life; contentment vanished the day Evan brought his bride into the family home. She'd tried valiantly to conceal her dislike of Elizabeth, but everyone who knew Caterina also knew that she'd never taken to her eldest son's choice of wife.

In her shrewd, common-sense way Caterina had summed Elizabeth Powell *née* Bull up as a cold, arrogant, snobbish woman but, concerned only for Evan's happiness, she would have forgiven Evan's love any failing other than hard-heartedness. Fearing for the emotional well-being of her unborn grandchildren, it was she who persuaded Evan to set up home with Elizabeth in the parlour and front bedroom of the house that her collier husband had bought for under two hundred pounds in the 'good times' before strikes and the depression hit Pontypridd and the Rhondda mining valleys. And she did it in full knowledge that Elizabeth would destroy the peace and harmony that reigned in the household.

Elizabeth fought hard against Evan's suggestion of setting up home with her mother- and brother-in-law, but Evan remained firm. Quite aside from his mother's wishes, finances dictated compromise. Not a man to shirk his responsibilities, he accepted that it was his duty as eldest son to support his mother and his wife, and the easiest way he could think of fulfilling both obligations was by installing them under the same roof. Besides, in his acknowledgedly biased opinion, his mother's house was amongst the best on the Graig.

Certainly the bay-windowed, double-fronted house in Graig Avenue had more than enough room for all the Powells – three good-sized bedrooms, a box room, two front parlours and a comfortable back kitchen complete with a range that held bread and baking ovens as well as a hinge-topped water boiler with a brass tap from which hot water could be drawn. Doors from the kitchen led into a walk-in, stone-slabbed pantry and a lean-to washhouse. The washhouse opened into the yard that housed the coalhouse and outside WC (all its own, not shared). It was a palace compared to the back-to-back, two-up one-downs at the foot of the Graig hill.

What Evan didn't discuss with Elizabeth, or his mother, was the full extent of the mortgage on the house. He had been fourteen, and his brother William twelve, when their father had collapsed and fallen in front of a tram at the Maritime pit. Jim Owen, the pit manager, sent Caterina Powell ten pounds to cover the funeral expenses. It was good of him. She knew full well that as the accident was her husband's fault, she was entitled to nothing. The Maritime's colliers organised a whip-round amongst themselves and raised another fifteen pounds. It was the largest sum ever collected after a pit death, and a fine testimonial to Evan Powell senior's popularity, but it wasn't enough to buy his widow, or his sons, security.

Evan and William left school the day of the funeral, and Jim Owen took them on as boy colliers out of respect for their father. So they began their working lives where Evan Powell senior had finished his, and without giving the matter a thought they also assumed his obligations, paying his bills, his mortgage, and providing their mother with housekeeping, the only money she ever handled. And she, too grief-stricken to realise what was happening, allowed her eldest son to assume the responsibilities of the man of the house – responsibilities he shouldered with a maturity far beyond his years. Time passed, Caterina's grief healed after a fashion – and then came Elizabeth.

The major alterations to the domestic life of the Graig Avenue household after Evan and Elizabeth's marriage came in the shape of the additions they were blessed with. Bethan was born seven months after their wedding day, Haydn less than a year later, Eddie on their fourth anniversary, and Maud on Bethan's sixth birthday. Caterina and Elizabeth were soon too busy to quarrel, and the initial resentment Elizabeth felt at her mother-in-law's insistence on holding on to the domestic reins of the household faded with the birth of Haydn. The babies generated enough work to keep a dozen pairs of hands occupied, let alone two. And although neither woman learned to like, let alone love the other, seven years under the same roof did teach them a wary kind of tolerance.

The thunder of Haydn and Eddie's feet hammering down the stairs shook Bethan out of her reverie. It would be wonderful to lie here for another two or three hours, staring at the walls, thinking of nothing in particular, but duty and her mother called.

Maud stirred next to her in the bed. Pulling the blankets close about her ears, her sister burrowed deeper into the feather mattress, making small, self-satisfied grunting noises as she curled complacently back into her dreams. Bethan looked enviously at the mop of blonde curls, all that could be seen of Maud above the blankets. What it was to be thirteen years old and still at school. If Maud got up two hours from now she'd still make it to her classroom in Maesycoed Seniors by nine – but there was little point in wishing herself any younger.

Grabbing the ugly grey woollen dressing gown that her mother had cut and sewn from a surplus army blanket three Christmases ago, Bethan sat up and swung her legs out of the tangle of flannelette sheets and blankets. Five o'clock on any morning was a disgusting hour to leave a warm, comfortable bed. On a cold,

4

dismal January morning it was worse than disgusting. It was brutal!

For all of her five feet eight inches, her feet dangled several inches above the floor. Mam Powell's bed was higher than any hospital bed. Easy to make, but painful to climb out of when there was ice in the air. Sliding forward she perched precariously on the edge of the mattress and ran the tips of her toes over the freezing floor in search of her pressed felt slippers. She found one, then, standing on her left leg, the other. As she shuffled across the room she thought wistfully of the last film she'd seen in the White Palace.

Claudette Colbert had floated elegantly around a vast, dazzlingly pale carpeted, beautifully furnished bedroom in a creamy lace and satin gown that she'd casually referred to as a 'néglige.' The actress would probably sooner have died than don a grey woollen dressing gown and flat tartan slippers with red pompoms. But then, Claudette Colbert looked as though she'd never had to trek out to a back yard first thing in the morning in her life. If the newsreels and Hollywood stories in the Sunday papers were to be believed, film stars had luxurious bathrooms with bubble-filled baths the size of the paddling pool in Ponty Park. And they could afford to keep fires burning in their bedrooms all night without giving a thought to the twenty-two shillings a load of coal cost a miner on short time and rations.

She twitched aside the curtains and tried to peer through the coating of frost on the window pane. Breathing on the glass, she rubbed hard with the edge of her hand and made a peephole. The street lamps burned alongside the houses in the Avenue in a straight line. Golden beacons radiating a glow that dispelled the navy-blue darkness, and lit up the high garden wall of Danygraig House opposite. Dawn was still hours away. She studied the unmade ground of the street beneath her. It was covered with a fine layer of white, but there were dark shadows alongside the stones. Too thin to be snow. Frost, and that meant a cold slippery walk down the Graig hill to the hospital.

She left the window and heaved on the bottom drawer of the dressing table. It jerked out sluggishly, with the stickiness of furniture kept too long in a cold, damp house. Rummaging impatiently through the tangle of clothes, she searched for an

5

extra pair of black woollen stockings. Nurses, especially trainee nurses, were only supposed to wear one pair, but her legs had been almost blue with cold when she'd left her ward at the end of yesterday's shift, and there hadn't been frost on the ground then. She found the stockings and tossed them on to the pile of underclothes and uniform that she'd laid out on the stool the night before. Warm legs were worth the risk of an official reprimand, even from Sister Church.

Heaving the drawer shut with her foot as well as her hands, she went to the washstand. She picked up the unwieldy old-fashioned yellow jug decorated with transfers of sepia country scenes, and tried to pour its contents into the washbowl. Nothing happened. Shivering as the chill atmosphere permeated her dressing gown, she brushed her dark hair away from her face and looked down into the jug. Pushing her fingers into the neck, she confirmed her suspicions. A thick frozen crust capped the water. Even if she succeeded in breaking through it without cracking the jug, the thought of washing in chunks of ice didn't appeal to her. Pulling the collar of her dressing gown as high as it would go, she tightened the belt and left the bedroom, stepping down on to the top stair.

Unlike the bedroom, the stairs were carpeted with jute, held in place with three-cornered oak rods. She trod lightly on the third and fourth stair from the top. Their rods were fragile – broken when her brothers, Haydn and Eddie, had purloined them to use as swords after watching a Douglas Fairbanks film. The rods had survived the fencing match, but neither had survived the beating her mother had inflicted on the boys with them when she'd found out what they'd done.

The light was burning in the downstairs passage as she made her way to the back kitchen. Her father, mother and eldest brother were up and dressed, breakfasting at the massive dark oak table that, together with the open-shelved dresser, dominated the room.

'Good morning, Bethan,' her mother offered frigidly with a scarcely perceptible nod towards the corner where their lodger Alun Jones was lacing up his collier's boots. Alun looked up and for all of his thirty-five years turned a bright shade of beetroot.

Irritated, Bethan pulled her dressing gown even closer around her shivering body.

'Good morning,' she mumbled in reply to her mother's greeting. 'The water in the jug is frozen, so I came down for some warm,' she added, trying to excuse her state of undress.

In middle age, Elizabeth Powell was a tall, thin, spare woman. Spare in flesh and spare in spirit. Bethan, like her brothers and Maud, was afraid not so much of her mother but of the atmosphere she exuded, which was guaranteed to dampen the most lively spirit. Elizabeth certainly had an outstanding ability to make herself and everyone around her feel miserable and uncomfortable. But she hadn't always possessed that talent. She'd acquired and honed the trait to perfection during twenty-one years of silent, suffering marriage to Evan Powell. Her silence. His suffering.

At the time none of the Powells' friends or acquaintances could fathom exactly why Evan Powell, a strapping, tall, dark (and curly-haired with it) handsome young miner of twenty-three had suddenly decided to pay court to a thin, dour schoolmistress ten years older than himself. But court her he had; and the courtship had culminated a few weeks later in a full chapel wedding attended by both families.

Elizabeth's relatives had been both bemused and upset by the match. In their opinion Elizabeth hadn't so much stepped down in the world, as slid. True, she had little to recommend her as a wife. Thirty-three years old, like most women of her generation she was terrified of being left on the shelf. She certainly had no pretensions to beauty. Even then, her hair would have been more accurately described as colourless than fair. Her eyes were of a blue more faded than vibrant, and her face, thin-nosed, thin-lipped, thin-browed, tended to look disapprovingly down on the world in general, and Pontypridd and the working-class area of the Graig where Evan Powell lived in particular.

She was tall for a woman. Five feet nine inches, and William, Evan's younger brother, rather unkindly commented that the one good thing that could be said about her was she looked well on his brother's arm . . . from the rear.

Before her marriage Elizabeth had possessed a good figure, and she'd known how to dress. But when marriage put an end to her career as assistant schoolmistress in Maesycoed junior school it also put an end to the generous dress allowance that had been her one extravagance. Not that she came to Evan empty-handed. She'd saved a little money of her own to add to the small nest egg her mother had left her, and Evan, generous and self-sacrificing to the last, had urged her to spend that money, or at least the interest it accumulated, on herself. However, her Baptist minister father had fostered a spirit of sanctity towards savings within the confines of her flat breast that was matched only by the feeling of absolute superiority to the mining classes that he had engendered in her narrow mind. She would have as soon pawned the family bible as used her deposit account to buy smart or fashionable clothes.

Their marriage, begun as an anomaly, continued in silence. Evan never discussed his feelings with anyone, least of all his wife, and Elizabeth, disgusted with herself for falling prey to what she privately came to consider a sad lapse into 'bestial passion', never divulged what had attracted her to Evan. Evan was extremely good-looking, even by Pontypridd standards, where well-set-up strongly built colliers were the rule rather than the exception. Six feet three inches in his stockinged feet, with an exotic, swarthy complexion that he'd inherited from his maternal Spanish grandfather, he was just the type to excite John Joseph Bull's suspicions.

John Joseph was Elizabeth's uncle, the brother of her dead father. A Baptist minister too, he knew, or thought he knew, everything there was to know about lust, as those who heard his sermons soon found out: 'A devil-sent demon to lead the weak and ungodly astray into a foul world of naked, hairy limbs, lewdness and lechery.' Small children sat bemused as he railed against both sexes for their fragile, miserable morals. Unlike some of his colleagues he realised that women could fall prey to the temptations of that particular cardinal sin as well as men. As an active revivalist, evangelist and minister of God, his knowledge was not based on personal experience, but on years of watching and noting the depths to which the people who lived within the boundaries of his chapel's sphere could sink. He ascribed his interest in the human condition to charitable motives. Evan, who

8

was considered remarkably well read even for a miner, called it by another name. Voyeurism.

John Joseph's wife Hetty, a small, quiet, mousy woman some twenty years younger than he, had a sense of duty that extended into every aspect of their joyless married life, from the kitchen to the bedroom and the Sunday night ritual during which, after lengthy and suitable prayer, John Joseph lifted her nightdress – the only night of the week he allowed himself to do so.

Hetty was a paragon, but John Joseph saw enough miners' daughters and wives to know that other kinds existed. Some were even brazen enough to eye men while they sat in his chapel pews. He'd caught sight of them after the service, walking off shamelessly, arm in arm with their paramours into the secluded areas of Ynysangharad War Memorial Park, or up Pit Road where they disappeared into the woods around Shoni's pond.

The thought of his niece and Evan Powell following either route incensed and disgusted him. But Elizabeth Bull was way past the age when she needed a guardian's blessing to marry. He could do nothing except voice his disapproval. Which he did, long, loud and vociferously, both before and after the ceremony.

He'd refused to give Elizabeth away on the grounds that he wouldn't be an active party to her social demise. But his contempt for Evan and the mining classes didn't prevent him from officiating as minister over the proceedings. It also gave him the opportunity to speak at the small reception that his wife Hetty had dutifully arranged in the vestry. He saw himself as a plain-speaking man, but even Hetty, who was used to his harsh, God-fearing ways, cringed when he pointed a long thin finger at Elizabeth, glowered at her darkly and bellowed that he was glad, really glad, that his dead brother and sister-in-law were not alive to see their daughter sink so low.

Elizabeth recalled his words every day of her married life. They came to her even now as she looked around her kitchen and saw her daughter in a state of undress; the unhealthy colour rising in the lodger's cheeks as he surreptitiously ogled the curves outlined beneath the thin cloth of Bethan's dressing gown; her son and husband sitting at the table, boots off, not even wearing collars with their shirts. She felt that not only herself but her children had sunk to the lowest level of the working-class life she'd been forced to live, and had learned to despise with every fibre of her being.

'I'll draw the water for you, Beth.' Haydn smiled cheerfully at his sister as he pushed the last piece of bread and jam from his plate into his mouth.

'Thank you.' Bethan walked past the pantry and unlatched the planked door that led into the washhouse. Switching on the light she sidestepped between the huge, round gas wash boiler and massive stone sink that served the only tap in the house. Opening the outside door, she caught her breath in the face of the cold wind that greeted her, placed her foot in the yard and slid precariously across the four feet of iced paving stones that separated the house and garden walls, grazing her hands painfully in the process.

She gripped the wall, desperately trying to maintain her balance while she regained her breath. The drains had obviously overflowed before the frost had struck, and the whole of the back yard was covered in a lethal sheet of black ice.

'Sorry, Sis, I would have warned you, but you came out a bit fast.' She squinted into the darkness, and saw her youngest brother Eddie brushing his boots on the steps that led to the shed and to the square of fenced-in dirt where her father kept his lurcher.

'I bet you would have,' she replied caustically. Rubbing the sting out of her hands she inched her way along the wall until she reached the narrow alley in the back right-hand corner of the yard that led to the *ty bach* or 'little house' that held the WC. Protected from the weather on three sides by the house, high garden wall, and the communal outhouse wall they shared with next door, it wasn't quite as cold as the yard, and, thanks to the rags that her father had wrapped around the pipes and high cistern, the plumbing worked in spite of the frost.

The heat blasted welcomingly into her stiff and frozen face when she returned to the kitchen. Haydn was sitting on the kerb of the hearth filling her mother's enamel kitchen jug from the brass tap of the boiler set into the range.

'Mind you top that water level up before you go,' Elizabeth

carped at Haydn. 'I've no time to do it, and if the level falls low the boiler will blow.'

'I'll do it now.' Haydn winked at Bethan as he handed the steaming jug across the table. Six feet tall, with blond hair, and deep blue eyes that could melt the most granite-like heart, Haydn was the family charmer. His looks contributed only in part to that charm. His regular features were set attractively in his long face, and his full mouth was frequently curved into a beguiling smile, but it was his manner that won him most friends. At nineteen, he possessed a tact, diplomacy and apparent sincerity that was the envy of every clergyman, Baptist as well as Anglican, on the Graig.

'You won't be topping up anything unless you hurry,' Elizabeth complained sourly. 'It's a quarter-past five now.'

'The wagons won't be leaving the brewer's yard until seven. I've plenty of time to get there, persuade the foreman to give me a morning's work, and load up before they roll,' Haydn said evenly, carrying his plate into the washhouse.

'It'll take you a good half an hour to get down the hill in this weather.'

'Don't look for trouble where there is none, Mam.' Haydn returned with a full jug of cold water, and pinched Elizabeth's wrinkled cheek gently as he passed. He was the only one of her children who would have dared take the liberty. 'I'll be in Leyshon's yard before I know it, with all that ice to slide down.'

'Taking the backside out of your trousers like you did when you were a boy. Well I've no money to give you for new ones.'

'I don't expect you to keep me, Mam.' Haydn dodged past and walked over to the hearth.

Not content with the sight of Haydn doing what she'd asked, Elizabeth turned on Bethan.

'And you, miss,' she said sharply. 'You'll have to get a move on if you're to be on your ward at half-past six.'

'I'm going upstairs now, Mam.' Despite what she'd said, Bethan still hovered uneasily next to Haydn. 'I'll just get a dry towel.' She unhooked the rope that hoisted the airer to the ceiling.

'And you can leave that alone when you like. I put a clean towel upstairs for you and Maud yesterday.'

'Thank you, Mam. I didn't notice,' Bethan said meekly. She

11

had achieved what she wanted. Her father and Alun Jones had pulled on their coal-encrusted coats and caps, picked up their knapsacks, and were heading out through the door. If she succeeded in lingering in the kitchen for another minute or two she wouldn't have to embarrass Alun, or herself, again by walking past him in her dressing gown.

'Good luck, snookems,' her father said with a tenderness that her mother never voiced. 'Not that you need it.' Snookems – it had been a long time since he had called her that. On impulse she replaced the jug on the tiled hearth, reached out and hugged him. His working clothes reeked of the acrid odours of coal and male sweat, but neither that nor the coal dust that rubbed off on her face stopped her from planting a hearty kiss on his bristly cheek.

'Thanks for remembering, Dad,' she murmured. 'I need all the luck I can get today.'

'Not you,' Haydn commented firmly, picking up the rag-filled lisle stocking that served as a potholder. 'You've done enough studying in the last three years to carry you to doctor level, let alone nurse.'

Bethan moved out of the way as he lifted the lid on the boiler. Clouds of steam filled the kitchen accompanied by a hissing, sizzling sound as water splashed over the hotplates as well as into the boiler.

'That's right, make a mess of it,' Elizabeth moaned. 'Just after I've blackleaded the top.'

'Looks like I have. Sorry, Mam,' Haydn apologised cheerfully. 'If you leave it, I'll clean it off this afternoon.'

'As if I'd leave it . . . '

'We're off then, Elizabeth,' Evan said softly, pushing the tin box that held his food and the bottle that held his cold tea into his blackened knapsack.

'About time,' she said harshly, angry at being interrupted.

'See you tonight, Bethan,' Evan murmured as he and Alun left the kitchen.

As soon as Bethan heard the front door slamming behind them she grabbed the jug and ran down the passage and up the stairs before her mother could find anything else to complain about. When she reached her bedroom she found the door closed and the room in darkness. She switched on the light and carried the steaming jug over to the washstand.

'I thought you'd gone,' Maud mumbled sleepily from the depths of the bed. 'I had to get up to turn off the light.'

'Sorry. Go back to sleep.' She tipped the hot water into the bowl and took the soap and flannel from the dish. The marble surface of the washstand was cold, the flannel encrusted with ice. Shivering, she stooped to look in the mirror while she washed, wishing herself shorter and more graceful, like Maud or her best friend and fellow trainee nurse, Laura Ronconi.

She was huge. Big and clumsy, she decided disparagingly, as she sponged the goose pimples on her exposed skin. Life was completely unfair. She was the eldest, why hadn't she been blessed with Maud's looks? Her younger sister was a fragile five feet four inches, with the same angelic blue eyes and blonde hair as Haydn. Not yet fourteen, she had the quiet grace of a girl on the brink of attractive, elegant womanhood. While she had a dark, drab complexion, and the height of a maypole.

She finished washing, tipped the water into the slop jar beneath the stand, and began to dress. Her hair wasn't *too* bad, she decided critically, studying the cropped black glossy waves, which Maud had coaxed into a style that wouldn't have disgraced an aspiring Hollywood starlet. And her eyes, large, brown and thickly fringed with lashes, were passable. Her mouth and nose were *all right*, taken in isolation, the problem came when the whole was put together. Particularly her enormous shoulders. Wide shoulders looked good on her father, Eddie and Haydn, but they looked dreadful on a woman. Life would be so different if she'd been born pretty. If not small, fragile and blonde like Maud, then at least petite, vivacious and dark like Laura.

The chill damp of the bedroom penetrated to her bones. Turning her back on the wardrobe mirror she pulled on her clothes as fast as she could. Chemise, liberty bodice, vest, long petticoat, fleecy-lined drawers, two more petticoats, one pair of stockings. She picked up the second pair and noticed a hole. Unrolling one of the stockings from her leg she reversed them, donning the one with the hole first, trying valiantly but vainly to manipulate the hole to the sole of her foot.

Uniform dress, belt with plain buckle; she tried – and failed –

13

to suppress an image of herself wearing the coveted silver buckle of the qualified nurse – apron, cuffs, collar and finally the veil that covered her one good feature, her hair. Marginally warmer, she stood in front of the oval mirror on the wardrobe and tried to see the back of her heels. There was a noticeable and definite light patch on her right heel. She debated whether to remove the extra pair of stockings, but the cold decided for her. If she was lucky Sister Church would be too busy, or too cold herself, to spend time checking the uniform of her final-year trainees.

'Could be your last day as a student nurse.'

Bethan looked from her reflection towards the bed. Maud's eyes were open.

'You're tempting fate,' she retorted.

'You're more superstitious than Mam Powell ever was. I'm tempting nothing,' Maud said grumpily. 'If you don't pass, no one will.'

'Well I'll find out soon enough.' Bethan hung her dressing gown in the wardrobe, and folded her nightdress before stuffing it under the pillow on her side of the bed. 'See you tonight?'

'If Mam will let me, I'll bake a celebration cake.'

'Don't you dare.'

Bethan switched off the light and left the room. Running down the stairs, she lifted her cloak from the peg behind the front door and returned to the kitchen.

'You're not leaving yourself much time to eat your breakfast,' Elizabeth complained as she walked through the door.

'I'm not that hungry.' She pulled a chair out from under the table. The kitchen was hot and steamy after the bedroom. Oppressively so. She cut a piece of bread from the half-loaf that stood, cut side down, on the scarred and chipped wooden breadboard that had been a part of the table furniture for as long as she could remember. The farmer's butter that had been bought on Pontypridd market was warm and greasy in its nest on the range, and the blackberry jam she had helped her mother make last autumn was freezing cold from the pantry.

'I suppose you'll get your results today,' her mother observed as she poured out two cups of tea.

'I hope to.' Bethan pushed her chair closer to the range so she could make the most of its warmth while she ate. The boiler and fires in the hospital were banked low with second-grade coal that smouldered rather than burned, barely warming the radiators and covering the yards with smut-laden black smog. She cut her bread and jam into small squares and began to eat. Elizabeth sat opposite her, sipping her tea with no apparent enjoyment. Bethan didn't attempt to talk. She'd never been close to her mother and didn't miss intimate conversations with her, because they'd never had one. Her father had always tried to help with her problems. He'd given her all the childhood hugs, kisses and treats that she'd received at home, and if she needed a woman to talk to now, she went to Laura or her Aunt Megan.

A month after Evan and Elizabeth's marriage, Evan's younger brother William began courting Megan Davies. Megan was the antithesis of Elizabeth. To use Caterina Powell's terms, she was 'a nice, warm-hearted Welsh girl, who knew where she came from' (a reference to Elizabeth's refusal to acknowledge her own mother's working-class roots). The daughter and sister of policemen, Megan Davies was smaller, prettier and stronger-willed than Elizabeth, and she point-blank refused to move into the Graig Avenue household. She wouldn't have minded sharing a home with Caterina, in fact she probably would have welcomed the opportunity, as her own mother had died when she was twelve, leaving her with a father and six brothers to look after, but as she put it baldly to William, 'I would as soon move into the workhouse as into the same house as Elizabeth.'

It was left to Evan to solve the problem. Unbeknown to Elizabeth, he took a morning off work, saw the bank manager, and extended the mortgage on the house so he could buy out his brother's share. Elizabeth was furious when she discovered what he'd done and, martyr to the last, took every penny of her hitherto untouched savings and paid off as much of the debt as she could. A lot more than Evan's pride was damaged by her gesture, but tight-lipped he said nothing and complained to no one.

Blissfully ignorant of Evan's pain, Megan and William were ecstatic. They put down a payment on a small, flat-fronted, terraced house in Leyshon Street. Its front door opened directly on to the pavement. A long thin passage (when she saw it Megan cried, 'God help if you're fat!') led past the tiny, square front parlour to the back kitchen. A lean-to washhouse, two skimpy bedrooms, a box room, and a back garden big enough to accommodate the coalhouse, outside WC, washing line, and precious little else comprised the rest of the house. But Megan and William were over the moon. Three streets down the hill from Graig Avenue, they were close enough to visit William's mother and brother whenever they wished, and far enough away to avoid Elizabeth – for most of the time.

Elizabeth disliked Megan from the first, not least because she had rich brown hair and eyes, a clear, glowing complexion and a slim petite figure that looked well in the discounted clothes that she bought from the shop where she worked. Pregnancy took a heavy toll on Elizabeth's health and looks, and by the time William and Megan fixed a date for their wedding she was on her second. Stubbornly refusing Evan's offer of a Provident cheque to buy a new outfit on the grounds that they couldn't afford the shilling in the pound a week repayment, she went to the wedding in a baggy old maternity dress that she knew full well he hated.

Her Uncle John Joseph, who did the honours for William and Megan as he'd done for her and Evan, publicly pitied her, telling her how ill she looked in a booming voice that carried to every corner of the chapel. Satisfied with her sacrificial gesture, she refused to enter the Graig Hotel where the reception was being held, and returned to the house with her baby, secure in the knowledge that she had ruined the day for Evan and upset Caterina. But the wedding was only the first of many irritants that Megan introduced into her life.

Although Megan had come from Bonvilston Road, which was across town and as alien to the people of the Graig as distant places like Cardiff, she was instantly accepted into the community. Elizabeth felt the slight keenly. Despite the fact that she'd lived most of her life in and around Pontypridd, everyone on the Graig referred to her as 'the young Mrs Powell' to differentiate between her and Caterina. In a village where first-name terms were the rule rather than the exception the title was an insult, particularly when Megan was Megan from the outset. As popular, well liked and accepted as Caterina, Evan and William.

Elizabeth burned at the injustice of it all. In the early days of her marriage she'd desperately tried to please her neighbours.

She'd joined several of the committees of her uncle's chapel. She'd visited the sick, cleaned the vestry, organised Sunday-school outings, and even offered to coach backward children with their school-work. But in doing all of that she'd failed to realise the potency of her neighbours' pride. Rough, untutored, self-educated, they earned their weekly wages the hard way, and held their heads high. Taught from birth to scorn 'charity', they mistrusted the motives that lay behind her overtures. And she, schooled by her father and uncle in 'charitable deeds', was incapable of helping people from a sense of fellowship or kindness simply because she'd never possessed either of those qualities.

It never crossed her mind to blame her own shortcomings for her isolation from the community. Uncultured and uneducated as her neighbours were, they could sniff out those who condescended and patronised a mile off, and she continued to condescend and patronise without even realising she was doing so. Outwardly she and Evan were no different from anyone else. They had no money to spare or to 'swank' with. In fact between the demands of her children, the mortgage, and what Evan gave his mother, most weeks she was hard put to stretch Evan's wages until his next pay-day. But close acquaintance with poverty did nothing to diminish her sense of superiority. If anything it entrenched it, along with her longsuffering air of martyrdom.

A year or two passed and she gave up trying to make friends of her neighbours. She decided she didn't need them. After all, they were hardly the type of person she'd associated with in training college, or during her teaching days. Instead she concentrated on domestic chores, filling her days with the drudgery of washing, cooking, cleaning, mending and scrubbing. Making herself a slave to the physical needs of her family, and keeping herself and them strictly within the bounds of what she termed 'decency'. But in the daily struggle whatever warmth had once existed between herself and Evan was irretrievably lost.

When war broke out and flamed across Europe in 1914 it affected even Pontypridd. In the early days before conscription some men, including miners, volunteered, sincerely believing they were marching to glorious battle and an heroic personal future that would return them to their locals by Christmas (with luck, covered with enough medals to earn them a few free pints). Evan knew better. So did William – when he was sober.

William and Megan celebrated their fourth wedding anniversary in 1915. Caterina looked after baby William, and William, excited by his and Megan's first night out together in a long time, went to town. They started the evening at six o'clock in the Graig Hotel then gradually worked their way down the Graig hill, via every pub, until they reached the Half Moon opposite Pontypridd Junction station, and just the other side of the railway bridge that marked the border between the Graig hill and town.

Concerned about the state William was getting himself into, Megan stuck to shandy; and even then she sat out a couple of rounds. There were over a dozen pubs either on or just off the Graig hill, and William had a pint in every one. Before he'd married Megan he'd been capable of drinking almost any man in Pontypridd under the table and walking a straight line home afterwards. What he hadn't taken into account was his lack of practice at sinking pints since his marriage. When money was tight, the man's beer was generally the first thing to go, and Evan had warned him, 'The price of getting a woman into your bed is every coin in your pocket.'

William was an inch or two shorter than Evan, but he was still a big man, and she worried about getting him home. Megan suggested that they catch the second house in the New Theatre. As it turned out, William didn't need much persuading. He was having difficulty in standing upright, let alone walking, and he loved the music hall. In his genial, euphoric state he treated himself and Megan to one shilling and threepenny seats in the stalls. It was an unprecedented extravagance that changed his life. If he'd bought his usual sixpenny gallery seats he wouldn't have been able to reach the stage as easily as he did.

The musical acts were good, very good. There was a ventriloquist, an American jazz band, and an extremely attractive blonde soprano who burst into rousing choruses of patriotic songs. Unfortunately for William, and a good ten per cent of the men in the audience, she was joined on stage by a recruiting sergeant, who beckoned them forward. Mesmerised by the blonde, and singing at the top of his voice, William took up the invitation. Happy, drunk and on stage for the first time in his life, he signed the paper that the sergeant thrust under his nose – and found himself an unwilling conscript in Kitchener's New Army.

Megan cried, but her tears softened nothing but her cheeks. William was shipped out that same night. She received a couple of abject, apologetic letters, then a postcard emblazoned with a beautifully embroidered bluebird, holding an improbably coloured flower in its beak and a banner proclaiming 'A Kiss from France'. A week later an official War Office telegram was delivered to her door in Leyshon Street:

'Regret to inform you Pte William Powell killed in action.'

His commanding officer wrote to her, a nice enough note that told her little about William's life in the army or the manner of his death. Six lonely, miserable months later she gave birth to William's daughter. She named her Diana after a character in one of the Marie Corelli novels that she'd borrowed from Pontypridd lending library.

Megan wasn't one to break under grief. She had two children, and a war widow's pension that wouldn't even cover the cost of the mortgage. Ever practical, she asked for, and got, a job scrubbing out the local pub in the early morning. But even that wasn't enough, so she put two beds in the front parlour, and took in lodgers. It wasn't easy to work even part time with little ones to care for, and Caterina used Megan's plight as an excuse to leave Graig Avenue and move into Leyshon Street.

Evan paid another visit to the bank manager. He took out a third mortgage on the house, this time for the maximum that the manager would allow, and insisted on giving his mother every pound that he'd raised. Elizabeth was devastated, and not only financially. Not realising how much she'd come to rely on her mother-in-law's assistance with her children, she'd barely tolerated Caterina's presence whilst they'd lived together, but after Caterina left, she felt her loss keenly. That, coupled with the crippling increase in the mortgage repayments, gave her yet another reason to feel rejected and ill used by Evan's family.

Bethan was six, Haydn five, Eddie two and Maud a baby when their grandmother moved into their Aunt Megan's house. They missed her warmth, her love and her cuddles, but fortunately Megan's was within easy walking distance even for small legs, and for once in his life Evan stood up to Elizabeth, overrode all her objections and actively encouraged his children to visit his mother and sister-in-law.

Much to Elizabeth's chagrin Evan also developed the habit of dropping into Megan's whenever he walked the Graig hill. The neighbours began to fall silent when she passed. She sensed fingers pointing at her behind her back; whispers following her when she left the local shops. She didn't need her Uncle John Joseph to tell her that, in Graig terms, 'Evan had pushed his feet under Megan's table'.

As jealousy took its insidious hold, Elizabeth reacted in typical martyred fashion. She became colder, and at the same time a more efficient housewife. Whatever else was being said, she made certain no one could cast a critical eye at her house or her children. Everything and everyone within the confines of her terraced walls shone and sparkled as only daily rubbing and scrubbing could make them.

In time the inevitable happened, the gossip-mongers tired of talking about Megan and Evan, and turned their attention to other things. But Megan, young, attractive, footloose and fancy free, was never out of the limelight for long. Interest in Evan was superseded by interest in Megan's lodgers, particularly one Sam Brown, an American sailor turned collier who'd made his way to Pontypridd via Bute Street, Cardiff, and the first negro to live on the Graig. Caterina's presence in Leyshon Street kept Megan just the right side of respectability – just – because other gentlemen callers besides Evan and Megan's brother Huw found their way to her door.

The most frequent visitor was Harry Griffiths, a corner shop-keeper. By Pontypridd standards Harry was comfortably off, by Graig standards he was a millionaire. Popular, and well loved by his customers because he and his father had almost bankrupted themselves by financing the grocery credit accounts of the miners during the crippling, hungry strikes of the twenties, he could do no wrong in the eyes of his neighbours. Megan couldn't have picked a better 'gentleman friend' if she'd tried. He was married, but the gossips had long since discovered that it was a marriage in name only as his wife refused to give him 'his rights'. They lived above his shop, which was housed in a large square building that dominated the corner of the Graig hill and Factory Lane.

Old Mrs Evans, who lived in rooms above the fish and chip shop opposite, saw him pulling the curtains of the box room less than a week after his wedding, and it wasn't long before everyone on the Graig became acquainted with the Griffithses' sleeping habits, as Mrs Evans continued her reports at regular intervals. The old iron *single* bedstead in the box room acquired a fresh coat of paint and a blue spread. Harry's clothes were hung on hooks behind the door, and a rag rug laid over the bare floorboards.

Mrs Evans was obliged to adjust her hours, and change to a later bedtime when Harry took to eating supper every evening with Megan in Leyshon Street, but then, as she whispered to Annie Jones who worked in the fish shop, 'A man's entitled to a bit of comfort, and if he can't get it at home, who can blame him for straying.' Certainly not the women whose credit was stretched by Harry when their husbands fell sick or were put on 'short time' by the pit owners. Megan had steeled herself to face worse. Fingers were pointed, but not unkindly. Only Elizabeth gave her the cold shoulder, but the relationship between her and Elizabeth was so strained already, she barely noticed the difference.

The war widows on the Graig generally fell into one of two categories. There were those who became embittered, afraid to love anyone, man, woman or child, lest they suffer loss again, and there were those like Megan who were prepared to reach out to anyone who needed them, hoping that in doing so they would, in some small way, assuage their grief. Megan found enough love and understanding for everyone she came into contact with. Her children, her mother- and brother-in-law, her nieces and nephews, her lodgers, her friends, her neighbours – her generosity became a byword on the Graig and an object of Elizabeth's scorn.

When Caterina died after a short bout of pneumonia Elizabeth expected her children to stop visiting Leyshon Street, but if anything their visits became more frequent. It was as if Caterina's death drew the children, Evan and Megan closer together, and shut out Elizabeth all the more. Caterina had always been the one to contact Elizabeth, and invite her to all the family births, deaths, marriages and celebrations. After she died Megan never climbed the hill as far as Elizabeth's house again, although she cleaned the Graig Hotel, which was practically on the corner of

Graig Avenue, six mornings a week; including, much to Elizabeth's disgust, Sunday mornings.

Bethan, like her brothers and sister, learned early in life that if she wanted, really wanted, anything other than plain food and carbolic soap and water she would get it in Leyshon Street, not at home. After Caterina's death Megan assumed the role of family confidante that had been Caterina's. And it was Megan who presented Bethan with her first lipstick and pair of real silk stockings, on her all-important fourteenth birthday. Thrilled, Bethan had rushed home to show them off. Tight-lipped, Elizabeth took the items from Bethan's trembling hands and threw them into the kitchen stove. Bethan retreated sobbing to the bedroom she shared with Maud, and later, when Evan came home from work, he wormed what had happened out of her.

He said nothing to either his wife or his daughter, but on payday Elizabeth's housekeeping was short by the amount he'd taken to replace Megan's gifts. Elizabeth learned her lesson. From that day forward she confined her disapproval of Megan and her presents to verbal lashings, nothing more.

Whenever Bethan, Maud or the boys returned from Megan's with something in their hands, Elizabeth would enquire coldly if it had been bought with Harry Griffiths' money. The children too learned their lesson. They hid the presents Megan gave them and ceased speaking about their aunt, their cousins or the visits they made to Leyshon Street in their mother's presence. So Bethan and her brothers grew up: unwilling participants in a conspiracy of silence.

Bethan learned about subterfuge before she even went to school. Whenever she did anything she knew her mother would disapprove of she ran to Caterina and later to Megan who would make it come right. She knew she could count on her aunt and grandmother to mend her dresses, or replace the pennies she lost on the way to the shops. They wiped her tears, and slipped her a few coins for treats and school outings when Elizabeth wouldn't, and until Bethan left home at fourteen years and three months old to work as a skivvy in Llwynypia Hospital she never questioned how her Aunt Megan, a widow with two children of her own, could afford to be so generous to her nieces and nephews.

22

And even when she was old enough to look at Harry Griffiths and see the answer in his frequent visits, she couldn't find it in her heart to condemn her aunt.

She loved Megan far too much to do that.

Chapter Two

'It's ten minutes to six,' Elizabeth said loudly, looking at the grease-stained face of the black kitchen clock that had been a wedding present from her Uncle John Joseph.

'I know, Mam. I'm not meeting Laura until six.' Bethan finished her tea and opened the cupboard set into the alcove between the range and tiny square of window that looked out on to the walled-in back yard. She took her toothbrush from the cracked coronation mug that held all the family brushes, and went into the washhouse. Rubbing the brush in the thick damp grains of salt that were spread out on an old saucer, she cleaned her teeth thoroughly under the running tap.

'Five to six, Bethan.'

'Yes, Mam.' She returned to the kitchen, replaced the brush and put on her cloak.

'I suppose you'll be late tonight.' Elizabeth's pronouncement was more of a condemnation than a question.

'I don't think so.'

'There's no celebration arranged then?'

'Not straight after work, Mam, no. If . . . ' She crossed her fingers behind her back, not to irritate Elizabeth, who abhorred all things superstitious. 'If I pass, we'll celebrate at the hospital ball tonight.'

'You're going then?'

'I said I was, Mam,' Bethan replied patiently.

'Fine state of affairs,' her mother railed bitterly. 'In my day a young girl would sooner die than be seen entering a public hall where drink was sold.'

'It's a ball, Mam. Doctor John and his wife are going, and Matron, and Sister Church.'

Elizabeth sniffed loudly to emphasise her disapproval.

'I'll be home about seven then,' Bethan said quietly with a touch of her father's resignation in her voice.

She laced on the boots she'd cleaned the night before, and

exchanged the warmth of the kitchen for the cold of the passage. The wind seared, needle sharp, into her face as she opened the front door. Drawing her cloak close, she stepped cautiously on to the doorstep and slammed the front door.

A frost haze haloed the street lamps, and her breath clouded foggily in her face as she pulled on a pair of knitted gloves. Placing one foot warily in front of the other she descended the sloping path and half-dozen steps that led down to the Avenue. Setting her head against the wind she walked in the shelter of the high wall that fronted the terrace. Large iron keys protruded from the doors, as they had done ever since she could remember. No one locked themselves into their home in Graig Avenue; the neighbours would have labelled anyone who tried 'strange'. A knock, followed by the turning of the key, was all that was needed to gain admittance to any house – although the neighbouring housewives seldom exercised their prerogative at Elizabeth's door.

Thin layers of ice cracked and crunched beneath her boots as she picked her way along. The one good thing about unmade roads was that they were easy to walk on in cold weather. The frost dried the mud so it didn't dirty boots, and the rough stones broke up any dangerously large expanses of ice.

Laura Ronconi was waiting on the corner, half hidden in the shadow of the high wall that fronted the six more forbidding grey houses at the beginning of the terrace.

'Today's the day,' Laura smiled brightly, her dark eyes gleaming in the light of the lamp above her.

'I've been trying to forget that ever since I got up.'

'You've nothing to worry about.' Laura led the way down the hill towards the main road. A shire horse, its nose and flanks steaming in the cold morning air, stood placidly, blinkered and harnessed, in front of the dairy as Alwyn Harries, a slightly deaf hunchback with a gammy leg, manhandled the milk churns on to the back of the cart.

'Good morning, Mr Harries,' Bethan shouted loudly, the clouds of her breath mingling with that of the horse.

'Morning, Nurse Powell, Nurse Ronconi.' He tipped his flat cap to both of them. 'Colder than yesterday.'

They nodded agreement as they went on their way.

The Graig hill was steepest at its foot, where it left town. That's not to say that it wasn't steep elsewhere. The incline from Graig Avenue to Danycoedcae Road, the last road built across the mountain side, and the street where Laura lived with her enormous family, was also lung-burstingly steep. Even the fittest men who took the short cut up through Iltyd Street, and the rough sheep track, were winded before they reached their goal. But the road below Graig Avenue flattened out, and the incline remained gentle until you reached Griffiths' shop on the corner of Factory Lane. So the two girls had no difficulty in crossing the Avenue below the dairy, rounding Vicarage Corner and out on to Llantrisant Road.

The frost on the main road had dissipated in the heavy morning traffic. Work began early for the fortunate few – those miners who'd been lucky enough to hold on to at least some of their six-thirty shifts in the depression-affected pits – even on cold January mornings. And besides the miners, who left their beds confident that there was work to be done and a wage packet at the end of the week, there was a small army of men like Haydn, and Eddie, who left their houses before six every day, in the hope of finding a few hours' paid work loading brewery wagons, or helping out on the carts that left the rag pickers' yard on Factory Lane.

The hill was nowhere near as slippery as Bethan had expected. Ice still lay in patches, but where it had been thickest it had already turned to a damp slush that clung to her boots. Her only fear was that they'd be filthy before she reached the hospital and that would gain her yet another lecture and black mark from Sister Church.

'Good morning, Bethan.'

She looked up to see her Aunt Megan, pouring buckets of warm water over the doorstep of the Graig Hotel.

'Aunt Megan, it's lovely to see you,' she smiled.

'Good luck, bach. It is today isn't it? Your results I mean.'

'Do you know, you're only the second person to wish me luck.' Bethan ignored the bucket, mop and dirty water, and hugged her aunt.

'Don't do that, you silly girl, you'll dirty your uniform.' Megan pushed Bethan away with her red, work-roughened hands.

'I don't care,' Bethan laughed.

26

'Had a super dress in yesterday, your size too,' Megan whispered, holding her mop in front of her like a weapon. 'Red silk, just right for the ball tonight.'

'I might not be going,' Bethan protested.

'You will,' Laura chipped in. 'She's being silly, Mrs Powell. She stands a better chance than any of us.'

'Even if I do go, I don't need a new dress,' Bethan protested. 'I've hardly worn my ringed black velvet.'

'You've worn it to every hospital ball for the past three years,' Laura said indignantly.

'I'll do the silk at a special price. You can pay me sixpence a week,' Megan offered persuasively.

'It seems such a waste to buy evening clothes that are only going to be worn once or twice.'

'It won't do any harm to look,' Laura suggested. 'And I have to call in on you on the way home from work anyway, Mrs Powell. If that's all right of course. I was hoping you'd have something to suit me. Have you?' she demanded eagerly.

'I've a lovely gold net, and a blue taffeta, both small sizes. I'll hold them for you until tonight.'

'Would you? Gold net sounds stunning. It would look good in the ball description in the *Observer*. After the hospital board ladies, and doctors' wives of course. Nurse Ronconi, in a stunning creation of gold net,' she murmured dreamily.

'Don't tempt fate,' Bethan warned. 'You haven't seen the dress, and you might not be able to call yourself Nurse tonight.'

'Job's comforter.' Laura stuck out her tongue.

'I'll see you both about seven.' Megan threw the last of her water into the gutter.

'Thank you, Auntie.' Bethan kissed Megan on the cheek. Avoiding the puddles, she and Laura hurried on.

'I really do have to call in on your aunt tonight,' Laura explained breathlessly, running to keep up with Bethan's long strides. 'I'm out of powder, perfume and lipstick.'

'After what you bought before Christmas?' Bethan asked incredulously.

'It doesn't go very far.' Laura shrugged her shoulders. 'Particularly in our house. Just be glad you've only got one sister pilfering your things. It's murder having five.'

27

Bethan dropped the subject. Laura was one of eleven, six girls and five boys. But they'd never gone as short as some of the other Graig children. Their parents were Italian immigrants, and their father had progressed from selling ice cream from a handcart in Market Square, to owning two cafés. One in the centre of Ponty-pridd, which Laura's eldest brother Alfredo 'Ronnie' Ronconi ran; and one in High Street, just below the hospital. All the Ronconi children were well fed and dressed, and whatever they earned, they kept. Unlike Bethan. Her father, along with the other miners in the Maritime, had been put on a three-day working week at the end of last year and, as her mother was so fond of pointing out, no one could keep a family on what he brought home. He did his best. Like every short-timer and unemployed man in Pontypridd, he tried to pick up casual work on the days he was free. There was fair amount of it – the rag and bone carts, the market traders, the brewery yards. The problem was that for every hour's work there were a hundred or more men prepared to undercut their fellows, and boys like Eddie were more often successful than their fathers, for the simple reason that they were prepared to work for less money.

Bethan earned twenty-five shillings a week. If (she couldn't even bring herself to think when) she qualified, it would go up to thirty-five. Good money by any standard. She already gave her mother fifteen shillings a week, and chipped in to help with expenses whenever she could. She knew her father found it diffi-cult to live with the notion that she was contributing more than him to the family kitty, but neither of them had any choice. The mortgage had to be paid; and the expense of keeping the boys, not to mention Maud, grew heavier with their increasing sizes. On top of the cost of food, extra coal to supplement Evan's reduced collier's ration, gas and electricity, there was the question of the boys' clothes. Bethan had been saving for months to buy both of them decent suits and overcoats. She'd managed to kit Haydn out on Wilf Horton's second-hand stall on the market, but only because he was into a man's size, and men who were out of work were queuing up to sell their good clothes. Boys' clothes were different. Every family in Pontypridd was anxious to buy their sons good outfits in the hope that smart clothes would impress a prospective employer. Poor Eddie was walking around in an overcoat that didn't cover his forearms, and trousers that had been twice turned. She had twenty-five shillings hidden in a wooden jewellery box that Haydn had made her in the school woodwork class, but decent overcoats Eddie's size started at two guineas in Leslie's stores, the cheapest shop in town. And that was without a suit.

'You're quiet,' Laura observed as they passed the yellow-lit window of Harry Griffiths' grocery shop.

'I was thinking about Eddie. He needs a good overcoat in this weather. The one he's wearing is miles too small for him.'

'Didn't you see the *Observer* on Saturday? There's a sale on in Wien's. All ladies' blouses and jumpers are down to a shilling from four and eleven, and youths' lined overcoats down from twenty-nine and six to four and eleven. Sale starts this morning. Our mam intends to be first in the queue.'

'Youths' sizes will probably be too small for our Eddie.'

'Our Joe wears youth sizes and he's bigger than your Eddie.'

'Oh if only I wasn't working,' Bethan complained in exasperation.

'You could slip out lunch time.'

'We're not supposed to leave the hospital.'

'Goody two-shoes. I'll go for you if you like.'

'So you can get caught instead of me? Do you think they'll have anything left tonight?' Bethan demanded anxiously.

'They might and they might not. Isn't that your Haydn?'

Bethan looked down the hill and saw her brother climbing, cap in hand, dejectedly back up it.

'No work today?' Bethan commiserated.

'There were fifty in Leyshon's yard this morning. Old Prosser said I'd had more than my fair share and it was the turn of the married men. Can't argue with that, I suppose.'

'Could be just as well,' Bethan said, trying to cheer him up. 'I need you to do me a favour.'

'What kind of favour?' Haydn asked suspiciously, his pride bristling at the thought of taking charity from his sister.

'There's a sale on in Wien's. Laura says they're selling youths' overcoats for four and eleven. You know where I keep my money?'

'Yes.'

'Take it and see what you can get for Eddie. If you like it, Eddie'll wear it.'

'Beth, you shouldn't have to do this . . . '

'If you see anything for yourself, get that too. If you and Eddie look smart I know, I just know, you'll get jobs,' she pleaded. 'You can pay me back then. Think what a difference it would make at home if you two were in regular work?'

'You'll let me and Eddie pay you back?'

'Of course I will. You'll go then? To the sale I mean.'

'I'll go,' he agreed dully.

'Thanks a lot,' she smiled.

'We'd best run, Bethan.' Laura grabbed her arm. 'If we don't, Sister will have us for breakfast. Bye, Haydn.' Laura flashed a look, half shy, half coquettish in Haydn's direction.

'Your Haydn?' Laura began as soon as they were out of earshot.

'Yes,' Bethan murmured absently, trying to walk carefully and quickly around the slush at the same time.

'Is he still sweet on Jenny Griffiths?'

'As far as I know.' Bethan looked at Laura, wondering if she knew more about Haydn's affairs than her.

'Shame,' Laura sighed wistfully.

'Laura!' Bethan exclaimed. 'He's a year younger than you.'

Laura halted at the huge wooden gates of the workhouse, and gazed after Haydn's retreating figure. 'When it comes to some things, age doesn't matter,' she said, grinning suggestively.

'Your father and Ronnie been chaperoning you everywhere again?' Bethan asked as she led the way around the corner to the main gates.

'Absolutely everywhere!' Laura complained. 'This morning Ronnie shouted at me for saying good morning to the paper boy. And he's only twelve, poor lamb.'

'Poor you, more like it,' Bethan laughed.

'It's all right for you,' Laura said testily. 'Your father's quite human. I told Ronnie straight last night that Italian men only lock up their wives and daughters because they know from personal experience that Italian men can't be trusted to keep their hands off any woman between fifteen and thirty that they're not related to.'

'That must have gone down like a lead zeppelin.' Bethan smiled at the porter on gate duty as he waved them through.

'Remember Cardiff Infirmary?' Laura murmured wistfully. 'There I could talk to anyone I wanted . . . '

'And generally did.'

'You can't blame me,' she retorted. 'Not after being wrapped up in cotton wool by Papa and Ronnie until the day I left home. And to think I was stupid enough to come back. I must have been insane to have even considered it.' They crossed the women's exercise yard and made their way towards the towering, grey stone maternity block. 'And now look at me,' she continued to grumble, 'working on a maternity ward of all things, when I really want to nurse on men's surgical.'

'Last time I looked in, I didn't see any tall dark handsome men waiting to fall in love,' Bethan teased.

'Were there any fair ones?' Laura mocked, still thinking of Haydn.

'None that would have interested you.' Bethan opened the heavy oak door of the ward block that housed the maternity unit.

'Oh well I can live in hope. And who knows, if Frederick March or Gerald du Maurier is brought in, they may mix maternity up with men's surgical. And even if they don't, by the end of the day we'll know whether we're qualified or not. And if we are,' she lifted her eyebrows suggestively, 'we can always request a transfer.'

'You're a hopeless case,' Bethan laughed as they climbed the steep flight of stone stairs. 'I really must remember to warn my brothers about you.'

'Both of them?' Laura asked indignantly.

'Both of them,' Bethan retorted firmly, as she unfastened her cape and prepared herself for duty.

As far back as she could remember Bethan had wanted to be a doctor. The proudest day of her life was when she passed the entrance examination to Pontypridd girls' grammar school, the saddest when she realised that a drastic cut in miners' wages had robbed her father of sufficient money to keep her there. Her mother's unemotional, realistic attitude had taught her to accept the inevitable. Enlisting the aid of a sympathetic teacher she applied to every hospital in the area, and at fourteen left home to take up the position of a 'live-in' ward maid at Llwynypia Hospital in the Rhondda. When she was sixteen the sister on her ward recommended her for nursing training in the Royal Infirmary in Cardiff. And she'd loved it.

Laura arrived to train alongside her, and they'd shared a cubicle in the nurses' hostel. Both of them soon discovered that trainee nurses were treated worse than domestics. The work was hard, the split shift hours impossibly long, their superiors demanding, but Bethan found her patients and their ailments fascinating, and when things were really tough, Laura was always there with a joke to lighten the load.

During the three years she'd trained she and Laura had scarcely seen their families. Trainee nurses' holidays rarely coincided with Christmas or Easter, and summer visits to Barry Island on the train with the other girls, and winter window-shopping trips around Cardiff had taken up most of their fortnightly free afternoons. But just as they'd finished their third-year finals, Bethan had received a letter from her mother suggesting a move to the Graig Hospital so she could help out with family finances. Realising that Elizabeth would only have made the suggestion as a desperate last resort, she saw Matron, and applied for a transfer without giving a thought to what her own plans might have been. And Laura, always the supportive best friend, decided to make the move with her.

Times were hard for everyone, but when she returned home they managed. Her father had three days' work guaranteed in the Maritime every week. The boys had left school, although Haydn, like her, had dreamt of going to college, and both occasionally brought home the odd few shillings. However, it was her own and her father's much-reduced wages that kept the family going.

'Only sixty seconds of freedom left and then it'll be twelve hours before we can call our souls our own again,' Laura muttered as they shuffled into line behind the qualified nurses ready for the ward sister's inspection.

'Ssh,' Nurse Williams, one of the qualified nurses, admonished as the squeak of rubber-soled boots over linoleum heralded the approach of authority.

Both Laura and Bethan had found the Graig Hospital very different to Cardiff Infirmary. The first thing she and Laura had discovered was that the place was known by many names, any one of which was enough to strike fear into the hearts of the poor and elderly who were terrified of dying alone and abandoned in one of its wards. The name least used was the official one, 'The Graig Hospital and Infirmary'. In newspaper reports of its social and fundraising functions it was generally referred to as the Central Homes, because all the wards, although housed in separate blocks, occupied the same vast tract of land sandwiched between the railway lines at the bottom of the Graig hill.

Despite the efforts of the staff to educate patients, few people differentiated between the hospital wards and those of the homes, although they were run as separate units, the hospital dealing with the sick, and the homes with the destitute. The destitute and 'casuals' generally entered the site through massive, high wooden doors that fronted High Street, and the sick and maternity cases by the huge metal main gates situated around the corner in Court-house Street. To the locals, the whole complex was known by its Victorian name, 'The Workhouse'. And they, like their parents and grandparents before them, knew many who had entered its high-walled precincts only to leave for an unmarked grave in a derelict corner of Glyntaff cemetery.

Bethan and Laura had only ever worked on the maternity ward in the hospital. A VD ward, euphemistically described as the 'clinic' because one was held there two days a week, and wards for the terminally ill were housed in the same block as the maternity unit. On these wards were mainly miners, young girls, and children who'd contracted tuberculosis or one of the other severe, and often fatal, respiratory illnesses that haunted the mining valleys. A separate block behind the maternity unit held 'J' ward, a unit for children under three, sick, orphaned and those whose parents had been admitted as destitute.

J ward was the only ward in the hospital where the sick and 'parish' cases overlapped. The rest of the homes side was virtually a closed book to Bethan. She came across the inmates often; it was difficult not to. Squads of young, pregnant girls from the 'unmarried mothers' ward wearing the 'workhouse' uniform of grey flannel were often commandeered to scrub the miles of stairs, corridors and outside steps of the complex. If it wasn't the pregnant girls and women who were hard at work, then it was the orphans from Church Village homes who'd reached the age of sixteen without finding a foster parent, job or sponsor. The council had no other recourse but to send these 'adult orphans' to the homes, where they carried coal, laid fires, swept yards and washed bedlinen for their daily bread and marge until they found either a sponsor or a job. And with the town strangled in the grip of a depression that was vacating shops and bankrupting longstanding, respectable traders at an alarming rate, most of the inmates could be forgiven for believing that they were in the workhouse for life.

Those who could no longer pay their rent, the elderly who couldn't look after themselves, girls who disgraced their families – they all ended up in the Graig. Occasionally Bethan heard cries from the yards as families were split up. Men to the male, and women to the female casual wards, their children under three to J ward, those over three and under eleven to Maesycoed Homes, a couple of miles away, and those between eleven and sixteen to Church Village homes several miles away. The elderly went to the geriatric wards. In addition to these semi-permanent inmates, every evening Bethan and Laura passed lengthy, verminous queues of 'occasionals' waiting to sign into a casual ward for the night. Three hours of coal shovelling or stick chopping earned them a delousing, bath, evening meal, breakfast and bed. There were always more casuals in winter than summer, but if they were capable of walking, they signed themselves out the next morning. Even in a snowstorm.

The nurses on the casual wards had a more difficult job in many ways than the nurses in the hospital, but Bethan sensed a 'looking down' by the medical staff on those who worked with the destitute. It wasn't simply that they spent their days delousing patients, and supervising menial tasks; it was the lack of any 'real' medical work. Bethan knew one or two of them, widows or women with unemployed husbands, who'd been forced to take on the role of family breadwinner. She felt sorry for them and, when she wasn't too busy to think, wondered why they didn't

34

apply for a transfer to the hospital. One of the reasons could have been Lena Church.

Sister Lena Church was the martinet who ran the maternity ward. She'd been christened 'Squeers' by a nurse when a stage production of *Nicholas Nickleby* had played at the Town Hall. The name had stuck, and not only because she had a squint. If she had any saving graces, neither her nurses nor her patients had seen any sign of them.

'Homes side has rung through. Unmarried has gone into labour.' Sister Church paused in the doorway of the sluice room where Bethan was scouring bedpans. 'I only hope they're not sending her over too early. The last thing we need is workhouse clutter on this ward. When you've finished that, get the delivery room ready and the bath run. But mind you don't skimp on those bedpans to do it. There's enough cases of cross-infection without you adding to them.'

'Yes, Sister.' Bethan fought the temptation to bite back. Sister's commands were like sergeant-majors' orders, never a please or a thank you. But three years on the wards of Cardiff Infirmary had accustomed her to routine brusqueness. What she found difficult to accept was the underlying hint that any job entrusted to her would not be carried out properly.

Head down, she continued to scrub until she heard the squeak of Sister's rubber-soled boots walking past the door and down the ward that housed the mothers. Then she turned on the cold tap, rinsed and disinfected the pans, and stacked them on the shelf above the sink. She washed and dried her hands, mournfully examining their cracked and sore state before removing her rubber apron. Straightening her veil, she left the sluice room and turned left, out of the main ward into a corridor. She walked into the principal delivery room and reflected, not for the first time, that it was a miserable place in which to make an entry into the world.

Its one small-paned window overlooked an inner courtyard hedged in by high, grey stone walls which darkened the atmosphere even further. The room itself was half tiled with brick-shaped tiles. Time and countless trolley knocks had cracked and stained their surface, transforming them from white into a patchwork of grubby beiges and greys. A mahogany dado separated

35

the tiles from the upper wall, which was glossed the same sickly shade of green as the rest of the hospital. A grey metal bedstead covered by a pink rubber sheet was the only furniture. No table, no chair, no pictures on the wall to relieve the monotony, only a cumbersome radiator built on a gigantic scale, that ironically did little to warm the room. Bethan laid her hand on it. It was warmer than the air. Marginally. Rubbing warmth into her hands, she left the room to fetch bedlinen and a birth pack.

'Patient's on the stairs, and Sister's screaming because the bath isn't run.' Laura poked her head around the door. 'Here, I'll finish that, you sort out the bathroom.'

Bethan ran.

There was only one bathroom on the ward, off the same corridor as the delivery rooms and linen cupboard. It contained two baths. Bethan sat on the edge of the one nearest the door and pushed the wrinkled rubber plug into the hole. She turned on the hot tap. A thin stream of lukewarm, brownish water trickled into the tub, covering a bottom long since denuded of porcelain covering by the friction of countless bodies and scourings with Vim. As soon as she sat down, she realised how tired she was. She'd been on her feet all morning, and her nerves were stretched. A porter had mentioned that Matron was calling the final-year students into her office one at a time to give them their examination results. Bethan hadn't worked in the hospital long enough to know whether this was normal practice. If it wasn't, did it mean that the results were dreadful? If she failed would she lose her job, or would the hospital authorities give her a chance to repeat the year and try the examinations again? So much depended on Matron's recommendations in cases of failure, and Matron based her decisions on Sister's reports. She really should have made more of an effort to get on with Squeers.

Reaching out she fingered a thin wedge of foul-smelling yellow soap in the dish at the side of the bath. It fell to pieces in her hand, melted and watery.

'Powell!'

She jumped as though she'd been scalded.

'Yes Sister.'

'What do you think you're doing?'

'Testing the bathwater, Sister,' Bethan lied promptly, standing stiffly to attention. Three months' training on Sister Church's ward had given her an aptitude to tell untruths she wouldn't have believed herself capable of acquiring a year ago.

'I see,' the Sister echoed sharply. 'Well, while you're "testing the water", the patient is waiting at the door of the ward. Bring her here and supervise her bath. I'll turn off the tap,' she said coldly, as though she couldn't even trust Bethan to complete that simple task.

The wards in the maternity section led into one another, and Bethan walked quickly out of the side corridor into the room that housed the mothers. Pushing open the double doors at the end, she went into the nursery. She loved this ward, with its aroma of talcum powder and fragile new life, and normally took time to linger among the rows of placid pink babies tucked up in their cots. Even now, rushed as she was, her steps slowed as she glanced into the cot of baby Davies; a sweet little girl with a mop of dark curly hair who'd rapidly become the staff favourite, although none of them would have willingly admitted such favouritism.

'Nurse! Nurse!' The cry was accompanied by a furious knocking on the far door that led into the main corridor. She broke into a run.

'She's in a lot of pain, Nurse.'

'All right, Jimmy.' Bethan smiled reassuringly at the tall, thin gangly porter who'd been sent from Church Village homes to the Graig Hospital on his sixteenth birthday, and worked his way up from the status of inmate to porter, a position he'd held for over thirty years.

'Breathe deeply . . . ' Bethan looked from the pale, strained face of the young girl to Jimmy.

'Maisie. Maisie Crockett, Nurse,' Jimmy supplied anxiously.

'Maisie?' Bethan looked for a resemblance between the young girl who stood, hunched and trembling before her, and her old schoolfriend from Danygraig Street.

'You remember me then?' Maisie clutched her abdomen as another pain gripped her.

'Of course I remember you.'

'I've seen you around the hospital. I didn't think you wanted to know me,' Maisie gasped.

37

'Now why should you think that?' Bethan wrapped her arm around Maisie's thin shoulders.

'You know . . . this . . . ' Head down, humiliated by her condition and weakened by pain, Maisie cried. Harsh, rasping sobs that tore violently through her throat.

'Don't worry, Maisie,' Jimmy was almost in tears himself. 'Nurse will see you all right.'

The girl clung to his arm, reluctant to release her hold.

'Sorry, Maisie, but Jimmy can't come in here.' Bethan looked meaningfully at the porter and he prised Maisie's fingers away.

'Sister on the homes side said to tell you she went into labour four hours ago. Shouldn't be long now,' Jimmy whispered. Bethan nodded.

'You're going to have to be quiet now, Maisie. We have to walk through the nursery.' She turned and pushed backwards through the double doors. Maisie stifled her sobs as Bethan led her, head bowed, through the nursery and mothers' ward into the side ward. Sister Church was waiting impatiently in the bathroom. Wearing her most intimidating expression she looked Maisie up and down before turning to Bethan.

'Bathed, shaved and in the delivery room in ten minutes, Powell,' she barked.

'Yes, Sister.'

Used to life in the homes section, Maisie began to undress without being told. Sister Church left. Bethan followed her as far as the linen cupboard. Unlocking the door from a bunch of keys that hung at her belt she removed a coarse grey towel, white cotton shift, grey striped flannel dressing gown and a new cake of carbolic soap. When she returned Maisie was sitting, shivering, in the water.

'They shaved me before I came over,' Maisie said plaintively.

'In that case, shout as soon as you've finished washing, and I'll help you out of the bath. I'll be outside the door.'

'Thank you.' Maisie smiled for the first time, grateful for the unaccustomed privacy.

Bethan returned to the linen cupboard. A pile of sealed cardboard boxes were stacked close to the fire door. She took the top one and ripped it open; the stench of carbolic sent her reeling. Struggling, she dragged the heavy box to the cupboard and began to stack the tablets of soap, the old ones to the front, the new ones at the back. Squeers could return at any moment and she was a stickler for order, and what she called 'stock cycling'. It was understandable in the drug cupboard, but there seemed little point in doing it with soaps and linens.

'Matron wants to see you.'

Bethan started at the sound of Laura's voice.

'You gave me a fright!'

'Did you hear what I said? Matron wants to see you.'

'Matron . . . ' The implication of Laura's words sank in and she dropped the soap.

'Now look what you've done,' Laura complained. 'You've dented the soap, and smeared it all over Squeers' nice clean floor.' She bent down and scooped up the cakes that were scattered from one end of the corridor to the other.

'Have you been up?' Bethan demanded.

'P comes before R. Remember your alphabet.'

Bethan straightened her veil, and her skirt. 'How do I look?'

'Like you're scared to death. Go quickly, before Squeers comes and finds some excuse to keep you here.'

Bethan scurried out of the door. Fortunately Sister was occupied with a patient at the far end of the ward. She left the maternity section and ran through the female exercise yard to the administration block as fast as she decently could, straightening her veil and apron again when she reached Matron's door. She hesitated for a moment to catch her breath. The lights still burned in the corridor although the sun had risen hours ago. Not that she could see any of it, only dismal grey rain clouds that shone wanly through the high corridor windows.

Breathing easier, she stared at the top half of the office door. Her heart was pounding so fast she could hear the rush of blood drumming in her ears. She waited, counting slowly to ten. One . . . two . . . three . . . The door opened.

'I thought I heard someone. Come in, Powell, come in.'

Straightening her back, Bethan walked in. The office was warm and cramped, its painted walls running with condensation between the book-lined shelves.

'Sit down.'

Two upright chairs were set in front of the desk. Bethan took the one nearest the fire. A few moments later she regretted her choice. This fire, unlike every other in the hospital, burned with a resolute, radiant cheerfulness that scorched her legs.

'Right, Powell, let's see what we have here.' Matron eased her bulk into the comfortable, padded chair behind her desk and thumbed methodically through the pile of papers before her, leaving Bethan free to study the room and fall prey to every spectre of failure that rose from the depths of her imagination.

Alice George was far too intimidating a figure to acquire a nickname. No one in the hospital from the ward maids and porters to the senior doctors referred to her as anything other than 'Matron'. She ran the wards and supervised her sisters with a rod of iron that was as even-handed and fair as it was inflexible. Rules were her lifeblood. It was rumoured that she'd been seen reciting hospital regulations during a service in St John's church instead of the Lord's Prayer, and no one, least of all Bethan, had thought to question the story's veracity.

The unkind described Matron as fat; the kind, plump. She was a short, dark woman, with beady black eyes that overlooked nothing. Every speck of dust in awkward corners and every trivial misdemeanour committed by probationers and domestics came under her scrutiny. Laura had been called up before her more times than she cared to remember. Bethan, with her more careful ways and healthier respect for authority, had never been in her office before now.

'You know why I sent for you, Powell?'

Bethan slid nervously forward to the edge of her chair.

'The results of my final nursing examination?' she enquired hopefully.

Matron smiled in an attempt to lighten the atmosphere, but the gesture was wasted on Bethan.

'You've passed, Powell. With distinction. Your name came top of your year.'

Bethan slumped in her chair. She'd passed. She'd really passed!

'I've recommended you for midwifery training.'

'Pardon, Matron?'

'I've recommended you for midwifery training. It means another full year's study, and I warn you now, the examination for the midwifery certificate is not an easy one. But there's a shortage of good midwives, and I believe you have the makings of a very good one indeed. Afterwards, may I suggest, you complete the six months' public health course. That will qualify you to work as a health visitor. God only knows,' Matron added irreverently, 'there's an even greater shortage of those, particularly in this area.'

'The midwifery certificate.' As the words sank in so did their significance. Another full year on Squeers' ward.

'I know another year of study is an unappealing prospect, Nurse Powell' – 'Nurse Powell.' Someone in authority, someone other than the patients had actually said it – 'But you will be on full pay while you train. Thirty-five shillings a week and a further five shillings when you qualify. You don't have to make your decision now.' Matron rose majestically and walked out from behind her desk. 'Think it over, and when you come to a decision make an appointment to see me. But remember,' she cautioned, 'you haven't much time. The list of candidates has to be in by the end of the month. Should your decision be a positive one, the board would want to offer you a contract. One year initially.'

'Yes, Matron. Thank you very much, Matron.' Bethan struggled to regain her composure.

'Is there anything you want to ask me?' Matron enquired.

'I can't think of anything. Thank you.' Bethan fumbled her way to the door. If she trained as a midwife, the board would offer her a contract. On Squeers' ward! But if she passed, it would mean two pounds a week. Two pounds!

She turned back as she reached the door.

'I don't need to think it over, Matron,' she said quietly. 'I'd like to put my name down for the course.'

'Good,' Matron beamed in approbation. 'It will be hard. Studying as well as working full time. But I think you'll find it rewarding, and you've already proved that you have the aptitude. When you return to your ward ask Ronconi to come here.'

Dismissed, Bethan returned to the ward at a much slower pace than she'd left it. She walked round a squad of young men sweeping the outside paths, without really seeing them. Stepping over two unmarrieds who were scrubbing the corridor, she pushed open the double doors and entered the nursery where the babies were beginning to whimper. The twelve o'clock feeding time was still three-quarters of an hour away. It was just as well that the ward was virtually soundproof; another half an hour and the din would be unbearable.

'Sister said would you please go to the delivery room the moment you get in,' one of the ward maids ventured shyly as Bethan passed the table where the babies were changed. Bethan tickled the squalling baby in the maid's hands, before moving on. Laura was taking the mothers' temperatures.

'I'll finish that,' Bethan offered, washing her hands at one of the sinks. 'Matron wants to see you.'

'I'll have to finish it,' Laura moaned, 'you're wanted in the delivery room. Well?' she demanded.

'I've passed.'

'Knew you would,' Laura crowed. 'Go on, you'd better get into the delivery room before Sister has your guts for garters.'

'I'll take over, Ronconi,' Staff Nurse Evans offered as she came into the ward from her tea break. 'Congratulations, Nurse Powell, I heard about your distinction. Top of the year isn't bad,' she winked.

'Typical,' Laura griped with a grin on her face. 'Leaving nothing for the rest of us to do.'

'Going to study for your midwifery?' Nurse Evans asked.

'Yes,' Bethan stammered. 'Yes I think so.'

'You won't catch me doing any more studying,' Laura said emphatically.

'You haven't been offered the chance yet,' Nurse Evans laughed. 'Go on off with you, Ronconi, you too, Nurse Powell.'

Laura suddenly realised that she was on the brink of moving up from the ranks of the unqualified. She was leaving the ward as Ronconi, but she could return as Nurse. It felt good, very good indeed.

'You'd best gown and mask up before you go into the delivery room,' Nurse Evans warned Bethan. 'Looks like a difficult one.'

When Bethan finally entered, she found Sister Church, Nurse Williams, the other staff nurse on the ward, and a doctor huddled around the bed.

'Powell, at last.' Sister glared at Bethan above her mask.

'Sorry, Sister, I was with Matron.'

'So I've been given to understand. Well, if you'd be kind enough to assist Doctor John and Nurse Williams here, I can get on with my other duties.'

Bethan took Sister's place alongside the bed. Maisie was lying on her back, her eyes rolling in agony, and even Bethan's comparatively inexperienced eye could see that something was seriously wrong.

'Chloroform, Nurse Williams,' Dr John ordered.

His voice didn't sound right to Bethan. She looked at his eyes, all that could be seen above the mask, and he nodded to her. 'Nice to be working with you, Nurse Powell.'

Flustered, she looked away. One of the first lessons she'd learnt was that doctors *never* talked to nurses. They were incomparably above and beyond the nursing staff in every hospital hierarchy. Besides, this Dr John was most definitely not the Dr John she knew. This Dr John was taller, broader and, judging by his voice, a good deal younger than the tall, thin, grey-haired man who visited the ward three mornings a week and sent Dr Lewis out on his emergencies.

Uncertain whether to reply or not she looked down at the bed, where Maisie had caught hold of her hand.

'Bethan, is that you?' Maisie squeezed her hand forcefully.

'You know the patient, Nurse?' The doctor's voice was soft, carefully modulated for a sickroom.

'We were at school together,' Maisie gasped.

'Old friends are the best, Maisie. That was quick, Nurse Williams,' he said pleasantly as she returned with the chloroform mask and bottle. 'Right, Maisie, we're going to put you to sleep for a little while, and when you wake up the pain will have gone. Keep hold of Nurse Powell's hand . . . '

'Bethan,' Maisie pleaded plaintively.

'Right, Bethan's hand.' His eyes wrinkled in amusement.

'Congratulations, Nurse Powell.' Nurse Williams clamped the mask over Maisie's face. 'Top of the year and a distinction, I hear.'

Bethan mumbled a reply as the doctor prepared the chloroform drops. It would take her a while to get used to this camaraderie from the senior staff, particularly if compliments were going to be offered over patients' heads.

'Well done, Nurse Powell,' Dr John congratulated enthusiastically.

'I had no idea I was working with such nursing talent. Now, if you could take over from Nurse Williams and steady the mask with your free hand?'

'Yes, Doctor.' Bethan took the mask and pressed it gently over Maisie's nose. The girl's eyes rounded in fear.

'Don't worry, Maisie,' she murmured, 'you'll be fine. A few moments and it will all be over.'

Maisie clawed at the mask with her free hand. To Bethan's embarrassment the doctor placed his hand firmly over hers, then slowly, drop by drop, he poured the chloroform. Maisie's eyes clouded, and her hands fell limply on to the bed. Nurse Williams moved quickly. She hauled back the sheet and strapped Maisie's legs into the stirrups while the doctor scrubbed his hands and picked up the forceps.

'This is going to be tricky. I'd be grateful if you could try to hold the patient still.'

Bethan clamped her hands on Maisie's shoulders. She looked down and watched as the doctor extracted one tiny wrinkled leg, then another. An interminable wait followed, during which she found it difficult to breathe. The cap covering the doctor's forehead moistened with sweat despite the chill in the room. Maisie moaned, a low bestial cry, as he worked frantically to free the tiny body imprisoned within her. Then suddenly, without any further drama, he lifted his hands. In them was the small, waxy, silent white form of a baby.

'Nurse?' he demanded urgently.

Nurse Williams took the child, leaving him free to cut the cord. The moment he severed it, she forced her fingers into the baby's mouth, and held it upside down. Nothing! The doctor tore the gloves from his hands and held the child by the heels, hitting it lightly on the back with his free hand.

A thin, weak wail filled the room. Bethan breathed again. She'd assisted at too many stillbirths to take life for granted.

'It's a girl.' The doctor wrapped her gently in the coarse towel that Nurse Williams handed him. 'A little small, but all there,' he announced cheerfully.

'I'll take her to the nursery,' the staff nurse volunteered.

'And when you've deposited her there, have a well-earned rest. Nurse Powell and I can wrap up here.'

44

'Can you?' the staff nurse asked eagerly. She hadn't had a break since she'd entered the ward at six-thirty, and the thought of putting her feet up, even for ten minutes, seemed like heaven.

'Of course we can, and Nurse?'

'Yes, Doctor?' She hesitated in the doorway.

'Thank you for your help.'

The staff nurse positively purred at the unaccustomed praise. Slightly embarrassed, Bethan turned her attention to Maisie.

Dr John pulled down his mask. When Bethan glanced up, he was leaning against the wall, his head in his hands. He saw her looking at him and shook his head.

'I hate the touch-and-go ones,' he said drily. 'Six years as a medical student and I'm still not used to death.'

'Then you've only just qualified?' Bethan asked, without stopping to think that she was talking to a doctor.

'Last summer. This is my first job. I'm assisting my father.'

'Doctor John?' she blurted out.

'You've worked out the family connection?'

She tried, and failed, to think of a witty retort. She'd never been one for spontaneous repartee, not like Laura. Maisie moaned again, he moved over to the bed and checked her pulse.

'The lady's waking up. Let's hope there'll be no more complications.'

The next hour was a busy one, and Bethan learned that young Dr John was nothing if not thorough. He didn't leave the ward until Maisie regained consciousness, and she still had to wash, change and make Maisie as comfortable as a patient who has just given birth can be made. Even awake, the girl seemed to be in a stupor. Bethan chatted as she worked, telling her that she had a lovely little girl, and that she'd be seeing her soon, but she failed to elicit a response. Undeterred, she persisted in talking about the child.

'She's small but all right, and with care, she won't be small for long.'

'Am I going back to the unmarrieds ward?' Maisie whispered finally.

'Not just yet,' Bethan replied calmly. 'You'll be with us for at least ten days. I'll be passing your house tonight. Do you want me to call in —'

45

'No!'

That single word said everything. Bethan finished doing what she had to in silence. As soon as Maisie was ready for the ward, she called one of the maids and told her to summon a porter. By the time Maisie was safely bedded down in a side ward away from the 'respectable' married patients, it was three-thirty in the afternoon and Bethan was free to take her lunch break. She went to the ward kitchen, hoping to find fresh pies and pasties cadged from the Hopkin Morgan van that delivered to the main kitchen. She was disappointed. There was a quarter-full tray of stale iced buns and a pot of stewed tea. Nothing more. She couldn't do much about the buns but she drained the tea down the sink, tipped the leaves in the waste bucket and started again.

'Laura did well then?'

'She did?' Bethan looked up from the gas that she was trying to light, and saw Glan Richards, the ward porter, who also happened to be her next-door neighbour.

'She got a distinction. Of course she couldn't make it to top of the year like you . . . '

Bethan switched off the gas that was refusing to light, tore a piece off a bun and threw it at him. It hit his nose, fell into the open kettle and blossomed over the surface of the water.

'Now look what you've made me do,' she complained, emptying and rinsing out the kettle.

'What I made you do? You just wait until tonight.' He tried to grab her by the waist but, too quick for him, she ducked and moved away. 'You are going to the hospital ball aren't you?' he asked anxiously.

'Yes, but that doesn't mean I want to see you there,' she said tartly, sticking her tongue out at him.

Glan smiled, a winning smile that he practised in front of the mirror every night.

'Why fight me, Beth?' He put his hand on her shoulder. 'You know you can't resist me.'

She tried the gas again. This time it caught and she dropped the taper she was holding into the sink, but not before it singed the tips of her fingers.

'Resist you! Times like this I could quite cheerfully brain you,' she exclaimed feelingly, brushing his hand off her.

Glan's smile never wavered. He took her outburst in good humour. He was used to being put down by the nurses, especially Bethan whom he'd known since their mutual school days in Maesycoed Infants. Above medium height with well-developed muscles, brown curly hair and pleasant open features, he was fairly good-looking and proudly aware of the fact. He lived at home with his mother and his father, a bullying collier who tried to dominate every single aspect of his timid wife's and children's life, which was why Glan was the only one left at home. But even Mr Richards senior had failed to prevent Glan from growing a moustache and fancying himself as a second John Gilbert; a fantasy founded in a surfeit of Hollywood films viewed from the bug run in the White Palace.

'Come on, Beth,' Glan crooned in what he imagined to be a seductive manner. 'Walk home from the ball with me tonight and I'll show you the moon as you've never seen it before.'

'I'd rather give the ball a miss.'

'You can't miss the ball. Rumour has it you're going to be the guest of honour.'

'Laura!' Bethan reached past Glan and hugged her friend. 'Congratulations.'

'Of course I couldn't do as well as you . . . '

'No one could,' Glan echoed.

'Is that tea you're making, because if it is, I'll have a cup.' Laura pushed Glan aside and sat on one of the hard wooden chairs that were ranged opposite the sink. 'Qualified nurses can demand to be put on early tea,' she winked at Glan.

'I'm on late lunch,' Bethan griped.

'Poor you. Have you seen the new doctor?'

'I have,' Bethan concurred, her mouth full of stale bun.

'Isn't he wonderful?'

'If you like the smarmy kind.'

'Smarmy!' Laura exclaimed indignantly. 'Smarmy! Bethan, you're the limit. He looks like Ronald Colman and has the manners of the Prince of Wales.' The kettle boiled, and she tipped hot water into the teapot to warm it. 'He can carry me off any time he likes.'

'Who? Glan?' Nurse Williams asked innocently, walking into the kitchen.

'Nurse Ronconi is smitten by Doctor John,' Glan glowered indignantly, sticking rigidly to his position in the doorway in the hope of getting a fresh cup of tea.

'Young Doctor John?' Nurse Williams proceeded to lay out cups and saucers. 'Forget it, ladies. Remember hospital rules, no fraternisation between doctors and nurses. Besides, rumour has it he's spoken for. Anthea Llewellyn-Jones,' she divulged archly.

'Good. That leaves all the more for us porters,' Glan leered, lifting his eyebrows.

'All the more what?' Laura demanded testily.

'Good times,' he suggested mildly, retreating from the belligerent tone.

'Haven't you got work to do?' Nurse Williams enquired.

'I have.' He ducked out of the doorway.

'Exiled to tea in the boiler room,' Laura laughed.

'You're not serious about Doctor John are you?' Bethan asked Laura after Nurse Williams had made two cups of tea and taken them to Sister's office.

'Depends on what you mean by "serious". I love a challenge. Not that Anthea Llewellyn-Jones would be that. And then again I wouldn't mind going to the New Theatre with him, or a dance. Not the hospital dance of course, that's a bit public. But a Saturday hop in Porth or Treorchy out of sight of the gossips, not to mention my brothers, with an opportunity to cuddle up on the train on the way home, now that's a different proposition.' Her dark eyes sparkled with mischief. She loved winding Bethan up.

Bethan poured out their tea.

'If you're angling for Prince Charming, you'd better sort out a better golden coach than your brother's Trojan van for tonight.'

'That's the fairy godmother department.'

'If you ask me, Pontypridd's a little short on those.'

'Then I'll improvise. If that gold net that your aunt has fits, it'll do for a start. Just remember, Miss Top of the Year, I laid claim to him first.'

'You can have him.'

'Such generosity. In return I give you Glan.'

'You can't, you'll need him yourself.'

Laura looked quizzically at Bethan.

'According to the fairy story, Cinderella needs a rat to turn into a coachman.'

'And mice to turn into horses. Fancy coming to the boiler room with me?' Glan interrupted from the corridor.

'People who eavesdrop deserve to hear nasty things.' Bethan tipped the remainder of her tea down the sink.

'Two waltzes and you'll change your mind about that moon-light walk,' Glan whispered into her ear as she passed him.

'One outing with you will last me a lifetime, Glan Richards,' Bethan muttered over her shoulder, referring to a visit she'd made to the Park cinema in his company.

'We'll see,' Glan muttered darkly. 'We'll see.'

Chapter Three

Darkness falls early on the Graig hill in winter. By the time Laura and Bethan left the hospital at seven, the street lamps had been lit for hours, throwing yellow smudges of light into an atmosphere filled with needle-sharp darts of rain, and on to roads spattered with glistening pools of black water.

'It's freezing,' Laura complained, pulling her cloak tightly around her shoulders.

'No it isn't,' Bethan contradicted. 'If it was this would be hail not rain.'

'Always have to be so literal, don't you?'

'Now that's a big word.'

'It comes from having a brother who's taking his matriculation next year.'

'Tony?'

'Who else?' Heads down, they ran out of the gates and walked up High Street as fast as they could. 'Papa thinks he's going to be a priest, but Papa's going to be disappointed. Tony follows Ronnie. He likes the ladies too much.'

'At sixteen?'

'You're never too young.'

'Our Eddie's sixteen, and all he can think about is boxing.'

'That's what he tells you. Evening, Mr Smart, off to buy sweets then?' Laura asked cheerily.

'Terrible craving to have, and by the way, congratulations, Nurse Ronconi, Nurse Powell.' He tipped his hat to them as he entered Davies' shop, the busiest sweet shop on the Graig. There were large cracks between the floorboards in front of the counter, filed wide enough to drop betting slips down to the bookie's runner who waited in the basement to catch them. Bethan knew that both her brothers worked there whenever they could. Haydn told her they couldn't afford not to, it was too well paid. Five shillings for a day's easy work. But ever since she'd found out what they'd been doing to boost their contribution to the family

50

kitty, she'd lived in terror of a knock on the door. The police picked up the bookie's runners in turn, and she'd read in the Pontypridd *Observer* only last week that one had been fined ten pounds with an alternative of six weeks inside. If it had been Haydn or Eddie, it would have had to be prison. There was no way they could raise that kind of money without getting into debt, and Elizabeth wouldn't stand for that.

'Congratulations, Bethan, Laura.' A young girl dressed in a thin cotton frock totally unsuitable for the time of year spoke shyly to them as she lugged a basket of potatoes out of the greengrocer's.

'Here, Judith, let me help with that.' Bethan hooked her fingers around the handle.

'And what do you mean by "congratulations"?' Laura asked.

'Glan told Mam that you both passed your examinations and that you,' she pointed a grubby finger at Bethan, 'passed as high as you can go.'

'He did, did he?' Bethan murmured.

'Thank you, Glan,' Laura said warmly. 'What's the betting that we've nothing to tell our families when we get home.'

'Everyone's ever so proud of you.' Judith tried to pull the shrunken cardigan she was wearing higher round her neck. 'Mam said if I work hard in school, I could be a nurse.'

'I bet you'd make a good one too.' Bethan released her hold on the basket as they approached the junction of High and Graig Street. 'Mind how you go now.'

'Thanks, Bethan, I will.'

Cold and wet, they left the gleaming shop windows of High Street behind them and began the long climb up the hill. The street was busy with shoppers. Women or errand-running children, spending the pennies or, if they were lucky, shillings, that their menfolk had scavenged during the day. The less fortunate among them putting a small piece of boiling bacon or a slice of brawn 'on the slate' until dole or pay-day. Every shopkeeper on the Graig had a book that in theory was worth at least twice his weekly takings.

A few men, caps pulled low, collars high, sidled out of the pubs. As they passed the Morning Star Bethan glanced in and saw their lodger Alun Jones sitting in the corner with a red-haired, blowzy-looking woman.

'That will be one less mouth for your mam to feed tonight,' Laura commented. They crossed the road, chilled to the bone, scarcely able to breathe through the cutting, driving rain as they turned up the narrow gully that led into the middle of Leyshon Street. Bethan tapped Megan's door and turned the key, shouting as she walked through. William, Megan's eighteen-year-old son, poked his head out of the kitchen door.

'Nice line in drowned rats you've brought with you, Beth.'

'Less of your cheek,' Bethan warned. She was as fond of William as she was of her own brothers. Tall, dark and handsome like Evan, the similarity between him and his uncle had often caused comment, but only among those who couldn't remember his father.

'Look out, Mam,' he called to Megan. 'Mermaids coming.'

'Get on with you, Will.' Megan pushed him aside as she bustled to the door. 'You poor creatures, come in, sit yourselves down next to the fire, and have a good warm.' She moved a pile of clothes off one chair and the cat off the other. Bethan and Laura felt as though a furnace door had opened in front of them. Hot and humid, the damp cooking and washing smells of the kitchen closed around them like a scalding wet blanket. A pan of stew was bubbling on the range, and an appetising aroma of lamb and vegetables wafted above the other odours. Bethan sniffed the air appreciatively; she hadn't realised how hungry she was.

'Here, take off those wet things and have some tea with us,' Megan ordered.

'We'd love to, Auntie Megan,' Bethan said quickly, 'but we daren't. They'll be waiting for us at home.'

'You had your results then.' Megan crossed her arms over her overall breast pocket and beamed. 'Two distinctions, I hear.' She was too tactful to mention she'd also heard that Bethan had come top of the year, but her pride in her niece's achievements shone in her eyes.

'Congratulations, Bethan, Laura.' They both turned around and saw Hetty Bull sitting perched in the corner on a kitchen chair.

52

'Aunt Hetty, I'm sorry I didn't see you there,' Bethan apologised. 'How are you?'

'Fine,' Hetty said automatically with a small, shy smile. 'Your uncle will be so pleased for you.'

'She came out best in the year,' Laura said, pointing a wet thumb at Bethan.

'I knew you'd pass. I just knew it.' Megan brushed a tear from her eyes and hugged her niece. 'I only wish Mam Powell was here to see it.'

'Knowing didn't stop her from paying a fortune teller to make sure,' William interrupted. 'Congratulations, girl. I always knew you'd come for something.'

'And me?' Laura flirted provocatively.

'I'll try to stay well, and out of the Graig Hospital.'

'Can I hit him, Mrs Powell?'

'Be my guest, but it doesn't do any good.' Megan released Bethan, dried her tears, and opened a suitcase half hidden behind one of the chairs. 'Here, as you're pushed for time you can pick what you want out of these.' She lifted a couple of large flat cardboard boxes on to the table. 'And while you're looking I'll get your skirt, Hetty, and the dresses I promised the girls from upstairs.'

'How much are these?' Laura held up a box of powder.

'Large boxes ninepence, small sixpence, all the lipsticks are fourpence. The small bottles of Evening in Paris are sixpence, the large ninepence. The bottles of essence of violets are ninepence, but they're really big.'

'I don't know how you do it, Mrs Powell,' Laura commented as she opened the lid of the largest box.

'Special prices?' Bethan raised her eyebrows.

'I won't deny that I don't make as much profit out of you two as I do out of some of my customers, but I do well enough,' Megan said as she left the room.

'First time I've heard customers complain that the goods are too cheap.' William took a wide-rimmed, thick white china bowl out of the cupboard and helped himself to a generous portion of stew from the pan. 'Sure you won't have some?' He offered the bowl to Hetty, who retreated even further into her shell.

'That's very generous William, thank you. But I must go and

make the minister's tea. I have it here.' She patted a bag that contained half a pound of best sliced ham for him and a small portion of salted dripping for her.

'Have you seen Haydn?' Bethan asked, remembering the overcoat she'd asked him to buy for Eddie.

'Yes,' William said mysteriously. He set the bowl on the table, took a spoon from the drawer and sat down. Dipping the spoon into the stew, he lifted it slowly to his lips and blew on it.

'And?' Bethan demanded.

'He looked very well.'

'William!'

'Is he teasing you again?' Megan burst through the door, her arms full of dresses.

'Need you ask?' Bethan retorted.

'Not when you call him William. He's just like his father was. Infuriating.' A momentary fondness flickered in her eyes. 'Here, Hetty, this is yours. Mrs Morris took it in a good four inches at the waist. She said it's the smallest waist she's ever sewed for, and it's about time you put on a few pounds.'

'I've always been the same size, Megan,' Hetty said mildly. 'And thank you for arranging this. How much do I owe you?'

'Nothing, love, Mrs Morris said it only took her a few minutes to do.'

'Oh I couldn't . . . '

'Course you could.'

'Well thank her very much. And tell her if there's anything I can do for her she only has to ask. Well I must be on my way, the minister will be wanting his tea straight after the deacons' meeting and I mustn't keep him waiting.'

'See you soon, love. William, see Mrs Bull out.'

'Here we go.' William took Hetty's parcels and carried them to the front door for her. They looked slightly ridiculous, the small mousy woman trailing behind the tall strapping young man.

'I'll never understand why Hetty always refers to John Joseph as "the minister",' Megan said when she heard the door close. 'Do you think she calls him that when they're alone together?'

'Even in bed I should think,' Laura said wickedly.

'Poor woman probably sleeps at his feet,' William added as he returned to his stew.

'That's quite enough, William. Laura, this is the gold net.'

Laura dropped the lipstick she was holding back into the box. 'Oh Mrs Powell, it's lovely. Really lovely.' She fingered the layers of net, pulling them back to inspect the underskirt of cream satin. 'I've never seen anything like this on the ten-bob rail in Leslie's.'

'And you won't.' Megan dumped the rest of her load on one of the armchairs. 'It's from my special stock, and it's only seven and six.'

'Really! It's absolutely gorgeous. It simply *has* to fit. Can I try it on?'

'William,' Megan turned to her son, who was sitting engrossed in his meal, 'out.'

'Mam, it's freezing in the passage,' he complained.

'And these poor girls have just walked up the hill in the pouring rain. They need a warm more than you. Out.'

'Mam!' Even as he protested, William picked up his plate and spoon and left his chair.

'The stew will keep you warm,' Megan consoled soothingly.

'It'll freeze out there.'

'I don't mind changing in the washhouse, Mrs Powell,' Laura offered.

'You'll do no such thing, my girl.'

Laura had her cloak and dress off the moment William closed the door.

'This is for you, bach.' Megan opened a thin, flattish box. A mass of flame-coloured silk burst out. 'A present,' she said proudly. 'From all of us to a clever girl.'

'Auntie, I couldn't possibly . . . '

'Yes you could. Come on now, let's see it on you.'

It fitted Bethan to perfection. A long, low waistline skimmed her narrow waist and slim hips, flaring out into a flowing, floor-length skirt that swirled elegantly around her legs. The sleeves were short and full, cut on the same bias as the skirt. She walked up to the sideboard and stooped to peer at herself in the oval mirror that hung above it. The neckline was low, lower than anything she'd ever worn before judging by the three inches of woollen vest that protruded above it.

'Oh Beth, it looks perfect on you,' Laura cried. 'You can wear it with your black crocheted shawl. You know, the one your grandmother left you.'

'Here, you can't see yourself like that. Look at yourself properly.' Megan lifted the mirror from the wall, and held it sideways, tilting it, so Bethan had a full-length view. The dress was truly stunning. Even the soaking wet veil that covered her hair and the heavily ribbed lines of her bulky underwear couldn't destroy its impact.

'Please Auntie Megan, let me buy it off you?' she pleaded.

'You won't take a present from me, now?'

'Of course I will. But not this. It must have cost a fortune.'

'I'll get William to put in an extra shift,' Megan winked.

'Auntie . . . '

'It's from all of us, for passing.' There was a tone in Megan's voice that Bethan knew from past experience wouldn't brook further argument.

'Thank you. Very much,' she said quietly.

'And don't go hugging me.' Megan pushed her away. 'At least, not until you put the dress back in its box. Don't you know silk creases, you silly girl?'

'When you've finished admiring yourself, perhaps you'd care to pass judgement on me.' Laura stood in the only clear space in the room, behind the table and in front of the tiny window that overlooked the back yard.

'You sparkle like one of those glittering angels you get in Woolworth's to go on the Christmas tree,' Megan smiled.

'You look beautiful,' Bethan complimented sincerely.

'Only beautiful?' Laura complained. 'I was hoping for sensational.'

'You won't get that wearing those shoes and stockings,' Megan laughed, 'but it does fit well. The colour suits you. Brings out your complexion nicely.'

'I'll take it, Mrs Powell, and these two lipsticks, the large powder and the Evening in Paris scent.' She pulled a ten-shilling note out of her purse and put it on the table. Megan took down a tin emblazoned with Lord Kitchener's portrait from the mantelpiece, pushed in the note and counted out four pennies.

'Thank you, Mrs Powell.'

'Don't mention it, love.' Megan turned to Bethan. 'You've got the silk underwear I gave you for Christmas?'

'Yes, I've been saving it for tonight.'

'Good girl, and here's two pairs of silk stockings, one for each of you. My present and no argument.'

'Can I come back in?' William pleaded pathetically from the other side of the door.

'In a minute,' Laura shouted, as she and Bethan shed their finery and struggled back into their damp uniforms.

'If you want to dress here tonight, you can,' Megan whispered to Bethan as she opened the kitchen door.

'Nurse Powell, Nurse Ronconi.' Charlie, Megan's latest lodger, was standing in the passageway hanging up his working coat. William, soup bowl in hand, retreated up the stairs to make room for the women to walk out of the kitchen.

'They really are nurses now, Charlie,' he called out. 'They qualified. With distinctions,' he added emphatically in a singsong tone.

'My very good wishes,' Charlie said solemnly in his thickly accented voice as he shook the rain from his white-blond hair.

'Thank you,' Bethan replied stiffly.

'Your tea's all ready in the kitchen, Charlie.'

'Thank you, Mrs Powell. I'll wash before I eat.'

Bethan and Laura followed William's example and stepped up on to the stairs to allow Charlie to pass.

Light-footed and athletic, Charlie gave the impression of being much larger than he actually was. William, at six feet three inches, was a good five inches taller, but Charlie was much broader, his square-shaped body thickly roped with well-developed muscles. He had lodged with Megan for only two months, sharing the front parlour with Sam the negro miner who'd boarded with her for over thirteen years. Unusually for the Graig where everyone knew all there was to know about everyone else, no one knew anything other than what was obvious about Charlie; not even Sam who'd introduced him into the house after meeting him at a party in Bute Street, Cardiff docks.

Charlie had sailed into Cardiff on board an Argentinian meat ship. On the strength of that experience he'd talked himself into a job with a wholesale butcher who supplied the traders on

Cardiff market. Deciding to expand his business into retail and anxious not to offend his existing customers, the butcher rented a stall on Pontypridd market and offered Charlie the chance to run it on a commission basis. If Charlie was pleased at the trust his employer was placing in him, he didn't show it. He accepted the job in the same flat, unemotional way that he accepted everything life threw at him. First he found his stall, then he set about looking for lodgings in Pontypridd.

Those who worked alongside him on the market said he was as strong as an ox and could just about carry a dead one on his back. He helped anyone who wanted a hand with lifting heavy weights or setting up a stall, but beyond those bare facts, his life remained a mystery. No one even knew his first name. Megan and Sam had heard it and said that it was Russian and unpronounceable; after a few futile attempts they simply gave up trying, and when Wilf Horton on the second-hand clothes stall christened him Charlie, the name stuck. Despite his size, pale complexion and white hair, which was unusual in the Valleys, he had an uncanny ability to melt into the crowd.

Rarely speaking unless spoken to, and then never beyond the usual pleasantries, he lived on the fringe of Pontypridd life. The best that could be said about him was that no one had a word to say against him, the worst, that no one had a word to say about him at all. Megan, William and Diana, used to strangers living in their home, took to him at once, simply because he was quiet, clean and helped around the house without being asked. Bethan, for no reason that she could put into words, was afraid of him. Whether it was the nature of his job, or what she saw as an unnaturally cold expression in his pale blue eyes, prickles of fear crawled down her back every time she found herself in the same room as him.

She'd voiced her misgivings about Charlie to Megan and William but they'd laughed at her, especially William who, much to her embarrassment, had taken great delight in telling Charlie what she'd said. She drew little consolation from the Russian's continued distant politeness. It was enough that he knew what she thought. And that knowledge brought a blush to her cheeks whenever she found herself in his company.

*

Kissing Megan goodbye and shielding their new acquisitions under their cloaks, Bethan and Laura left Leyshon Street and cut up Walter's Road, past Danygraig Street, to Phillips Street. Although the backs of the houses in Phillips Street faced Graig Avenue there was no thoroughfare between the two roads. But there was Rhiannon Pugh.

Bethan and Laura climbed the steps of the first house in Phillips Street, knocked on the door, turned the key and walked into the passage.

'It's all right, Mrs Pugh, don't disturb yourself, it's only us,' Bethan called out.

Mrs Pugh hobbled to her kitchen door and opened it.

'Come in, come in.' Her broad smile of welcome was like winter sunshine touching a withered landscape. 'Nice to see you, girls. I've got the kettle on, all ready.'

'Sorry, Mrs Pugh, no time for tea today, we've got to get dressed for the hospital ball, but we'll have two cups tomorrow to make up for it,' Laura apologised.

'Heard that you both passed your examinations with flying colours,' the old lady smiled. 'Good for you.'

'They're so short of nurses they couldn't do anything but give us our certificates,' Laura joked as she led the way into the kitchen. 'Mm, fresh Welsh cakes, they smell delicious.'

'I baked them specially for you two. Our Albert used to love Welsh cakes.'

'In that case we'll make time to eat one,' Bethan said.

Rhiannon Pugh was a widow. Her only son Albert had been killed in the same pit accident that took her husband. Alone in the world, she was happy to allow her friends and neighbours to use her house as a thoroughfare between the three terraces of Leyshon Street, Danygraig Street, Phillips Street and Graig Avenue. Universal concern for the old lady's welfare meant that the short cut was put to frequent use.

Mrs Pugh took two garish blue and yellow plates from the dresser, and laid a couple of Welsh cakes on each.

'Here you are, girls, pull the chairs close to the range, it's cold outside.'

'And wet,' Laura complained, watching the steam rise from her damp cloak. She took the plate from Rhiannon's shaking hand and bit into one of the thick flat cakes. 'These are good,' she mumbled, her mouth full. 'You really must give our Ronnie the recipe for them.'

'The secret's in the kneading,' Rhiannon winked. 'I keep telling him that. The kneading. But mind, you need a good griddle iron. And then you've got to watch them.'

'You certainly do that, they're a lovely colour,' Bethan agreed.

'When you see your brother, Laura, thank him for the meat pie he sent up with Mrs Morris from the Avenue. I had it for my tea. Don't forget now.'

'I won't forget.' Laura popped the last piece of cake into her mouth.

'And you, thank your Haydn for the potatoes he brought me this afternoon, Bethan. He said Mr Ashgrove gave him more than your mother could use when he delivered for him this morning.'

'I'll do that.' Bethan followed Laura's example and swallowed the last of her cake. 'Thank you for the Welsh cakes, Mrs Pugh. See you tomorrow. Don't come out now, we'll close the door.'

'I will stay here if you don't mind, love. This damp doesn't help my rheumatism one little bit. See you tomorrow?'

'Same time. Bye.'

Laura and Bethan carried their dishes out to the washhouse and put them in the enamel bowl in the sink. They left, latching the door securely behind them. They weren't worried about the washing-up they'd created. Mrs Pugh had a lodger, Phyllis Harry, who worked as an usherette in the White Palace. She'd been engaged to Albert, Mrs Pugh's son and, more like a daughter than a lodger, she moved in after Albert's death and took care of whatever Mrs Pugh couldn't. And for Rhiannon Pugh's sake, she welcomed the neighbours who treated the house as a thoroughfare.

It was very dark in the garden, and Bethan and Laura fumbled their way up the steps. Graig Avenue seemed positively floodlit when they finally emerged opposite Bethan's house.

'Our Ronnie will take us down at half-past eight. We'll pick you up here to save you dirtying your shoes.'

'That gives me barely half an hour to have tea, wash, dress and do my hair,' Bethan complained.

'You don't need to do a great deal to yourself besides wear that dress. Sixpence says that Glan asks you for first dance.'

'He can ask all he likes,' Bethan laughed.

She ran across the road and up the steps. Opening the door, she shook out her cape and hung it up. She was depositing the box containing her precious dress and stockings on the floor of the front parlour when her father called out.

'That you, Beth love?'

'It is.' She made her way to the kitchen. It was warm and humid just like Megan's and Mrs Pugh's. The table was laid, and a pile of the same type of thick earthenware soup bowls that William had used were warming next to a simmering pan of faggots and mushy peas on the range.

'Heard you passed.' Her father waylaid her and gave her a hug. 'Clever girl.'

'Aren't I just?' She kissed his cheek.

'Knew you'd do it.' Her brother Eddie came up from behind and tapped her across the bottom.

'Taa . . . raaa . . . ' Maud walked in from the pantry, bearing a rather lopsided sponge cake bedecked with a thick coating of icing sugar and blazing candles.

'Stuff and nonsense,' Elizabeth said tersely, irritated by the fuss the family was making of Bethan's results. She recalled the time when she'd gained a teaching certificate with distinction and received no more than a passing 'You did what was expected of you, Elizabeth' from her parents. 'And who told you that you could waste candles, Maud Powell, when it's no one's birthday? Do you think money grows on trees?'

'It's my birthday next and I'll do without them on my cake,' Maud said, almost in tears.

'It's not every day our daughter passes her examinations, with distinction,' Evan interposed.

'And comes top of her year,' Maud added proudly.

'There's plenty of others that have done as well,' Elizabeth commented coldly. 'And I'm sure their families aren't losing their heads over it.'

Without looking at one another, or Elizabeth, everyone tacitly ignored her contribution to the conversation. Time and constant exposure had made the entire family, with the exception of Maud,

61

immune to all but her bitterest pronouncements. And Maud was learning.

'Glan has a lot to answer for,' Bethan said after she ceremoniously blew out the candles.

'Next door's Glan?' her father asked.

'He sneaked out lunch time to buy cigarettes and gave Mrs Lewis in the newsagent's our results. By the time we left the hospital it was over the whole of the Graig. Even Mrs Pugh knew. We've been congratulated all the way up the hill.'

'You deserve it, love,' her father smiled proudly. 'Hospital ball tonight?'

'Yes, Ronnie's taking us down in his van.'

'When will he be here?' Maud asked.

'Half-past eight.'

'It's five-past now. You'd better get your skates on.'

'Not before she's eaten a proper meal,' Elizabeth said sharply, spooning two faggots and a ladleful of peas on to the top plate.

It wasn't until they sat at the table that Bethan realised that not only the lodger but also Haydn was missing. Her father saw her glance at her brother's empty chair.

'Haydn was mad when he realised he'd miss you tonight, but he brought good news home before we heard yours today.'

'What?' Bethan asked hopefully, thinking of the coat she'd asked him to buy.

'He's got a job. Full time. Twelve and six a week,' Eddie said a little wistfully.

'Where?' Bethan asked excitedly.

'Town Hall,' Elizabeth snapped. 'Low wages, and unchristian hours. The Lord only knows what kind of people he'll come up against there. Working every evening except Sunday if you please. Four until midnight.'

'It's permanent, Elizabeth, and a start for the boy,' Evan interposed.

'A start in what, that's what I'd like to know?' She slapped a plate on the table in front of Evan, splashing mushy peas over his shirt front.

'He's stagehand and callboy, and helps out at the box office,' Eddie whispered to Bethan.

'Twelve and six a week is no wage for a nineteen-year-old boy,' Elizabeth railed bitterly.

'It's a wage that plenty round here would like to have.' There was a note in Evan's voice that quietened Elizabeth. She continued to dish out faggots and peas in a tight-lipped martyred silence. She'd had her say, made everyone uncomfortable, but that was as far as it would go. She'd always balked at out-and-out argument, because she thought scenes 'vulgar'; the kind of thing only the uneducated, unrefined working classes indulged in.

Her reticence infuriated Evan. He'd grown up with parents who'd made a point of frequently 'clearing the air'. They'd also periodically cleared the dresser of plates, and broken the odd window pane or two, but they'd never failed to kiss and make up before bedtime, and Evan was conscious that his own marriage lacked the passion that had characterised his parents' relationship. Loving or hating, at least they'd felt something for one another. The only things left between him and Elizabeth were the children they had made, and mutual irritation. But twenty-one years of marriage had taught him how to handle his wife, including how to utilise her fear of open discord to gain silence when he could no longer bear the sound of her carping.

Rhiannon's Welsh cakes had taken the edge off Bethan's appetite, but she forced herself to eat, finishing the faggots and peas in less than five minutes.

'I have to get ready,' she said, rising from her chair.

'Can I help you?' Maud pleaded.

'You sit down and eat your meal, young lady,' Elizabeth commanded.

Bethan filled a jug with hot water from the boiler as Maud spooned up the last of the mess from her plate.

'Now can I go?' she pleaded.

'You may, though I don't know why I bother to cook a decent meal when all you do is wolf your food and run. When I was a girl, my family made a point of conversing with one another at the table.'

Elizabeth almost smiled at the memory of her childhood. When she wasn't consoling herself with thoughts of her teaching days, which time and nostalgia had endowed with a rosy hue that had little basis in reality, she sought comfort in inaccurate memories of her upbringing in the parsimonious home of her minister father.

Haydn Bull had, unfortunately for the emotional well-being of his daughter, disregarded the actual situation of his house, flock and purse, and elevated himself to the ranks of the middle classes. Apart from the Leyshons who owned the brewery and lived in Danygraig House, the bleak, grey stone villa set in its own grounds below Graig Avenue, there had been no middle-class families on the Graig. And there was only a handful in Pontypridd to challenge his belief in his change of station. The only tangible result of his adopted airs and graces was the further isolation of his family from the community, and a dwindling congregation in his chapel, which had pleased the Methodists if not the chapel elders.

Evan glanced despairingly at Elizabeth before leaving the table for his chair, which was to the right of the range facing the window. He delved under the cushion at his back and produced a copy of Gogol's *Dead Souls* which he'd borrowed from the Central Library. Eddie finished his meal and carried the dishes through to the washhouse. Maud refilled the boiler, and Bethan left the room, stopping to pick up the box from the front parlour as she went upstairs.

She switched the bedroom light on with her nose, set the jug down on the washstand and threw the box on to the bed, before walking over to the window to close the curtains. The rings grated uneasily over the rusting rod as she shut out the darkness. Facing the wardrobe mirror she tore the veil from her head and looked in dismay at her hair. It clung, limp and lifeless, to her head, as straight as a drowned cat's tail. Grabbing the towel she rubbed it mercilessly between the rough ends of cloth until it frizzed out in an unbecoming halo.

'Here, let me do that.' Maud closed the door behind her and took the towel from Bethan's hands.

'I haven't got time to set it.'

'Yes you have.' Maud leaned over and opened one of the small drawers built around the dressing-table mirror. She took out a dozen viciously clipped metal wavers. Combing Bethan's hair, she marked a parting and fingered a series of waves, crimping them firmly into the metal teeth.

'That's the two sides done –' she surveyed her handiwork critically – 'and there's six left for the back. You could tie a scarf over your head and leave them in until you get to the Coro,' she suggested, referring to the Coronation ballroom, where the hospital ball was being held.

'I could,' Bethan agreed doubtfully. 'But where would I put them? I can hardly cram them into my evening bag.'

'Leave them in Ronnie's van and pick them up on the way back. Mind you do. I need them for Saturday.'

'Going to Ronconis' café with the girls?' Bethan raised her eyebrows.

'And the boys,' Maud replied disarmingly. 'Right, that's your hair finished.'

Bethan leapt up from the dressing-table stool, and tried to unbutton her uniform dress and tip water into the bowl at the same time.

'Shall I get your ringed velvet out of the wardrobe for you?'

'No.' Bethan nodded towards the bed.

'Someone's been to Auntie Megan's,' Maud sang out, lifting the top off the box. She stared at the dress. 'Bethan, it's tremendous. Oooh, it's real silk . . . '

'Be an angel and get the underwear Auntie Megan gave me for Christmas. It's the top drawer of the dressing table. And the essence of violets Eddie gave me, the powder and lipstick you gave me.'

'What did this cost?' Maud probed tactlessly, holding the dress up in front of her and swaying before the wardrobe mirror.

'It was a present. For passing my exams.'

'You lucky duck. I'll never be clever enough to try, let alone pass anything. What are you going to wear on top? Surely not your old black coat?'

'Mam Powell's shawl, and the only coat I possess.'

'It would look better with furs.'

'Anything would look better with furs. I must ask Haydn to borrow Glan's gun and go up the mountain and shoot something. Mind you, it will take an awful lot of rats to make a coat.'

'When I'm old enough to go to balls I'm going to have furs,' Maud pronounced decisively, laying Bethan's dress on the bed.

'The underclothes?' Bethan reminded.

She finished washing, picked up a bowl of talcum powder from the dressing table and puffed it liberally over herself, then looked down. She was standing in a puddle of white dust.

'Don't worry. I'll wipe it up before Mam sees it,' Maud offered.

'You won't forget?'

'Promise.' Maud extricated the underwear and scent. Picking up Bethan's jewellery box she lay down on the bed next to the dress and rummaged through the trinkets. Bethan slipped on the silk underwear. Checking the seams in the mirror, she rolled and clipped on the stockings Megan had given her, then sat in front of the dressing table. She dabbed a little rouge high on her cheekbones, face powder on her nose, combed Vaseline on to her eyelashes, pencilled over her heavily plucked eyebrows and liberally coated her lips with 'flame-red' Hollywood stick, 'as worn by the stars'.

'Scent,' Maud prompted.

Bethan dabbed scent behind her ears, on her throat, hair and in the crooks of her elbows and knees. Then, on hands and knees, she scrabbled in the bottom of the wardrobe she shared with Maud. After throwing out two worn pairs of plimsolls and a pair of rubber boots, she finally came up with the black patent strapped sandals she wanted. As soon as she buckled them on she picked up the dress. Holding it carefully she slid it over her head and Maud buttoned up the back.

'What jewellery?' Maud asked.

'The black glass necklace and earrings Haydn gave me for my birthday. They'll match the shawl.'

'You don't want to wear the Bakelite piggy I gave you?'

Bethan looked hard at her sister. Maud had a peculiar sense of humour, but she could also be over-sensitive at times.

'Got you going, didn't I?'

Bethan threw her powder puff at her.

'Great, now I get to clean up the bed as well as the floor.'

'Serve you right.'

At twenty-five minutes to nine Bethan stood in front of the mirror. She turned on her heel and tried to view herself from the back. The dress was incredible. Beautifully cut, it clung tightly, if a little too revealingly, to her bust, waist and hips and swirled fashionably around her long slim legs. For the first time in her life she felt very nearly pretty.

'Will you lend me that frock when I go to my first ball?'

'If you grow another six inches. I'm not lopping that much off the bottom.'

'I wish I was tall and dark like you.'

'And I wish I was small and blonde like you.' Bethan leaned over and kissed Maud's cheek carefully so as not to smudge her lipstick. 'Thanks for the help. I couldn't have done without you.'

'Your bag,' Maud reminded. Another two minutes were spent frantically searching the back of the wardrobe for the black sequinned bag that Bethan had bought in a mad moment of extravagance from Wilf Horton's second-hand stall on the market. Bethan draped the shawl around herself while Maud filled the bag. She managed to stuff a lace handkerchief, a small bottle of essence of violets scent, a comb and Bethan's lipstick into the cramped interior.

'All I need is some change and I'm set to go.'

'What happens if your nose gets shiny? You've no powder.'

'I'll borrow Laura's compact.'

'You'd better pull that shawl higher or Mam won't let you out of the house.'

'It's not too low is it?' Bethan asked anxiously, checking her reflection one more time.

'Depends on what you mean by low. It'll be too low for Mam but I dare say the men who dance with you will find it interesting. There goes the door.'

'It'll be Ronnie.'

'Don't panic, I'll stall him.'

'Who's panicking?' Bethan demanded hotly.

Maud reached the foot of the stairs just as Bethan left the bedroom.

'My word!' Ronnie, all slicked-back hair, dark eyes and flashing white teeth, grinned up at Bethan. 'We are beautiful tonight. Iron curlers must be all the rage. Laura's wearing hers too.'

Bethan stuck her tongue out at him, hitched her shawl higher around her throat and descended the stairs. 'I'm off then,' she called to the back of the house. Evan and Eddie came out of the kitchen, followed by her mother.

'That's some dress,' Evan commented.

'Scarlet woman,' Eddie grinned.

'I needn't ask where you got that!' her mother exclaimed sourly. 'All I can say is that you must have more money than sense.'

'Auntie Megan gave it to me,' Bethan muttered, pulling on her shabby black coat and buttoning it to the neck.

'As I said, more money than sense,' her mother retorted.

'When will you be home?' Evan asked.

'Don't worry, Mr Powell, I'm picking the girls up,' Ronnie said in a tone more paternal than fraternal. 'The ball finishes at twelve, so even allowing for their gossiping I should have them home before one.'

'That's good to know,' Evan nodded.

'Don't forget you have work tomorrow morning,' Elizabeth reminded.

'She's not likely to do that.' Evan leaned over and kissed Bethan on the cheek, scratching himself on one of the iron wavers. 'Have a good time, love,' he murmured, rubbing his chin.

'I will.' Bethan pulled a coarse woollen headscarf from the peg above her head, folded it cornerwise and tied it over the metal curlers. 'Bye.' She squeezed Maud's hand, waved her fingers at Eddie, picked up the hem of her dress and took a deep breath before stepping out of the house.

Chapter Four

The Coronation ballroom was built on the second floor of the arcade of the Co-operative stores. The Co-op occupied two whole blocks between Gelliwastad Road and Market Square, with the intersecting road of Church Street terminating in the Co-op arcade. The windows of the ballroom overlooked both the arcade and Gelliwastad Road, and there was a fine view of the solid grey stone police station. Through the wired-off grilles that shielded the station's basement windows, shadowy figures could sometimes be seen pacing the cells, and the town wags insisted that the Coro had been sited so that potential drunks could view their overnight accommodation.

As ballrooms go, the Coro was not wonderful. It couldn't hold a candle to the beautifully moulded elegance of the blue and cream ballroom in the New Inn, or the white and gold function room of the Park Hotel. Viewed in harsh daylight, it was no more than a bleak assembly hall, proportioned too long for its narrow width, the floor covered with thick brown rubberised linoleum, the walls painted an unprepossessing dingy cream. But that night, by dint of imagination and a great deal of hard work, the ball committee had transformed it into a glittering fairyland.

Silver tinsel and fetching blue and red crêpe paper decorations, tortured into fabulous shapes by pressganged nurses and idle ladies of the crache (those rich enough to employ servants to do their dirty work), hung in clusters from the ceiling and walls. Even Bethan and Laura had done their bit by 'donating' an evening to help pin up the home-made ornaments.

The manager of the Co-op had entered into the spirit of the evening. The windows in the arcade shone with electric lights as though it were Christmas, not January, and there were no shoddy sales goods on offer. He was astute enough to realise that more customers with money in their pockets would pass his windows that night than on the last Saturday before Christmas, and so had arranged lavish displays of his most luxurious and expensive clothes and trinkets.

The hospital ball was the charity event of the year. Everyone who considered themselves anyone wanted to be seen to be supporting the cottage hospital. Entirely funded by voluntary contributions, money from the depression-depleted miners' union, and as many five-guinea-a-year subscriptions as the Hospital Board could muster, the hospital was in dire need of cash. Particularly as the board had taken it upon themselves to build a new wing to house a four-bedded children's ward and an up-to-date X-ray room: additions that had been completed and were now operational, but not yet paid for.

The ball was organised by, and mainly patronised by, the crache. The doctors belonged to that social group; the nurses did not, but they along with anyone else who could afford the ten and sixpence that the tickets cost were invited, and generally only those nurses who were on duty on the night turned down the invitation.

Ronnie slowed the cumbersome van to a crawl as he entered the top end of Taff Street. He steered carefully through its narrow precincts until he reached Market Square. Swinging the wheel abruptly to the left, he bumped over the cobbles of the square and ground the van to a halt in front of the entrance to the arcade. Laura and Bethan were still frantically unclipping the metal wavers from their heads when Ronnie stopped the engine.

'My hair's damp,' Laura said mournfully.

'It'll be even damper when you go out there,' Ronnie observed happily.

'It's not raining is it?' Bethan asked, dreading the prospect of water splashes staining her silk dress.

'Just miserable and misty. I'll come in at twelve.' He looked at his sister. 'Buy you a night-cap.'

'Must you?' Laura wailed.

'Oho, now you're the great qualified nurse you're ashamed of your brother?'

'No, only the way you interrogate whoever I'm with.'

'If you spent your time with decent boys I wouldn't need to interrogate them,' Ronnie retorted warmly.

'And you wouldn't know decent if you saw it,' Laura dismissed him contemptuously. 'I've seen some of the girls you go out with.'

'Who I go out with is none of your concern.' Ronnie rammed his index finger close to Laura's nose. 'But I know spiv when I see it. That porter Glan you primp and wiggle —'

'Wiggle! *Wiggle!*' Laura's face reddened in fury.

'If Papa knew the half of what you do . . . '

'That's right, bring Papa into it. We all know you can't breathe without Papa's say-so.'

Laura threw the remainder of her wavers into the front pocket of the van and wrenched open the door. Bunching up the skirt of her gold net she teetered on the side of the bench seat, poised to jump down.

'Here, you haven't even got the sense to wait for me to help you.' Ronnie leapt out of his side, walked around the front of the van and lifted Laura down, dumping her unceremoniously on the pavement. 'Your turn.' He looked up at Bethan.

'I'm quite capable of climbing down myself,' she said primly. The last thing she wanted was any man, even one she'd grown up with like Ronnie Ronconi, comparing her weight to Laura's.

'Nursing's softened your brains,' he groused angrily. 'You're as stupid as Laura.' He grabbed hold of her by the waist, lifted her out of the cab and deposited her next to the seething Laura. 'See you at twelve,' he said stiffly. He climbed back into the driving seat of the Trojan and revved the engine.

'Men!' Laura snarled furiously. 'They're all stupid, but Italian men are stupider than most.'

'Ronnie's more Welsh than Italian.'

'That's as may be, but he thinks like an Italian,' Laura said illogically, walking into the arcade and flouncing up the stairs.

A wave of warm scented air greeted Bethan as she followed Laura. People were milling in every available inch of space. Men in dark dinner suits, boiled shirts, stiff collars and white or black ties. Ladies in frocks of every hue and fabric known to the fashion trade. Laura made a bee-line for the cloakroom only to find it as crowded as the foyer. Bethan queued to deposit their coats while Laura fought for a space in front of the single mirror. The anteroom was packed with nurses not only from the Central Homes, but also from Llwynypia and the Cottage Hospitals, as well as the ladies of the town's prominent citizens.

Bethan found Laura, and they spent five minutes squashed together, reapplying their lipstick and teasing their damp hair into waves.

'That dress makes you look entirely different,' Laura commented, as, much to the relief of the other ladies, they finally walked away.

Bethan glanced at the subdued gold and cream shades in Laura's dress and contrasted them with the crimson swirls of silk that flowed around her own ankles.

'You don't think it's too much do you? The neck . . . '

'Is perfect. Where's your confidence, Nurse? Good evening, Doctor Lewis,' she called out to Trevor Lewis, Dr John senior's assistant.

Trevor Lewis, a thin, diffident man whose clothes always hung on him as if they'd been handed down by a much larger older brother, walked over to them. 'Nurse Ronconi, Nurse Powell. Can I book a waltz with each of you?'

'For you, Doctor Lewis, anything,' Laura flirted outrageously. Giggling like a pair of schoolgirls they heaved and pushed themselves into the room.

'So much for the grand entrance,' Bethan muttered between clenched teeth.

'Ladies, I have your drinks.' Glan waylaid them with three glasses of orange juice balanced precariously.

'I'm not thirsty.' Laura waved her fingers dismissively as Bethan breathed in and slipped sideways between an elderly plump dowager and her equally plump, cigar-smoking husband.

'But . . . but . . . '

Bethan could still hear Glan's spluttering 'buts' as Laura caught up with her. Tables had been placed around two sides of the room, and most were already taken. At the far end, opposite the door, a raised dais had been erected, and Mander's Excelda dance band was in full flow, playing a jazzed-up, foxtrot version of 'They Didn't Believe Me'.

'Bethan, Laura, over here.'

'See what passing exams has done for us? First-name terms, no less,' Laura said in a loud voice.

'Ssh.'

'That's a fabulous dress,' Nurse Williams enthused, pulling out the chair next to her own for Bethan to sit on. 'I saw it in Howell's window in Cardiff. It was an absolute fortune . . . '

'Twelve guineas,' Nurse Fry interrupted.

'This was never in Howell's window,' Bethan said quickly. 'My aunt gave it to me.'

'Rich aunt, lucky you,' Nurse Fry said maliciously.

'She's not rich, she's an agent for Leslie's stores.'

'She never got that from Leslie's.'

'She also sells "specials",' Bethan explained impatiently. 'Clothes that local dressmakers pass on to her to sell. It's one of those. It hasn't even got a label.'

'Clever dressmaker,' Freda Williams mused. 'It wasn't made by Mrs Jenkins was it? Lewis Street?'

'I'm sorry, I don't know. I didn't think to ask.'

'The bodice would look better without the shawl wrapped around your throat,' Laura whispered in her ear.

'Nurse Ronconi, Nurse Powell, your drinks.' Glan plonked the orange juices in front of them, slopping the liquid.

'Thank you,' Laura said heavily. 'But I prefer my drink in the glass.'

Uncertain how to take the comment, Glan hovered uneasily next to their table.

'Doctor John's in fine form,' Freda said conversationally, in an attempt to lighten the atmosphere.

Bethan looked towards the front of the hall where Dr John senior was holding forth at a round table set in prime position to the left of the band. He had a large party gathered around him. His wife, his assistant Trevor Lewis, the matron Alice George, the Reverend Mark Price, the vicar of St John's church on the Graig, and his wife Angela were all sharing his table and, judging by the way they were laughing, a joke.

'There he is,' sighed Nurse Fry, 'over by the bar. Isn't he heavenly?'

'Young Doctor John?' Laura looked to her for confirmation. 'Who else?'

'That's young Doctor John?' Bethan cried.

'You should know, you worked with him all afternoon.'

'He was gowned up and had a hat on.'

'Hat or no hat, you gave me first claim,' Laura muttered into her ear.

Bethan had noticed that Andrew John was tall, broad-shouldered and well built, but she'd failed to realise how concealing a surgeon's hat and mask could be. He was easily the most handsome man she'd seen off a cinema screen. The dark brown hair that had been hidden under the theatre cap held a rich tint of auburn, and his face, oval, smooth-skinned and with a dark Ronald Colman moustache, attracted the attention of every female under forty, married as well as single, in the room. He smiled and nodded to her and she blushed crimson with the knowledge that she'd been staring at him. She turned abruptly and knocked one of the orange juices Glan had placed on the table. None of the juice touched her own or Laura's dress, but Glan's trousers were soaked.

'I'm dreadfully sorry,' she apologised, jumping up and delving into her handbag for her handkerchief.

'I bet you are,' Glan said viciously, all too aware of who she'd been staring at.

'You can borrow my handkerchief, Glan.' Laura added insult to injury by tendering a purely decorative scrap of silk and lace.

'Keep it.' Glan's temper boiled dangerously close to eruption.

The band chose that moment to stop playing, and Bethan sensed the attention of the dancers focusing on their table. Glan threw Laura's handkerchief to the floor and glowered at Bethan. She stepped back, and promptly trod on a foot behind her. She turned to find Andrew John's face inches away from her own.

'I was going to ask you for the next dance, but now you've broken my foot I'm not sure I'm capable of a limp, much less a foxtrot.'

'I'm terribly sorry, I didn't mean to . . . '

'I don't think there's any serious damage, but it might be just as well to make sure,' he said gravely. 'As you're a qualified nurse now, would you help me into the cloakroom so you can make a thorough examination?'

Bethan stood dumbfounded for a few seconds, then saw a peculiar glint in his eyes. 'You're not serious?'

'No,' he said slowly. 'I'm not serious.'

The MC's voice crackled over the microphone and the strains of 'If I Should Fall in Love Again' filled the room. Andrew took her by the hand, nodded to the fuming Glan, and led her on to the floor.

'That porter has blood pressure,' he commented blandly. 'Just look at his colour.'

Bethan was too mortified to do anything other than stare at the left shoulder of his tailored dinner suit.

'Are you always this quiet, or is it something I've said?' he asked on the second circuit of the room.

'It's what I've done,' she murmured miserably.

'Tipping orange juice over that porter? I assumed it was a clever ploy calculated to cool his ardour.'

'I didn't do it deliberately,' she protested.

'I know you didn't,' he said gently. 'It's been quite a day for you hasn't it? Qualifying. Helping to deliver your friend's baby, and now this?'

'I'm beginning to think I should have had an early night.'

'And lost an opportunity to air this frock.' He held her at arm's length for a moment. 'Now that would have been a crying shame.'

Bethan managed a nervous smile as they resumed dancing. She would have been happier if he'd chosen Laura. Laura was more his type. They could have laughed and been witty together, and she could have sat in the corner and watched enviously with all the other nurses. Unlike her, Laura took good-looking, well-heeled men in her stride. But she, for all of her training, or perhaps because of it, was always intimidated by the likes of Andrew John. The first lesson she'd learned in hospital was that doctors were second only to God. And everything about Andrew John – his conversation, his clothes, his accent – confirmed his superiority. She was used to men like her father who spent their lives grubbing for pennies to buy the bare essentials. What little free time they had was spent earnestly reading and discussing communism as a possible solution to the problems of the working, or unemployed, classes.

Even youngsters like Haydn, Eddie and William were too busy trying to scratch a living to have much time or money for fun. In contrast Andrew looked and behaved as though he hadn't a care in the world. But then, she reflected, his father was not only a doctor who didn't have to fear the spectre of rising unemployment, but also the landlord of several houses, and that, at a time when most families in Pontypridd were hard pressed to keep a roof over their heads, put him firmly in the crache.

The band droned softly on. Perspiration trickled down her back. She became more nervous with every step she took. Yet, much as she wanted to, she couldn't blame Andrew for making her feel awkward; she couldn't fault the way he held her. A dance with Glan, or any of the other porters for that matter, would have turned into a wrestling match by now.

'I don't suppose I could interest you in an orange juice when this dance is over?' he asked, breaking the silence.

'Nurses aren't supposed to fraternise with doctors,' she retorted primly.

'They have to at hospital balls,' he protested. 'If they don't who are we supposed to dance with?'

'The town's socialites.'

He laughed. 'You have a tongue in your head after all. Now tell me, just who in Pontypridd do you call a socialite?'

'Well,' she looked around the room, 'there are the Misses Rees-Davies, the solicitor's daughters.'

'They're a trifle elderly for me.'

'That's unkind.'

'Unkind maybe, but true.'

'Miss Henrietta Evans? Now you can't say she's too old.'

'No, but she hasn't had an original thought since the day she was born, and I'm not sure she had one then.'

'You don't need original thoughts to dance.'

'No, but dancing is such a repetitive exercise it helps to have a partner capable of some conversation.'

'Anthea Llewellyn-Jones?' Bearing the gossip in mind, she watched his reaction carefully. 'You can't accuse her of not having any thoughts?'

'No, she has too many and all of them boring. I danced with her at the tennis club ball and as a result I can now recite the entire catalogue of recent flood and mine disasters and the names of all the committees that have been set up to assist the afflicted. Please,' his dark eyes gleamed as he looked at her, 'don't suggest I repeat the experience.'

'I think people can make all the suggestions they like, but I don't believe for one minute that you'd be affected enough by anyone's opinion to do anything you didn't want to,' she smiled.

'Good Lord, you can smile as well as talk. This must be my lucky night.'

'Are you always like this?'

'Like what?'

'Like turning everything into a joke.'

'Joking is an extremely serious business.'

'Really?'

'You must allow me to teach you just how serious, some time.'

The band ceased playing and she broke away from him and applauded.

'I think, Doctor John, it's time that you danced with someone else; nurse or socialite, it really doesn't matter.'

'And if I don't want to?'

'If you want to continue dancing you're going to have to. If I remain with you, people will notice. And I don't intend to attract any gossip, especially with Matron sitting in the room.'

He shook his head dolefully. 'So beautiful, and so hard-hearted.'

She turned her back on him and returned to the table, which had been washed down and dried by the barman. A crowd of porters had gathered around Laura and the two senior nurses. Glan, she noted gratefully, was not among them. There was no shortage of partners for the next dance, or the one after that. But no matter which porter she danced with, her attention wandered, and she found herself looking at her fellow dancers hoping to catch another glimpse of Andrew John. Flippant and frivolous as he undoubtedly was, he'd breathed colour and life into an existence she'd never considered drab or dull until that moment.

The hours blurred by in a haze of scented heat and soft romantic music. Just before the bar closed at eleven she and Laura treated themselves to a sherry, and bought a conciliatory pint of beer for Glan. They'd only just returned to their table when Laura glimpsed Ronnie entering the room.

'Oh blast, here comes trouble,' she complained, hiding her sherry glass in her hands.

'Haydn's with him.' Bethan waved to her brother and he joined them. She pushed out Nurse Fry's chair. 'I heard about the job. Congratulations.'

'The wages aren't wonderful, it's only twelve and six for a six-day week, but it's steady, and Wilf said I can still help out on his market stall two mornings a week, so that'll make it fifteen shillings. Not up to your standard,' he grinned, 'but there's prospects.'

'Here you are, mate, get that down you.' Ronnie dumped two overflowing pint pots on the table.

'I thought stop tap had been called,' Laura complained, edging away from the glasses.

'It has, but Dai Owen's behind the bar and he owes me a favour.'

'When you get to hell you'll try to tell the devil that he owes you a favour,' Laura snapped acidly.

'Been eating razor blades?' Ronnie enquired mildly.

'How would you like to dance with me?' Haydn left his chair and offered his hand to Laura.

'I would love to.' Laura glared furiously at her brother as she walked away.

'I hope that wasn't one of dear sister's hints that I should ask you to dance.' Ronnie sank laconically into the seat Laura had vacated. 'Because if it was, I'm simply not up to it. I've had a swine of a night in the café, if you'll pardon the expression. Nothing but cups of tea, packets of PK and people warming themselves at my expense.'

'Look on the bright side, at least you weren't rushed off your feet.'

'I'd rather be rushed off my feet than lose money on heating and lighting and listen to the moans of my underworked cook. Take my advice,' he swallowed a large mouthful of beer in between words, 'never employ an Italian cook. They're all raving mad.'

'As I'm never likely to be in a position to employ anyone I'll take your word for it.'

Ronnie swung his feet on to a vacant chair, took another mouthful of beer and let out a large satisfied burp as the MC called the last waltz.

'May I borrow your lady?' Andrew asked, climbing over Ronnie's legs to get to Bethan.

'Be my guest, take her,' Ronnie offered expansively.

'That's uncommonly generous of you.'

'Not at all, old boy,' Ronnie accurately mimicked Andrew's public school accent. 'It's not as if you're asking me to do anything that requires effort.'

'Nice boyfriend you have there,' Andrew observed as he led Bethan away from the tables.

'Ronnie is Laura's brother and nobody's boyfriend.'

'I'm not surprised.'

'Ronnie's all right,' she laughed. 'He just takes a bit of getting used to.'

'I'd rather not try if it's all the same to you. But talking about getting used to people, how about you getting used to me? There's a Claudette Colbert film showing in the Palladium the second half of this week.'

'I know. Laura and I are going on Saturday.'

'Laura?'

'She's dancing with my brother over there.'

Andrew peered in the direction Bethan had indicated.

'I've seen her somewhere before.'

'She works on the ward with me.'

'Ah, a fellow nurse. In that case she won't mind if I tag along with you?'

'Nurses aren't supposed to . . . '

'I know, I know . . . aren't supposed to fraternise with doctors. But have a heart. I've just returned to Pontypridd after six years in London. Apart from my parents and their friends I don't know a soul here. Now tell me, what possible harm can a trip to the cinema with both of you do?'

'That depends on who sees us.'

'I thought people went to the cinema to watch films, not the audience.'

The band stopped playing and streamers of finely cut crêpe paper cascaded down from nets strung close to the ceiling.

'I'm saying please nicely, just as my mother taught me.' He brushed a clump of red and blue streamers out of his hair. There was such a pitiful expression on his face she burst out laughing.

79

'We pay our own way,' she said firmly.

'In this day and age of the emancipated woman, I wouldn't dream of treating you.'

'All right.'

'What did you say?' he shouted above the strains of 'Auld Lang Syne'.

She stood on tiptoe and whispered into his ear, 'I said all right.'

Glan, who'd spent the whole of the last dance standing on the sidelines watching Bethan and Andrew John, chose that moment to step forward. Catching her unawares, he gripped her right elbow painfully and propelled her forwards, away from Andrew into the thick of the crowd who were linking arms and singing in the middle of the room.

'Should auld acquaintance be forgot . . . '

The music resounded in her ears, closing out all other sounds. Dr John senior was standing opposite her, his face flushed with heat and whisky. She turned and saw the top of Andrew's head, but he seemed very far away, separated from her by a mass of chanting, swaying bodies.

'Happy New Year, Beth, a little late, but better late than never.' Glan bent his head to kiss her, she ducked and he kissed thin air.

'Don't you dare take liberties with me, Glan Richards,' she hissed vehemently. She broke away and pushed backwards.

Laura was waving to her from the doorway, her arm full of coats. She pointed down and mouthed, 'I've got yours as well as mine.'

'Come on, Sis, follow me.' Haydn appeared at her side. Pushing ahead, he cleared a path through the crowd. 'Here.' He took her coat from Laura and helped her on with it.

'Thank you.' Bethan looked around as she slid her arms into the sleeves. Dr John senior was shaking hands with everyone who'd sat at his table, but she could see no sign of Andrew.

'Come on then, before the rush,' Ronnie shouted impatiently, from the foyer.

Dragging her feet, Bethan reluctantly followed the others down the stairs and into the arcade. The Co-op windows were still lit. No expense spared on hospital ball night. They walked towards

Market Square, their footsteps resounding over the tiled floor, echoing upwards to the high vaulted ceiling.

'Holy Mother but it's cold,' Ronnie complained, buttoning his coat to the neck.

'That's blasphemy,' Laura crowed victoriously.

'I was merely making an observation to the Blessed Virgin,' Ronnie contradicted.

Ignoring their bickering Bethan looked out from the shelter of the arcade into the deserted square. Gwilym Evans' windows were in darkness. No lights burned to celebrate the ball there. The fine misty rain had turned to a cold, penetrating icy sleet that burnished the cobblestones to pewter. She turned up her coat collar and pulled her gloves out of her pocket.

The heavy footsteps of someone running thundered up close behind them.

'Goodnight, Nurse Powell, Nurse Ronconi.'

'Starting a marathon, Doctor John?' Laura asked.

'No. Getting my father's car out of the New Inn car park before the rush starts.'

'You could have gone the back way, mate,' Ronnie said helpfully. 'Quicker.'

'It would be if the shutters weren't down and locked at the Gelliwastad Road end.' He stepped close to Bethan. 'Ronconis' café on the Tumble. Six o'clock Saturday night,' he muttered under his breath.

He was gone before she could reply. She looked back. The arcade stretched out behind her, full of laughing, chattering people. She watched as they swarmed towards Gelliwastad Road. The shutters were clamped back, exposing a square of dark sky, cut midway by the dour grey outline of the police station. A gentle smile played at the corners of her mouth. He'd lied – he'd run to catch up with her! That had to mean something. Bracing herself, she followed the others into the freezing cold of Market Square.

She was still smiling when she and Haydn let themselves into the house. They paused on the doorstep to wave goodbye to Ronnie and Laura who, judging by the erratic way in which the van turned in the narrow street, were still at it hammer and tongs.

81

'Italians!' Haydn said, stepping inside as the van finally drove off down the street.

'Lovely, warm people.'

'Like that doctor you were dancing with?'

'Doctor John?'

Haydn reached past her to hang up his coat and she saw that he was watching her closely.

'I hardly know him,' she protested. 'I only worked with him for the first time today. We delivered Maisie Crockett's baby. It was touch and go. The baby nearly died.'

'Maisie from Phillips Street?'

She nodded.

'I didn't even know she was married.'

'She's not.' Bethan brushed the surface rain from her coat as she hung it up. 'She's living in the homes.'

'Poor bugger,' Haydn said with feeling.

'Haydn! Bethan! Is that you?'

'Yes Mam.' Haydn frowned as he walked down the passage. 'I thought you'd all be in bed.'

'It's just as well we're not,' Elizabeth complained. 'No one could possibly sleep through the racket you and Bethan are making.'

He opened the door and they walked into the kitchen. 'What in hell . . . '

'And I'll have none of that language in this house.'

'Sorry, Mam,' Haydn apologised automatically, as he rushed across the room to where Eddie sat slumped in Evan's chair. 'What happened to you, mate?' he asked, pushing aside the damp cloth Evan was holding over Eddie's swollen right eye.

'I would have thought that was obvious.' With a look of pure venom Elizabeth wrung out a second cloth that was soaking in an enamel bowl on the table.

'You had a fight?' Bethan asked, pushing Eddie's hair back and peering into his eye.

'They were looking for sparring partners for the boxers down at the gym,' Eddie mumbled from between split and swollen lips. 'Look, I got two bob.' He put his hand in his pocket and pulled out a coin. 'I wanted to give something towards the silver nurse's buckle Dad and Haydn have been saving for. Here, Dad. Take it.'

Tears blinding his eyes, Evan fumbled at Eddie's hand and palmed the coin. Bethan held her father's hand for a moment, then she took the cloth and dabbed at the swellings on her brother's face.

'Being a sparring partner is a mug's game,' Haydn said angrily as he checked over the rest of his brother's body.

'I know.' Eddie's left eye shone with excitement in the firelight. 'That's why I asked Joey Rees to train me. You can win as much as five pounds in a good fight. Think of it, five pounds for one night's work. I won't get it yet, of course. But Joey says that I could be a first-class lightweight. Haydn —' he reached out and grabbed his brother's arm — 'I could make more money than I ever would working down the pit or in the brewery yard. I just know I could. A few months of that and we'll all be rich.'

'Over my dead body,' Elizabeth proclaimed.

Evan slumped back on the kitchen chair and looked at the two shillings he was holding. 'There's not many rich boxers, son,' he warned.

'But there are an awful lot of punch-drunk ones,' Haydn said acidly. 'You only have to look as far as Cast Iron Dean in Phillips Street.'

'He made his money.'

'And spent it. What's he got to show for it now?' Haydn demanded.

'What about Jimmy Wilde?' Eddie bit back. 'He's been every-where. London, America . . . stayed at the best hotels, eaten the best food. He bought his own farm —'

'There's a lot more to life than money, son,' Evan interrupted softly.

Eddie opened his left eye and looked around the shabby kitchen, the white strained faces of his family.

'If there is I haven't found it,' he said stubbornly. 'All I know is there's got to be more than getting up in the morning and queuing for the dole, or half a day's work. And if boxing puts money in my pocket and the best food on my plate instead of bread and scrape here, then I'm going to box. And no one in this family is going to stop me. Now or ever,' he added defiantly.

The silence after Eddie finished speaking was total and crushing. Bethan continued wiping and cleaning the mess on his face. But after a while she couldn't see the cuts and bruises. Her tears obliterated everything. Even the look of impotent misery on her father's face.

Chapter Five

'Look, are you going out with Andrew John tonight or aren't you?' Laura demanded of Bethan as she carried two cups of tea over to the corner table of Ronconis' café that they'd commandeered. 'Because if you are, I'm leaving now. I'm not in the habit of playing gooseberry . . . '

'I've told you,' Bethan repeated impatiently. 'He's only just returned to Pontypridd after six years away. He knows no one and he's lonely.'

'Lonely my eye!' Laura exclaimed scornfully. 'Men who look like him are never lonely, they . . . '

'For goodness' sake keep your voice down,' Bethan hissed. She looked up and smiled at Ronnie, who was leaning sideways on the counter within easy listening distance. 'For the last time, he wanted me to go to the Palladium with him and when I told him that I was going with you he asked if he could tag along, and I said yes,' she continued in a whisper.

'Do you, or do you not, want me to scarper?'

'Of course not.'

'I would if I was in your shoes,' Laura said philosophically, as she tipped sugar into her tea.

'You're the one who fancies him, not me.'

'All's fair in love and war.'

'This is not love,' Bethan protested vehemently.

'But it could be. Just look at who's coming through the door.'

Bethan glanced up and choked on her tea. 'Honestly, Laura, isn't there anything in trousers that you don't fancy?'

'Not much between the ages of eighteen and thirty. Cold enough for you, William?' she shouted to Bethan's cousin.

'It's real brass monkey weather out there!' William replied as he breezed into the café along with a draught of freezing air. Charlie walked in behind him, and closed the door with a resounding clang of the bell.

'Two hot teas to thaw out two icemen, please, Ronnie.' William stood in front of the chipped and scarred wooden counter, and rubbed his hands vigorously together. 'Charlie and I are blue already and there's three hours to go before the bell for the bargain rush.'

'I thought they'd drop the prices early on a night like tonight.' Laura eyed William coyly. He gave her the full benefit of his most beguiling smile, but it was the blazing coal fire alongside her table that had really taken his eye.

'No such luck.' William left the counter and squeezed a chair in between Laura and the fire. 'Nine o'clock bell, not before.'

'Be kinder to the poor people waiting to buy their Sunday meat to ring the bell now.' Bethan looked out through the steamed-up window at the women and children huddled in layers of shabby clothes, who were walking up and down, shivering and waiting for the moment to come.

'Be kinder to the poor devils behind the stalls.' William pulled off his fingerless gloves and blew vigorously on his frozen white hands. 'Thanks, mate.' He took the tea Charlie brought over from the counter. Bethan shifted her chair, making room for Charlie to sit alongside her, in front of the fire. The Russian moved a chair into the vacant space, and nodded his thanks.

'Is a man allowed to ask where you two are going all tarted up like that?' William studied them over the rim of his thick earthenware mug.

'No,' Ronnie shouted above the noise of the steamer from behind the counter, 'they'll bite your head off.'

'We're not "tarted up",' Bethan protested indignantly. 'I've had this coat for five years.'

'It's not the coat,' William smiled snidely. 'It's the perfume, the silk blouse you bought off my mother yesterday, when a jumper would be more serviceable, not to mention the smile and the whiff of excitement in the air.' He winked at Ronnie. 'I think you'd better warn every man who walks in here that these two are out on the razzle and looking for husbands.'

'The men are safe enough,' Ronnie drawled as he polished the water urn with a damp rag. 'Five minutes of Laura's company should be more than enough to make any man run a mile. If he doesn't, he's either a fool or a madman.'

'Why, you –' Laura looked around for something to throw, but Bethan had already put the salt and pepper pots out of reach. 'Oh . . . Oh . . . Oh . . . '

'Doing impressions of Father Christmas?' Bethan asked William caustically. 'Little late aren't you?'

'Or early,' he said absently, staring at the door.

She looked up and saw Andrew standing in the centre of the café. 'Time we went, Laura.' She jumped to her feet and promptly knocked over her chair.

'Can't wait to get at him, can you?' William leant over and picked up the chair. 'And by the way, Beth,' he muttered in a stage whisper, 'you need more powder on your cheeks. They're *very* red.'

She lifted the spoon out of William's hot tea as she passed and laid it on the back of his hand. He yelped, but she ignored his cry and carried on walking.

Andrew smiled when he saw her.

'I hope you don't mind, Trevor was at a loose end so I invited him to join us. He's waiting outside.'

'Trevor?'

'Doctor Lewis. Trevor Lewis,' he explained.

'Of course we don't mind.' Bethan gave William a sharp kick on the ankle for pulling on her coat. 'I don't think you've met my cousin William?'

'Your cousin?' Andrew raised an eyebrow. 'How do you do, Mr . . . '

'Powell.' William extended his hand.

'Ah yes, it would be wouldn't it?' Andrew's smile broadened. 'If you don't mind I won't get up, I haven't thawed out yet.'

'It is cold,' Andrew agreed.

'Not so you'd notice.' William reached out and fingered the cloth of Andrew's coat. 'Cashmere,' he nodded approvingly. 'Nice stuff. If you ever want to sell it, I'll get you a good price.'

'William!' Bethan admonished indignantly.

'I appreciate the offer, Mr Powell, but as I've only just bought it I think I'll hang on to it for a year or two,' Andrew said evenly.

'The offer'll hold until then. This is a mate of mine, Charlie Raschenko.'

'Mr Raschenko.' Andrew winced as Charlie took his hand in a bone-crushing grip.

'You've met my brother,' Laura said over-sweetly, smiling at Ronnie who was leaning on the counter.

'I've had the pleasure.' Andrew extricated his bruised hand, and walked towards the counter, happy to be heading towards the door and the outside. He shook hands gingerly with Ronnie, then turned to Bethan. 'I don't want to rush you, but if we're to get there on time, we'll have to make a move.'

'Town Hall pantomime for the kiddies?' Ronnie enquired condescendingly.

'That's your taste, dear brother, not ours,' Laura replied, gathering her things together. 'Bye, everyone.' She waved as she followed Bethan and Andrew out of the door.

'Don't be late or Papa will shout,' Ronnie called after her.

'That depends on what we're doing,' Laura countered cheekily as she closed the door. 'Some things are worth a shout or two from Papa.'

'The car's in the station car park.' Andrew held up his hand, halting a dray-cart so they could cross Taff Street.

'Wouldn't it be easier to walk to the Palladium?' Bethan asked suspiciously.

'It would be if we were going there, but Trevor has tickets for the Moss Empire Circus.'

'At the Empire Theatre in Cardiff?' Laura demanded eagerly.

'Where else?' Andrew answered for Trevor, who left a circle of young men to join them.

'Boys from my YMCA drama class,' he apologised briefly. 'Hope you don't mind me coming with you?'

'Of course we don't,' Laura said generously, thinking about the tickets. 'Well, what are we waiting for? Let's go.'

Bethan trailed behind Andrew and Laura as they wove through the crowds who were pouring up the alleyway steps alongside Gwilym Evans and into Market Square. She'd been looking forward to a night out with Andrew and Laura. But a foursome with Trevor Lewis and a trip to Cardiff put quite a different complexion on the evening that lay ahead. A threesome could be put down to innocent friendship, a foursome could be construed as men chasing women. And quite apart from the doctor/nurse fraternisation embargo, there was the question of where Andrew lived.

The Graig and the Common were situated at opposite ends of Pontypridd for very good reasons. Their residents didn't mix. They had very different life-styles and lived in entirely different worlds, and although the depression had affected both, on the Graig it had cut essentials such as food down to two scrap meals, or in extreme cases one a day. On the Common it had merely cut the servants' wages.

She knew that her father would disapprove if he could see her now, and that thought upset her. Too many girls on the Graig had been dazzled by middle-class boys dangling middle-class riches, only to end up as inmates on the 'unmarrieds' ward in the Central Homes.

'Andrew can be a bit overpowering, but he means well,' Trevor ventured, stepping alongside her.

'Yes I know,' she agreed noncommittally. 'Have you really got tickets?'

'Yes. A friend of mine offered them to me when I was having a drink with Andrew after work last night.'

'And Andrew bought them?'

'He did,' Trevor confirmed sheepishly. 'He said you wouldn't mind making tonight a foursome.'

'Of course we don't mind,' Bethan said warmly. Even under the uncertain light of the street lamps she could see the shiny patches on the cuffs and elbows of Trevor's overcoat. She and Laura had noticed soon after going to the Graig that, for a doctor, Trevor's shoes and clothes were distinctly shabby. But Bethan liked him all the more for his down-at-heel appearance. It gave him a kinship with her own background. Perhaps his wages, like hers, were needed by his family for more important things like rent and food. And she had elaborated on the few bare facts that she knew, imagining either an unemployed father, or one on 'short time' like hers.

Trevor couldn't have been more unlike Andrew. Quiet, rather shy, even with patients, he exuded diffidence rather than confidence. He was a favourite with the nurses because his 'in need of care and attention' appearance coupled with his gentle manner appealed to their maternal instinct.

'Congratulations, by the way, I haven't had a chance to compliment you or Laura on your results,' he said suddenly.

'Thank you.'

'Quite a boost for the Graig, getting the nurse with the top marks in the examination. How do you like nursing with us?'

'It's different from the Royal Infirmary.' She stepped into the road to avoid a young woman carrying a baby in a shawl wrapped around her coat, Welsh fashion. She was pushing a battered pram loaded with another two children, who were half buried under a mound of newspaper-wrapped potatoes and swedes.

'The patients can't be all that different. I grew up in the dock area of Cardiff. There's a lot of similarities between the back streets there and the Graig.'

'There's always similarities between one poor area and another.'

'Cockles, love, halfpenny a pint. Cockles, sweet cockles. Go on, sir, buy the lady a bag of cockles.'

Bethan shook her head at old Will Cockles who stood on the corner of Market Square. 'Have you any family left in Cardiff?' she asked curiously.

'My mother, two sisters and a brother.'

'Four children,' she smiled. 'Just like us.'

'My father was killed ten years ago. He was a docker, in Cardiff. The rigging broke as they were unloading a ship. Two days before it happened I won a scholarship to County School. I didn't want to take it, but my mother insisted I went. She said she could keep the family until I began work. I don't think she bargained on my getting a second scholarship to medical college. I was twenty-three before I earned a penny.'

'You were lucky your family could hold out that long.'

'Very,' he agreed drily. 'My brother and sisters could have done with some of my luck. They're all out of work now.'

'My father's on half-time and my youngest brother can't find work,' Bethan commiserated.

'Come on, Trevor,' Andrew called from the bridge opposite Rivelin's. 'We don't want to be late.'

Conscious that they'd been dawdling, Bethan and Trevor quickened their pace, but they didn't catch up with Andrew and Laura until they reached the station yard.

Andrew's car was pale grey with chrome trimmings, very shiny and, judging by the strong leathery smell of the interior, very new. He unlocked the door, and the interior light showed rich, gleaming walnut facias and pale grey upholstery. Bethan caught a strong whiff of expensive men's cologne as Andrew held the door open for her and Laura to climb into the back. When he closed the door behind them she glanced out of the window, to see if anyone was watching. The usual ladies of the town were standing in front of the old stone and red-brick wall that enclosed the yard. One of them sidled up to a passing man, her garishly painted face shining like a clown's under the artificial light.

'Nice car,' Laura commented, settling her skirt around her knees.

'Glad you like it,' Andrew called over his shoulder. He grinned at Trevor. 'Crank's under your seat.'

Trevor fumbled beneath his seat, lifted out the crank and went to the front of the car. Three turns and the engine purred into life. Once Trevor had climbed in again, Andrew slid the car in gear and manoeuvred out of the station yard.

Bethan and Laura sat back and tried to look as though they drove out to take the air every night of their lives. Apart from a few odd trips in Ronnie's Trojan baker's van, it was the first time either of them had ever travelled by private transport. But whereas Laura revelled in the experience, allowing the sense of luxury to wash over her like a warm, perfumed bath, Bethan was beset by guilt. It was more than just the fact that Andrew and Trevor were doctors. It had something to do with her own sense of self-value – as though Andrew, the trip, the car were too good for her, and any moment he'd find out the truth. That she, Bethan Powell, simply wasn't worth the time and attention he was expending on her. Or, worse still, was the outing simply a ploy on his part to get her alone and defenceless in an isolated spot where he could 'take advantage' of her?

Laura, bubbling over with excitement, began to talk about the last circus she'd seen. Trevor was infected by her mood and joined in, with Andrew, who was concentrating on driving, chipping in with the odd remark. They reached the outskirts of the city just after seven o'clock, and Andrew dropped them outside the Empire Theatre while he went to find a parking space. As they waited for him in the foyer, Bethan used the time to study the clothes of the women around her; she wished she'd taken the trouble to dress up a little more, although as she was wearing the new grey crêpe de Chine blouse she'd only just bought from her aunt, and her best navy-blue serge skirt, it was difficult to know what, besides the red dress or her black figured velvet, she could have put on.

Trevor dug into the pockets of his overcoat and produced the tickets. Laura shrieked in excitement.

'You've got a box!'

'Purely by default. A friend of mine bought it for his family, but they've gone down with influenza. He sold it cheap. He said he owed me a favour,' he added as an afterthought.

'You must belong to the same tribe as my brother.'

'Tribe?' He looked at her blankly.

'Someone always owes my brother a favour.'

'Then he's luckier than me.'

'The favours Ronnie's owed never extend to theatre boxes.'

'This was a one-off.' Trevor looked around the crowded foyer searching for a glimpse of Andrew.

'I hoped you'd wait.' Andrew suddenly appeared behind them, his hat pushed to the back of his head, his face glowing pink from the cold. 'Shall we go up?'

Neither Laura nor Bethan had been to the Empire Theatre before. Their acquaintance with the glamorous world of live show-business had been restricted to the dog-eared, slightly grubby New Theatre and the Town Hall in Pontypridd. Shortage of money in both theatres had meant that the tarnished gilding remained tarnished, the marked paintwork stayed marked, and the once plush seats in the auditoriums stood as shiny, bald pink monuments to the depression.

Here everything gleamed, newly restored, painted and sparkling in royal, opulent colours of red, gold and cream. There wasn't a speck of dust or dirt anywhere, and as they mounted the stairs to the circle Bethan noticed that even the people crowding into the doors that led to the stalls seemed better groomed than those in Pontypridd.

They were shown to their seats by an usherette who fluttered her eyelashes and pouted seductively at Andrew. Trevor relieved them of their coats while Andrew went to the confectionery kiosk.

'Do you know the cheapest seat in the stalls is two shillings?' Laura whispered while Trevor was hanging their coats on the back of the box door. Bethan shook her head and peered over the edge of the balcony. The theatre, like Laura, was buzzing with suppressed excitement, and she wished that she could relax enough to be swept up in the tide of gaiety.

Andrew returned with two programmes and an enormous box of chocolates. Handing them to Bethan he pulled a chair up alongside hers, leaving Trevor no other option but to sit next to Laura. Discordant notes filled the air as the orchestra began to tune up. The curtain twitched intriguingly, the lights dimmed and a hush fell over the auditorium.

Bethan passed the chocolates and a programme on to Trevor. Leaning forward she stole a sideways glance at Andrew under cover of the darkness. He smiled at her. Embarrassed, she looked away quickly, upsetting herself with the thought that he'd probably visited hundreds of theatres before, no doubt in the company of dozens of different girls. Perhaps she was reading too much into the evening. It could be just as he'd said, he wanted friendship and companionship, nothing more. They'd enjoy themselves, and afterwards, when the show was over, he'd shake her hand, drop her off at the corner of Graig Avenue and that would be that. A memorable night for her, just another amusing evening for him.

Once the orchestra struck up the opening number, and the curtain rose, she forgot her preoccupation with Andrew. Multi-coloured images whirled around the stage as acrobats dressed in red and blue silk jumped on and off circling horses. The music raced, quickening to a foot-tapping, pulse-racing speed.

The horses circled for the last time, left as the curtain fell and a troop of performing dogs yapped in front of the footlights, accompanied by their trainer. To 'Oohs' and 'Aahs' they went through their paces until the last black and white mongrel jumped through the final hoop and the curtain rose on a tightrope act. Bethan leaned forward on the balcony, resting her chin on her hand, completely enthralled. Her father had taken all of them to the circus once, when a touring company had pitched a tent in Pontypridd park. But it had been nothing like this.

Human act followed animal act in bewildering variety. Monkeys, trapeze artists, camels, clowns, elephants, jugglers, a knife thrower, flame eater . . . they took their bows, the curtain fell, the music stopped and light flooded the auditorium.

'It's not over is it?' she asked, blinking at the brightness.

'No,' Andrew laughed. 'Half time.' He rose from his seat. 'Can I get you a drink? Ice cream?'

'Ice cream if you let us pay,' Laura said pertly.

Trevor coloured, but Andrew held out his hand. Laura delved into her bag and produced half a crown.

'Ice cream for everyone?'

'Yes please,' Bethan answered.

'I'll help you carry them,' Trevor offered, following him out.

'This is the life.' Laura rifled the box of chocolates and popped one into her mouth.

'You'd better not get too used to it. Work tomorrow.'

'Don't be a grumble-grumps and remind me.' Laura took another chocolate. 'Tell me, how come you get the rich handsome one when I laid claim to him first? Not that I'm complaining, Trevor is rather sweet in a little-boy-lost way, and he does have prospects.'

'Laura, we're out with them for the evening, not heading up the aisle.'

'Speak for yourself. I could do a lot worse than marry a doctor, even a poor one.'

'If you want to swap seats . . . '

'If I want to?' Laura dug her elbow into Bethan's ribs. 'Where've you been looking. The eminently eligible Doctor John is smitten, and alas not with me. But don't worry, I know how to retire gracefully from the fray. And I'm suitably grateful for my consolation prize.'

'Now you're being ridiculous,' Bethan said irritably.

'Here you are, ladies.' Andrew pushed his way into the box, his hands full of ice-cream wafers.

'I feel like Orphan Annie on a Christmas treat,' Laura said, wrapping her hanky around her wafer.

'You're that hard done by?' Andrew asked drily.

'You're a doctor, you should know. "Nurse get me this, nurse get me that, nurse bow your head the doctors are passing. Run water into the sink for him, make sure it's not too hot, not too cold, no, not that soap, a new piece. Hold out a clean towel so he can dry his hands, and pick it up when he's done and dropped it to the floor." '

'It can't be that bad,' Andrew protested.

'Believe me it is. You should try standing in our shoes some time,' Laura replied.

'Sorry I took so long, there was a massive queue.' Trevor pushed his way awkwardly into the box, carrying a tray of glasses filled with orange juice.

'I didn't give you enough for orange juice,' Laura protested. 'Not at these prices.'

'My treat,' Trevor insisted.

'In that case, thank you,' she smiled and took a glass.

Andrew took the tray from Trevor and handed a glass to Bethan as he resumed his seat.

'I take it you're enjoying the show.'

'It's wonderful . . . ' She hesitated, seeing a mocking glint in his eye.

'Chocolate, before Trevor and Laura eat them all?' he asked, taking the box and putting it on the balcony next to her.

'No thank you.'

'You don't like chocolates?' he asked incredulously.

'Not very much,' she admitted.

'What do you like?'

'Oranges. I love oranges.'

'In that case you must marry me, I have this horror of middle-aged fat ladies who eat too many chocolates.'

'Ssh!'

The hissing came from the neighbouring box as the lights dimmed and the band started playing. The curtain rose on a fenced-in stage. Laura grabbed Trevor's arm as an immense tiger prowled towards the footlights. The creature lunged forward and rattled the bars and a couple of women in the front stalls screamed.

'You can hold my hand if you're afraid,' Andrew teased.

Bethan ignored his offer, but noticed that Laura was still pressing her cheek against Trevor's shoulder.

The second half passed even more quickly than the first. A

95

whirl of tigers, more clowns when the cage was being dismantled, Cossack dancers, more ponies – this time accompanied by cowboys and Indians, a snake-charmer, a balancing act, and eventually the grand finale. But no matter how vigorously she and the rest of the audience clapped, cheered and called for encores, all they got was another bow from the performers.

'Supper?' Andrew enquired, helping her on with her coat.

'I should get back,' she said doubtfully. 'My parents think I'm at the Palladium.'

'It's only ten o'clock, I'll have you back by twelve I promise.'

She looked to Laura, hoping for moral support, but Laura and Trevor were already discussing the merits of one café as opposed to another.

'As long as we go straight to Pontypridd afterwards,' she relented.

Supper was a bottle of wine and an omelette in a small café close to the dock area, and by the welcome they received, it was obvious that Andrew and Trevor had both been there before. True to his word, as soon as their plates were cleared and the wine bottle emptied Andrew drove to Pontypridd; this time Laura sat in the back with Trevor, leaving the front seat free for Bethan.

Bethan saw only two houses with the lamps lit as they travelled up the Graig hill, and even those lamps were in the bedrooms. She gripped the front of her seat nervously, hoping that her mother hadn't taken it into her head to wait up for her, or worse still, come out on to the doorstep to greet her. Andrew steered up High Street into Llantrisant Road, and bypassing the turning to Graig Avenue he stopped the car at the end of Danycoedcae Road. Trevor stepped out and opened the door on Laura's side.

'If you don't mind, I'll get out here too,' Bethan said as she struggled with the door handle.

'I thought you lived in Graig Avenue?' Andrew waved goodnight to Laura.

'I do.'

'Then I'll drive you down. I can always come back for Trevor.'

'The road isn't made up on Graig Avenue. It would play havoc with your car.'

'I'm a doctor. I make house calls on all kinds of roads, so one more rough surface won't make any difference.'

'You'd wake the neighbours.'

He looked at her, trying to decipher her features under the indistinct light of the street lamps. 'You're ashamed to be seen with me?' he asked.

'Not ordinarily,' she tried to make light of her reluctance, 'but it is nearly twelve o'clock.'

'Oh dear, don't tell me, you're about to turn into a pumpkin.'

'No.' Bethan struggled to keep her rising irritation in check. 'I have a family and neighbours who may resent being woken up by a car engine at this time of night.'

'In that case I'll walk you home.'

'No really, please. I don't want you to go to any trouble.'

'No trouble I assure you, and as you won't let me drive you it's the least I can do. Besides, your family really would have cause for complaint if I allowed you to walk home alone at this hour.'

He turned off the engine and dimmed the lights. She got out of the car. The air was bracing on this part of the mountain, even in summer. Now it sliced through their overcoats like the cutting edge of an icicle. He called out softly to Trevor.

'I won't be long.'

Bethan turned up her collar and walked across to the footpath that led down to Iltyd Street.

'Wouldn't it be better to go by the main road?' he suggested as he joined her.

'It's much quicker this way.'

'I don't doubt that it is, but I'd rather not break my neck.'

'The path is quite straightforward. Here –' without thinking she held out her hand – 'just be careful when you step over this rock, it's the only one the boys couldn't move.'

He intertwined his gloved fingers with hers, and hung on to them as they walked down the dark hillside. He didn't let go, even when the lights of Iltyd Street burned overhead. Hands locked, huddled into their coats, they walked quickly, crossing into Graig Avenue and the shadow of the wall of Danygraig House.

'That's it, there,' she whispered. All the houses were in darkness. The cost of heating and lighting ensured that most of Graig people went to bed early. Even on Saturday nights.

He looked up at the twin bays, the square of etched glass above the door, and the upstairs sash windows. All were in darkness.

'Everyone in bed?' he whispered.

'I hope so,' she said fervently, not wanting to explain that they lived in the back kitchen.

He held her hand briefly. 'Thank you, Bethan, for a lovely evening.' For once she could detect no hint of mockery in his voice.

'No, it's I who should be thanking you.' She hesitated, expecting a kiss, a fumbling, demanding hand beneath her coat after all the money he'd spent on her.

'I'm glad you enjoyed it. I hope you and Laura will join us again some time.'

'I'd like to.'

'Good.' He glanced up at the star-studded, clear night sky. 'I must come up here more often. I never knew the stars shone so brightly over the Graig mountain.'

'There's no smoke to cloud the sky because we can't afford to keep our fires in all night.'

'That's what I like about you, Bethan, you're so prosaic.'

Unsure of what he meant, she didn't answer. He bent his head and brushed his lips lightly across her forehead, so lightly that afterwards she wondered if he'd kissed her at all.

'Goodnight.'

He turned to face the wind and walked away. She watched his tall dark figure merge into the shadows around the corner. Then, crossing the road she mounted the steps to her front door. The evening had ended as she'd hoped: with him leaving without making a pass, groping beneath her coat or creating a scene. All the things that Glan would have done as a matter of course. He hadn't even tried to set a date for another outing, just a vague, 'I hope you and Laura will join us again some time.' But then, it didn't matter. Did it? She'd had a good time. Seen the circus from a box she could never have afforded. Ridden in a car. Eaten supper in a café late at night. Drunk her first glass of wine with a meal.

Andrew John had treated her to an absolutely perfect evening. Given her a taste of a glittering, sparkling world she thought she'd never experience. She should be feeling on top of the world.

Instead she felt unaccountably depressed, restless – and angry. Angry with him for introducing her to something she could never have – for ending their relationship before it had even begun.

Chapter Six

'And just where do you think you've been until this hour young lady?'

'Sorry, I know it's late, Mam. Laura and I . . . '

'That was Laura who walked you home was it?' Elizabeth sneered. 'Taken to wearing men's clothes, has she?'

'Mam, if you'll let me explain . . . '

'There's nothing to explain. I know exactly what you've been doing, my girl. I can smell the drink on you from here.' Elizabeth's face darkened with a contemptuous, naked anger that Bethan had witnessed only a few times in her life.

'I had a glass of wine with my supper,' she retorted defensively.

'Wine is it? I suppose you think wine is one step up from beer?' Elizabeth's voice rose precariously close to hysteria as she followed Bethan down the hall into the back kitchen. 'Do you think it's any better to be a rich man's whore than a poor man's?'

'Mam!' Bethan whirled around and faced her mother only to see her father standing in the passageway behind them. They'd been so wrapped up in their quarrelling they hadn't even heard him come down the stairs.

'That's enough, Elizabeth.' Evan advanced towards them bare-chested, his trouser belt hanging at his waist, his shirt flapping loosely on his arms.

'Look at her! Just look at her!' Elizabeth screeched. 'Your darling daughter. The whore!'

'I said that's enough, Elizabeth,' he repeated sternly. He turned to Bethan. 'Go to bed, girl. Now,' he commanded.

'That's right. Send your little darling to bed,' Elizabeth mocked. 'We all know she can do no wrong in your eyes. Your little darling . . . the whore,' she hissed, repeating the word, conscious of the effect it was having on Evan. 'My father always said that colliers, not the devil, invented whores. Well, collier or not, Evan Powell, I'll not have a whore under my roof. I'm telling you

100

now . . . ' she ranted, pointing at Bethan. 'Get her out, or I'll put her out. She's no daughter of mine.'

'You don't know what you're saying, woman.' Evan pushed himself between her and Bethan.

'Oh yes I do, and she goes . . . '

'That suits me fine,' Bethan shouted, goaded to breaking point. 'I'll pack my bags now.'

'Don't be silly, love. Where would you go at this hour?' her father said testily.

'She can go back to wherever she's been until now.'

'For Christ's sake, woman, shut up.' Evan turned fiercely on Elizabeth.

'Don't worry, Dad. I'm going.'

Bethan saw her parents through a red haze of anger that had been slow in coming, but smouldered all the fiercer for its tardiness. 'Just remember one thing,' she flung the worst thing she could think of in her mother's face, 'I didn't ask to come back here. You begged me because you couldn't make ends meet. I can have a place in a nurses' hostel any time for the asking. And I'll be a damned sight better off —'

'Bethan!' The cry came not from her mother, but her father. Her hand flew to her mouth. 'Dad,' she whispered. 'Dad, I'm sorry, I never meant . . . '

'See,' Elizabeth crowed. 'See what an ungrateful wretch you've spawned.'

'Go to bed, Bethan.' Evan leaned wearily against the door frame so she could pass him in the narrow doorway.

'I didn't mean . . . '

The words died on Bethan's lips. Her father wasn't looking at her. He was staring at her mother, a strange expression in his eyes. Head down, she ran along the passage and up the stairs.

Haydn and Eddie were sitting side by side on the top step, hunched and shivering in the nightgowns Elizabeth had patched together from Evan's old shirts.

'What's happening, Beth?' Haydn whispered.

'Nothing.' She brushed past him tearfully.

'Noisy nothing,' Eddie said tactlessly.

She slammed the bedroom door on them.

'Beth?' Maud's voice echoed sleepily from the dark lumpy shadow that was the bed.

'Go to sleep,' Bethan ordered, banging her ankle painfully in the blinding darkness.

She almost fell on to her side of the bed and began to undress, allowing her clothes to fall any shape on to the floor. Fumbling beneath her pillow she finally found her nightdress and pulled it over her head before she stole between the sheets. Tensing her body she strained to listen to what was happening downstairs.

At first Maud's heavy breathing seemed to drown out all the other noises of the house. But then she heard the boys blunder their way back to their bedroom. Still listening intently she lay awake until the first cold fingers of dawn crept through the thick curtains to lighten the shadows from black to grey. No other sound reached her during those hours. No voice was raised in the kitchen, and no foot stepped on to the stairs.

Elizabeth sat up in the parlour all night. She was conscious of one thing and one thing only. Of the depth to which her children had sunk. Haydn working night after night in the Town Hall rubbing shoulders, and heaven only knew what else, with chorus girls, drunken spivs, played-out musicians – the dregs of the theatrical world. Eddie practically living in the gym at the back of the Ruperra Hotel, fighting, smashing men's faces in and having his own beaten in for a pittance, and – even more sickening – because he enjoyed the feel and smell of violence. Bethan spending her evenings in public halls where drink was sold. Going out with men, drinking – and no doubt allowing herself to be pawed like an animal.

She recalled the time when she'd been able to control almost all of their waking moments. Almost all – because she'd never been able to prevent them from visiting Leyshon Street. They'd been such plump, pretty children. She'd taken pleasure in bathing them, dressing them in warm flannel nightgowns and tucking them up in cosy beds.

Most of the time they'd paid heed to her and done what she'd wanted them to. Now . . . now she felt as though her world was breaking up, her values shattering, and the children she'd struggled to keep clean and fed had gone the way of all the worthless working-class children around them.

She finally had to accept that none of them would now aspire to climb out of the back streets of the Graig, let alone to greatness. Neither Haydn nor Eddie would become a minister of God like her father and uncle. The girls wouldn't teach as she had done. Instead, Bethan, the most intelligent of all of them, had become a nurse. She wrinkled her nose at the thought of what Bethan did every day of her life. Messing with people's naked bodies. Women in childbirth . . . she shuddered in disgust, wishing she'd never borne any of them. All motherhood was pain. The pain of conception, of birth, and this – the ultimate and worst pain of all. The pain of losing them.

At a quarter to six in the morning Bethan lifted down the card-board suitcase she'd carried her clothes home in from Cardiff. Then she remembered the look on her father's face when she'd threatened to move out. Swallowing her pride she put it back on top of the wardrobe, and washed and dressed ready for work.

She had to walk through the kitchen to go out the back. Her mother was alone, engrossed in blackleading the stove. If she heard her entering she made no sign of it; nor did Bethan acknowledge her.

For the next few days a mixture of mortification and smoulder-ing anger kept Bethan away from the house as much as possible. She went there only to sleep. She ate her breakfast, dinner and tea, such as they were, on the ward, and had supper at Megan's, buying bloaters, meat pies, pasties and slices of brawn in the grocer's opposite the hospital to offset the cost to her aunt. Megan, used to the vagaries of her brother-in-law's household, was quietly supportive. Her father and her brothers tried to smooth things over, and Maud complained that she hardly saw her, but she excused her absences with brief references to pres-sures of work.

She wasn't exaggerating about that. Her shifts began at six-thirty in the morning and finished at seven at night. Afterwards she stayed behind in Sister's office, studying until ten or eleven o'clock. The midwifery certificate covered a vast amount of both text and practical knowledge; following Matron's suggestion, she made full use of the small library kept locked in the cupboard of Squeers' office.

She soon found out that Matron had told her the truth. It was difficult to do a full day's work and study at the same time. When she'd been a probationer in Cardiff Infirmary, concessions to studying time, scant though they'd often been, had at least been made. Squeers didn't even pay lip service to the idea. And now she and Laura were qualified the sister took care to see that every minute of their ward time was spent on their feet and working. But although the job was demanding she enjoyed it, and she was grateful that it left her very little time to think of what was happening at home – or of Andrew.

She looked for him constantly and even saw him occasionally, but never alone. He was either on ward rounds with his father and Trevor, or they were both gowned and masked with a patient lying between them. It didn't help when Laura returned from a day off in the middle of the week with bright, shining eyes, a definite lilt to her voice and tales of an outing with Trevor, whose free time had miraculously coincided with hers. Flushed with, if not love, at least the beginnings of fond affection, she renounced all her claims to Andrew in favour of Bethan. Bethan scoffed at Laura's teasing, but it didn't stop her from manoeuvring to get close to Andrew whenever he visited the ward.

Envy hadn't been part of Bethan's nature until she watched Trevor and Laura during the week that followed. She grew taciturn and silent, particularly in Laura's presence. Totally preoccupied with thoughts of Andrew, she regretted what she saw as her dark, amazonian figure, contrasting it with Laura's pert, petite appearance. Would Andrew have asked her out again if she'd been prettier? More talkative, like Laura?

She grew pale, lost weight, and close to the end of her unbroken stint of duty, she felt both physically and emotionally drained. She had a two-day break coming to her, but she was dreading it. She'd toyed with the idea of spending most of it in the reading room in Pontypridd's lending library, resolving to get up early and study in the morning; after buying a few dainties in town, she would invite herself to Megan's for tea and supper. But she took no pleasure in the prospect. In fact she took pleasure in very little except Haydn's good fortune in finding work, and the rapid progression of her studies.

Two days before she was due to take her leave, Squeers came down with influenza. The night sister was shifted to day duty, and Matron sent for Bethan and asked if she'd work two nights, to cover for the sister's absence. Pleased to be singled out for the responsibility, she agreed, leaving late in the afternoon to catch a few hours' sleep before returning for the night shift.

She tossed restlessly on the bed from three o'clock until five, then finally rose to wash and dress. Downstairs she walked in on the entire family, who were sitting around the table in the kitchen eating tea. Her father, Maud, Haydn and Eddie greeted her warmly, and for the first time in over a week she was persuaded to join them. Her mother had made an enormous bread pudding, heavy on the stale bread and light on the fruit, like all the others she'd baked since Evan had been put on short time, but it was topped by a thin layer of delicious sugary pastry. Cooking, like the other domestic skills, had been studied by Elizabeth until she had passed from mere proficiency to mastery. The only factor that blighted her recipes was the quality of food she could afford to buy.

Evan, airing paternal pride, asked Bethan how she was progressing with her studies, but the rest of the family were even more silent than usual. Maud had caught a cold, and coughed violently between mouthfuls of warm pudding and tea. Bethan laid her hand on her sister's forehead and, discovering that she had a temperature, suggested that her sister go to bed after the meal. Before Elizabeth could complain about walking up and down stairs with trays, Evan offered to make a batch of the home-made, vinegar-based remedy that Caterina used to brew whenever one of the family went down with a cold.

Eddie had been withdrawn and sullen since the night he had been used as a punchbag in the gym, and he ate quickly. Without a word he carried his plate to the washhouse and disappeared out of the back door and up the garden, ignoring Haydn's shouts.

'I was going to walk down the hill with him,' Haydn complained, finishing his pudding.

'I'll walk down with you,' Bethan offered, picking up his plate as well as her own.

'I've got to go in five minutes.'

'So have I.'

Bethan left the plates in the enamel bowl on the wooden board next to the sink in the washhouse, and looked for the stone foot-warmer that only came out when one of them was ill. She found it behind a sack of carrots on the floor of the pantry.

'Who's that for?' Elizabeth demanded when she saw her filling it with hot water from the boiler.

'Maud, she has a fever,' Bethan replied when she'd recovered from the shock of hearing her mother speak directly to her.

Elizabeth sniffed loudly, but said nothing more. Bethan followed Maud upstairs, and tucked her into bed with a scarf around her throat, a handkerchief under her pillow and the foot-warmer at her feet.

'Dad will be up in a minute with some of Mam Powell's tonic. See you in the morning.' She smoothed Maud's hair back, away from her face.

'Thank you,' Maud croaked, snuggling under the bedclothes.

'What are big sisters for?'

'To pay for little sisters to go to the pictures?' Maud suggested hopefully.

'You're not going anywhere,' Bethan pronounced authoritatively, lifting the blankets up to Maud's chin.

'Not now, but I might be on Saturday.'

'We'll see. Sleep well, see you in the morning.'

Although the sky was heavy with the promise of rain, it was still dry when Haydn slammed the door behind them.

'Long time no talk, Beth,' he said cheerfully.

'Sometimes I think all there is to life is work, work and then more work.'

'I know what you mean,' he sympathised. 'It's the same in the Town Hall. Haydn get me this, Haydn get me that, Haydn clean this floor. Haydn sweep up between the seats. Haydn . . . '

'Last in always gets the dirty work to do. I thought you knew that.'

'I do. I just didn't realise there were so many bloody awful jobs that needed doing.'

'Haydn!'

'Sorry, Beth.'

'You didn't think it would be all glamour did you? Delivering flowers to the chorus girls, and wild parties backstage after the show.'

'No . . . oo . . . o,' he said slowly. 'I've hung around the Town Hall too long for that. But then again a man can live in hope.'

'Hanging around isn't the same as working in a place.'

'I've found that out. Take no notice, Beth. You've caught me at a bad time. Other people get early morning willies, with me it's evening. Besides, I know I'm damned lucky to have any kind of a job. And this one – ' he grinned slyly – 'well it does have its compensations. Some of those chorus girls you mentioned aren't half bad.'

'I see.' She gave him a telling look. 'Does Jenny Griffiths know how you feel about them?'

'That's the other thing,' he said mournfully. 'Working these hours, I only get to see her on Sundays.'

'You could give her a ticket for the show and walk her home afterwards.'

'Now that's an idea.'

'If you do, don't forget to check with her father that it will be all right for her to be out so late.'

His mouth fell into a downward curve. 'Harry's all right, but her mother thinks Jenny could do a lot better than me.'

'Then she's a fool!' Bethan protested indignantly.

'Thanks, Sis, I could always rely on you to stick up for me. By the way,' he said casually, 'while we're on the subject, who's this doctor?'

'What doctor?'

'Don't give me that. The one that brought you home early Sunday morning.'

'It wasn't Sunday morning. It wasn't even midnight.'

'Whatever.' Haydn refused to be sidetracked. 'Who is he?'

'He works in the hospital. I hardly know him. He just happened to have a couple of spare tickets for the circus . . . '

'In the Empire Theatre Cardiff?'

'I haven't noticed a circus in Pontypridd this week,' she said sarcastically.

'Beth, you don't just happen to have a couple of spare tickets for something like that. Bill Twoomey's been trying to get hold of some for his family for weeks, and working in the Town Hall he's in the know. They're like gold.'

'People always feel they owe their doctor a favour,' she said carelessly. 'Which reminds me, I've a bone to pick with you. Thank you for putting my money back in my box, but where's the overcoat I asked you to get our Eddie?' she asked, deliberately steering the conversation away from her personal life.

'I wouldn't have made a dog's bed out of the ones in Wien's.'

'I was afraid of that when Laura told me the price. You're still working for Wilf aren't you?'

'Yes, and I'm always on the lookout, you know that.'

'Have you been paid yet?' she asked shrewdly.

'By Wilf? Every shift I do. On the nose.'

'Not by Wilf, by the Town Hall?'

'Got to work a week in hand,' he grumbled.

'I thought so.' She unzipped her shopping bag and reached down for her purse.

'Here.' She tried to slip him half a crown.

'No, Beth. We can't keep relying on you to bail us out.'

'Did Dad say that to you?' she asked suspiciously, remembering her outburst.

'No.'

'Go on, take it,' she insisted. 'Pay me back next week. You'll be moneybags then.'

'I don't need it.'

'I know you don't, but I don't like the thought of you walking around without any money in your pocket. And if you see something that will suit our Eddie you can always put a bob down so they'll hold it. Quick, take it, or I'll be late.'

'All right then,' he agreed finally. 'Thanks, Beth.'

'See you in the morning.'

'It's funny to have a sister working nights.'

'It's funny to have a brother working,' she smiled.

'It'll be funnier still to have two working.'

'Is there any chance of our Eddie finding anything?' she asked hopefully.

'Not that I've heard.'

'Then he's still going down the gym?'

'Did you really think he'd stop because of what we said?'

'No. Just wishful thinking.'

'He's got to make his own life, Beth. We all have.'

'Said with the wisdom of old age?' she laughed.

'You don't do any near enough of that, Sis.'

'What?'

'Laugh,' he said seriously as he walked away down High Street.

She had little time to think about what Haydn had said as the tail end of the evening dragged on into night. The maternity ward was never peaceful. As soon as one babies' feeding time was over, there was the next to superintend. In between there were restless mothers to soothe, and an unexpected admission who'd gone into labour three weeks before time.

With only one second-year trainee and two ward maids to help her, she did the best she could, detailing the maids to the routine tasks of feeding and changing the babies, and entrusting the care of the patient to the trainee when she had to leave the labour ward. At a quarter-past midnight the baby was born with the minimum of fuss, but before the trainee could take him to the nursery the mother began to haemorrhage.

Bethan's first instinct was to shout for help, then with a sinking heart she realised she was it. The senior nurse on duty wasn't even a qualified midwife. Taking a deep breath, she subdued the tide of panic.

'Take the baby to the nursery, then bring a sterile pack and the drugs trolley straight here. Then telephone for the duty doctor. *Hurry!*' she shouted as the trainee stared, mesmerised by the rapidly deepening puddle of blood on the rubber-lined bed sheet. The girl looked from the bed to Bethan, wrapped a towel tightly around the baby, and ran.

At that moment the responsibility she had so proudly assumed crushed Bethan with the devastating effect of a collapsing pit shaft. The woman on the bed was slipping away, already in the semi-comatose state that precedes death from massive blood loss. Bethan lifted the thin, calloused hand, took the barely perceptible pulse and studied the patient. Her face was prematurely aged, lined by years of worry, childbearing and trying to make ends meet. The admission card had detailed this as her eleventh preg-

109

nancy, but Bethan had no way of knowing how many of her other children had survived, or how many orphans there'd be if she died.

The trainee returned with the trolley, and Bethan set to work. Praying that her fumbling efforts would be enough, she spent the following hour and a half pounding and kneading the patient's uterus, desperately trying to recall everything that had been done in similar cases when she'd sat by as an interested pupil. Long before the hour and a half was up she had good cause to regret her lack of foresight in not realising then just how swift and sudden the transition from onlooker to nurse in charge would be.

'Trouble, Nurse Powell?'

She turned her head. Andrew was standing in the doorway of the delivery room, cool, unflustered and incredibly handsome in a black evening suit, boiled shirt, black tie and white collar.

'The patient's haemorrhaging,' she said harshly, turning back to the bed. 'I'm doing what I can, but it's not enough.'

He stepped closer, taking off his coat.

'What do you think?' he asked briefly. 'Operate?'

'You're the doctor.'

'And you're the nurse,' he said evenly. 'You must have seen a dozen cases like this.'

'Operate,' Bethan agreed.

He used the small theatre in the outside corridor, and as Bethan couldn't leave the ward in charge of a trainee, he asked the sister from the men's ward who had a qualified staff nurse in attendance to help him. As soon as the duty porters wheeled the patient out, Bethan checked her ward. The maids had just finished the two o'clock feed and, for once, all the mothers were either sleeping or resting peacefully. She told the trainee to clean the labour room and change the bed, and asked one of the maids to make tea and bring her a cup in the sister's office. Emergency or not, she still had to update the patients' record cards, and she felt as though someone, or something, had pulled her plug. It would be difficult to keep her eyes open until her shift finished at seven.

She closed the office door behind her. The fire was smoking miserably behind its tarnished mesh guard. She unhooked the

110

metal screen from the iron grate and tried to poke some life into the coals. The crust of small coal broke, revealing glowing embers beneath. She replaced the guard and kicked off her shoes, resting and warming her feet on the hearth kerb. The ward maid knocked and carried in her tea. For once it was fresh, not stewed.

Revelling in the luxury of being able to put her feet up she leaned back on her chair and glanced up at the uncurtained windows. White streaks of rain were lashing down on the black glass. She felt warm, cosseted and comfortable, ensconced in an overworked nurse's idea of heaven.

After half an hour of writing, she left the office to check the ward. Everything had remained quiet, so she returned to the record cards. She was still sitting, pen in hand, cards on lap, in front of the fire when Andrew returned.

'She's very weak.' He shook the flat of his hand from side to side. 'We'll know one way or the other tomorrow.'

'The birth was straightforward. No problems,' she explained defensively. 'When it happened it was so sudden. . . . '

'Believe me, she wouldn't have lasted until I got here if you hadn't done what you did.' He untied the green gown he was wearing and pulled down the mask. 'I'll get rid of these. Want some tea?'

'I ought to see to the patient.' She rose stiffly from her chair, putting the record cards on to the desk.

'There's nothing for you to do.' He pushed her back into her seat. 'Sister Jenkins from upstairs is staying in the theatre with the patient. I thought it best not to move her for an hour or two. She'll call if we're needed. Tea?' he repeated.

'Yes please.' She sank back down and checked her watch. Half-past three. Another three and a half hours before the night shift ended.

Andrew returned. He was in shirt-sleeves, his black tie hanging loose around his neck, his coat slung over one shoulder.

'Obliging ward maids you have there. They said they'd bring in fresh cups as soon as it's made.' He sat in the chair behind the desk and swung his feet on to the wall. Crossing his hands behind his head he closed his eyes and leaned back. The clean, sharp smell of male perspiration tinged with the heady scent of his

111

cologne filled the warm office. Shy and a little embarrassed by the unaccustomed intimacy, Bethan returned to the record cards.

The maid brought the tea with a quick curtsy and a shy glance at Andrew. He sat up. Leaning over the desk he lit a cigarette with a heavily engraved gold lighter.

'Cigarette?' He pushed his case and lighter towards Bethan.

'I don't smoke.'

'I should have remembered. Sorry I took so long to get here.' He inhaled deeply and blew long thin streams of smoke from his nostrils. 'I was at the tennis club ball in the Park Hotel. The message bounced from home to the Park Hotel twice before the porter found me.'

Bethan knew from his dress that he'd been at a formal 'do'. There was no reason for her to be upset, but the thought of him laughing, dancing and talking to other girls hurt her with a pain that was almost physical.

'I would have asked you to come with me, but you were on duty,' he murmured as though reading her thoughts.

'How did you know I was on duty?' she broke in quickly. Too quickly. She could have kicked herself when she saw his wry smile of amusement.

'I read the duty roster for this ward.'

'You read the rosters?'

'Among other things. You're off on Wednesday and Thursday this week.'

'Off the ward, but I still have to work for my certificate.'

'All work and no play makes Jill a dull girl.'

'Possibly, but I'm not Jill.' She paused, as it hit home that the sour note in her voice sounded exactly like the one that dogged her mother's speech.

'Laura and Trevor spent their free day in Cardiff. I had hoped we could follow their example.'

'And do what?'

'Window-shop, see a film, eat. The things that normal people do outside of hospitals and infirmaries. I'll pick you up in Station Square at ten on Wednesday morning.'

'I can't afford the time.'

'Of course you can,' he said in exasperation. 'That's why you're given days off. To do nothing in particular. Even the hospital board recognises that you can't work people like machines. Ten, Station Square?'

She stared into the fire, refusing to look at him. She was honest enough to admit to herself that she would rather go out with Andrew than any man she'd ever met. One evening in his company had been enough for her to fall for him, to use Laura's language. But the sheer intensity of her feelings terrified her. He was a doctor. He was rich. He could have any girl he wanted – and probably had, she thought cynically.

She realised already that she wanted him to regard her as something more than just a diversion from boredom, and she doubted that he'd see a nurse from the wrong side of the tracks as anything else. She also had a shrewd suspicion that one date with Andrew John could, if she wasn't careful, make her reject out of hand anything less that other men had to offer.

'I assure you, that although I'm a doctor and you're a nurse, my intentions are strictly honourable.'

'I don't doubt it.'

'It's more than just this doctor/nurse thing isn't it?' he asked. 'Is it Laura's brother, or that porter? Because if it is I'll bow out now.'

'No, nothing like that,' she replied swiftly.

'Then what?'

'Nothing,' she said decisively, sweeping her doubts to the back of her mind. 'I'll meet you in Station Square, only at twelve, not ten. I'm on nights again tomorrow, and I'll need a couple of hours' sleep.'

'Good,' he smiled. 'Now that's settled I can go and check on my patient, with luck on my way home.'

The money Bethan had saved for an overcoat for Eddie went on a green wool dress and a down payment on a new navy-blue coat at her Aunt Megan's. She tried to justify the extravagance with the thought that there'd be extra money in her pay packet at the end of the week, but she still hid her new clothes from everyone except Maud.

Her sister's cold had worsened, settling into a hacking, feverish chest infection that Elizabeth had been forced to acknowledge, but even Maud's illness couldn't dampen Bethan's excitement at

113

the prospect of a day out with Andrew. On Wednesday morning the routine update of patients' notes and ward handover to the sister who was standing in for Squeers seemed to take for ever.

It was a quarter-past eight before she reached Graig Avenue, tired and breathless from running all the way up the hill. Haydn had gone to work on Wilf's stall in the market and her father and Eddie had walked down with him, hoping to pick up some work themselves. Her mother had cleared away the breakfast things and changed out of the overalls she wore in the house, ready to go shopping. After a stern injunction to Bethan to clear up any mess she made, Elizabeth left.

Bethan checked on Maud, who was still coughing despite Evan's remedy. She returned to the kitchen to make a fresh pot of tea. While it was brewing she looked at the kitchen clock. Half-past eight. No one would be in before ten at the earliest. She ran outside and unhooked the tin bath from the nail hammered into the garden wall. Her father and their lodger Alun bathed after every shift, out the back in summer, and in the washhouse in winter. Eddie and Haydn bathed in the washhouse before bed on a Friday night, but she and Maud weren't so lucky. Her mother frowned on them bathing, preferring them to wash in the privacy of their room where there was no risk of their father, the lodger or their brothers walking in on them.

She carried the bath into the washhouse, and wiped it over with the floorcloth before taking it into the kitchen. She stood it on the rag rug in front of the range. Lifting down the enamel jug from the shelf where Elizabeth kept her pots and pans she drew off hot water from the boiler, careful not to allow the level to get too low before topping it up. After she'd filled the bath with as much hot water as she dared, she tipped in a couple of jugfuls of cold.

She took Maud's tea upstairs. Shivering in the freezing bedroom she tucked Maud in before returning to the kitchen with her scent, dressing gown and the flannel, towel and soap from their washstand. Closing the curtains in case any of the Richards should happen to walk into their yard, she stripped off and poured a little of the essence of violets into the water. Two minutes later she was sitting in the tub, sponging her back, revel-

114

ling in the feel of the warm scented water trickling over her bare skin.

Forgetting that she only had a limited amount of time she decided to wash her hair. Ducking her head between her knees she soaked it before rubbing the bar of soap into a lather that covered her hands, and then her head. Luckily she'd left the enamel jug on the hearth, so all she had to do was refill it with the now cool water from the boiler to rinse off the suds. When it was squeaky clean, she wrapped it in the towel, closed her eyes, and wriggled down as low as she could. When she opened her eyes again the water was cold, the hands on the clock pointed to twenty past nine, and her fingers were as wrinkled as her mother's scrubbing board.

Jumping up she pulled the towel from her hair and hastily rubbed herself as dry as she could in the soaking cloth. Moving quickly she stepped out on to the rug and tied on her dressing gown. Her mother never lingered any longer in town than she had to, and if she came back and found out that the bath had been carried into the kitchen there'd be hell to pay.

Bethan emptied the bath with the jug. It was long slow work, particularly as she had to watch that she didn't spill a drop of telltale water on the kitchen rugs. It was a quarter to ten before the bathwater was low enough for her to grab hold of both handles and carry it out through the door.

'What do you think you're doing?'

She jumped, slopping a good pint of water on to the floor.

'Sorry, didn't mean to scare you.' Eddie walked into the kitchen. 'Here, let me take the other handle. Haven't you got enough sense to realise that you could do yourself a permanent injury trying to carry that out by yourself?'

'I was trying to be quick before Mam comes back.'

'I saw her going into Uncle Joe's house as I crossed the Graig mountain.'

'Thank God for that.'

Eddie's eyes were shining, his face filthy, blackened by a thick layer of coal dust.

'What have you been doing?' She didn't need to ask. She already knew.

'Getting coal.'

'Off the wagons in the colliery sidings?' she accused him heatedly.

'Maud needs a fire in that bedroom. It's freezing.'

'You could cop a two-pound fine for that. Jail, because we couldn't pay.'

'They'll have to catch me first. And before you ask, the coal's already safe and sound in the shed along with what's left of Dad's ration. There's no telling it apart, and as soon as I've given you a hand with this, I'll lay a fire in your bedroom.'

Bethan gripped hold of the bath handle. She was too ashamed to say any more. As the only one earning any real money she should have done something about the temperature in the bedroom before this. Spent the money she'd wasted on a new dress on coal. She'd been so wrapped up in Andrew and the row with her mother that she'd managed to forget Maud's illness for hours at a time.

'One two three, lift,' Eddie ordered. Shuffling along, they carried the bath through the washhouse towards the back door.

'You can't step out here without slippers on.' Eddie heaved her out of the way, stumbled and tipped the water all over the yard, soaking the flagstones.

'That will never dry before Mam comes,' she wailed.

'I'll tell her I washed it down.'

'She won't believe that,' Bethan rejoined crossly.

'She will if I tell her next door's cat dragged a dead rabbit across it. Right, you go and dress and I'll wash here,' he ordered, embarrassed by the amount of cleavage she was showing.

She saw what he was looking at and pulled the edges of her dressing gown closer together. 'I won't be long.' Grabbing the towel, her discarded clothes and her scent from the kitchen floor, she raced through the passage and up the stairs.

Maud was sleeping fitfully, her cheeks bright red, burning. If the fever didn't break soon Bethan resolved to ask Andrew to call in and take a look at her. Dressing as quietly as she could, she started with the silk camiknickers and petticoat that she hadn't worn since she'd washed and aired them in her bedroom. (Elizabeth had taken one look at the flimsy garments and refused to hang them on the airing rack in the kitchen.) She finished with the new green wool dress and plain black low-heeled shoes. She looked herself over in the mirror, her thoughts an uneasy mixture of guilt over the new dress and regret for her decidedly worn shoes, handbag and dated hat. All things considered, she didn't look *too* awful. She screwed her eyes in an attempt to view her profile in the wardrobe mirror, and gave up when Maud tossed restlessly from her back on to her side.

Stealing out, she closed the bedroom door softly and shivered her way down the stairs and along the passage to the kitchen.

'Want some tea, Beth?' Eddie asked.

'Not if I've got to make it.'

'It's all done.' There was a hurt tone in his voice.

She pulled one of the kitchen chairs close to the range, unwrapped her hair and began to towel it dry.

'Mam'll go berserk when she finds out that you've gone to bed with wet hair.'

'I'm not going to bed,' she said, blessing Eddie's lack of observation. Haydn would have spotted the new dress and smelt the scent by now.

'Then where are you going?'

'To Cardiff.'

'Cardiff's even worse. Going out with wet hair, just after a bath? You out to catch pneumonia?'

'You sound just like Mam.'

'Does she know what you're up to?'

'No. And you're not going to tell her. Are you?' she asked anxiously.

'What's it worth?'

'Sixpence.'

'Make it another seven bob and you're on.'

'You little. . . . '

'I need the money.'

'What for?'

He picked up the teapot from the range, took off the cosy and filled the cups he'd taken down from the dresser.

'What for?' she repeated, forgetting her hair for a moment.

'Gloves,' he answered reluctantly.

'Boxing gloves?'

'I'm good, Beth. I really am.'

'I saw how good you were the other night.'

117

'No you didn't,' he broke in angrily. 'That was the first time I'd ever climbed into a ring. I really am good, everyone in the gym says so. Once I get gloves I'll go round the fairground booths. A few weeks of that and I'll make enough to pay you back and chip in my corner here. Come on, Beth, a month at the most and I'll give you a quid. I'd ask Dad but he's never got any money, Haydn hasn't been paid yet and Mam won't give me a penny. You know what she is,' he added acidly.

'I haven't got it to give to you.'

'It's like that, is it,' he said sourly.

She opened her handbag. 'I can give you half a crown now, and five bob on Friday when I've been paid.'

His face lit up. 'If I put half a crown down today, George will hold them until Friday.'

'George?'

'It's his gloves I'm buying. Beth, you're a darling.' He hugged her out of sheer excitement, then, realising what he was doing, he dropped his arms.

'Fool, more like it.' Her face fell, serious at the sight of one or two cuts and bruises that hadn't quite healed. 'Just don't go getting yourself into a real mess, or I'll never forgive myself.'

He grinned. 'Me? I'm immortal, Beth, I thought you would have realised that by now.'

She tried to quell her misgivings. Eddie was entitled to his dreams. She'd found out long ago that they were the only thing that made the harsh reality of life on the Graig bearable. Since she'd qualified, her fantasies of Florence Nightingale nursing had been replaced by hazy, formless desires that somehow encompassed Andrew John. Haydn had hopes of a theatrical career that would sweep him from dogsbody in the Town Hall to success on the London stage. Her father dreamt of a workers' uprising that would revolutionise the face of the Valleys. Maud had mapped out a future rags-to-riches plan for herself roughly based on the plot of *Jane Eyre*. The only problem with Eddie's dream was that it was easier to put into practice and far more dangerous than any of the others. But fear for Eddie's health and life gave her no right to stop him from trying. For all she knew he might be the lucky one: the next Jimmy Wilde to come out of the Valleys with enough talent to earn himself a slice of the good life he craved for.

And even if he was on a hiding to nothing, who was she to stop him? Better for him to hold on to his dream, no matter how hopeless, than lose all hope for something beyond the grim reality of the present – like their mother.

Chapter Seven

Andrew had parked his car and was sitting waiting for Bethan in the station yard car park. She saw him as soon as she emerged from under the railway bridge, her face flushed with the walk down the hill, her hat and new coat damp from the fine misty rain. She quickened her pace and ran towards him. He stepped out and opened the passenger door.

'I'll start the engine.'

'I'm sorry, am I late?' she asked breathlessly.

'Not at all.' He turned up the collar on his burberry and closed the door for her. Taking the crank from under his seat, he paused for a moment to admire her long slim legs clad in shining, flesh-coloured silk. A few minutes later they were dodging brewery carts and grocers' wagons on Broadway heading towards Treforest on the Cardiff Road.

'Well,' he looked across and smiled, 'you have a whole day free, Cinderella, what would you like to do with it?'

'Window-shopping, the cinema, tea?'

'Those were my suggestions.'

'I haven't any better ones.'

'Lunch first? Or have you eaten?'

'I haven't eaten,' she admitted.

'Then lunch it is.'

He drove off the road in Taffs Well. Turning right he steered the car up a small country lane that meandered through the woods surrounding the romantic, fairytale Castell Coch.

'Where are we going?' Bethan demanded, a sharp edge of concern in her voice.

'To have lunch.'

'Up here?' A chill prickled down her spine. Her mother's frequent and disturbingly graphic warnings sprang to mind as she realised she was on her own, miles from anywhere with a man she scarcely knew.

'Look on the back seat.'

She did, and saw the corner of a wickerwork hamper poking out from under a rug.

'That – is lunch. I asked Cook to pack it for us. Now all we need is the right spot.'

He found it almost at the summit of the mountain. A small dirt-track, its far end barred by a rotting wooden gate that looked as though it hadn't been opened in years. He pulled to a halt and turned off the engine. Evergreens and conifers hedged them on both sides, so closely that if they hadn't travelled along the lane Bethan would have doubted its presence. The only open view was over the gate in front of them.

Andrew turned round and knelt on his seat. He handed her the blanket while he unbuckled the strap that secured the lid of the hamper.

'It will soon be cold without the warmth of the engine so wrap the rug around yourself,' he ordered briskly. 'Now what have we here?' He lifted out two steep-sided glass bowls topped with squares of gingham tied with string. He handed them to her, and took out two forks and a plate wrapped into a parcel of grease-proof paper. 'Brown bread, and lemon.' He balanced the plate on the dashboard and gave her a fork. 'And prawns in aspic – ' he took one of the bowls from her – 'try it.' He removed the gingham and squeezed a slice of lemon liberally over the food. 'It's good. I know picnics should be held in summer, but I couldn't resist the temptation to have one now. I love picnicking, brings back memories of childhood and all that.'

She took a wedge of lemon. Conscious of her vulnerability, she contrasted Andrew's childhood memories with her own. The present fare couldn't be further removed from the jam sandwiches wrapped in newspaper, a bowl of whatever wild berries were in season, and the bottle of water that she and her brothers had devoured on the side of the Graig mountain when they were small.

Thrusting his fork into the aspic, Andrew began to eat. 'Don't you like prawns?' he asked as she picked one out of the jelly and examined it closely.

'This is the first time I've tried them.' She put it into her mouth and began to chew. Her mouth was dry, and she almost choked when she tried to swallow it.

'They're not unlike cockles. Fishy and salty, with the taste of the sea.'

'They don't look like cockles.' She extricated another from its bed of aspic. 'They look . . . they look naked,' she blurted out, without thinking what she was saying.

'Naked?' He lifted his left eyebrow.

She blushed. 'It's just that they're so pink.'

He burst out laughing. 'What it is to have the mind of a child.'

'I haven't. . . . '

'I'm sorry.' He held up his hand in front of her. 'I didn't mean that the way it sounded. Glass of wine?'

'Wine?'

'It's probably not as cold as it should be. . . . ' He leant close to her and she backed away, hitting her spine painfully on the door handle. Sliding his hand under her seat he pulled out a green bottle wrapped in wet towels. 'There's a couple of glasses and a corkscrew in the glove compartment.'

'Do you always think of everything?' She handed him the corkscrew and held on to the glasses.

'Only where picnics are concerned.' He finished forking the prawns into his mouth, tossed the bowl into the back seat, and jammed the bottle between his knees. It was open in a minute: the wine was clear, sparkling. Unlike anything she'd drunk before.

'If you finish the prawns, we can move on to the next course.' He pulled open the door of the glove compartment, and placed both glasses on it. Then he produced two large plates individually wrapped in damp muslin and thick folds of greaseproof paper. Uncovering hers, she discovered slices of cold chicken breast, lean ham and neatly turned-out moulds of potato salad, grated carrot and rice. She tried her best to eat, but could barely manage a quarter of what was on her plate. Even his food emphasised the difference between them. When she organised a picnic the best she could manage was bread and dripping, brawn, sliced cold heart and dry bread. For the first time she found herself wondering what his home was like. He'd casually mentioned Cook. There would undoubtedly be other servants – kitchen and parlour maids, the sorts of position Maud would apply for when she left school, and count herself lucky to get. A daily 'skivvy' for the heavy work, someone like her Aunt Megan – an odd-job man cum gardener, young like Eddie – or an unemployed miner like her father.

'And here we have the *pièce de résistance*.' Andrew held a glass preserving bottle in front of her. 'It looks disgusting I grant you,' he said, struggling with the top, 'but looks can deceive.'

'Preserved fruit salad,' Bethan ventured, staring at the mishmash of pale fleshy bits floating in murky liquor.

'My father's idea of a winter fruit salad.' He wrenched open the lid and decanted the contents into two china bowls decorated with red and burgundy-coloured cherries.

Bethan tentatively dipped her spoon into the mess, extracted a piece of soggy, colour-bled strawberry and put it into her mouth.

'What is it?' she gasped.

'Summer fruits in Jamaican rum.' He spooned a generous portion into his own mouth. 'My father's favourite dessert. And the only thing in the house made entirely by him. As the season progresses he puts a couple of pounds of every fruit that ripens in the garden into a huge earthenware pot that he inherited from his father, covering it with rum as he goes along. By the time winter sets in, the pot is full enough to keep his after-dinner conversations genial until the next lot is ready.'

Bethan felt as though her mouth was on fire, but for politeness' sake she dipped her spoon into the mess again. This time she found a cherry.

'There's oranges in here,' she said in surprise. 'Surely you don't grow those in your garden.'

'Only in my father's imagination. Here.' He refilled her wine glass.

'Are you trying to get me drunk?' She wouldn't have asked the question if the mixture of rum and wine hadn't already gone to her head.

'No,' he replied quietly. 'Just trying to get you to relax a little. I don't think I've ever met anyone who's been quite as nervous or suspicious of me before.'

She took the glass and stared into it.

'Don't you like it?' he asked.

'It's better than the fruit salad.'

He picked up the bowl from her lap, and winding down his window tipped the contents outside. She sat back in her seat and looked over the gate down into the valley below. She followed the course of the river Taff as it wound between patchwork fields, wooded copses and narrow threads of stone houses.

'I hope the rain stops when we get to Cardiff,' she said for the sake of saying something.

'It won't make any difference to us if it does. The arcades are best for window-shopping, and I'll try and find a film with plenty of sun in it. It'll be black and white sun of course,' he said earnestly.

She smiled.

'That's better. Here, let's finish this.' As he emptied the last of the wine into their glasses, his hand accidentally brushed against her arm. She jumped as though she'd been scalded.

'I didn't bring you here to have my evil way with you,' he said quietly, gazing into her eyes.

'I'm sorry.' She was close to tears.

'You really are in a state, aren't you? Here – ' He wedged the bottle of wine in the hamper and handed her his handkerchief. She dabbed at her eyes with it. It smelt of fresh air and new starch.

'Would you like anything else?'

She shook her head.

'In that case I'll pack up and we'll go.'

He folded the dirty plates and crockery into a cloth, then drained his wine glass and laid it on top before closing the lid.

'I won't be a minute.' He picked up the starting handle.

'Andrew, I'm sorry. Really sorry,' she said with difficulty.

'For what?' he smiled. 'Being a nice girl?'

He glanced at her frequently as they continued their journey. She sat perched on the edge of her seat, smiling tautly with her mouth but not her eyes, very obviously what his mother called 'sitting on pins'. He recalled the first time he'd seen her tall, slim figure striding briskly along the hospital corridors. Even the convent veil that covered her hair, and her pale complexion drained by overwork and the drab surroundings, had failed to detract from her exotic Mediterranean beauty. Then she'd turned, and a single glimpse of her magnificent dark eyes had been enough to make him forget his current girlfriend and offer to cover for his father on all maternity ward emergencies.

At the hospital ball he'd seen the humour and intelligence that lurked beneath the surface of basic insecurity, and the evening at the circus had shown him how very different she was from the self-assured, middle-class, somewhat selfish and often mindless girls he'd known in London. When he'd moved to Pontypridd to join his father he'd assumed that he would follow the carefree path of many and varied girlfriends and happy off-duty hours spent in search of the good times that he'd had in London. But he'd reckoned without the effects of the economic slump. The dour grey stone buildings and air of grim poverty that clung to the streets in the town soon came to epitomise the word 'depression' for him.

'Good times' in Pontypridd were few and far between, even for the young. Survival, not fun, was the major concern and preoccupation. He knew from something Laura had said that Bethan's father was on short time and her brother out of work. That made Bethan with her regular job the family breadwinner. So he put her serious outlook down to too much responsibility too soon. And that made him want to introduce some harmless frivolity into her life. If anyone needed it, she did. Every time he looked at the patients in the maternity ward he saw her as she might be ten years from now. Married to an unemployed miner. Her slim, lithe figure bloated from bad food and constant child-bearing; her pale, delicate skin chapped, roughened and reddened by cold weather, even colder water and a life lived out in a smoky back kitchen. The prospect saddened him. He liked her, felt sorry for her, and at the same time longed to protect her from the miserable effects of the soul-destroying poverty that ultimately crushed most women of her class.

Part of her attraction lay in her vulnerability. As an incurable romantic, her plight brought out the Sir Galahad in him that his mother had nurtured with frequent readings of Arthurian stories. But he recognised that his romantic feelings for Bethan were just that – romantic. And he knew from previous liaisons just how transient romanticism could be. As his father light-heartedly but frequently pointed out, it was one thing to court a girl, quite another to marry her, and he was astute enough to realise that

125

whatever happened between him and Bethan probably wouldn't last very long, simply because she didn't fit into his world any more than he fitted into hers.

He'd never known anyone like her. Unlike all the other girls he'd gone out with, she was working class and, despite her diffidence, possessed a mind of her own. The differences between them were far greater than the common threads that bound their complementary professions, but if anything the disparities made him more interested in her as a person. Or at least that was what he tried to tell himself. He'd never been quite so confused about what he felt for a girl before. Wary of the stage and film stereotype of the caddish middle-class male who deliberately sets out to seduce the poor working-class girl, he decided that for once he would be the perfect gentleman, opting for platonic friendship in the true tradition of Sir Galahad. So with a sharp pang of regret he pushed from his mind all thoughts of enjoying the kind of sensual and easy physical relationship with her that his looks, carefree manner and open purse had brought him with the London ladies.

Not for one minute did he consider that he wouldn't have thought her friendship worth cultivating if she'd been fat, frumpish or looked other than she did. His paternalistic desire to give her and, incidentally, himself the elusive good time closed his mind to everything except the kindness he sincerely believed he was bestowing on her.

He parked the car close to Queen Street station, and from there they walked to the shopping centre. Bethan had often spent afternoons in Cardiff with Laura when they'd been at the Royal Infirmary, but Andrew stopped to browse in small out-of-the-way shops she never knew existed: second-hand bookshops, crammed to the ceilings with musty, leather-bound volumes and framed prints; galleries that displayed black-framed oils and watercolours on crooked walls above rickety staircases. And antique shops – real antique shops, as different from Arthur Faller's pawnbroker's shop in Pontypridd as chalk from cheese.

These shops didn't even hold goods against future payment. The merchandise on display was uniformly old, in good condition, and not an item of clothing amongst the stock. Fine French china and porcelain. Elegantly turned, mahogany Regency furniture. Scenic oils of rural landscapes no longer recognisable as part of modern industrial Wales. Ornate, highly wrought late Victorian jewellery, heavily encrusted with precious and semi-precious gems, and lighter, more tasteful early ornaments that Andrew examined with interest.

They were in a small booth in the arcade when he appealed to her for assistance.

'It's my mother's birthday next week,' he explained. 'Would you help me choose a piece for her?'

'But I don't know her taste,' Bethan protested.

'Good.' He smiled at the perplexed look. 'Good taste,' he qualified patiently. 'Which is what I suspect yours to be.'

Flattered, Bethan bent over the glass display table and studied the pieces.

'I like that,' she said slowly, a little uncertain of herself.

'The blue enamelled and gold locket?'

She nodded.

'My suspicions are correct. You do have good taste.' He called the proprietor.

'Very nice, sir, very nice,' the man repeated, sensing a sale in the air. 'The lady has an eye for excellence if you don't mind my saying so.' He unlocked the cabinet with a key that hung on his watch chain and delicately removed the locket, laying it out, face uppermost in the palm of his hand. 'Late Regency and in superb condition, which isn't surprising considering where it came from. Can't say any more than that, sir. Confidentiality you know,' he whispered close to Andrew's ear. 'The maker's mark is on the back,' he continued in a louder voice. 'French, authenticated early nineteenth century, and I can offer it to you for a very good price.'

The very good price sent Bethan reeling. Twenty pounds! She thought of what her family could do with twenty pounds.

Andrew carried the locket over to the window, and while he examined it more closely she wandered round the rest of the shop. Judging by the mound of black leather jewel cases on display, there was no shortage of women prepared to part with their rings and necklaces, and there was an abundance of other valuables: silver and gold cigarette cases, watches, hairbrushes and ladies' toilette sets. She couldn't even begin to imagine having enough money to buy such luxuries and envied the people who had them to sell. One gold cigarette case would buy new outfits for Haydn, Eddie and her father. And put Sunday dinners on their table for a month or two.

'Ready? Ready to go?' Andrew repeated in reply to her quizzical look.

The shopkeeper opened the door for them with much bowing and scraping. The heavens had opened while they'd been in the shop, and Andrew turned up the collar of his coat and opened his umbrella as they reached the mouth of the arcade, placing it more over her head than his own.

'Here, take my arm,' he said as he looked up and down the street. 'Is there anywhere special you'd like to visit?'

'Nowhere.'

He pulled his pocket watch out of his waistcoat and flicked it open.

'It's too early for the cinema. We could have tea? Are you hungry?'

'Not really.'

'We could visit my favourite place in Cardiff. Game for a mystery tour?'

'I'd be interested to see your favourite place.'

'Favourite place in Cardiff,' he qualified. 'Let's go.'

He walked past a large department store and into another arcade that opened out next to a churchyard.

'It's so quiet here,' she murmured. The only sound was the rain pounding on the gravestones and the thick leaves of the yew trees. 'You'd never think you were in the middle of a city.'

'Or next to the market,' he agreed. 'Sometimes when I come to Cardiff in the summer I just sit here for a while, watching the world go by.'

'You watch the world go by?'

'Occasionally,' he replied unconvincingly.

He clenched her arm tightly in the crook of his elbow as they left the shelter of the arcade for the open street. Turning left he led her up a step into a building. He shook the umbrella and folded it while she wiped the raindrops from her eyes and hat, then she looked around in amazement.

'I've never seen anything like it.'

'I have, but not in Wales. Isn't it magnificent?' He was as pleased with her reaction as if he'd been personally responsible for the décor.

They were in a long corridor, the ceiling plastered, arched and moulded after the Norman style. The walls were tiled – but with tiles that would have done justice to an Oriental mosque, brilliantly patterned and coloured in a multitude of blending and contrasting styles. The narrow tile borders were moulded, thrown into sharp relief above and below the bands of squares that bore designs in every conceivable colour and flow of lines.

She walked slowly, running her fingers along the walls, allowing the textures and colours to assail her senses. The corridor finally ended in a sharp left turn and she looked back to see Andrew smiling.

'Watching your reaction is almost as good as seeing it again for the first time.'

'What is this place?' she asked.

'Public library.'

'I wish I'd joined when I was in the Royal Infirmary.'

A pointed, rather forced coughing echoed towards them.

'Reading room around the corner,' he whispered. 'If we creep along quietly, we can take a look at it on the way out.'

Embarrassed, she hung back, but Andrew forged ahead oblivious to her discomfort. She followed shyly and found herself in a large, pillared and niched room, as beautifully decorated as the corridor but far lighter and altogether airier.

'It takes very little to imagine a stunning harem girl sitting at one of those windows,' he whispered in her ear as they left.

'Is that why you like it?'

He laughed out loud, throwing his head back as he opened his umbrella.

'No. I'll like it even when I'm too old to appreciate beautiful girls.' A sudden violent downpour drowned out his words. Taking her arm he quickened his pace, steering her into a Lyon's tea shop. He helped her off with her coat, and they sat at a table resplendent with white linen tablecloth and napkins. An impeccably turned-out waitress came to take their order, and without

129

consulting Bethan he ordered a plate of mixed cakes and a pot of tea for two.

'I think we've exhausted the arcades, and we can't really walk around the streets in this.'

'No we can't,' she smiled, beginning to relax. The unease she'd felt when she'd been alone in the car with him had vanished during their walk around the city. She glanced at the occupants of the other tables then looked back at him, managing to sustain eye contact even when he winked at her.

'We have an hour to kill before the film. We may as well wait here in comfort.'

'Yes,' she agreed.

'I thought we'd go to the Pavilion in St Mary Street. It has talkies.'

'All singing, all dancing, all talking . . . ' she began in the manner of the promotional trailers in the cinema. Suddenly she felt happy. Very happy indeed.

'I don't know about all singing or all dancing. There's a court-room drama showing this week. With Pauline Frederick and Bert Lybell.'

'I love Pauline Frederick.'

'Who doesn't?' he asked drily, leaning to one side so the waitress could lay out the cakes and teapot. The girl dropped a curtsy, straightened her cap and with a backward glance at Andrew left. Bethan poured out the tea, feeling very grand and privileged. It felt good to know that other women in the room were admiring Andrew and probably envying her.

'Tomorrow?' he asked. 'Would you like to do anything special?'

'You're off duty tomorrow as well?'

'I told you. I read rosters.'

'I don't know. I really should work.'

'Nonsense. You must be way ahead with your studies.' He helped himself to a large cream bun, dividing it into two with his fork and spoon. 'Pity it's not high summer. I could think of lots of things to do in fine weather.'

'Such as?'

'Motor to the coast.'

'I love the sea.'

'Really? Most girls don't like the beach because the wind and the sand mess up their hair.'

'I'm not most girls.'

'I noticed that the first time I met you, which is why you're sitting where you are.' He put three lumps of sugar into his tea, hesitated and added a fourth. 'The beach in winter is very impressive, and if the weather's like this I know a very good tea shop in Porthcawl.'

'No picnic?'

'You'd like another picnic?'

'Yes please.' She lifted a chocolate éclair on to her plate. He stared at her for a moment.

'Then a picnic it is,' he mumbled through a mouthful of cream and choux pastry.

'I wish you'd let me drive up your street.'

'So you can bring all the neighbours out on their doorsteps. No fear,' she said firmly.

'You had a good day?'

'A very good day. Thank you.'

'You enjoyed the film?'

'Very much.'

'And you'll still come out with me tomorrow? Even after this?' He leaned towards her and brushed his lips over hers.

'Even after that,' she whispered. Her lips tingled, tantalised by the light touch of his. For the first time in her life she felt as though she actually wanted a man to kiss her, and kiss her hard.

'I parked outside the vicarage so you could call for help if I became too ardent,' he joked, seeking her hands with his.

She looked up at him, glad of the darkness that concealed the colour flooding into her cheeks, embarrassed by his veiled reference to her earlier behaviour. Shyly, tentatively she lifted her face to his. He needed no other invitation. His lips bore down on hers. She raised her arms, and running her fingers through his thick, curling hair she pressed her head against his. Weak, breathless, she was conscious only of the crushing of the heavy layers of woollen clothing that separated their bodies – his breath, warm, moist as it mingled with hers – the smell of his cologne as it filled her nostrils – the sensation of slow-burning, heavily restrained passion.

'I think I'd better walk you up the Avenue before you're the talk of the neighbourhood,' he said huskily as a light flicked on in one of the cottages opposite the car.

They walked in silence. When they reached her house he whispered, 'Ten o'clock tomorrow.'

'Station car park?'

He nodded and walked away quickly. Taking a deep breath she climbed the steps and opened the front door. The kitchen clock was chiming the hour. Eleven. Heart pounding, she switched on the light and walked down the passage, bracing herself for another ordeal with her mother.

The room was in darkness, but not deserted.

'Hello, love.' Her father's voice floated from his chair. 'I've been enjoying a quiet time. Want to sit with me a while? There's a fresh pot of tea on the range.'

'Thanks, Dad.' She unbuttoned her coat, and asked the question uppermost in her mind. 'Where's everyone?'

'Your mother's gone to bed with a headache. Eddie's walked down the hill to meet Haydn, and Alun's out. Want to tell me what you've been up to?'

'I've been picnicking.' She kicked off her shoes and sat in the chair opposite his, waiting for her eyes to become accustomed to the gloom.

'In this weather?'

'In this weather,' she laughed. 'And then I window-shopped in Cardiff. Had tea in Lyon's café. Saw a talkie, a really good one, and ate fish and chips on the way home.'

'This boy of yours. Is he a good one, Beth?' he asked gravely.

'I think so, Dad.' She leaned forward and hugged her knees. 'I think so,' she repeated slowly.

'That's all right then.' He reached for the cups and put them slowly and deliberately on the table. 'We all want to see you enjoy yourself, love. But none of us wants to see you get hurt.'

'Don't worry, Dad.' She picked up the teapot and began to pour. 'I won't.'

Bethan's relationship with Andrew, and Laura's with Trevor,

soon became the worst-kept secrets in the Graig Hospital. And within a very short time Bethan discovered that despite the embargo she no longer cared what anyone, even Squeers and Matron, thought about her or her liaison with Andrew.

Some of Andrew's self-confident, happy-go-lucky attitude rubbed off on her. Haydn no longer complained that she rarely smiled. Now she not only smiled but frequently laughed, even in her mother's presence. She only had to catch a glimpse of Andrew across one of the yards in the Central Homes or in the corridor of the hospital to get a surge of happiness that would lighten her step and last her the whole day.

Eligible, charming and incredibly handsome – and out of all the girls he could have chosen, he'd chosen her. Everything he said to her, every place he took her to, every moment they spent together, became precious memories to be mulled over, and dwelt upon.

Hidden beneath her underclothes in her drawer lay the chocolate box Andrew had bought at the circus. She'd distributed the last of the chocolates to Maud and her brothers, and as winter faded she filled it with mementoes of her outings with Andrew.

There was the streamer that she had found caught in the neckline of her dress after the hospital ball. One of the programmes he'd bought at the circus; a sugar cube from the Lyon's café, and the ticket stubs from the film he'd taken her to in Cardiff (stubs that she'd retrieved from under his seat when he thought she was picking up her handbag). A perfect round pebble he'd pulled out of a rock pool at Rest Bay, Porthcawl. More cinema ticket stubs – from Pontypridd this time. A programme from a variety show they'd seen in the New Theatre, another from the Town Hall, a wrapper from a bar of chocolate they'd shared . . . every day off brought a new addition.

Two or three nights a week Andrew and Trevor would sit in his car around the corner from the hospital in Courthouse Street, and wait for her and Laura to finish their shifts. Then he'd drive up the Graig hill and drop them off at Leyshon Street, where they changed clothes in Megan's bedroom. With their uniforms folded into bags, they'd spend what remained of the evening in one of the villages on the outskirts of Pontypridd. They visited cinemas in Aberdare, Abercynon, Llantrisant and the Rhondda, and after-

133

wards they ate fish and chips out of paper bags and newspaper in Andrew's car. And when Trevor finally saw Laura to her house in Danycoedcae Road, Andrew walked Bethan the long way home, over the Graig mountain.

When she was with Andrew, Bethan was happy – happier than she'd ever been before. When she was alone, particularly in the early hours of the morning, she fell prey to ugly fears and insecurities. What she feared most was that he'd desert her for a prettier girl from his own class. But even that fear receded as days of unbroken courtship turned into weeks. Then one day as she and Laura walked through the female exercise yard on their way to the maternity unit they saw the green spikes of daffodil shoots pushing their way up in the narrow strip of soil beneath A and B ward windows, and she realised that her relationship with Andrew had survived a whole half-season.

'The first signs of spring,' Bethan observed triumphantly.

'You know what that means,' Laura commented significantly.

'Warm weather, light clothes, outings to the park and the seaside. Trips into the country, lots of fresh air, and if Andrew's right, the disappearance of Maud's cough.'

'Lazy afternoons spent lying next to Trevor on the beach. Warm evening walks up the mountain. . . . '

'Have you mentioned these thoughts to Ronnie?' Bethan teased.

'Don't have to, his mind runs like a sewer.'

'If he suspects that you're still going out with Trevor he won't let you out without a chaperon.'

'Ah, but he thinks I finished with Trevor weeks ago. And he can't say anything to wholesome outings with my girlfriends, now can he?'

Laura leaned back against the wall of the main dining room and breathed in deeply, but all she could smell was the strong odour of cabbage water wafting out of the kitchens. Bethan stood next to her, still smiling at the thought of all she had to look forward to. The Easter Rattle Fair would be held soon, closing the streets of the town to traffic and opening them to stalls and crowds. Andrew had promised to teach her tennis on the courts in Pontypridd Park and put her up for membership of the tennis club. He'd offered to take her to the beaches at Barry Island and Porthcawl, and even mentioned Swansea.

And there was always the hope that things would improve at home. Haydn's job had worked out well; perhaps it was Eddie's turn next. There had been a lot of talk about changes coming to the Maritime. The pit might open five days a week and revert to full-time working, in which case Maud could stay in school. . . .

The hysterical screams of a woman shattered the peace in the yard and with it went all the castles that Bethan had built in the air.

'If that's someone in labour, tough,' Laura said emphatically. 'I've got another ten minutes of this tea break to go.'

Glan and Jimmy appeared in the doorway of K ward dragging a girl between them. She was shouting obscenities at the top of her voice, kicking, spitting and scratching at everyone unfortunate enough to be within her reach.

'Isn't that Maisie Crockett?' Laura asked.

Bethan ran across the yard.

'Stay clear, Nurse Powell,' Sister Thomas, the nurse in charge of K ward ordered loudly. 'You could get hurt.'

'Went berserk when they took her baby from her,' Glan explained as he struggled to pin Maisie's arms behind her back. 'Come on, girl,' he addressed Maisie irritably, 'you're on to a loser. You can't fight me and win.'

'Maisie, listen to me. Rules are rules.' The sister stood in front of Maisie, trying to force the girl to look at her. 'You've done nothing but sit around and look after your baby for six weeks. You can't expect that to go on. You have to work to support you both. And if you work hard, you'll see her for an hour on Sunday. It's not as if they've taken her to the ends of the earth,' she explained gently. 'J ward's behind the maternity unit, not in Africa. Now come along, be a good girl, say you're sorry and we'll forget about this outburst.'

'I want my baby,' Maisie hissed, spitting like a cornered cat.

'You're not doing your baby or yourself any good with all this nonsense,' the sister said in a firmer tone.

'Bastards!' Maisie screamed venomously, going wild. 'Bastards, you've no right to take my baby. She's mine!' She pulled away and kicked Glan in the shin. He relaxed his hold for an instant and she lashed out at Jimmy, broke free and ran back towards J ward, where the babies and toddlers under three were kept.

'Sister Thomas, what is the meaning of this?'

'Oh Christ, the Master, that's all we need.' Glan stopped rubbing his leg, and grabbed Jimmy's arm. Together they ran past the dispensary after Maisie. Sister Thomas was in the middle of her explanations to the Master when Glan and Jimmy returned, frogmarching the still defiant Maisie between them.

'I've heard enough, Sister Thomas.' The Master glared at Maisie. 'There's only one way to deal with recalcitrant paupers, my girl, and you're going to find out what that is.' He turned to Glan and Jimmy. 'C ward,' he commanded.

'The men's ward?' Glan countered in amazement.

'Padded cell, and don't release your hold on her until she's safely inside. Sister Thomas, don't expect her back, I'm telephoning the police. Maisie'll be spending the night in the cells down the station. Where she goes after that will be up to the magistrate.'

Bethan went to Sister Thomas and picked up her hand, which was bleeding badly.

'Maisie bit it,' the sister explained.

'I'll clean it up if you like,' Bethan offered.

'That would be good of you.'

Maisie screamed just one more time before Glan and Jimmy, with the assistance of the Master, heaved her round the corner and out of sight. Feeling faint, the sister sank down on the steps of K ward. Bethan rubbed her temples.

'Sometimes,' Sister Thomas said weakly, 'just sometimes I hate this job.'

'I'm not surprised,' Laura said mildly. 'I'd better be getting back. Don't worry, Beth, I'll tell Squeers where you are.'

'Thanks.'

Bethan sat alongside Sister Thomas and looked up at the square of clear blue sky framed by the rooftops of the workhouse buildings. It seemed paler, more washed out than a moment earlier. The air held an uncomfortable damp chill. She glanced down the yard towards the daffodil shoots. They were very small, no more than buds. Spring was as far away as ever. She'd been a fool to think otherwise.

Chapter Eight

On Easter Sunday the sun beamed down on Graig Avenue, softening the harsh grey outlines of the buildings and the drab brown
and black tones of the pressed dirt streets. It directed brilliant
spotlights on to the few daffodil buds brave enough to poke
their heads out of the dry, barren mountain soil that filled the
handkerchief-sized gardens, and it shone warmly on Bethan as
she stepped out on to her well-scrubbed doorstep.

'You going to chapel, Beth? Or high church now you're keeping
company with a doctor?' Glan enquired snidely.

She looked over the low wall that separated the front of her
house from next door, and saw Glan togged out in his best navy-
blue rayon suit, sitting cap in hand in front of the bay window
closest to her. 'None of your damned business where I go, Glan
Richards,' she replied briskly, pulling on the white gloves she'd
taken out of mothballs to wear with the long-sleeved blue and
mauve floral cotton frock she'd bought from Megan the day
before.

'Swearing. On Easter day too. Well I'm a forgiving sort of a
chap, and seeing as how we're both dolled up in our Sunday best,
how about some company to walk down the hill with?' He took
a comb out of the top pocket of his jacket and ran it through his
heavily creamed hair.

'I have enough company,' Bethan answered sharply.

'I wish you didn't,' Eddie observed glumly as he, Maud and
Haydn came out of the house.

'Didn't the Easter bunny bring you any chocolate eggs to sweeten your temper?' Glan jumped down his steps and followed them
on to the Avenue.

'Maud made us some beauties,' Haydn gloated, hooking his
arm around his sister's shoulders. 'Little chocolate ones in sponge
cake nests.'

'Lucky you,' Glan grumbled. 'Mam thinks chocolate eggs are
a lot of nonsense. All I managed to scrounge was one of the

hardboiled eggs left over from those our Pat and Jean painted for their kids. And being Pat and Jean they used red paint that went through the shell and dyed the whites pink.'

'Different,' Haydn said pleasantly. 'Talking about your mam, where is she?'

'Went down early to help lay out in the hall ready for the chapel tea.'

'Some people are gluttons for punishment,' Eddie grumbled mutinously, straightening an old crumpled tie of Evan's that he wore at the neck of his only collar.

'You'll eat the tea this afternoon, same as everyone else,' Maud rebuked. 'And if we don't step on it, we'll be late for the service.'

'Mustn't upset Uncle John Joseph,' Eddie cautioned.

'Sooner we get there, sooner we'll be back.' Haydn pulled his cap over his face, and offered Bethan his other arm.

'That doesn't apply to chapel. Sooner we get there, longer we'll sit on hard benches, and the number our bums will be,' Eddie said crudely, trying to wind Maud up. Maud refused to be wound up.

'Isn't it a beautiful day,' she said as they walked, glancing coquettishly at Glan from under her eyelids.

'And you're too young to be doing what you're doing,' Haydn admonished, pulling her away from Glan.

'How am I ever going to learn how to flirt if you get in the way every time I try to practise?' Maud protested.

'Practise all you like,' Glan offered with a sly look at Bethan. 'I don't mind little kids.'

'I'm not a little kid,' Maud complained furiously.

'Boxing tomorrow?' Glan asked Eddie, looking at Maud in a new light.

'Thought I might visit the booth in the Rattle Fair,' Eddie murmured.

'That's a mug's game if ever there was one,' said Haydn, very much the big brother.

'Uncle Joe's going to collapse when he sees us all walking in together.' Maud changed the subject, trying to smile at Glan behind Haydn's back.

'He'd only do that if Dad walked into chapel,' Eddie said.

'Communists don't go to chapel,' Maud commented primly.

'I think Dad would, if anyone other than Uncle Joe was the minister,' Eddie contradicted.

'What about your father, Glan?' Haydn asked. 'He's not a communist and he doesn't go to chapel.'

'He's not much of anything except a drinker.' Glan glanced over his shoulder in case someone was eavesdropping. 'He says time's too precious to waste sitting about in chapel listening to preachers who've never got off their arses to do a day's work in their lives.'

'Bethan, Maud!' Diana shouted to them as they rounded the corner by the Graig Hotel. She was wearing a light green and white flower-sprigged dress and a white straw hat. William had on a new three-piece suit.

'I wish I had a mother who was an agent for Leslie's,' Glan said enviously, thinking, but not daring to speak his mother's opinion that Megan and her children made more out of her relationship with Harry Griffiths than she did from her agency.

'Bad case of jealousy, Glan?' Bethan asked.

'Nice suit,' Glan conceded to William, staring at the grey and blue wool cloth pin-stripe.

'I'd sell it to you if I thought that taking it in a yard or two at the shoulders and a foot or two on the trouser bottoms wouldn't spoil the cut.'

'You're barely an inch taller than me,' Glan protested.

'But what an inch.'

'You. . . . '

'Easter. Good will to all men,' Bethan interrupted, sensing a fight brewing.

'That's Christmas.' Eddie halted in front of the chapel. The reedy strains of the organ floated out into the street along with a heady mixture of Evening in Paris, camphor and mothballs. 'As this was your idea, Beth, after you.'

Aunt Hetty was playing the organ as usual, the music resounding to the arched roof of the fifty-year-old building. Bethan led the way into the back pew, pushing Maud next to the wall so she could keep an eye on her. Haydn followed, with Eddie next to him and Glan on the end of the bench. The pew in front of the pulpit was packed with sober-suited deacons. Her mother had taken her place in the second row, alongside the deacons' wives, an honorary position granted to her in accordance with her status as John Joseph's niece, and only living relative after his wife.

A thud followed by a chorus of subdued titters came from the gallery overhead, traditionally the province of the children. Bethan had happy memories of sitting up there, chewing ends of 'sweet tobacco' and the 'sweepings' that Haydn used to bring back from the stalls on the market. Even as small boys he and Eddie had haunted the place, begging for odd jobs, carrying parcels for heavily loaded customers, laying out gimcracks on the displays, clearing up the rubbish that accumulated around the traders' feet. Once the stallholders realised that they could trust the boys, they paid them in halfpennies, sweepings (whatever they could glean from the rubbish) and spoiled and leftover goods. The halfpennies had been hoarded, the hard goods traded or swapped and the edibles devoured in chapel on Sunday mornings, out of sight and reach of Elizabeth.

The music became vibrant, the vestry door to the right of the pulpit opened and John Joseph Bull, resplendent in white wing collar, dark suit and black bow tie, entered the chapel and climbed on the rostrum to the pulpit. He pointed to the board that carried the hymn numbers and the congregation rose to the opening bars of 'There Is a Green Hill Far Away'.

The only part of chapel that Bethan really enjoyed was the singing, particularly when it was bolstered, as it was now, by the full choir. Clear waves of pure music echoed down from the rafters, breaking into crescendos that carried with them the swell of absolute emotion. And croaking along with the tide of sweet voices were the discordant, hoarse, gravelly chants of the old men, John Joseph's foremost amongst them.

As a child Bethan had never understood the see-saw arrangement of chapel services. The up side of the singing which lightened people's spirits was invariably followed by a depressing down side, when her uncle began his own particular brand of hellfire sermonising. Today, after the prayers and a second hymn, he laid his handwritten notes on the pulpit and stared down at the assembled men, women and children. Each curled into their seat, desperately trying to appear small and inconspicuous as his powerful voice began to recite a catalogue of dire, red-hot torments that the devil kept in readiness for those who transgressed from the straight and narrow.

His bony index finger sought and pointed, and even tough, hardened miners shuddered, closing their eyes and knotting their hands into fists, as guilt coursed swiftly through their veins.

'You. Yes you there, Robert Jones!' The full force of his wrath descended on a hapless miner sitting in the pew opposite Bethan's. 'You know what you've done! So does God. And I know.' He appealed to the deacons' wives in the second pew. 'He took his pay. His three-day pay. Money which his wife needed to keep his children's bodies and souls together. And what did he do with it?' He whirled, a dervish in a flapping black coat. 'He drank it. Every penny! And while he lay retching in the gutter his wife was forced to beg shopkeepers for food for her crying babies. He drank the devil's brew, and let his family starve.'

In the shocked and absolute silence Robert stared down at his feet, too mortified to move or attempt to reply. A child tittered out of sheer nervousness, and John Joseph's hawk-like eyes scanned the hushed crowd searching out the culprit.

'Well might you laugh, Freddy Martin,' he shouted. 'I know and God knows what you stole from the market last Saturday. He sees into the black and sinful hearts of boys who slide sugar crumbs from the edge of sweet stalls into their pockets. Crumbs that aren't theirs to take. And you – ' He turned on two unemployed boys who'd been fined for playing cards in the street, moved on to a wife who'd quarrelled publicly with her neighbours – no one in the congregation was safe from his prying, self-righteous condemnation.

Anniversary of the Resurrection it might be, but for all that John Joseph's anger remained harsh and unabated. He'd never made any allowances for the weakness of his fellow man, and he wasn't about to begin now. His voice rose to a fever pitch of indignation as he shouted out the names of those who had sinned, followed by details of their transgressions. Bethan stared down at her gloved hands. She found it difficult to meet her uncle's eyes over the tea table in the back kitchen of Graig Avenue, let alone when he was preaching.

She glanced surreptitiously around the pews, lowering her lashes whenever anyone caught her eye. The deacons' wives had decorated the chapel with vases of daffodils and catkins, but the clothes of the congregation alone would have testified to the season. Everyone had made an effort, no matter how little they had. Even old Mrs George, who'd worn the same rusty black cotton dress to chapel for as long as Bethan could remember, had taken the trouble to wash, press and trim it with a twopenny lace collar. All the men's collars were stiff with starch and gleaming white, in some cases whiter than the shirts they topped. Best shirts generally lay wrapped in tissue paper in drawers between one Sunday and another. Even the hats that the women wore, and the men held in their hands, had been brushed until the felt had piled into balls.

Studying her neighbours' clothes was infinitely more diverting than listening to her uncle. Shutting her ears to the sound of his voice Bethan picked out the women from Leyshon Street. She'd met most of them in Megan's house. Betty Morgan who had six children, and whose husband was on short time like her father, was dressed in a smart, white-trimmed navy crêpe de Chine. Her next-door neighbour Judith Jones was dressed either in green silk or the best imitation of it that Bethan had seen, and all six Morgan children were wearing new white socks and sandals. Little wonder that William and Diana could afford new clothes. Megan's business must be booming, though heaven only knew how her customers were affording it.

A crash rocked the pulpit and jolted her sharply back to awareness. Her uncle appeared to be staring straight at her although it was difficult to be sure, as his eyes were deep set, half hidden beneath bushy grey brows. The blood rushed to her face, burning her skin. The tension in the atmosphere grew bitter, almost tangible, unbearable in its intensity. Slowly, ever so slowly, John Joseph uncurled his fingers from the edge of the wooden lectern. He lifted his hand, pointed and spoke the one word dreaded above all others by the women in his flock.

'Harlot!'

Every eye in the chapel focused on the hapless victim. Phyllis Harry, shoulders hunched, head lowered beneath the brim of her cheap straw hat, cowered in the corner of her pew.

'Scarlet woman! Follower of the devil's ways. She carries the child of sin within her. God knows, and it is by His will that we are no longer deceived by a wolf in sheep's clothing.' John Joseph's eyes remained focused on Phyllis as he stepped backwards out of the pulpit on to the rostrum. 'We must, all of us,' his eyes scanned the silent, expectant congregation, 'follow God's Law.' His voice deepened, booming with a strength that matched that of the organ. 'If thy right eye offends thee, pluck it out.' His hand moved up to his eye and a collective gasp rippled through the assembly. 'If thy right arm offends thee, cut it off,' he decreed, slashing the flat of his hand towards his shoulder. 'If thy son or daughter walks hand in hand with the devil, shun them. If thy brother or sister ceases to follow in the steps of the Master then. . . . ' He paused and waited expectantly for his sentence to be finished. He was not disappointed.

'Cast them out!' The cry was taken up by those sitting in the front pew, and people further back who wished for a place on the privileged benches.

'Cast them out.' John Joseph echoed the words softly, thoughtfully, as he gazed into the mesmerised faces. 'It is not a step we take lightly. But didn't the Lord Himself overturn the tables of the Pharisees in the temple? Pharisee!' He homed in on Phyllis. 'Neglected, her sin will spread like a cancer.' He stepped down from the rostrum and moved into the central aisle. 'We dare not be complacent,' he thundered. 'Its seed lies within us all.' He bore down on the rows of silent people. 'You – ' he pointed to Jimmy, the porter from the Central Homes. 'And you – ' this time it was a deacon's wife. 'But you, good people, fight to suppress your baser instincts. As does every decent man and woman. We must be ever vigilant. We must strive every day, every hour of our lives. We must fight with every inch of strength we possess. Fight though it costs us our last breath. And even as we fight – the devil lies in wait. He sits there – ' he stretched out his arm to Phyllis – 'fat, complacent, licking his lips as he leads the weak into hell. He sits in God's House, masquerading as the meek. Shun him. Root him out. Destroy him and all his works. As he knows no pity, neither shall we.'

He lowered his voice to a whisper that carried to every dusty corner. 'Should we fail, should we show mercy, the rot that lies within will contaminate us all. It will contaminate you.' He turned to Mrs Richards, Glan's mother who sat in the centre of the middle pew, the layers of her well-covered body quivering. 'And you – ' He clamped his hand on Mrs Evans who lived above the fish and chip shop. 'Should we turn our backs and ignore the cancer, it will grow. Feed upon our fragile hearts of godliness. We *must* be strong.' He paused for breath, allowing the full effect of his words to sink in. 'The Lord taught that there are times when to be merciful is to be weak. There is only one path open to us. We must cast out the devil that is among us. Cast out . . . Cast out. . . . '

The deacons and their wives took up the chant. Soft at first, it built into a deafening crescendo.

'Out! Out! Out! Out! Out! Out!'

Maud gripped Bethan's arm, pinching her flesh until it burned. Casting fallen women out of chapel was a rare feature of John Joseph's ministry. As far as Bethan knew it had only happened twice before, for the simple reason that John Joseph, flanked by a full complement of deacons, visited the miserable girls in their homes as soon as the news broke, before they had time to set foot in chapel. But infrequency didn't make these occasions any the less dreaded by most of the women in the congregation. Even now the only ones who seemed to be enjoying the proceedings were John Joseph, his deacons and the privileged women in the second pew.

Bethan gritted her teeth and held Maud's hand. The object of her uncle's scorn was trapped in the centre of a pew four rows in front of them. Her heart went out to the pathetic creature. Phyllis Harry? The Phyllis who lived with Rhiannon Pugh? Bethan turned to Haydn, and saw shock register on his face. The same thought was in both their minds. Phyllis was in her late thirties, plain . . . she'd never done any harm. In fact there probably wasn't a child on the Graig she hadn't been kind to at some time or another. Turning a blind eye when they'd smuggled baby brothers and sisters into the White Palace under coats, or in through toilet windows. Handing out boiled sweets in the intermission to those who didn't have the halfpennies to buy ice-cream cornets. . . .

A buzz hummed around those who weren't chanting. Only one word was intelligible above the noise. A word that voiced the question uppermost in Bethan and Haydn's minds. 'Who?' Who could the father possibly be?

Coat billowing, John Joseph sailed down the aisle with the deacons following, a tide of grim-faced lieutenants in his wake. He halted alongside the pew in front of the one where Phyllis sat, white-faced and immobilised by terror. It emptied as if by magic, the occupants melting into the aisles on either side as they tried to lose themselves amongst their fellows. John Joseph walked into the wooden pen and halted in front of Phyllis. Only the back of the pew stood between them. He leaned over and jabbed his forefinger into her chest. She shrank from him, hitting her back on the pew. Wincing, her eyes fogged by tears, she edged sideways in a futile attempt to escape.

'Only the devil would have the gall to sit here, in His house. You . . .' He lunged after her, stepping out of his pew before she could reach the end of hers. 'You are not fit to walk the same earth that our Lord trod.'

Eddie rose to his feet. Haydn, realising what was in his brother's mind, grabbed hold of Eddie's coat. Crouching on hands and knees Phyllis slid out of the pew backwards, trying to edge around John Joseph. Then, as the chanting increased in intensity, the first stone was thrown, hitting Phyllis high on her left cheek-bone, drawing blood.

Neither Bethan nor Haydn saw where it came from. Afterwards Bethan realised that her uncle must have primed the deacons for them to have carried stones into the chapel. Phyllis screamed, more from fear than pain. The congregation, whipped into a frenzy, surged towards the back of the chapel . . . and Phyllis.

She struggled upright but the crowd hemmed her in on every side. One of the deacons' wives spat on her, the spittle trickling down the sleeve of her yellow and green print dress. Another threw her hat to the floor and pulled her hair. Sickened, Bethan turned away, pulling Maud close to her.

'Eddie!'

She heard Haydn's cry and saw her younger brother, fists flying, fight his way towards Phyllis. But before he could reach her John Joseph fell silent. He held up his hand and the crowd parted, allowing the choking, sobbing woman to stumble towards the closed doors at the back of the chapel. Eddie clambered over

145

their pew, forced his way through and reached the doors before Phyllis. He wrenched them open and in the only gesture of sympathy he was able to make smiled at her. She didn't even see him. Tripping over the worn doormat she fell, grazing her knees on the pavement outside. Eddie tried to go after her, but a bellow from John Joseph froze him in his tracks.

'Only the devil's paramour would run after the devil.'

Colour flooding into his cheeks, Eddie slammed the door shut, thumping his fist impotently on the jamb.

'The hymn.'

Flustered, Hetty began to play, mixed up the notes, and began again. It took another curt command from John Joseph for her to realise that she was still playing 'There Is a Green Hill Far Away'.

People shuffled back to their seats. John Joseph returned to the rostrum, singing every step of the way. He'd stage-managed the affair brilliantly. The words that resounded into the air, thrilling the congregation were 'Fight the good fight with all thy might.'

Eddie didn't return to his seat. When Bethan looked back she saw that he'd remained standing in front of the closed door, staring at John Joseph.

'Christ is thy strength and Christ thy right,' John Joseph bellowed. 'Lay hold on life and it shall be. . . . '

The deacons picked up the collecting plates. Another musical note joined in with the singing – the quiet clinking of coins. Bethan reached for the white straw bag she'd bought to go with her new dress and fumbled for her purse. She clicked it open and felt the coins inside. Taking out two joeys – silver threepenny bits – she slipped one to Maud and held the other in her gloved hand. The collecting plate was full by the time it reached her. It always was at Easter. People who couldn't afford to put food on their tables more than once a day always seemed to find pennies for the collecting plate. They were too afraid of John Joseph not to.

She waited for Maud to lay her offering on the plate, then turned to pass it to the pew behind her. As she did so she glimpsed one of the deacons handing Eddie a server. Eddie took it, and passed his hand over the plate before returning it to the deacon with a wry smile. She couldn't be sure, but she thought she'd

146

seen Eddie remove, not add, coins. The notion troubled her, and she glanced back when the hymn had finished. Eddie slipped his hands into his pockets as he returned to his seat alongside Haydn. Then she knew for certain. She looked nervously at John Joseph. He'd closed his hymnal and was beginning the prayers. If he'd noticed anything he would have announced it to the assembly. Of that much she was certain. Two castings out in one day would have been too good an opportunity to miss.

Eddie was the first to leave the chapel. William and Haydn weren't far behind him. Bethan followed as soon as she mustered Maud and Diana.

'Straight home?' Haydn asked, looking to Bethan.

'I'm calling in on Rhiannon Pugh.'

'There's nothing you can do, Beth,' Haydn said.

'What you're trying to say is I've my reputation to think of,' she retorted hotly.

'Our mam'll already be there,' William chipped in, trying to defuse the situation.

'Your mam hasn't got a reputation to care about,' Glan smirked as he joined them.

'You take that back right now.'

'Or?' Glan taunted.

'Or I'll punch you on the mush.'

'Not here, later on the mountain if you have to,' Haydn whispered, looking to the chapel doorway as he stepped between them.

'Name the time and place,' Glan retorted.

'The old quarry, three o'clock this afternoon.'

'I'll be there.'

John Joseph, with a deacon and three middle-aged women walked into a puddle of sunshine on the pavement and remained there talking. Diana forced a smile, took hold of her brother's arm and pulled him round the corner, the others following at a slower pace.

'Push off, Glan,' Diana ordered vehemently once they were out of earshot.

'It's a free country.'

'You're not wanted.' Eddie crossed his arms over his chest and blocked Glan's passage. 'Get the message.'

Glan took the hint. As the others climbed the flight of stone steps that led from Graig Street to Leyshon Street, he retreated round the corner.

'Beats me why she came to chapel in the first place.' William brought up the topic uppermost in everyone's mind.

'Beats me how John Joseph knew.' Haydn leaned against the railings and waited for Bethan and Diana to walk up the steps. 'I didn't even realise she was knocking around with anyone.'

'Whoever he is, he's a right bastard to leave her to go through that on her own.'

'Eddie. Language,' Haydn reprimanded.

'Well he is,' Eddie protested.

'I agree with Eddie,' Diana said warmly. 'From a woman's point of view . . . '

'Woman.' William choked on the square of chewing gum he'd put into his mouth.

'We are women too,' Maud insisted. 'Everyone knows that girls mature long before boys.'

'And who told you that, rat's tails?' Eddie pulled the plait that stuck out beneath her straw hat.

'Never you mind.' She linked arms with Diana and they walked on up the street, their noses in the air.

'Look out!' William shouted to the neighbours who'd moved their kitchen chairs into the street to enjoy the spring sunshine. 'Their ladyships are airing their maturity.'

'Don't you three ever let up?' Bethan said irritably.

'Sorry, Beth,' Haydn apologised.

'You could at least *sound* sorry!'

'I am. I really am.' He held out his hands, palm up.

'You're going to have to do better than that if you want to tread the boards in the Town Hall instead of scrubbing them.'

'Ouch, Beth, that hurt. Come on, I've said I'm sorry. What more do you want me to do?' He dropped the pose and slipped his arm round her shoulders. 'Don't let it get to you.'

'Don't let what get to me?' she asked, removing his arm.

He shrugged and grinned at her. 'The weather?' he suggested mildly.

'Now you're being ridiculous.'

'I see that uncle of yours has been at it again.' Mrs Plumett, who lived two doors down from Megan, nodded to Bethan and Haydn.

'He's no uncle of ours,' Eddie said warmly.

'Shame on him,' Mrs Plumett continued as if he hadn't spoken. 'Nice girl like Phyllis too. She deserves better than that. Caring for Rhiannon the way she has all these years. Your mam's up there doing what she can,' she said to William. 'And Rhiannon's already said that Phyllis will go to the workhouse over her dead body. As long as she has a roof over her head, she'll see that Phyllis has one too. Mind you,' she whispered, dropping her voice, 'if you ask me Rhiannon hasn't been looking too well lately, and then . . . well . . . ' she pulled the edges of her cardigan together, trying to make the sides meet across her vast bosom, 'there's no saying what'll happen then. Phyllis could end up on the street yet. You know what Fred the dead is like?' she prattled on, referring to the local undertaker cum builder who owned a fair number of the houses in both Phillip and Leyshon Street. 'He won't let a woman like Phyllis take on the rent book. You can be sure of *that*,' she finished, triumphant in the knowledge that she'd been the first to think that far ahead.

'I'm sure that whatever needs doing to help Phyllis or Rhiannon will be done,' Bethan replied noncommittally.

'Oh, I wouldn't be too sure of that if I were you. You know John Joseph and his brigade. Holier than thou and a moth-eaten blanket. Still, you being a nurse and working on the labour ward, you could do a lot if your uncle lets you.'

'You can count on me to do whatever I can.'

'And I'm sure Phyllis will be grateful. I must go or my old man's dinner will be burnt.' With that she ran through her open front door, down the passage and into her back kitchen. Bethan heard the washhouse door slamming and Mrs Plumett calling to her neighbour over the garden wall.

'In five minutes it'll be all over the Graig that you approve of Phyllis. And that, dear sister, as far as the gossips go, makes you no better than her.'

'Seems to me Maud's right.' Bethan glared at him. 'It's always the women who are left to clear up the mess.'

Before going to chapel Elizabeth had prepared the Sunday dinner of rolled breast of lamb, stuffing, mint sauce, roast potatoes, cabbage and gravy to celebrate Easter. She'd also given her children strict instructions to hurry home after the service to help put the finishing touches to the meal. But angry and restless, Bethan stuck by her decision to visit Phyllis. She went to Rhiannon's house alone, making Maud and the boys walk the long way home past the Graig Hotel, but she saw neither Rhiannon nor Phyllis. Megan had taken charge of the house, and she was keeping most of the neighbours, particularly the gossips, firmly at bay.

Rhiannon and Phyllis were sitting in the front parlour, in itself an event, for no one had entered the room except to clean it since the funeral of Rhiannon's husband and son. The door was firmly closed and Megan was ferrying cups of tea through from the kitchen when Bethan knocked and walked in.

'Oh it's you, love,' Megan said, dropping the aggressive stance she'd adopted.

'I came to see if I could help,' Bethan murmured rather inanely. Now she was actually in the house she felt quite useless. And nosy. Just like Mrs Plumett.

'If I thought you could do anything to help I'd take you in, love, but they're best left on their own for a bit. Rhiannon needs to get used to the idea of Phyllis being in the family way. Look, I'll be back in a minute.' Megan pushed open the door with her hip and took in the tea. When she came out she carried two empty cups and saucers stacked in one hand. She closed the door and took Bethan into the back kitchen.

'I'm staying for a bit,' Megan continued. 'Just to see to the callers.'

'It was awful. . . . ' The tears she'd kept buried beneath a surface of anger welled into her eyes.

'You don't have to tell me, love,' Megan said bitterly. 'I've seen John Joseph's casting outs for myself.'

'I should have done something.'

'What?' Megan demanded.

'I don't know. Something. I could at least have helped her to get out of the chapel quicker.'

'If you'd tried to help Phyllis you'd only have given them an excuse to throw stones at you as well. No, love, it's my guess that you did the same thing I did when your uncle cast out Minnie Jones the year our William was born.'

'Sit tight and watch,' Bethan said disparagingly. 'That doesn't make me feel any better.'

'I never said it would. But I made my protest afterwards,' Megan said proudly. 'I swore I wouldn't set foot in the chapel again while John Joseph preached there, and I haven't.'

'Are you telling me to do the same thing?'

'No one can tell you to do anything like that, love.' Megan filled the kettle in the washhouse and walked back into the kitchen to set it on the range. 'That has to be between you and your conscience. But I do know this much. If you decide to boycott chapel you'll have your mother as well as John Joseph to contend with. And that's without bringing God into it.'

Chapter Nine

'Cat got your tongue?' Andrew asked Bethan as he changed down into second gear in preparation for the long slow drive up Penycoedcae hill.

'No,' she said abruptly. Too abruptly.

'Come on, something's the matter,' he pronounced with an irritating superiority. 'I know it is, so you may as well tell me first as last.'

'Are you church or chapel?' she demanded.

'Now that's a strange question. Why do you ask?'

'I just wondered.'

'Church. St Catherine's.' He named the largest church in town that stood, resplendent in its Victorian glory, in the centre of Pontypridd, next to the police station on Gelliwastad Road. A church that catered unashamedly for the crache of the town.

'You would be,' she said bitterly.

'What's that supposed to mean?'

'Nothing. Take no notice. It's just me.' She stared blindly out of the car window, oblivious to the fresh spring beauty of budding trees and green fields.

'Look, baa lambs.'

'Second childhood?' she enquired frostily.

'I always think the mothers look so old and grubby compared with the young,' he continued, unabashed.

'Bit like the difference between young girls and old women.'

'You sound like one of the old women.'

'I feel like one.'

'I don't know, you get Easter Sunday and Monday off, the two days any one of the staff nurses would give their souls, if not their virtue, for. Presumably you've had nothing more taxing to do this morning than go to church and eat lunch with your family. And now you have a highly desirable and amusing bachelor like myself at your disposal, and what do you do? You growl in a mood more fitted to a night of thunderstorms than a heavenly spring day.'

Lunch, she thought bitterly. Just one more word to remind her of the gulf between his family and hers. The crache consumed lunch on the Common, the working class downed dinner on the Graig.

'I don't go to church, I go to chapel,' she snapped.

'I beg your pardon,' he apologised heavily. 'I didn't mean to upset your ladyship.'

'I know you didn't.' Her anger deflated into shame. 'I told you, it's me.'

'Would it help to talk about whatever it is?'

She closed her eyes against the glare of the sunshine and remembered the events of the morning. Each and every shameful detail was recalled in appalling clarity. John Joseph, his dark eyes shining, elated as he stood triumphant and secure in the midst of his deacons. Phyllis pathetic and cowed, spittle running down her spring dress, blood on her cheek where the stone had hit her. . . .

'No,' she said decisively.

'In that case do you mind telling me where we're going?'

'Anywhere.'

'Mumbles Pier so I can throw you off?'

She looked at him. He stuck his tongue out. She laughed in spite of herself.

'That's better.' He narrowed his eyes against the strong sunlight. 'Pass my sunglasses please, they're in the glove compartment. Now can we discuss where we're going?'

'Anywhere you want to.'

'Anywhere?' He raised his eyebrows, and adopted an excruciating foreign accent. 'Right, young woman, how about I carry you off somewhere warm and exotic. Like – ' he leaned across and whispered close to her ear – ' 'a silk-draped harem in the wilds of the Sahara.'

'Saw too many Rudolf Valentino films when you were young did you?' she enquired sarcastically.

'Of course, didn't every child? My mother used to drag me along every chance she got. Life with Father was so very, very humdrum.'

'That I don't believe.'

153

'You've only ever seen my father directing patients' treatments and hospital policy. At home my mother won't allow him to be important.'

'Just how many other women would you like in this harem of yours?'

'That depends on how quickly you wilt in a hot climate.'

'Why, you. . . . '

'Don't hit me when I'm driving or we'll end up in a ditch.'

He swung the car around the corner past the Queen's Hotel, carried on for a couple of miles until the few cottages that were Penycoedcae were well and truly behind them, then pulled into the side of the road. Leaving the engine running he reached across, wrapped his arms around her and kissed her full on the mouth. She relaxed against him, warm and secure in his embrace. They'd come a long way since the awkward beginnings of their first outing to Cardiff.

'Right, for the last time where do you want to go?' He released his hold on her and turned to face the wheel.

'The sea?' she suggested.

'Don't you have to be back early?'

'No. I told my father to expect me when he sees me.' She could have added 'and now my mother knows better than to interfere' but her strained relationship with her mother was something she'd kept from Andrew.

'Good.' He pulled his watch out of the top pocket of his silk shirt and flicked it open. 'Two o'clock.' He did some quick calculating. 'If we get a move on we can have at least four hours there, and still be back before midnight.'

'Four hours where?'

'You'll see when we get there.'

He put the car into gear and pulled out into the lane; with his arm round her shoulders he steered skilfully along the winding road. She snuggled up to him, conscious of the warmth of his body beneath the blue blazer and thin shirt, the smell of his cologne as it clashed with and finally overpowered the essence of violets she was wearing.

'Share a cigarette?' he asked.

'Do I ever?'

'It sounds more polite than asking you to light one for me.'

She slid her hand into the blazer pocket closest to her and removed his gold lighter and cigarette case. Lighting one, she placed it between his lips.

'Thanks.' He wound down the window and rested his elbow on the open ledge. 'Settle down, we've a long way to go.'

'How long?'

'The Sahara side of Porthcawl.'

Knowing she wouldn't get any sense out of him while he remained in this mood, she did as he suggested. Resting her head on his shoulder she closed her eyes, pushing the images of the morning's service to the back of her mind. She wondered at the miracle that had enabled her to build a happy, relaxed relationship with Andrew despite the strain of their first outing together.

Although they went out in a foursome with Trevor and Laura as often as staff rosters allowed, she preferred and treasured the times, like now, when she and Andrew were alone. He was less of a public entertainer, more sensitive and aware of her feelings without an audience. And although she still occasionally woke up in the small hours, cold at the thought of where their relationship might end, afraid because she knew she had come to rely on him far too much, she continued to be free of such worries while they were together. She felt incredibly alive when she was with him, a kind of elation that blocked out every other aspect of her life. It was as if she only really lived in his presence.

Those who were closest to her – Megan, her father, Laura, her brothers and Maud – suspected that she was in love, but she continued to stop short of analysing her feelings. If anyone had tried to present her with the evidence she would have laughed. For quite apart from the social gulf, underlying the strong emotions she felt for him was an inherent fear. She had seen at first hand the damage that love could cause. Her mother wielded the power it gave her like a lash, using it to strip her father of everything he valued and held dear – dignity, independence, even the small pleasures he tried to take in the simple everyday facets of life.

She was aware that there were other kinds of relationship: those in which gentleness and consideration prevailed over the desire to subjugate. Some marriages were undoubtedly based on mutual understanding and affection. She only had to look as far

155

as her father and contrast the air of patient, resigned sadness he wore like the proverbial hair shirt whenever he was in her mother's company with the jolly exuberance of Laura's father, who was always hugging and kissing his plump, happy wife.

But until now she'd never considered such a partnership relevant to her. When she'd taken up nursing she'd mapped out her future in terms of a career where hard work and celibacy came before any thought of a personal life.

There'd never been much time for boys. An occasional, unmemorable trip to the cinema in Cardiff with Laura and one or two of the porters from the Royal Infirmary. And before that, outings with her brothers, William, and Laura's brothers. They'd gone out as a crowd, visiting the cinema when they had a few pennies to spare, and Pontypridd park, Shoni's pond or the Graig mountain when they didn't.

Once, soon after she'd returned home from the Infirmary, she'd visited the White Palace with Glan. Neither had forgotten the episode, but for different reasons. He, because he was continually nagging her to repeat the experience; she because the evening had ended with her slapping his face soundly when he'd tried to kiss her. Now . . . she wrapped her arm round Andrew's and snuggled closer to him; now, she actually liked being kissed.

'We're here.'

Disorientated, she opened her eyes and looked around. She hadn't known the world could be so green. Even the air seemed green, filled with a clear jade light that danced off the thick, curling new leaves of trees and bushes.

'Come on, I'll introduce you.' He turned off the car engine, opened his door and walked around to hers. She stretched her cramped limbs and stepped out of the car, shivering in the cool spring air.

'Over there, look.'

A breathtaking view over a thickly wooded hillside swept down towards a wide, flat, grassed valley floor branded with a meandering snake of silver river. And beyond the river, towering green-capped cliffs sheltered pale golden sands fringed by crashing breakers.

'You wanted the sea?'

'It's beautiful. It's like it's never been touched.'

'Oh but it has.' He opened a low barred gate that she hadn't noticed and beckoned her forward. She followed him up a narrow gravel path bordered by hedges of white-blossomed may, or 'bread and butter' trees as the children on the Graig called them, eating the leaves when they had nothing more tasty to put into their mouths. Encroaching on the path were clumps of poppies. Andrew halted in front of a wooden door, bleached dry by the sun.

'It's not much,' he smiled. 'Just a wooden summer chalet, but we used to have great fun here when we were kids.' He produced a large key from the top pocket of his blazer and unlocked the door. Pushing hard he scraped it over a flagstoned floor. 'Faugh.' He wrinkled his nose in disgust. 'I hate being the first one in after the winter.'

She followed him into a small, pine-boarded kitchen.

'Welcome to the John summer residence.' He opened a casement window set over the sink. 'It may look dirty, damp and musty now, but there's nothing amiss that a good scrub and a summer's warmth won't cure. Do you like it?'

'Like it? I love it.' She looked around. A square pine table, four pine wheelback chairs round it, stood in the centre of the room. A pine dresser, its shelves bare, its cupboard doors closed, stood against the wall opposite the door. Brightly coloured rag rugs lay on the floor next to the door and in front of an old stone sink with a brass tap.

'All the comforts of home.' He turned on the tap. Nothing happened. 'Well almost, water's still turned off.' He crouched beneath the sink and twisted the stopcock. 'My mother bought the rugs at a church sale of work. She used to enjoy shopping for this place when we were small.'

'The "we" being you and your sister?' He nodded. She knew from hospital gossip that he had a married sister a couple of years older than himself. But this was the first time he'd mentioned her.

'Come on, I'll show you the rest. Not that it's much.'

He walked out of the kitchen into the gloom of an inner hallway. There was no window; from the light that filtered in from the kitchen she could see that the wood planking walls were painted cream. There were four doors. Three led into good-sized double bedrooms with large windows overlooking the woods. Two of these contained sets of twin beds, the third a double. The bedsteads were plain unvarnished pine, with mattresses wrapped in rubber sheeting to protect them from the damp. The walls and floors were of stripped pine planking, the furniture pine chests of drawers and ottomans, no wardrobes. And like the kitchen all the rooms had a pervasive, thick musty atmosphere of neglect and disuse.

'My father got a local chap to cover this area in when he bought the place. Must be over twenty years ago.' He opened the fourth door. An overpowering dry warmth wafted out to greet them. 'It used to be a veranda, but he planked the walls and put in windows. The door from here to the garden stuck three or four years ago, and I never bothered to plane it. If you want to get out in a hurry you have to use the windows.'

'Sitting here must be like sitting in a goldfish bowl in the woods.'

He laughed. 'I suppose it is. The best view is down this end.' He walked past the two large picture windows that framed the woods, turned left around what had been the corner of the house, and paused before a massive window that looked out over the headland towards the bay.

'Three Cliffs,' he said as proudly as if he were showing her a painting. 'The finest view on Gower.'

'It's wonderful.'

'Isn't it just? Here, help me pull off these dust sheets. I don't know why I bothered to lay them out last autumn, there's so much glass here the damp disappears as soon as the sun shines.' They uncovered a rattan three-piece suite with cushions upholstered in thick, faded but serviceable green linen. She pressed down on one with her hand. It was quite dry.

He sank down on a chair, and pulled her on to his lap.

'I'd forgotten how much I love this place. Strange, I used to spend more weekends here when I was living in London than I do now. Get the train from Paddington to Pontypridd on a Friday night. Borrow one of my father's cars, motor down, eat supper here, and stay until Sunday afternoon.'

'You used to come down here a lot?' She left his lap and stood in front of the window, a maggot of jealousy worming away inside her at the thought of all the girls he must have brought here. Girls like Anthea Llewellyn-Jones who would have been only too happy to go away with him for a weekend.

'Every time my tutors threatened to kick me out for not doing enough studying. This became my work base. The family gave up on it years ago. I don't think my parents have been here more than once or twice in the last five years. Sometimes they lend it out to friends. Fanny. . . . '

'Fanny?' she turned to face him.

'My sister,' he explained. 'Her name's Fiona but I call her Fanny, mainly because she hates it. She loathes this place. No hot and cold running water, no bathroom. Only an old thunder-box out back.'

She remained silent, angry with herself for falling prey to jealousy. He hadn't made her any promises. She had no right to question him about the women in his past.

He left the chair and joined her at the window. 'Would you like a walk? It's too late to go to the beach, it's a lot further than it looks. But we could walk across there.' He pointed to some grey stonework barely visible through the trees on the hillside. 'Those are the ruins of an old Norman castle. If you won't let me play at harems with you, then perhaps I can persuade you to play at knights and ladies.'

'Are you sure the beach is too far?'

'We'll come here early on your next day off.'

'Tomorrow?' she asked hopefully.

'I thought you wanted to go to the Rattle Fair?'

'I do.'

'Then it'll have to wait until the next one.'

'Promise?'

'Promise.' He unlatched the windows and threw them wide. 'Come on, if we leave everything open this place will air out by the time we get back, then I'll make you tea. Totally from tins,' he said gleefully as if it would be a great treat.

They took it in turns to visit the outhouse before they left. He apologised for the primitive facilities. She said nothing, wondering if he realised that the only house that could boast a bathroom on the Graig was that of the Leyshons.

She enjoyed the walk. It blew away cobwebs accumulated

159

during a winter spent working in the hospital, and she even managed to forget the events of chapel that morning in the novelty of the clifftop scenery. Until that moment the sea had meant either Barry Island or Porthcawl. Built-up resorts with rows of stiff wooden chalets, bathing huts, funfairs and railway stations large enough to accommodate the thousands of day trippers that swarmed down on them from the coal-mining valleys. This charming, unspoilt bay set in a wilderness of green pastures and trees entranced her, and although Andrew assured her that there were other chalets close by, she refused to look at the red and grey roofs, preferring to cling to her first impression of total and absolute solitude.

When they returned after an hour's hard walking her feet were blistered from her new shoes, but the air in the chalet was definitely fresher. She sat at the table while Andrew ran the water, first washing out then filling a kettle he produced from the walk-in pantry.

'Last one to leave before winter sets in makes sure there's a fire laid for spring. Not that it always burns, mind you.' Using his cigarette lighter he lit a ball of newspaper and pushed it beneath a pile of logs in the grate, which was built beneath a chimney, the only stone-built part of the chalet.

The paper smouldered reluctantly, then just when Andrew decided to pull the fire out and relay it, it burst into flames. He hung the kettle on a chain over the fire.

'Now, like the three men in a boat we have to pretend that we really don't want tea. Then the kettle will boil, which is more than it will do if we watch it. Let's see, what have we here?' He left the fireplace and walked into the pantry. 'Tinned fruit, tinned sardines, and,' he frowned as he held up a jar filled with dark greenish liquid and some very dubious-looking solids, 'what do you think? Pickled gherkins or eggs?'

'Medical specimen?'

'You could be right. The last time I came here I was studying for my finals.'

'All of a sudden I don't feel very hungry.'

'Coward. How about we settle for tea and I buy you fish and chips on the way home?'

'It's Sunday.'

'So it is. Oh well, we'll have to make do with what's in the car.'

'You brought a hamper? I thought you only decided to come here when we were in Penycoedcae.'

'You know me and picnics. I like them even on slag heaps. If you use the water to wash a couple of plates and glasses I'll bring it in.'

'What about tea?'

'Why drink tea when we can have wine?'

He went to the car while she rummaged through the dresser. She came across a set of thick blue and white clay pottery plates, cups and saucers, and a tray of bone-handled knives and forks. The glasses she found on a high shelf in the pantry, along with a stack of tea towels, tablecloths and enamel bowls. By the time she'd washed some dishes he'd rifled the hamper, laid the cloth and set out a plate of rolls filled with ham and cheese, a bowl of fresh fruit and opened the bottle of wine.

'If we fill our plates we could take this through to the veranda,' he suggested.

They ate and drank sitting side by side on the rattan couch, watching the flaming ball of the dying sun sink slowly over the horizon.

'How would you like to retire here with me? We could grow old together, watching sunsets, drinking wine. . . . '

'Without work there wouldn't be any money to pay for wine.'

'Always the practical one.' He took the wine glass gently from her hand and set it on the floor next to her chair. Then he leaned over and kissed her. She responded, slipping her hands beneath his jacket, running her fingers over the smooth silk of his shirt.

'If we're going to do this we may as well do it in comfort.'

He undid his tie, took off his jacket, unbuttoned his braces and flung them on to one of the chairs. Then he kicked off his shoes without undoing the laces. 'Come here, woman,' he commanded, pulling her down alongside him, until they both lay full length on the couch.

His body, hard, unyielding, pushed her into the soft cushions at her back. He kissed and caressed her, embracing her body with his own, arousing the slow-burning passion that he had carefully

161

nurtured in her since the night she had first trusted him enough to return his kiss.

His hand sought her breast, stroking its contours through the thin material of her dress, awakening sensations that were new and wholly strange to her. Face burning, she clung tightly to him, wrapping her arms around his neck, hoping that he'd stop. Kissing she enjoyed, but she wasn't ready for anything more. Not yet. Not now. And when she felt his fingers fumble at the buttons on her bodice she clamped her hands firmly over his.

'Bethan.' His eyes, dark, serious, stared intently into hers. 'Darling,' he pleaded. 'Just this. I promise you, it will go no further.'

He kissed her again, but she froze, tensing her muscles until her entire body was rigid. Too embarrassed and ashamed to look at him she kept her eyes tightly closed, furious with herself for failing to control the tears that welled beneath her eyelids.

'Bethan, what's wrong?' he demanded.

When she didn't reply he swung his legs on to the floor and reached for his jacket. Searching through the pockets he extracted his cigarettes and lighter. 'I knew there was something on your mind when I picked you up. Is it something I've done?' he asked, cursing himself for losing control. He didn't want their relationship to end. Not this way. Besides, he should have known better. The first thing he'd discovered as a probing adolescent was that there were no girls so moral as those brought up in the ways of the Welsh chapels.

'It's not you, it's me.' Clinging to him she buried her head in his shoulder.

He lit his cigarette, pulled a table with an ashtray closer to the sofa and inhaled deeply. 'Are you fed up with me?' he asked simply.

'No.'

'Well that's a relief.' He leaned back against the cushions. 'Look,' he waved the cigarette he was holding towards the window, 'the sun's shining, spring's here, you have me. Now what can be dreadful enough to spoil all that?' he joked nervously.

'If you'd been there this morning you'd know,' she retorted vehemently, frightened by his questions. (That the thought she didn't care about him should even cross his mind!) 'But as you're not chapel you can't even begin to imagine it.'

'Imagine what?'

'The stoning.'

'Stoning.' A frown appeared between his eyebrows. 'Stoning out of unmarried pregnant women?'

She nodded.

'I've heard of it happening in chapels in the Rhondda. But surely to God it doesn't go on today. And on the Graig of all places?'

She blurted out everything. John Joseph's triumph in condemning Phyllis from the pulpit. The way he and the deacons had rounded on Phyllis as she'd fought to get out of the building. The women spitting, the stone being thrown. He listened in silence, holding her, stroking her hair away from her face, and when she finally ceased talking, he kissed away the tears that fell despite her efforts to contain them. Tears of sympathy for Phyllis, and rage against her uncle.

'You poor, poor darling.' He pulled her head on to his shoulder. Wrapping her arms around his chest, she was acutely aware of his heart beating beneath her hand.

'This minister, he's your uncle?' he murmured, breaking the silence when he had to move to stub out his cigarette.

'Yes.'

'Good God, no wonder you're mixed up. But you're a nurse, sweetheart, and half a midwife to boot. Surely I don't need to tell you what causes pregnancy?' He smiled, shaking his head as she blushed. 'Darling, I respect you, and I love you.' He was as surprised by his spontaneous declaration as her, but he continued, not wanting to think too hard about the implications of what he'd said. Not yet. 'If I didn't I wouldn't be spending as much time with you as I am, and the last thing I'm going to do is leave you alone and pregnant to face a chapel full of monsters. Bethan,' he lifted her chin, forcing her to look into his eyes, 'I care about you. I'll never do anything to hurt you. You must believe that. The problem is you're beautiful, extremely desirable and I'm weak. But I promise you now. I'll never be weak enough to forget myself. Never.'

She tightened her arms, holding him close with every ounce of strength she possessed. The only sound in the room was their soft, rhythmic breathing. The peace was absolute, the air warm from the sun's rays beating on the windows throughout the day. She could smell the dust, the odour of his perspiration mingled with the perfume of cologne, the aroma of wine wafting from the open bottle standing on the floor next to the sofa.

He ground his cigarette to dust in the ashtray before kissing her again.

'Do you think you could trust me enough to pick up where we left off?' he asked softly.

Her eyes were huge, liquid, almost luminous pools in the gathering dusk. She lifted her hands to the back of his neck and pressed her lips to his. Without his braces his shirt worked loose from the waistband of his trousers. Shyly, hesitantly she pushed it aside, running the palms of her hands over his naked back. He gripped his collar and pulled his shirt off over his head. His skin was unbelievably white and smooth, smoother than the silk of the shirt he had thrown to the floor.

Moving his hand he slipped the buttons of her bodice from their loops. Excited, and more than a little afraid, she dug her nails into his back, but this time didn't try to stop him undressing her. Gently, very gently, he pulled her dress and chemise down over her shoulders, exposing her breasts. Her cheeks burnt crimson as his fingers gently teased her nipples.

'You're beautiful, Bethan,' he murmured thickly, staring at her.

'I love you, Andrew.' She lay back and closed her eyes, trying to forget her mother's warnings, the events of the morning, everything except his declaration of love, and the feel of his fingers on her skin as he caressed her.

Slowly, gradually she warmed to his touch, relaxing enough to allow his sensuous stroking to hold sway over both her body and her mind. And even when his hands were supplanted by his lips she made no effort to stop him. He loved her. Really loved her, and she him. What could possibly be sinful about that?

'Bethan, it's Easter Monday,' William complained as she walked through Megan's front door at eight o'clock in the morning. He turned his back and hitched the cord of his pyjama trousers higher, concealing a bruise he'd got, courtesy of Glan. His only consolation was that Glan had more, and blacker ones. 'Don't they sleep in your house?' he moaned.

'Not during the day.' Ignoring his state of undress, she pushed past into the kitchen. Megan was outside, unpegging the salt fish that she'd soaked and hung out the night before.

'Just in time for breakfast, love.' She bustled in with an enamel bowl full.

'I've had mine, thanks, Auntie.'

'But you'll have a cup of tea.'

'Love one. I called in to see if you've anything new.'

'Had some smart two-pieces in on Saturday night. Specials. One's your size, lovely dark green, linen. And there's a nice cream silk blouse that will match it to a T. Are you in a hurry, or have you got time for that cuppa?'

'I could murder a cuppa.' Bethan pulled one of the kitchen chairs from under the table and sat down.

'Not meeting him early then today?' Megan said archly.

Bethan coloured. 'Not till eleven o'clock.'

'When are we going to get a chance to see this young man of yours then?'

'Some time.'

'Soon I hope. I want to give him the once-over. Make sure he's the right one for you.'

'He's the right one for her,' William called out as he walked through the kitchen on his way to the outside privy. 'Doctor who's not short of a few bob to put a nice bit of stuff on his back, or on his arm, eh Beth.' He winked at her as he ducked out of the washhouse door, still bare to the waist, his pyjama trousers flapping in the breeze.

'Take no notice of him, love, he can't bear the thought of anyone having money when he's got none.' Megan took two cups and saucers from the dresser and set them on the table. Removing the teacosy, she felt the side of the pot before pouring it out. 'I'll make some fresh in a minute but this will do to be getting on with.' She spooned a generous helping of fat from her dripping bowl into the cast-iron frying pan on the range. 'By the way, I've something else in that might interest you.'

'I think I'll settle for the suit. I've got to start saving. . . . '

'Why bother, love? If there's one thing I've learned over the years it's that the rainy days are always here and now. Besides – '

165

Megan swirled the melting fat in the pan – 'you're only young once. Look as pretty as you can while you can, that's my motto.'

'I've nothing to show for my pay rise.'

'You've a wardrobe full of clothes, and God knows you needed them.' Megan tipped the fish into the pan. 'And the something's not intended for you. I've two men's suits upstairs. One your Eddie's size and one your Haydn's. They're brand spanking new. Six bob each.'

'Six bob! Wilf Horton's are ten, and they're second-hand.'

'Specials,' Megan said airily.

'Specials out the back door of a tailor's warehouse?' Bethan asked suspiciously.

'Nothing like that.'

'We don't need handouts.'

'Even if you did I haven't any to give. Six bob includes my profit. When you've finished your tea take a look at them.' Megan turned the fish over carefully. 'They're in a brown paper sack in my bedroom behind the dressing table. The women's suits are on top of the wardrobe.'

Bethan carried her empty cup into the washhouse, bumping into William, who was washing under the cold tap.

'Comes to something when a man can't strip off in his own house,' William complained.

'Man! It's not that long ago I helped your mam bath you in that sink,' Bethan retorted.

'I can vouch for that,' Megan joined in from the kitchen. 'Will, when you've finished messing out there, take Bethan upstairs and show her where I keep the men's suits.'

'No peace for the wicked.'

'Breakfast!' Megan yelled in a voice loud enough to carry half-way down the street. Charlie came in from the garden where he'd been cleaning his shoes. He nodded in reply to Bethan's quiet hello as he waited patiently for William to finish at the sink. Bethan returned to the kitchen where Diana and Sam, washed and dressed, were already sitting at the table helping themselves to fish, and the bread that Megan was cutting and buttering at a rate of knots.

'No breakfast for you, young man, until you dress,' Megan said sharply as William walked in.

'Nag nag nag.' William planted a smacking kiss on Megan's cheek. 'She loves me really,' he grinned at Bethan.

'Do I now?' Megan asked.

William led the way upstairs, lifting out the sack of men's suits from behind Megan's dressing table before disappearing into his box room. Bethan looked around. She could barely move for piles of boxes and cardboard suitcases. Lifting the sack on to the home-made patchwork quilt that covered the bed, she opened it. It held two suits. A navy-blue, shot with a fine grey pin-stripe, and a plain mid-grey flannel. Both had waistcoats complete with watch pockets, but the grey flannel was shorter in the leg than the pin-stripe so she presumed that was the one Megan intended for Eddie. She felt the cloth between her fingers. It was a good lightweight wool mix. Although she didn't know much about men's clothes she could recognise quality when she saw it.

'Smart, eh?' William walked in behind her, his braces dangling down over his trousers, his fingers busy as they tried to push his collar through the studs in the neck of his shirt.

'Here, let me.' Bethan pushed his hands aside and took over.

'Ow! Your nails are long.' He rubbed his chin ruefully. 'Doctor into vicious women is he?'

'Lay off.'

'Lay off what?' he enquired innocently.

'You know what.'

'If I did I wouldn't ask.'

'What do you think of these?' she asked.

'The suits?'

'What else?' she snapped irritably. 'There are times when I could brain you, William Powell.'

'Promises, promises,' he sighed. 'But going back to these,' he picked up the grey suit, 'I liked them enough to buy two off Mam with the money I earned on the stalls last week.'

'Then they'll be all right for our Haydn and Eddie?'

'I should cocoa. Here – ' he lifted one of the largest cardboard suitcases on to the bed and opened it. 'Shirts, ties and socks. Everything a young man about town could want to go with his new suit, and,' he sidled up to her, 'for you, madam, very cheap.'

'When you've finished practising your sales patter, find me a

167

shirt and tie to go with each of these. The socks I can manage myself.'

'What size is Eddie?'

'Sixteen.'

'I wouldn't have said he was a bull neck.'

'It's got worse since he started going down the gym.'

'Haydn?'

'Sixteen and a half.'

'Two white linen shirts, four collars to match, one set sixteen, the other sixteen and a half, half a crown the lot and studs thrown in for free. You can't do better than that.'

'You should be on the market full time instead of down the pit three days a week.'

'I'm working on it. Socks – ' He tossed her a bundle. 'Pure wool, and only fourpence a pair. How many would madam like?'

'Four pairs.' She pulled out two pairs of grey and two of navy.

'Ties – ' he looked thoughtfully at the suits laid out on the bed – 'what do you think? This red and blue stripe for the grey, the plain grey for the pin-stripe.' He held them up.

'Looks good to me.' She piled them on top of the shirts and socks.

'Then I take madam is satisfied.' He left the bedroom and picked up his waistcoat and jacket from the banisters.

'Now look at you,' she teased. 'All done up like a dog's dinner.'

'Easter Rattle Fair.' He raised his eyebrows. 'Never know what a fellow like me might find down there.'

'Stalls to put up?'

'You don't think I'd wear this,' he shrugged his waistcoat over his shoulders, 'to put up stalls do you? Besides, I did that last night. We didn't finish till four, that's why I slept in.'

'Haydn and Eddie with you?'

'And your father.'

'That's why none of them stirred this morning.'

'And what time did cashmere coat bring *you* home last night?' he asked pointedly. 'It must have been late seeing as we didn't walk down the Graig hill until eleven.'

'Late,' she replied succinctly.

'Be careful with that one, Beth,' he warned, dropping his bantering air. 'He's crache.'

'I hadn't noticed.'

'I'm serious. Wouldn't want to see you get hurt by the idle rich.'

'He's hardly idle, he's a doctor.'

'He seems to have all the time in the world to run around in that car of his.'

'You look after your concerns, I'll look after mine,' she snapped.

'Speaking of my concerns,' he slipped his arms through the sleeves of his jacket, 'you and Laura going to the fair?'

'Yes,' she answered warily, wondering what was coming next.

'Anyone going with you?'

'No one you'd be interested in.'

'I was wondering if any of Laura's sisters were going?'

'Like Tina for instance?' she asked shrewdly. Tina was six months younger than William. They'd gone to school together and become far too friendly for Laura's father and Ronnie's peace of mind. So much so that Signor Ronconi had expressly forbidden Tina to talk to William when her brothers weren't around.

'Maybe,' he murmured casually.

'And you say you're worried about me getting hurt. You're on a hiding to nothing there, William Powell.'

'You know something I don't?'

'I know that nice Catholic girls don't go out with chapel boys.'

'I can become a Catholic,' he said brightly.

'Uncle John Joseph would stone you down the Graig hill let alone out of chapel if he heard you say that.'

'He's not my uncle, thank the Lord,' William said irreverently. 'And after yesterday's uplifting experience I'm looking for a new place to spend Sundays. I might . . . just might take a walk down Broadway to see what Father O'Rourke has to offer.'

'Are you sure you know what you're doing?'

'Put a good word in for me with Tina, Beth, and I'll stop annoying cashmere coat.'

'You are serious aren't you?'

'You serious about cashmere coat?'

'That's different.'

'How?'

'I'm older. . . . '

169

'Oh ho ho. Age has nothing to do with it, Granny. Bet you a pound that I catch Tina before you catch cashmere coat.'

'Will you stop calling him that?'

'I will if you promise to talk to Tina.'

'Like marries like, Will,' she warned. 'The Ronconi girls are all earmarked for nice Italian boys.'

'I can be a nice Italian boy. Wanna hear me talk?' he asked, imitating Laura's father's accent.

'I'm being serious.'

'So am I.' He picked up the bundle of clothes from the bed. 'I know I can be a nice Italian boy, Beth. But be honest. Can you see yourself running a ladies' committee for the "Miners' Children's Boot Fund" in a house on the Common?'

Before she had a chance to answer he turned his back on her and carried the clothes downstairs. There was no need for her to mull over what he'd said. Andrew's declaration that he loved her had sent the same thoughts worming through her mind like maggots in a rotten apple. All William had succeeded in doing was stirring the whole mess up.

Chapter Ten

After William clattered downstairs Bethan picked up the box from the top of the wardrobe. Inside were two ladies' costumes, one a bottle-green coarse linen, the other a light blue wool. Both were styled along the same lines, with close-fitting jackets and long, narrow skirts. Closing the bedroom door she tried on the green linen. Beautifully cut, fully lined in silk, it might have been tailored for her. She turned around slowly in front of the dressing-table mirror whilst doing some rapid calculations in her head.

The boys' clothes came to fifteen shillings and tenpence. Even allowing for Megan's prices the costume would be at least another ten shillings. Twenty-five shillings and tenpence, and she barely had fifteen shillings in her purse to last her until pay-day . . . and she really needed a hat. . . .

'Mam sent me up to see if you needed help.' Diana walked in, still chewing a mouthful of bread and butter. 'Ooh that does look good on you. It's only seven and six too.'

'How does your mother manage to keep her prices down?'

'He who asks no questions gets told no lies.'

'I really need a hat to go with it,' Bethan murmured more to herself than Diana.

'They're over here.' Diana produced a hatbox from under the bed. Lifting out one hat after another she shook a plain black felt with a small brim from the pile. 'This looks good and it will go with practically anything.'

'It will, won't it,' Bethan agreed, perching it on the front of her head.

'And that's only two bob, making nine and six in total, and here's the silk blouse Mam was talking about.' She produced yet another package from under the bed, and handed Bethan a blouse. 'Pure silk, hand-embroidered collar and only ninepence.' Bethan fingered the silk. It felt cool, luxurious. The kind of blouse the crache would wear. If she didn't get it now, at this price, she never would. She was earning good money. If she didn't buy any more for a while . . . . The excuses whirled around her head as she wrestled with her conscience. Finally she decided. She took the hat from her head and unbuttoned the jacket.

'Keeping it then?' Diana asked.

'We'll see.' She folded the costume carefully and laid the hat and blouse on top of it before slipping her dress back on. When she turned round Diana had already replaced the hatbox under the bed. She helped tidy away the shirts, ties and socks, while Diana packed away the blue costume. Then both of them lifted the suitcase off the bed, smoothed over the counterpane and checked the room before going downstairs.

'All right, love?' Megan was clearing the table when Bethan and Diana returned to the kitchen. Charlie and Sam were sitting, like a pair of bookends, in the easy chairs either side of the fire, but William was still eating.

'I think so,' Bethan replied doubtfully, still trying to work out what her 'tab' stood at.

'You out to give your boys a good Easter treat?' Megan nodded at the clothes that William had heaped on the dresser.

'And myself if I can run to it,' Bethan said wryly, holding up the hat, blouse and costume.

'Nine shillings for the three. And with the discount on the boys' stuff we'll call it twenty-five bob.'

'I make it more than that,' Bethan insisted.

'I make my profit. Besides, customers like you save me a lot. You buying in bulk means that I've less stock sitting around gathering dust and losing money.' Megan pulled a black card-covered exercise book out of the drawer in her dresser.

'I owe you three pounds at the moment. . . . '

'Two pounds ten, love, you paid me ten bob last week, and with today's little lot it comes to . . . ' Megan scribbled a few figures in the margin of her book and bit her bottom lip in concentration.

'Three pounds five shillings,' Bethan interrupted.

'Spot on, love,' Megan agreed.

'I can give you ten bob now. . . . '

'Don't you go leaving yourself short. Not on Rattle Fair day.'

'She doesn't need money. She's got her fancy man to treat her,' William winked, as he finished his breakfast.

Bethan glared at him and he burped loudly.

'Piggylope,' Diana remonstrated from the scullery, where she was rinsing dishes in the stone sink.

'William picked up his plate and carried it out. 'Miss starched knickers,' he whispered into Diana's ear.

'Mam! William said a naughty word,' Diana protested.

'Here's the ten bob.' Bethan took advantage of the altercation between her cousins to push the note on to Megan.

'You sure you're not making yourself short now?'

'I'm sure.'

'William, wrap and carry those suits up to Graig Avenue for Bethan.'

'Aw, Mam, I promised to meet the boys. . . . '

'The boys can wait,' Megan said firmly.

'I'll carry them, Mrs Powell.' Charlie lifted his boots from the hearth and took off his slippers. 'I want to see Mr Powell about some business. That's if you don't mind walking with me, Nurse Powell?' He looked at Bethan.

'Of course not.' Bethan took the sheet of brown paper William handed her and laid the boys' clothes in the middle of it.

'Here, love, I've a carrier bag for your suit.' Megan produced a brown paper and string bag from behind one of the easy chairs. 'See you later at the fair?'

'I expect so.' Bethan finished tying the parcel and folded the costume and hat inside the bag.

Charlie left his chair and took the parcel from the dresser. He waited quietly for Bethan to precede him. She led the way out through the front door. The street was teeming with people: children playing with sticks, stones and empty jam jars in the gutter, their parents gossiping in doorways. One or two of the women had carried chairs and bowls on to the pavement and were peeling vegetables and keeping up with the gossip at the same time.

'Mrs Morgan – ' Charlie tipped his hat to Megan's immediate neighbour as he shut the door.

'That's a big parcel you have there, Charlie. Megan doing business even on Easter Monday?'

'Not really, Mrs Morgan,' he answered evasively. 'Mrs Jones – ' He removed his hat as they passed another neighbour.

To every other adult on the Graig, Mrs Morgan was Betty, Mrs Jones, Judy, but Bethan had noticed that Charlie addressed everyone, even Megan, formally. It was as if he wanted to maintain the barriers that he'd erected between himself and those he'd chosen to live amongst. Walking side by side, the parcel swinging heavily in Charlie's hand between them, they turned the corner of Leyshon Street and made their way towards the Graig Hotel. Bethan glanced up Walter's Row to Phillips Street. The curtains were still drawn in number one. Her heart went out to Phyllis.

Charlie stopped and looked at her. Flustered she moved on, and they covered the distance between Walter's Row and the vicarage on the corner of Graig Avenue in silence. If the lack of conversation bothered Charlie he showed no sign of it, but Bethan felt she had to say something. Finally she resorted to an inane 'The weather's quite nice today isn't it?'

'Yes,' he agreed flatly.

She made no further attempt to talk. Half-way up Graig Avenue they met the vicar of St John's, his young and extremely pretty wife clutching his arm as she teetered along the rough road on heels that were too high for safety.

'Wonderful Easter weather, Bethan, Charlie,' he greeted them as his wife smiled warmly.

'It makes a welcome change after the winter,' Bethan agreed.

'We've just called in on Mrs Pugh and Miss Phyllis Harry,' he said with a significant look at Charlie. 'They're very grateful for your efforts on their behalf, Charlie. And your support, Bethan,' he added as an afterthought.

Bethan looked at Charlie, wondering what his 'efforts' might be.

'It's Mrs Powell you should be thanking,' he mumbled.

'I'll call in later to thank her, never fear. But the assistance Mrs Powell has given Miss Harry in her hour of need in no way depreciates the value of what you've done for the unfortunate household. As a vicar of the Church I know how scarce real Christian charity is in cases like Miss Harry's. The ladies would like to see you so they can thank you in person. Will you promise me that you'll call on them?'

Charlie nodded but said nothing.

'And both Miss Harry and Mrs Pugh are grateful for your kind wishes, Bethan.'

'I didn't think they knew I'd called.'

'They knew,' the vicar said drily. 'In a week or two when things are quieter I'm sure they'll welcome another visit.'

'I'll make a point of calling in.'

'Good. See you both at the Rattle Fair.' He tipped his hat and he and his wife went on their way.

Charlie crossed the road and Bethan had difficulty keeping up with him, but he hung back when they reached her house. She ran up the steps to the front door, turned the key and shouted for her father. Evan opened the kitchen door and ushered Charlie through the passage, parcel and all. The front parlour door, usually kept firmly closed, was open. Bethan glanced into the room that Haydn and Eddie usually referred to as 'the holy of holies'. Her mother had taken the dust sheets off the Rexine-covered suite and was busy straightening and dusting the ornaments on the mantelpiece. A sure sign that Uncle John Joseph and Aunt Hetty were going to visit.

'Where are the boys?' Bethan asked.

'Out the back with Maud,' Elizabeth replied tersely. 'Are you here to help or just passing through?'

'I'm meeting Laura in half an hour.'

'I suppose you'll be out all day?'

'Probably.'

'You won't be back for dinner or high tea?'

'No.'

'I don't know what your uncle and aunt are going to say about that,' Elizabeth pronounced stiffly.

'I'll see them another time.'

'When, that's what I'd like to know?' Elizabeth called after her as she walked away. 'You haven't got a minute to spare for your family these days.'

'Sorry, Mam,' Bethan said automatically. She wasn't in the least bit sorry. As a child she'd loathed holiday tea times when her uncle and aunt came to visit. Her mother always forced her father to wear a collar, and the whole family to sit stiffly upright around the kitchen table taking small bites and chewing quietly. If anyone dared deviate from Elizabeth's idea of correct behaviour they received the full force of the cutting edge of her tongue in front of Uncle John Joseph, who could never resist putting his oar in and belittling the culprit further. And after tea the entire family 'retired' (John Joseph's expression) to the front parlour to listen to his diatribes on how the advent of the wireless set and the cinema had caused the downfall of morality and religion in Welsh society.

As a small child Bethan had confused her uncle with the devil, and Sundays spent in the front parlour with hell. Looking back, it was an understandable mistake for a small child to make. John Joseph's entire conversation had always revolved around sin and the threat of eternal damnation, and his tall, thin, sardonic figure presiding over the gloomy gatherings in the front parlour wasn't that far removed from the traditional warning posters of hell.

She was looking forward to her day out at the Rattle Fair with Laura, Andrew and Trevor, but if there'd been no Andrew and no Rattle Fair, a brisk walk through the fresh young nettles that grew in wild abandon on the north side of Shoni's pond would have been infinitely preferable to the afternoon's entertainment mapped out by her mother.

She tried to creep into the kitchen, pick up the parcel and tiptoe out through the washhouse door without disturbing her father and Charlie. But her father was watching for her. Interrupting his conversation with Charlie he looked up quizzically as she reached for the parcel.

'Aunt Megan found a suit for Eddie,' she explained.

'And you bought it for him?'

'It's on trial. To see if it fits.'

'And if it does?'

'Aunt Megan will put it on her book. It's very cheap.'

'When you say Megan's book, you mean the one you've opened with her?'

'Eddie's been promised three mornings' work in the brewery yard next week. He'll soon pay for it himself.'

A sharp frown creased Evan's forehead. He was sitting hunched forward, leaning towards the range, his shoulders rounded like those of an old man. There were faint touches of grey in the roots of the black hair at his temples, grey that Bethan hadn't noticed before. If Charlie hadn't been in the room she would have

176

attempted to caress and kiss the frown away. She'd tried to help, and only succeeded in hurting his pride, even more than her mother did with her constant nagging.

'Do you really think the union strong enough to make these demands, Mr Powell?' Charlie asked, breaking the tense silence.

'The strength of the union is not the issue. The demands have to be made. If they're not, we'll none of us have jobs to go to.'

Bethan listened to them for a moment, and when she was certain that her father's attention was firmly fixed on what Charlie was saying she took the parcel and went through to the back yard. Sunshine blinded her after the gloom of the house. Narrowing her eyes she saw Maud and Haydn sitting on the top step talking to Glan over the wall that separated the two backs.

'Enjoy your morning walk?' Haydn asked.

'Yes. Here's something for you and Eddie.'

'Something for me?' Eddie shouted from the fenced-off upper yard where he was filling the lurcher's water bowl. 'What is it? Something nice, I hope.'

'Got something nice for me, Beth?' Glan leered.

'Eddie's cheerful today,' Bethan observed, deliberately ignoring Glan.

'For a change.' Maud looked slyly at Haydn.

Haydn took the parcel from Bethan and fought with the knot on the string. He unfolded the brown paper and lifted out the grey suit that was on top.

'We supposed to just take these off you, Beth?'

'Auntie Megan had them in last night. They were too good a bargain to miss so I took them on spec hoping they'd fit.'

'This for me?' Haydn asked, holding up the grey.

'No, the stripe is. And I got you a few other things while I was at it.'

'Lucky sods,' Glan muttered enviously, peering over the wall at the contents of the parcel.

'How much was this little lot, Beth?' Haydn demanded.

'Not a lot. Auntie Megan has the account.'

'What's not much?' he pressed.

'Hadn't you better try them on to see if they fit before asking how much they are? And before you say any more, I only brought what you both need. Have you thought what you're going to

177

wear to work when your one and only suit needs cleaning? And Eddie hasn't even got a one and only.'

While Bethan was glaring at Haydn, Maud tried to ease the situation by holding up the grey suit to Eddie as he latched the gate on the dog pen.

'Fancy yourself in this then, boyo?' she asked.

'Mmm.' Eddie flicked the jacket over gingerly with the tip of his grubby forefinger. 'Waistcoat as well.'

'Of course,' Bethan said defensively. 'Nothing but the best.'

'How much do we owe you, Sis?' Eddie asked.

'Nothing yet. I've taken them on spec.'

'Well what do you say, Haydn, shall we try them on?'

'No harm in that.' Haydn folded the paper back over the suits and dusted off his trousers as he rose from the step. Bethan breathed easier. She hadn't expected them to give in so easily.

Maud moved so Eddie and Haydn could walk down the steps. Bethan rested her elbow on the wall and allowed herself a small smile of triumph as they passed.

'You'll either get the money or the suits back tonight, Beth.' Eddie dumped the can he'd used to fill the dog's bowl in the corner of the yard. Bethan looked up and saw a cut on his chin that she hadn't noticed when they'd eaten breakfast together the day before. His left cheekbone was also bruised, but there was a look of quiet determination in his eyes that made her blood run cold.

'The Rattle Fair! Of course. You're going to fight.' It wasn't a question.

'As soon as they open the boxing booth. Come and watch. If you've any money to spare you can place a bet. You won't lose,' he said cockily.

She shuddered.

'And I won't get hurt either,' he insisted. 'I've learned a lot in the last couple of months. Joey's been training me, and training me good. I'll be the breadwinner in this family soon, Beth. Not you. And I'll make enough to pay for half a dozen suits for each of us, Mam and Dad included. You'll see if I'm not right.'

The Rattle Fair was held every Easter in Pontypridd. Every other fair that visited the town pitched on the vacant lot, sometime

178

cattle market, known as the Fairfield opposite the Palladium cinema at the north end of town. But the Rattle Fair was held courtesy of a charter which enabled it to pitch in the centre of the town itself. The Dante family, who owned and ran most of the fairs that visited Pontypridd, erected their rides and booths along the main thoroughfares including Taff Street and Market Square. The police in compliance with the order closed the town to all traffic, diverting non-fair carts and vans around Gelliwastad Road.

Roundabouts and brightly painted garish stalls that sold every conceivable kind of useless object and edible delicacy cluttered the streets from one end to the other, and in prime position in Market Square stood the coughing, wheezing engine that drove the machinery and powered the organ that announced to everyone within a mile's listening distance that the fair had arrived. It was *the* place to visit after dinner on Easter Monday. But it was just after eleven o'clock in the morning when Laura, wearing a new and most becoming (from Megan's stock) lilac spring suit, and Bethan in her green costume and cream silk blouse emerged from under the railway bridge. The Ronconis always opened their café in town on Rattle Fair afternoons, but today they had decided to hold a family dinner in the place first, and Laura had invited not only Bethan but also Trevor and Andrew to join the family party.

More nervous than Bethan had ever seen her before, Laura tripped along the streets on heels twice as high as those she normally wore. Both of them were careful to avoid the grimy outstretched hands of the street urchins who'd camped among the stalls since before dawn in the hope of cadging scraps from the food vendors or winning free rides from the 'softer' fair folk.

'Ronnie's told the cook to make a chicken dinner. Roast potatoes, peas, stuffing, all the trimmings,' Laura said fussily. 'There'll be brown soup first, and apple pie and Papa's ice cream for afters. Do you think Andrew and Trevor'll be happy with that?'

'They'll be hard to please if they aren't.' Laura's edginess was beginning to irritate Bethan.

'It's just that I want everything to be absolutely perfect. You know what bears Papa and Ronnie can be.'

179

'It's serious between you and Trevor, isn't it?' Bethan asked suddenly.

'Yes,' Laura admitted, pulling nonexistent wrinkles out of her new cotton gloves. 'Promise you won't breathe a word of this to Andrew.'

'A word about you being serious?'

'About what I'm going to tell you, you clot. If you tell Andrew he'll only go blabbing everything to Trevor. Those two are like Tweedledum and Tweedledee.'

'I hadn't noticed.'

'You haven't noticed anything except Andrew's dark brown eyes since New Year's Eve.'

'Don't be ridiculous . . . ' Bethan began coldly.

'Oh come on, Beth, it's not a sin to be in love.' Laura paused, then giggled. 'And then of course it might be.'

'A sin?'

'In the eyes of the Church what Trevor and I do is classed as sinful. But I don't see anything wrong with it,' she lifted her chin defiantly, 'particularly as he's far too caring and careful to see me land in the same mess as poor Phyllis.'

'You mean you and Trevor. . . . ' Bethan paused, too embarrassed to continue.

'Of course. Are you saying that you and Andrew don't?' Laura exclaimed incredulously.

With her face burning, Bethan shook her head.

'To think of Andrew . . . ' Laura's eyes grew round in amazement. 'He's lived in London, and everything. He never struck me as backward about coming forward, not like Trevor. Now he needed a bit of pushing.'

'Pushing?'

'You know what I mean.'

Bethan crossed the road in advance of Laura. She had a fair idea what Laura meant by pushing, but she didn't feel like discussing the details in any great depth.

'Being a doctor has its advantages,' Laura continued when she caught up with Bethan. 'For one thing Trevor doesn't have to sidle up to old Dai Makey in the market to buy his French letters. You know our Tina is friendly with Dai's daughter Pru? Well when she called in on Pru one day she caught Dai and his wife

rolling the . . . the letters,' she giggled, 'in talcum powder. Trevor
told me Dai charges half a crown just for one. No wonder the
unmarrieds ward is so full. If you ask me, the quickest way to
empty it would be to hand out free French letters to everyone
who wants them.'

'Ssh.' Bethan pulled her out of the path of a group of gaping,
dumbstruck children.

'Anyway,' Laura continued lowering her voice, 'Trevor might
not be as well heeled as Andrew, but he does have prospects.
And although his car isn't quite in the luxury class, it gets us to
where we want to go. You wouldn't believe the quiet lanes that
he knows. . . . ' She gave Bethan a hard look. 'You're not having
me on about you and Andrew are you?'

'No,' Bethan protested indignantly, leading the way round the
back of the stalls to the canvas-walled alleyway that had been
created on the pavement in front of the shops.

'I just find it hard to believe. You do know he's absolutely mad
about you?'

'I'm not so sure.'

'Beth, you're *impossible*. He jumps through hoops, switches
duties, and breaks all kinds of engagements with his family just
to spend his days off with you.'

'Who told you that?' Bethan asked suspiciously.

'Who do you think?'

'Trevor?'

'They are best friends.'

'And Andrew told Trevor that we were. . . . '

'Good Lord, no. I don't think they talk about anything as
personal as that.' Laura skipped over a pile of debris at the back
of the candyfloss stall.

'Why not? We do.'

'I suppose we do. How did we get on to this subject in the first
place?'

'You were telling me about the dinner Ronnie organised and
your father. . . . '

'That's right, Papa,' she mused thoughtfully. Her expression
changed completely. 'Beth, you wouldn't believe what he did
when I told him about Trevor on Friday night! Doolaly Tap
wasn't the word for it. And as soon as he started performing

181

everyone ran and hid except Mama and Ronnie. Mama wanted to, but I stood in front of the kitchen door and wouldn't move, leaving her with the choice of either staying or sitting in the washhouse. Nothing would have budged our Ronnie of course. He loves Papa's tempers. When he's not on the receiving end of them, that is,' she added bitterly.

'Have you warned Trevor what he's walking into today?'

'I didn't dare. He'd never have agreed to come if I had. Besides, Papa did eventually calm down, a little,' she qualified. 'At least he went from raving lunacy to ordinary temper when I told him Trevor was a doctor. Ronnie was no help. The only comment he made in Trevor's favour was that an Irish Catholic doctor was better than a Protestant Welsh miner, but only just. Then Papa turned on Mama and blamed her for talking him out of sending me to my grandmother in Italy, as he wanted to when I was sixteen. When Mama pointed out that I was a qualified nurse, he said he'd rather have a decently married Italian housewife for a daughter.'

'Sounds fun,' Bethan said ironically.

'Oh it was. Papa finished off by screaming up the stairs at my sisters. He swore blind that he won't let any of them out of his sight until they reach sixteen and then he's packing each of them off to Italy in turn. That makes Tina overdue for the journey. I don't think she's recovered from the shock yet. Not that she's talked to me about it. I've been sent to Coventry for making Papa angry in the first place.'

'Does your father mean it?'

'You know Papa. At the moment he does.'

'Poor William,' Bethan said feelingly.

'He's still sweet on Tina?'

'Isn't Tina still sweet on him?'

'I've just told you, she's not talking to me. Oh Beth, I'm so worried. What if Papa hates Trevor on sight? It was as much as Mama could do to persuade him to let Trevor come to dinner in the café today.'

'I don't know whether I should thank or kick you for inviting Andrew and me.'

'Don't you see, I need you and Andrew there. Papa's always liked you, and Andrew can charm the birds off the trees when he wants to. And with you two sitting at the table I don't think Papa'll dare make a scene. At least that's the plan. And as he can't very well ignore someone who's eating with us he's going to have to talk to Trevor, and when he does he's bound to see how wonderful he is.'

'And if he doesn't?' Bethan probed.

'I'll have to elope. I'm old enough.'

'Elope as in get married?'

'Of course. What do you think I've been talking about for the last half-hour. Trevor asked me to marry him on Friday evening after work. We've nothing to wait for except more money, and we can save as well when we're married as we can now.'

'You'll have to give up nursing.'

'That won't matter, I never really saw myself as the Florence Nightingale type. Besides I spend every penny I earn on clothes, and thanks to Megan my wardrobe should last me until Trevor gets a better-paid post. He earns four pounds a week now,' she said proudly. 'Another two years should make it six. And although we haven't enough money to buy a house straight off, we certainly have enough to rent one. Glan says there's one going in Maritime Street for ten bob a week, and we shouldn't spend more than a pound a week housekeeping, so with luck we'll manage to save the deposit for a decent place of our own within a year. Maybe even a house on the Common.'

'Sounds like you've got it all worked out,' Bethan murmured wistfully. While Laura had been talking, her mind had painted a picture of the terraced houses in Maritime Street, or rather one in particular. Newly decorated and papered, tastefully furnished, and her caring for it, cooking delicious meals in the kitchen while she waited for Andrew to return from the hospital in the evening. Suddenly it all seemed so very attractive, and Laura had it within her grasp.

'Neither Trevor nor I have saved a bean,' Laura prattled on, 'me because . . . well you know where my money goes, and Trevor's been supporting his mother and his brother and sisters. But I'm sure we'd be able to scavenge everything we need, and what we don't need we'll do without. Once his sisters and brother are settled his mother can move in with us. She's so sweet, Beth. And she really likes the idea of Trevor marrying me. . . . '

'You've met her?'

'On Saturday. I was dying to tell you all about it in work yesterday but you had to be off, didn't you. I know we won't quite have the start you and Andrew'll have. His father will probably buy you a mansion on the Common. . . . ' She stared at Bethan. 'Don't tell me you and Andrew haven't even talked marriage?'

'We're just good friends.' Bethan repeated the trite phrase without even thinking what she was saying.

'Just good friends my eye. The man's besotted. God, you're either a cold fish or a slow worker, Bethan Powell. I thought you'd have chosen the ring pattern by now.'

'Ring pattern?' Bethan asked blankly.

'Engagement ring,' Laura explained impatiently. 'Trevor and I are going to choose one in Cardiff on my next day off. . . . Oh God there he is!' Laura muttered, catching sight of Andrew and Trevor, cigarettes in hand, waiting outside the café door.

'Do you think they've already knocked and your father wouldn't let them in?'

'Don't tease, Beth, I'm in no mood for it. What's the time?'

Bethan opened her handbag and looked at her nurse's watch that she'd pinned inside the flap.

'Nearly half-past eleven.'

'Dinner won't be until twelve. Back me up if I suggest a stroll round the town.'

'Hello darling.' Andrew winked at Bethan, before turning to Laura. 'What have you done to this fellow?' he demanded mischievously. 'He's an absolute wreck.'

'I think we should go for a walk around the town. See what's going on,' Laura suggested loudly.

'Not on your life.' Andrew pushed a large cardboard box towards Trevor with his toe. 'For one thing your brother's already seen us, and for another, Trevor couldn't carry this another step.'

'What is it?' Laura asked.

'A case of decent wine to sweeten your father,' he grinned. 'If a quarter of what I've heard about Italian fathers is true, we're going to need every drop.'

The warm Italian welcome that the Ronconis extended to Bethan

184

was as cordial as usual. It even embraced Andrew, but it stopped short of Trevor. A German spy captured during the Great War couldn't have been put through a more intense interrogation than the one Papa Ronconi subjected him to. Half a dozen of the largest tables had been pushed together in the centre of the room and covered over with Mrs Ronconi's biggest damask tablecloth. Gleaming like freshly cut coconut it was graced by the family's best silverware and china that had been specially brought down for the occasion in the back of Ronnie's Trojan van the night before.

Unwilling to sit alongside Trevor and Andrew and listen to what her father was saying, Laura donned an apron and busied herself, cleaning the tables and straightening the chairs that Ronnie had cleaned and straightened the night before. Bethan hid in the kitchen with Mrs Ronconi and Laura's sisters. But when the soup thickened and the chickens turned a dark brown at their extremities Laura's mother had no choice but to begin serving the meal. She laid the tureen proudly in the centre of the table, and Ronnie opened one of the bottles of wine that Trevor had presented to Laura's father. Bethan recognised the label: the bottles were from Andrew's father's cellar, the same vintage that Andrew took on their picnics.

The meal wasn't as bad as Laura had expected. Thanks to Andrew there were no embarrassing silences. He excelled himself. One amusing story followed another, and he took every opportunity to present Trevor in a good light. He deferred to Trevor's judgement on all things from politics to current medical advances – not forgetting to sketch in glowing colours the brilliant career that every doctor of note in the area confidently predicted for Trevor. And when he wasn't praising Trevor, or the cooking, or the Signor Ronconis' (father and son) business acumen, he was complimenting Laura's mother on her children, or smiling and joking with Laura's sisters until all of them, even Tina, fell madly in love with him.

After the apple pie and ice cream had been cleared away he even succeeded in winning Ronnie over by producing a bottle of Napoleon brandy to complement the cigars that Trevor handed round. Bethan studied them as Andrew clipped off the ends, noting that they too were the brand that Dr John senior smoked.

185

Following the example of the women of the family Bethan gulped her coffee and rose to help clear the table, but Andrew forestalled her.

'That was a wonderful meal,' he thanked Mrs Ronconi effusively, 'and we'd love to stay longer, but unfortunately I promised my parents that we'd pick up my sister and her husband from the station at one-thirty. They're coming in on the London train. Please forgive me for cutting such a pleasant time short, and having to take Bethan with me.'

'We understand the value of family promises,' Laura's father said ambiguously, as he struggled to his feet. His vast stomach shook in unison with his arm as he pumped Andrew's hand enthusiastically. 'Good of you to join us. You must come again.'

'I hope next time it will be our turn to play hosts,' Andrew said with a significant look at Trevor. 'Thank you so much for inviting us. Mrs Ronconi, Ronnie, nice to see you again. Tina . . .' he went around the table shaking hands, and kissing blushing cheeks. 'See you later, Trevor, Laura.'

If looks could have killed, Laura would have slain Bethan there and then. Andrew waited impatiently as Bethan untied her apron and fixed her hat on, securing it with the neat pearl-headed hat pin that had been part of her inheritance from her grandmother. Then he ushered her smartly out of the front door before she even had time to say her goodbyes properly.

'We're not really meeting your sister are we?' she asked as the door clanged shut behind them.

'Of course.'

'Andrew, not now. I look dreadful.'

'For pity's sake, she's my sister not the Queen. Come on, we've barely ten minutes before the train comes in.'

The two glasses of wine she'd drunk with the meal swam fuzzily in her head as she marched briskly alongside Andrew, or at least as briskly as the fair paraphernalia would allow, towards the station. Andrew bought platform tickets in the ground-floor office and raced up the wide stone staircase that led to the trains. Bethan tried to keep up and failed. He waited for her by the ticket collector's booth.

'Unfit, Nurse Powell?'

'After a meal like that, yes,' she panted.

'It was rather good wasn't it,' he agreed. He handed the tickets to the uniformed official. 'London train?' he enquired.

'Platform two. Due in three minutes, sir.'

'I love the certainty of railway staff,' he whispered as he took hold of her elbow and ushered her down the platform.

'I wish you'd given me some warning about this,' she pleaded. 'I must look dreadful.' She rummaged in her handbag for her powder puff.

'You look beautiful. Here – ' He took a clean handkerchief out of his top pocket and wiped a smut from her chin. She glanced down her nose trying to see if there were any grease stains on her costume from the café kitchen.

'You look absolutely perfect,' he grinned. 'Come here, woman.' He wrapped his arms around her. 'You know, the best thing about railway stations is that people turn a blind eye to things that they'd "tut" at in the park. I don't know why we haven't thought of coming here before.' Bending his head to hers, he gave her a long, lingering kiss.

'Now you'll have to reapply your lipstick,' he laughed as he released her.

'Thank you very much, Doctor John,' she said peevishly. Suddenly weak at the knees, she looked at the benches, saw the dirt on them and decided against sitting down.

'How was Laura this morning?' Andrew asked, staring up the line in the direction the train would come in. 'Frankly there were times when I wondered if Trevor would make it to the café in one piece.'

'I've never seen her so nervous,' she mumbled as she dabbed lipstick on her mouth. 'Did you know that Trevor had asked her to marry him?'

'He told me when he came round on Friday night, late. Or should I say early Saturday morning.'

'You didn't say anything to me yesterday.'

'Laura warned Trevor against saying anything, she wanted to tell you about it herself. So I could hardly pass on information that I wasn't supposed to know. Look, here's the train. Three minutes to the dot.' He checked his watch. 'I take my hat off to British Rail. For once they're spot on time.'

187

Chapter Eleven

Laura wasn't the only one in town who was nervous that day. At two o'clock Eddie entered Captain Dekker's boxing booth flanked by his trainer Joey, and Haydn. The bravado that had sustained him at home fled in the face of the large crowd pressed tightly around the roped-off makeshift ring.

'You'll be fine, boyo. Don't think about them, just pretend you're in the gym.' Joey, who knew exactly what Eddie was feeling, slapped him soundly on the back. Eddie looked coldly at the old man, and for the first time saw him as he really was. Teeth missing, nose broken and pushed sideways, eyes bloodshot, sunk into a prematurely aged and wrinkled face, jaw broken and badly set. He'd told everyone he was the one who'd make it. World champion? But Joey had once believed in his own ability every bit as much as Eddie believed in himself now. And you only had to look around the town or the gym to see those who were even worse off than Joey. Punch-drunk, with slurred speech that no one could understand, not that they said anything worth understanding. Men like Cast Iron Dean. Once hailed as the strongest man in the world, now a blind wreck that the kids ran from on sight, and jeered at behind his back.

'It's not too late to walk away, Eddie,' Haydn murmured, blanching at the sight of the dried bloodstains on the canvas floor and walls of the booth. It was the best, or perhaps the worst thing he could have said.

'I'm here to stay,' Eddie snapped. 'But if you want to go, feel free.'

'That's not what I meant and you know it.'

'Haydn, Haydn, over here!' Four of the chorus girls from the current show at the Town Hall were sitting on one of only two benches in the booth. Sandwiched between them was the show's comedian.

'Come on, I'll introduce you,' Haydn offered.

'To them?' Eddie stared at their faces, heavily painted to

188

announce to the world that they were on the stage. He'd never seen so much make-up on a woman close up before. Not a young one, and certainly not out of the station yard.

'Come on, they don't bite.' Haydn pushed Eddie ahead and Joey, reluctant to allow his protégé out of his sight, followed.

'Eddie, Joey, meet Polly, Daisy, Doris, Lou, and the best comedian in Wales, Sam Spatterson.'

'Best comedian in the British Empire, old boy,' Sam corrected.

'My apologies,' Haydn smiled. 'Best comedian in the Empire. Everyone, this is my kid brother Eddie and his trainer Joey.'

'Trainer. Oo . . . ooh you're a boxer,' Daisy squealed as she caught hold of Eddie's arm and pulled him down on to the bench next to her. 'I just love strong, powerful men,' she purred.

Too embarrassed to say anything, Eddie stared at his feet.

'He's a world champion in the making, miss,' Joey said proudly.

'He doesn't look much like you, Haydn,' Doris said pertly. 'Sure your mother didn't stray from the nest?'

The blood rushed to Eddie's face.

'I'm sure.' Haydn gave Eddie a warning frown. Even he occasionally found it hard to reconcile the risqué talk of showbusiness people with that of 'normal' life. He couldn't expect the same kind of latitude from Eddie, who'd never been backstage in the Town Hall in his life.

'Tell me, Eddie,' Daisy whispered in his ear as she fingered his biceps, 'are you doing anything later, after you've boxed?'

'I hadn't thought about it,' he mumbled.

'If you aren't you could come and see me in the show.' She puckered her bright red lips as though preparing to kiss him. 'I have a spare ticket here.' She pulled a warm crumpled ticket out of the front of her low-cut blouse and thrust it into the breast pocket of his new suit. 'Don't forget now,' she crooned seductively. 'Afterwards we could paint the town red. What about it, strong man?'

'Lay off, Daisy,' Haydn warned. 'That's my kid brother you're talking to.'

'Ooh, big brother can get masterful.' Doris opened her eyes wide. 'I never knew you had it in you, callboy.'

'I'll see you ladies tonight,' Haydn retorted suggestively.

189

'Promises, promises,' Daisy cooed as Eddie extricated himself from her grasp and rejoined Haydn and Joey.

'Will you really see those girls tonight?' Eddie asked as they walked back towards the ring.

'Of course, I'm working, remember.'

'I forgot.'

'Girls like that aren't worth a farthing,' Haydn said with all the assurance of his nineteen years. 'It's nice girls you should be making cow's eyes at.'

'Like Jenny Griffiths?' Eddie couldn't resist the taunt.

'Yes. If you must know, like Jenny Griffiths. But if on the other hand you're looking for a bit of skirt to take up Shoni's pond tomorrow you couldn't do better than Daisy. By all accounts she's made men of many boys.'

'Sure you don't mean mincemeat?' Joey interrupted. Eddie turned to the old man in surprise. He'd almost forgotten he was there. 'You want to win fights, boyo? You stay away from women. That's my advice. Women concentrate the blood where it's not needed or wanted in a fight. And they stop it from flowing to where it is.'

'Can you see Bethan anywhere?' Eddie asked, embarrassed again.

'She said she'll be here this afternoon, and that means she will,' Haydn reassured him.

A voice boomed from the centre of the ring: 'Here we have big bad brutal Billy . . . '

Joey pressed close to Eddie. 'This is where you start fighting, boy. Watch. Eyes and ears. Remember. Eyes and ears. Listen to the ref. Watch their boy's movements, think about his training. After you've seen two or three of the Captain's lads you'll be able to pick out their weaknesses. And there's always weaknesses. Knowing your opponent is half the battle, boy. And when you know enough to take him on, we'll make our move. And not on one of your venture five bob, win a quid challenges either.'

'Five bob. Only five bob a challenge. Any man who can go for more than five minutes in the ring with Bad Billy Bater and stay on his feet gets a crisp, crackling pound note. Now who's going to be the first taker to down this man. . . . '

The crowd gasped as Big Billy stepped over the ropes into the ring and stripped off his robe. He was an enormous hulk of a man. His face battered, his back and chest above his shorts black and blue from the punches he'd taken in the last town. He grinned vacantly at the crowd and held his hands high.

'Please, Joey. Let me have a go at this one?' Eddie pleaded, dreading the encounter but anxious to have it over and done with at the same time.

'Not yet, boy. Not yet.' Joey put his arm round Eddie's shoulders. 'See those bruises. No boxer worth his salt would let an opponent get close enough to leave marks like that. His brain's gone. No medals to be won flattening a has-been like Bad Billy. He's Jim Dekker's punchbag. The real talent comes out with the five-pound offer not the quid. Remember. Eyes and ears, boy. Eyes and ears.'

Eddie leaned uneasily against one of the posts that held the canvas ceiling over the booth. Haydn put his hand into his pocket and pulled out a packet of PK. He offered one to his brother. Waiting was definitely the worst part of this game.

'Andrew's kept your existence quiet enough. But then he always was tight-lipped about his girlfriends, even when he practically lived with us in London. Heaven knows why, because I've been dying to have a sister-in-law.' Fiona Campbell-White, *née* John, pressed her hand over Bethan's as they sat together in the back seat of Andrew's car. 'There's so many things I could tell a sister-in-law that I couldn't tell a brother,' she confided in a voice that carried to Andrew.

'Perhaps now Bethan can see why I've kept her away from you for so long.' Andrew changed gear, ready to take the hill to the Common.

'Why, dear brother?' Fiona purred sweetly. 'Were you afraid that I'd tell her what a rotter you really are?' She glanced slyly at Bethan.

Bethan was amazed at the similarities between brother and sister. Fiona was a beautiful feminine version of Andrew. They had the same dark eyes, smooth tanned skin, and glossy black hair. But Fiona's curls had been tamed into the classic, perfect bob that belonged to the world of advertising posters, not real life. Expensively dressed in a tan, fur-trimmed costume, set off

191

by matching crocodile-skin shoes and handbag, she exuded wealth and confidence with every whiff of her exotic perfume. Even her husband seemed to be one of her accessories. Good-looking in a smooth, matinée-idol, middle-parting sort of way, he was beautifully dressed in an immaculately tailored pin-stripe suit. The whole image of well-heeled affluence that they projected contrived to make Bethan feel grubby, working class and more inadequate than ever.

'So what's new in the medical world down here, Andrew?' Alec Campbell-White asked heartily.

'Not a lot.'

'Have you decided to take up my father's offer of a post in the surgical department of Charing Cross?'

'No. Not yet.' Andrew glanced in his mirror at Bethan who was sitting very stiffly and quietly.

'Here we are, home!' Fiona exclaimed excitedly. 'And everything looks just the same.'

'It would, wouldn't it,' Andrew commented wryly.

'It was good of you to meet us, old boy, I know you and. . . .'

'Bethan,' Andrew supplied.

'Bethan must have had a million other things to do.'

'Nothing as important as meeting my favourite brother-in-law and unfavourite sister. Here, I'll give you a hand with the cases.' Leaving the engine running he stepped out of the car and opened the boot.

'But you are coming in, aren't you?' Fiona demanded of Bethan as Andrew and Alec swung the set of matching brown leather cases out of the car and into the front porch.

'Afraid not, Fanny,' Andrew answered for Bethan. 'We've promised to meet friends in town. But we'll be back for dinner.'

'Look forward to it, old boy,' Alec said cheerfully as Fiona rang the doorbell.

Andrew slammed the boot shut. Climbing back into the car he patted the vacant passenger seat.

'Join me?' he asked Bethan.

She did as he asked, waving shyly at Fiona in return to her enthusiastic goodbyes.

'I didn't know we were dining with your family tonight,' she said as he left the driveway for the road.

'I'm sure I told you.'

'And I'm sure you didn't.'

'It's no big deal, Beth.' Instead of turning down the road into town he steered the car along the rough road that skirted the Common and the bleak moor that surrounded the cenotaph.

'Where are you going?'

'Somewhere where we can talk.'

'I promised to go to the boxing booth this afternoon.'

'The boxing booth!' he exclaimed in horror. 'Bethan, have you ever been in one?'

'No, but my brother Eddie is fighting.'

'In that case I'll take you. But they don't even open until two and nothing much happens for the first couple of hours. If I promise to get you there in the next half-hour, can we talk for ten minutes now? I want to explain. . . . '

'There's no need to explain anything,' she said quickly. She had a sudden premonition that jarred uneasily with his decision to introduce her to his family. He was going to London to take up the post that Alec had mentioned. Laura and Trevor were getting married and Andrew was saying goodbye. She began to shake, terrified at the thought of a future without him.

'You just took me by surprise,' she gabbled hastily. 'You never said anything about meeting your family. . . . '

'You don't want to meet them?'

'No . . . yes. Of course I don't mind meeting them. It's just that. . . . ' She fell silent, conscious that she was talking simply so she wouldn't have to listen to what he had to say. He continued driving until the road ended in a narrow lane. After a mile of winding turnings and sharp corners he pulled into a lay-by beside a farm gate. He switched off the engine and turned to face her. She was staring at her handkerchief, knotting its corners into tortuous shapes with her tensed fingers.

'Don't you think it's time you met my family?' he pressed.

'It's good of you to ask me.'

'Do you or don't you want to meet them?' He lifted her chin with his finger, forcing her to look at him.

'If you want the truth, I'm scared to death of meeting them,' she admitted.

'Why, Beth? You already know my father, and my mother's

sweet and old-fashioned. Not in the least bit modern or strident like Fanny.'

'Sounds to me as if you don't like Fiona very much,' she observed neatly, attempting to divert his attention from his father. How on earth could he say that she knew his father? Nurses bowed their heads in the hospital when the senior doctor passed. He talked about him as if they were used to exchanging pleasantries.

'Take no notice of Fanny,' he said glibly. 'Sibling rivalry. We've hated each other since cradle days.'

'Why?'

'No reason. All reasons. Don't you hate your brothers and sister?'

'No.'

'Oh dear. I had no idea you belonged to a perfect family.'

'My family's anything but perfect.'

'At last. We have something in common.'

'Imperfect families?'

'Come to dinner? Please?' he smiled. 'I'd lose all credibility with Fanny if you didn't. And I told my mother to expect you.'

'When?'

'This morning.'

'I could have made other arrangements.'

'I told you to keep the whole day clear.'

'All right I'll have dinner with your family tonight.' She summoned up her courage. 'On one condition,' she blurted out quickly before she could change her mind.

'Name it.'

'After we've been to the Rattle Fair, you take me home to change, then you can meet my family first.' She wanted to add, 'so you can see who and what I really am' but pride held her back. If he really loved her, home, background and family would make no difference.

'I thought you were never going to invite me,' he smiled. 'Now that's settled how about picking up where we left off in the station.'

He cupped his hands round her face. Drawing her close he kissed her, effectively preventing her from voicing any of the mass of questions that slithered through her mind. But his lovemaking failed to still her doubts. Was he leaving? Going to London? If so why did he want her to meet his family? Yesterday he'd said he loved her. Was that a trite, meaningless remark – a product of passion – of the moment – or the truth? Laura and Trevor were to marry and they. . . .

'I don't think we'd better go too far down this road,' he said huskily pulling away from her. 'Not here. Not in daylight.' He buttoned her blouse and jacket. 'Of course,' he murmured looking into her eyes, 'I could take you home this way tonight after dinner, or better still invite you to my rooms.'

She thought of what Laura had said – 'Are you sure you're not having me on about you and Andrew?' Was that the way to become an indispensable part of a man's life? Because if it was . . . 'I'd like that,' she agreed softly. He smiled as he reached for the starting handle. He'd always dwelt upon the differences between Bethan and the other girls he'd spent time with. But there were similarities too. And it was reassuring to know that once warmed up a Welsh chapel girl wasn't that far removed from her London counterpart after all.

The boxing booth was warm, humid and airless beneath the thick canvas walls and ceiling. The atmosphere within was gloomy in the half-light, heavy with unhealthy excitement and the fetid smell of stale male sweat. Andrew paid the shilling admission fees for himself, Trevor, Laura and Bethan to ensure they'd get a seat on the benches. Those who paid sixpence were fortunate if they got standing room that allowed them to see over the heads of the ex-professional and amateur boxers who'd laid claim to the prime area around the ring.

'Can you see Eddie anywhere?' Bethan asked Laura anxiously.

'Once we're on the benches we'll get a better view.' Trevor wrapped his arm protectively around Laura's shoulders. 'This really is no place for women.'

'And why not?' Laura demanded, spoiling for an argument after the stresses and strains of the afternoon.

'If you're serious about marrying this lady you'll have to learn that anything a man can do, a woman, particularly this woman,' Andrew pointed at Laura with his wallet as he pushed it back into his inside pocket, 'can do better.'

'Not boxing,' Trevor said firmly.

'Oh I don't know,' Andrew mused airily. 'Would you fancy going three rounds with Squeers?'

Bethan giggled as a sudden, very real image of Squeers in boxing shorts and vest sprang to mind.

'The moment we've all been waiting for, Gentlemen . . . and Ladies.' Jim Dekker himself stepped into the ring. He bowed towards Laura and Bethan and the bench where Doris and Daisy were still sitting. 'The supreme challenge, and the supreme purse of the day. A single, crisp five-pound note for any man brave enough to step into the ring with Dekker's champion. Ladies and Gentlemen. Let's have a round of applause for Daring Dan Darcy.' He swung round and a tall, well-built man climbed into the ring behind him. Holding his gloved hands high to the shouts and applause of the crowd, Daring Dan took his bow.

'God, how the mighty have fallen,' Trevor mumured under his breath.

'Blasphemy.' Laura nudged him in the ribs.

'It's starting,' Andrew warned Trevor. 'Another month and you'll be wearing a ball and chain.'

'What did you mean about the mighty falling?' Bethan asked nervously, scanning the crowd for a glimpse of Eddie as she took her seat.

'Ever heard of Dan Farrell?' Tevor replied.

'No. Should I have?'

'Five years ago he was the best. Tipped for world champion. And that's him now.' Trevor nodded towards the ring, where Dan had stripped off his robe and was flexing his biceps.

'What happened?'

'Could be any one of a number of things. Drink, high living. . . . '

'Women?' Andrew suggested innocently.

'Are you going to hit him, Bethan, or shall I?' Laura enquired frostily.

'Vicious too,' Andrew continued to tease Trevor.

'Come on, lads, don't be shy,' Jim Dekker shouted. 'First man to stay on his feet for three rounds with Daring Dan takes the pot. Five pounds! Who'll be the first taker? Five pounds for ten-bob entry fee?'

'Oh no you don't, Jim Dekker,' Joey shouted. 'You don't pull that one. Not in this town. It's five not ten bob.'

'Trying to put an honest man out of business, Joey,' Jim bit back humorously.

'Fair's fair,' someone in the crowd heckled.

'It's always been five bob,' Joey retorted sharply.

'Fair's fair,' the same man chanted.

'Show me your challenger,' Jim answered. 'And I'll show you what's fair.'

'Here.' Joey pushed Eddie's hand up, and Bethan started, almost falling off the bench.

'That your brother?' Andrew asked, trying to size up Eddie's chances.

'That's my brother.' Bethan fought back the tears that welled into her eyes.

'Seeing as how's he's a nipper, Joey, I'll allow him a try at five bob,' Jim conceded. 'Over here, lad.' He pointed to the pegs where contenders could hang their clothes.

Bethan watched Haydn follow Eddie to the corner of the booth. Then she saw her father push his way through the crowd towards the boys. The bookie who fixed the odds on the fights and made the real money for Dekker eyed Eddie carefully as he stripped off his suit, shirt and tie. He was wearing his shorts under his trousers.

'I never realised Eddie was so skinny, Beth,' Laura whispered in a voice that carried above the hubbub of noise.

'Neither did I.' Bethan paled as she compared her brother's underdeveloped figure with that of the seasoned boxer who was preening and parading in the ring.

The bookie, hat pushed back on his head at a rakish angle, sidled up to Andrew. 'Enjoying yourself, sir?' he enquired.

'Yes thank you,' Andrew replied with an amused glance at Trevor.

'Men of substance like yourselves,' he touched his hat to Trevor, 'tend to enjoy the sport a little better if they've a small matter on the outcome. If you know what I mean?'

'We know what you mean,' Andrew muttered under his breath, putting the poor man out of his misery. 'What are the odds?'

'Ten to one against the youngster pulling it off, sir.'

Andrew took out his wallet. 'Tenner on the challenger, all right?' he asked, folding a note into the bookie's palm. The man glanced at Eddie to check his prognosis. He nodded and slipped his hand into his pocket.

'I want to put some money on too.' Bethan fumbled in her handbag. The bookie looked anxiously around the booth at all the heads tall enough to be policemen. Andrew put his hand into his wallet again. 'Fiver for the lady.'

'Andrew. . . . '

'Pay me later.' He pocketed the slips the bookie handed him.

The man moved on past Trevor, who handed him a pound, to the people sitting behind them. Bethan stared at Haydn and Eddie, willing them with all her might to look at her. But as her father reached them they went into a huddle with Joey, the crowd closed in and they were lost to view.

'We're in the wrong business,' Andrew observed as he watched the bookie circle the booth. 'He must have taken the best part of fifty pounds in the last five minutes.'

'He'll be in the wrong business if Bethan's brother wins,' Trevor replied. 'Is he good, Bethan?'

'I don't know.' Worried about the five pounds that Andrew had handed over so glibly, and that she had no hope of repaying if Eddie lost, she couldn't bring herself to think about his prospects. 'If the way he talks is anything to go by, he's brilliant.'

'Believing in yourself is half the battle with a boxer,' Trevor commented.

'You know a lot about boxing all of a sudden.' Laura eyed Trevor suspiciously.

'Used to box in medical college.'

'You're joking.'

'Now why should I joke about something like that?'

Ignoring the bickering Andrew closed his hand over Bethan's. 'They stop these things long before anyone gets really hurt,' he asserted quietly.

'I've seen just how careful *they* are,' she answered scathingly. 'Eddie's been beaten to pulp in the gym once. Perhaps it would be different if he could get a steady job. It's not as if he hasn't tried, but his efforts don't seem to get him anywhere, and now he sees this as a way out.'

'It might prove to be just that. That old boy with him looks as though he knows what he's doing. I'm sure he wouldn't put your brother in the ring if he didn't think he stood a chance.'

'But he's much smaller than the one he's going to fight.'

'That can be an advantage.' Trevor leant towards her. 'Think of Jimmy Wilde.'

'Ladies and Gentlemen, give a big warm Pontypridd welcome to Eddie Powell.' Dekker shoved Eddie into the centre of the ring. 'He's one of your own. From the Graig.' The crowd went crazy. Shouting, cheering, cat-calling and stamping as if it was the Saturday penny rush in the pictures.

Bethan looked past Eddie and saw the bookie who'd taken Andrew's money standing alongside her father and Haydn. Both had their hands in their trouser pockets. If Eddie went down they'd be in the pawn shop with the new suits, her costume, and the jewellery she'd inherited from her grandmother tomorrow.

A very tense Eddie returned to his corner. Haydn pushed on his gloves. Joey laced them. The final knot was tied. Jim Dekker waved him forward. Eddie gave one quick last conscious look at Joey who stood, towel slung over his shoulder, behind his corner.

Dekker spoke, but Bethan didn't understand a word he said. The atmosphere swirled, a hot black whirlpool pierced by flashing red arrows. At the centre was Eddie, alone, skeletally thin. Dekker moved backwards. A bell clanged and Dan and Eddie raised their gloves. She gripped the edge of her seat as they circled one another warily around the canvas-covered boards.

The champion was playing with Eddie. Even Bethan with her limited knowledge of boxing could see that. A sudden swift right – a left – another right – Eddie dodged them as fast as they came. Then came a resounding whack which cracked through the air like a whiplash. She closed her eyes tightly and bit her bottom lip until she could taste salt blood.

The crowd booed. She opened her eyes. Blood was streaming from a cut high on Eddie's right cheekbone. He stumbled. She cried out. He threw a wild punch. By sheer fluke it landed on Dan's unguarded left jaw. The tension in the booth grew to explosive dimensions as the champion closed in.

Fists pummelled into naked flesh; close punches jabbed into Eddie's ribcage. Dekker shouted. The clinch broke and the crazy

dance began all over again – circling – shadow boxing – feinting
– circling . . . .

Andrew prised Bethan's fingers from the bench. She gripped
his hand fiercely, digging her nails into his wrist. Eddie threw a
punch that again connected with Dan's jaw. Dan retaliated with
a blow that landed high above Eddie's eye. Blood spurted, joining
the flow from the cut on Eddie's cheek. Fresh stains were added
to the rust-coloured splashes that spotted the canvas floor.

'Why won't someone stop it?' Bethan pleaded impotently; her
fingers were knots of pain she was barely aware of.

Smiling triumphantly, Dan swayed drunkenly on his feet. Half
blinded by his own blood Eddie threw all his strength into a left
targeted at the same spot he'd attacked throughout the bout. The
crowd roared as it hit home. There was a crack followed by a
dull thud. Bethan couldn't bear to look. She clung to Andrew,
burying her face in his tweed-covered shoulder. The sound of a
child's number chant filled the air:

'One . . . two . . . three . . . four. . . . '

She blocked out the sound. Eddie was bleeding. From his head.
She recalled all the punch-drunk boxers she'd seen. Harry
Mander, Joey Rees. . . .

'It's safe to look if you want to. The first round's finished and
your brother's still on his feet.'

She peered over Andrew's arm. White and trembling, Eddie
was sitting on a three-legged stool in the corner of the ring. Joey
held a wet towel over his eye. Haydn had handed him a water
bottle and he was swilling his mouth out and spitting into a
bucket that her father held in front of him.

'You shouldn't have bet so much money,' she breathed without
looking at Andrew.

'The odds were too good to miss.'

'Your brother,' Trevor patted her hand. 'He's good.'

'He is?'

'You don't know?'

The bell rang and Andrew gripped her fingers. The insane
dance began again, only this time the punches were flung wider,
but not by Eddie. He kept himself taut, compact. Presenting a
small, flitting target that darted around the ring – a flea teasing
a floundering rat. Bethan cried out and crushed Andrew's hands

fiercely every time Dan aimed a punch. But time after time he hit thin air. The blood rushed to Dekker's face as he strove to contain his irritation.

Eddie's right shot out of nowhere, hitting Dan soundly on the jaw. The crack of the impact was followed by a crash as Dan's head hit the canvas. The bell rang. No one noticed it was half a minute early.

'I'm taking you outside,' Andrew whispered, rising from the bench.

'No,' she hissed.

'You can't stand much more of this. You're as white as a sheet.'

'I couldn't bear not being able to see.'

'I didn't know you could through closed eyelids.' The sarcasm was lost on her.

Dekker and two of his fighters were working vigorously in their corner trying to revive Dan with wet towels and vinegar. Joey crouched in front of Eddie, mouthing last-minute instructions. Her father looked up at the crowded benches, saw her and smiled. He bowed his head towards Eddie. Eddie nudged Haydn and they both waved.

'Who's that with your brother?' Andrew asked.

'The tall dark one is my father,' she said proudly, 'the fair one is my older brother.'

'Close-knit family. Where's your mother?'

'At home making tea for my uncle,' she answered automatically, not really registering what he'd asked.

'The minister?' he persisted, trying unsuccessfully to divert her attention.

The crowd, growing restless, heckled, booed and stamped their feet, drowning out any further chance of conversation. Sensing trouble in the air Dekker signalled to the timekeeper. The bell rang. Bethan clutched Andrew and screamed in horror as Dan flung himself forward and threw his whole weight into a blow aimed at Eddie's head. Her brother ducked, and the booth faded. She was aware only of a blackness tinged with red, a distant roar that pained her ears.

'He's won,' Andrew shouted. 'He's won. Your brother, Bethan. He's won!'

She struggled to focus her eyes. Dan was flat on his back on the canvas. Eddie, blood streaming down his face, stood wild-eyed and panting in the centre of the ring. Joey clambered over the ropes and lifted his hand high into the air.

'Next world flyweight champion,' Joey shouted ecstatically above the noise of the crowd.

'Some brother you've got there, Bethan,' Trevor complimented.

'I always knew that.' She was crying. Tears streamed unchecked down her cheeks as she stared at Eddie. Shocked no longer, he was grinning at the crowd, confident and victorious. But all she could think of was that neither she nor Haydn nor her father would ever be able to stop him from boxing again – and again.

Chapter Twelve

'Table for – ' Andrew checked the size of his party – 'eight please, Mr Rogers.'

'Of course, Doctor John.' Dai Rogers, under-manager of the New Inn Hotel bowed, fawning not so much because of Andrew but Andrew's father, and his influence. 'This way please, Doctor.' He led them past the magnificent central staircase that dominated the entrance hall to the hotel, and into the comfortably furnished lounge. He beckoned brusquely to a waiter, who immediately finished scribbling down the order he was taking and rushed to his side.

'We have a nice table in the corner, Doctor John,' the waiter ventured, pointing to a low round table surrounded by comfortably padded red plush chairs.

'It will do fine,' Andrew agreed briskly. 'And as it's thirsty work watching boxing I'll have a beer. Trevor?'

'Pint as well, thank you.'

'Haydn, Eddie, William?'

'I think pints will be fine for all of us,' Haydn said quickly, forestalling William, who was on the point of asking for whisky, and looking out for Eddie who was was still a little shell-shocked as well as overawed by the surroundings.

'Five pints please,' Andrew said to the waiter. Dai Rogers continued to hover at the waiter's elbow, making sure that he wrote the order down correctly.

'Ladies?' Andrew looked to Bethan, Laura and Jenny Griffiths who sat nervously on the edge of the chair next to Haydn's.

'Sherry,' Laura said decisively. 'A large one. I need it.'

'Anyone would think you'd just gone three rounds with Desperate Dan, not Eddie. Bethan?'

'I'll have a sherry as well please.'

'Miss Griffiths?'

'Jenny,' she said shyly. 'Could I have a lemonade please?'

'Most certainly. Two large sherries, one lemonade and sandwiches for eight. Ham and pickle, and cheese and cucumber all right with everyone?'

'Cakes?' Laura enquired hopefully.

'And a plate of cakes. Cream and plain.'

Rogers nodded to the waiter, who disappeared in the direction of the kitchens.

'Pleasure to serve you, Doctor John. As always.'

'Thank you, Mr Rogers, it's a pleasure to be here.'

Left to the peace of the secluded corner, Andrew sat back and pulled out his cigarette case. He offered it around. William, Haydn and Trevor helped themselves, Eddie declined.

'What does it feel like to have won your first important bout?' Andrew asked, wanting to break the ice.

'All right,' Eddie answered briefly, resting his battered face on his hand.

'It's good of you to come with us. I suspect you would rather have stayed in the booth with your friend.'

'I think it's just as well Eddie left when he did,' Haydn said. 'Jim Dekker was about to make him an offer and Joey has other things in mind for his protégé.'

'That's not to say I won't try my hand in a boxing booth again,' Eddie contradicted truculently.

'You'll never make odds again like the ones you made today,' Andrew commented. 'I hope you put the maximum you could afford on yourself?'

'We all did.' William smiled, cheering up at the sight of the beer arriving. 'If he'd lost there would have been a queue of Powells a mile long outside the workhouse in the morning.'

Bethan set her mouth into a thin hard line at William's bad joke. She loved William as much as she loved her brothers, but she knew their faults and failings. It wasn't difficult to read the small signs of resentment against Andrew and the privileged world he represented. And she was furious with Haydn and William for playing down to Andrew, deliberately setting themselves out to be coarser, less educated and less intelligent than they really were.

The way they were acting made her ashamed. She hated them for forcing her to face up to the changes Andrew had wrought in her in such a short space of time. A few months with him had been enough for her to adopt his ways – to deliberately refine the roughened edges of her Welsh accent, to watch what she said, and the way she said it, in his company. To take good food, drink, and things like tea out in hotels for granted. For the first time she realised that the boys had noticed the changes and despised her for it. Almost as much as they despised Andrew for being crache.

There was a flurry of activity; the waiter laid the sandwiches, cakes, plates, knives and forks on the table. As soon as he left, Andrew, still very much the host, handed around the sandwiches. They all began eating with the exception of Eddie who sat supping his pint slowly.

'I wish you'd let me look at your face.' Bethan moved her chair closer to his.

'It's fine,' he insisted irritably.

'It doesn't look fine.' She touched his bloodied cheekbone with the tips of her fingers.

'The cuts are superficial,' Trevor said authoritatively. 'It's the bruising you're going to have to watch.'

'I bet they don't feel superficial.' Andrew smiled amicably at Eddie in an attempt to win him over.

Eddie didn't return the smile. Instead he sat sullenly staring down into his beer. He didn't feel like talking. In fact he didn't feel much like anything. He'd been looking forward to winning his first real, meaningful fight for so long that now it had actually happened he felt flat. He'd wanted to stay in the booth and discuss the possibility of a job with Dekker, but Dekker had been put in a foul mood by his champion's failure, and Joey had pushed him out with a sharp 'Play the booths, boy. Don't work in them. That's a sure road to nowhere.'

He drained his beerglass and put it down. Sliding his fingers inside his starched collar he tried to loosen it. He felt on edge, out of place, ridiculous. Like when he was seven years old and his mother had forced him into an angel's costume for the chapel pageant. He glanced across at Bethan's boyfriend, and put the man into the smarmy, not to be trusted category. The doctor probably meant well, he allowed grudgingly, but everything Andrew John did and said smacked of condescension. It was as if he wanted the whole world to know he had money and could afford to spend it. He'd bought Bethan and now he wanted to buy them all. Well he for one wasn't impressed. If Dr high-and-mighty John had wanted to treat them to tea he should have met them half-way and taken them all to Ronconis' café. There at least they would have been on familiar territory, not this . . . this stuffed-shirt place.

He decided he'd had enough. He'd just won a fight. He had a fiver in his pocket and he didn't have to put up with anything he didn't want to. He left his chair awkwardly, kicking the table and slopping the beer and sherry on to the cloth.

'Where you off to?' Haydn asked.

'See Joey.' He fumbled in his pocket. All he had was the five-pound note he'd won, and a penny-farthing, and that wouldn't cover the cost of a pint, not in the New Inn.

'This one is on me, Eddie,' Andrew said quietly, seeing Eddie's hand slide into his pocket.

'Buy you one next time I see you. Bye everyone.'

Bethan's voice floated after him as he left the room. 'Haydn, is he all right? Shouldn't one of us go after him?' Then came Haydn's voice uncharacteristically cutting and impatient. 'For pity's sake, Beth, he's seventeen. It's time you broke the apron strings.'

Eddie paused to straighten his tie in front of the large gilt-framed mirror that filled the end wall of the lounge. He took a moment to study their reflections. Haydn, his hand on Jenny's knee under the table where he thought it couldn't be seen, still arguing with Bethan. William oblivious to everything except his beer and the food, helping himself to another sandwich. Laura grinning like a miner who'd just been put on double rate drooling over the skinny fellow she was with, and that dark, smarmy sod eyeing Bethan as though she were on offer in the cattle market. He just hoped Bethan wasn't too dazzled to keep her wits about her.

He left the hotel and walked out into the sunshine. The street was packed with people, the music from the organ blasting at full tempo. He pulled his flat cap down low, covering his damaged eye, and walked up towards Market Square.

'Cockles, sir? Sweet cockles?'

'Candyfloss, sir. Candyfloss for your lady?'

'I've got no lady,' he replied gruffly.

'You have now, Eddie. Bye, Doris.' Daisy waved goodbye to her friend as she hooked her arm into his. 'I was hoping I'd see you again.' She smiled at him, displaying two rows of pearly white teeth set into very pink gums between even pinker lips.

'Come on, sir. Buy the lady a ride on the wooden horse.'

'Swinging boats, sir. Be amazed what you can do with a lady in a swinging boat.'

'Cheeky beggar,' Daisy retorted, pulling Eddie along with her as she struggled against the tide of people towards the top end of Market Square.

'Shooting, sir. Nothing like a gun to impress the lady. Win her a prize?'

'I'd love that little monkey, he's cute.' Daisy's eyes sparkled with reflected sunshine as she gazed adoringly at Eddie.

'The monkey's not up for a prize, miss.' The stallholder stroked the small creature clinging to his shoulder. 'But you can have a nice ornament for your bedroom?' He held up a grotesque chalk figure of a shepherdess.

'The monkey or nothing.' Daisy made a sulky mouth.

'Goldfish, miss.' He held up a large sweet bottle in which fish were circling one another in a stew that was more fish than water.

'How about a toy monkey?' Eddie pointed to one pinned to the side of the booth.

'Twelve hits of the target, sir, and he's yours.'

'I'll take twelve shots.'

'Penny a shot. Four for threepence.'

Eddie handed over his precious fiver.

'Four pounds nineteen and threepence change, sir.' The stallholder shovelled four pound notes into Eddie's hand and topped them with a pile of change. Eddie counted the whole amount carefully from one hand into the other, calling the stallholder back sharply when he realised he'd been short-changed by half a crown.

'Can't blame a chap for trying, sir,' the man said cheerily, handing over the missing coin together with the rifle and pellets. Eddie loaded a pellet and looked down the barrel. 'North,' he murmured to himself.

'Did you say something?' Daisy asked.

'They bend the barrels to lengthen the odds in their favour. Whenever my father took us to the fairs when we were little he always used to make for the shooting galleries so he could point out the defects in the guns. If they were bent upwards it was north, downwards south. This one's north.'

'No bent gun barrels here, mate,' the stallholder shouted angrily.

Eddie didn't bother to answer. Instead he lifted the rifle, took aim and fired. It was difficult to know who was the more surprised when he made bull's-eye, Daisy or the stallholder. He fired his remaining shots in quick succession. Each one hit the centre of the target, and the man grudgingly unpinned the toy from the canvas.

'Here you are, miss.' He leaned over and handed it to Daisy, brushing her hand with his own as he did so.

'Sure you won't change your mind about giving away the real thing?' Daisy smiled.

'Depends on what you've got to offer,' the man said, eyeing her appreciatively.

'The lady's with me,' Eddie snarled.

'Looks like she'd prefer a monkey.'

'I'd be careful what I say if I were you.' Daisy wrapped her arm around Eddie's. 'He's just knocked out Dekker's champion.' Eddie pushed his cap to the back of his head, and glared furiously, unwittingly exposing his cut and bruised eye.

'Sorry, mate. Didn't mean nothing,' the stallholder apologised.

Eddie turned away and Daisy, still clinging to his arm, tottered alongside him.

'Well you've got your monkey,' Eddie said. 'Where to now?'

'Ride on the horses?'

They waited for the largest roundabout in the fair to stop. Painted gold, with beautifully carved red and gold wooden horses and cockerels riding three abreast, it was the oldest ride in Dante's fair and his pride and joy. Caught up in the rush of people clambering off and on, Eddie pulled Daisy up the steep wooden steps. He sat on one of the inside horses and she climbed up in front of him, sitting demurely in a side-saddle position, her right arm low around his waist. It was the first time Eddie had been physically close to a woman outside of the family and a peculiar mixture of pride, shyness and embarrassment beset him as he delved into his trouser pocket for two pennies to pay the boy who was collecting the fares.

The organ music rose to a crescendo as the roundabout began to turn. Slow at first, it gradually rotated faster and faster. The horses moved up and down with a speed that seemed geared to the music, and Daisy squealed and wriggled closer to Eddie on each downward movement. The warmth of her hand burned his back even through the thick layers of his suit jacket and trousers. Then, without warning, she wrapped both her arms around his waist. Bending her head to avoid the pole that stood between them she brushed her lips over his. A peculiar excitement coursed through his veins, leaving an odd deflated, tinny taste in his mouth when the ride finally ended. Buffeted by the crowds they left the roundabout and stood in the middle of Market Square.

'Where to now?' Eddie asked.

Daisy pulled up the sleeve of her long white cotton glove and squinted at her rolled gold watch. 'I have to be in the theatre soon. Two shows tonight.' She made a face.

'Oh.' He didn't know what he'd hoped for, but it certainly hadn't been that. He should have known. After all, Haydn had introduced them, and he'd moaned enough about having to work tonight. He waited foolishly, feeling clumsy and ham-fisted next to her small, perfumed, feminine figure.

'I do have time for a quick drink.' She smiled at the crestfallen expression on his face. 'And if you want to watch the show I could leave a ticket at the box office for you. Second house finishes at half-nine. I'm free then if you want to take me somewhere.'

'I'd like that.' His spirits soared at the prospect.

'Where's a good place to drink?' she asked.

It may have been his imagination but he thought he saw her glance towards the New Inn. 'Two foot nine,' he said boldly, giving the town's pet name for the back bar of the Victoria at the top end of Taff Street. From what Haydn had said some of the theatrical crowd from the New Theatre went there, and perhaps Daisy might feel at home in the surroundings.

'Two foot nine?' She looked at him and giggled. 'Where *did* it get its name from?'

'The length of the bar.'

'Ooh. I didn't think of that.'

She took his arm and they walked past the New Inn. Eddie saw a few boys from the Graig and a couple of men from the gym. He spoke to all of them, taking care they saw that Daisy was with him, but when the coins in his pocket began to disappear over the bar of the two foot nine on gin and tonics for her, beer for him and a couple of pies he began to regret picking her up. The five pounds meant a great deal to him. He'd never had so much money in his life, and he'd intended to take care of it. He stared at the clock on the white-tiled wall and tried to focus his eyes. The room blurred around him and his hand shook as he replaced his empty glass on the table.

'Time I left.' Daisy made a face as she downed the last of her gin. 'Tell you what,' she ran her fingers along the lapel of his coat, 'why don't you walk me to the theatre via the park?'

'The park isn't on the way to the theatre,' he protested dully.

'But it could be, sweetie. It could be.' She picked up her handbag. They walked out of the pub and retraced their steps towards the centre of town, turning right by the Park cinema and crossing the bridge that led from Taff Street into Ynysangharad Park. The revue that Daisy was in had only been in town for a week, but she'd obviously taken time to find her way around and Eddie allowed her to lead the way. She turned right again after the bridge and they walked past the tennis courts along the bank of the river. Not many people walked that way, especially when the fair was in town, and Eddie in his drink-fuddled state wondered where she was taking him.

'This will do nicely.' She sat down in a patch of high grass behind a bank of bushes and trees, and patted the ground beside her. 'Join me?'

He bent his knees and landed heavily next to her. The greenery appeared to be swimming and the sky was revolving above his head. She pressed him back against the tree and slid her hands inside his coat, running her nails over the buttons on his waistcoat.

'I do love fighters.' She unfastened his waistcoat and moved on to the buttons on his shirt.

'What are you doing?' he asked thickly.

'What do you think?'

She kissed him, thrusting her tongue inside his mouth. He tried to kiss her back but he was impotent, helpless, overwhelmed by the soft feel and exotic smell of her body. Her face powder cloyed in his nostrils, mixing with the warm, musky scent of her perfume, so different from the light flowery toilet waters that Bethan and Maud used. Pulling her skirt high she straddled him, her hands busy with the buttons at the waistband of his trousers. He held her, lightly at first then as her kisses grew more intense he found courage enough to hold her tight.

She pulled back from him and he felt her fingers unfasten the buttons on his fly.

'Relax,' she whispered into his ear. 'No one can see us.' She took his right hand and laid it above the stocking top on her naked thigh. He left it there, stiff and immobile.

'I think you need a little more help, sweetie.' She leaned back and unbuttoned her blouse. She wasn't wearing underclothes, and he found himself staring at the small pink nipples on her naked breasts. He watched mesmerised as she shrugged off the blouse and tossed it on to the grass behind them.

'Are all Welsh boys as backward about coming forward as you?' she laughed. She laid her hand on top of his and pushed it up until he could feel the lace that trimmed the edge of her silk French knickers. 'How about we get this out of the way as well?' She unbuttoned her skirt, pulled it over her head and threw it on to the blouse.

'You're . . . you're beautiful,' he choked.

'I know.' She tossed her head back confidently. 'But thank you for saying so. Come on, sweetheart,' she wheedled impatiently, 'this body isn't just for looking at. It won't break if you touch.'

Steeling himself he ran his hands over her naked back, inadvertently pulling down her knickers as his hand slipped on her smooth skin.

'That's it, sweetie, *now* you're getting the hang of it. Try sliding your hand down a bit more.' She opened his trousers wide, and moved her fingers expertly, teasing him to a throbbing erection that made his face burn.

'You really are slow,' she complained playfully, rearranging his clothes. 'Most men would have tossed my knickers in the river by now. Here, do you want me to do it for you?' She arched backwards, wriggling out of the scrap of silk and lace, and lay down on the grass.

'What you waiting for? I'm here ready, willing and able.'

Eddie stared at her for a moment, studying the exposed curves and contours of the female form that had remained a mystery to him for so long. Then slowly, tentatively he reached out and laid a hand on her naked breast.

She smiled. 'Do you want me to undress you, sweetie? Or can you do it yourself?'

The suit jacket he had been so proud of that morning was flung, a heap of crumpled cloth, on the ground. She scratched his chest with her long, sharp, red-varnished nails as she undid the buttons on his shirt and wrenched it off his back.

'Steady now,' she warned as he lunged towards her. 'Oh my God, you haven't done much of this before, have you?' she gasped as he fell clumsily on top of her. 'Here,' she opened his trousers wide and pulled them down over his buttocks, 'can't get far with these on either, that's for sure.' She yanked down his underpants. 'Take your time now, ducks. Aim true and get it right, for my sake. That's it, slow and steady,' she sighed, helping him inside her. 'Not too quick, no sense in hurrying, it'll be over before we start the way you're going at it. Don't look down. Just put your hands here, and here – ' She planted his hands firmly, one on each breast. 'And if you can manage three things at once you could try kissing me as well.'

'Easy isn't it?' she giggled as he came up for air. 'Just like riding a bike.'

'It's a damned sight better than any bike I've ever ridden,' he cried feelingly as she wrapped her legs around his back. 'It's bloody marvellous,' he crowed as she thrust herself hard against him.

'If you're going to do this sort of thing regular, love,' she offered kindly, wincing and digging her nails into his back, 'you need to organise yourself a bit of practice. It'll do wonders for you. May even rub the rough edges off this caveman technique of yours.'

Eddie was too far gone to hear what she was saying. He was

off, sailing on a wondrous sea of sensual pleasure that had opened into a whole new world. One he never wanted to leave.

The sun was low on the horizon when Andrew drove Bethan out of the station car park and up the Graig hill.

'Sunshine can brighten anything, even the homes,' he observed, noticing how the last rays of the dying day played on the grey stonework of the eight-foot wall around the infirmary and work-house.

'It's been a lovely day,' Bethan answered mechanically. She was fighting a headache that came from wine and sherry drunk too early in the day, followed by too many roundabout rides.

'For some,' he answered. 'Trevor's like a dog with two tails.'

'Laura said it went well between her father and Trevor after we left. It must have. They're getting engaged officially next weekend.' She screwed the handkerchief she was holding into a tight, damp knot.

'Are we invited?'

'Yes. Ronnie's organising a party in the café on Saturday night.'

He stopped the car in front of the Graig Hotel.

'I'm not going for a drink in there,' she said quickly. 'Someone would be knocking the door to tell my mother before you even got to the bar.'

'And your mother doesn't know that you have the odd glass of wine or sherry?'

'No.'

'Your secret is safe with me.' He removed the keys from the ignition. 'And I wasn't suggesting that we should drink in the Graig Hotel.' He pointed across the road to a small lane that opened out between two rows of terraces. 'Does that lead to the famous, or should I say infamous, Shoni's pond?'

'Yes,' she answered shortly. Apart from being a lovers' haunt, Shoni's was inextricably bound up with her childhood memories. It was the place where her father had taught them all to swim, and to fish with bent pins tied to string, and empty jam jars. They'd picnicked there on bread and dripping inexpertly put together by either herself or her father, for Elizabeth would never go to Shoni's, referring to the small lake and surrounding greenery as a filthy place, fit only for animals and beggars.

213

'Would you like to show it to me?' Andrew asked.

'I have to dress for dinner, remember?'

'We dine at eight. It's only six now.'

'You promised to meet my family.'

'Not for two hours, I didn't.' When she didn't answer, he opened his door. 'I'm not suggesting a quick roll in the hay,' he said lightly. 'Only a short walk. I need some peace and tranquillity after the noise of that fair.'

'It'll take us about three-quarters of an hour to walk there and back,' she warned.

'The sooner we start, the sooner we'll be back.'

'This will cause a stir,' she said as she stepped out of the car.

'What?'

'Your car parked here.'

'No one will notice it.'

'Oh yes they will, and as everyone knows exactly who it belongs to, tongues will wag about us and Shoni's tonight.'

'All the tongues are at the fair.' He crossed the road and began walking up the lane.

'Not all,' she said, glancing back at the hotel. A group of women were congregating outside the jug and bottle bar of the pub.

'I can put up with a bit of gossip if you can,' he said glibly.

'Doesn't anything ever bother you?' she asked in exasperation.

'Bethan my sweet,' he put his arm around her waist, 'you're a lovely girl, but you'd be even lovelier if you didn't take life so seriously.'

'Round here life is serious,' she said with an edge of resentment.

'All the more reason for me to introduce you to other places.'

They continued to walk along the path in silence. The track was well trodden, black with coal dust, the worst of the potholes filled in with stones and dirt by the children who rode their home-made go-carts and old pram wheels to Shoni's every chance they got. The further they went from the houses, the greater the profusion of wild flowers. Bethan saw the first of the season's bluebells peeking out amongst the celandine, buttercups and harebells. Then came the infinitely sweet, sad song of a solitary lark. She'd felt angry and bitter, for reasons she hadn't examined too closely because of an ugly suspicion that they stemmed from

214

jealousy of Laura and Trevor's happiness, but all of that dissipated as the countryside closed in around her. For the first time
that day she felt quiet and at peace with herself.

'Who would have thought there could be so much beauty so
close to such ugliness?' Andrew said spontaneously as they stood
before the dark expanse of water surrounded by trees that was
Shoni's pond.

'Ugliness?' she questioned, picking up a stone from the shore
and skimming it across the surface of the pond. 'Are you saying
that the Graig is ugly?'

'No uglier than a few other places,' he said in an attempt to
soften his declaration. 'In fact it's not half as bad as some areas
of London.'

'It's strange,' she said thoughtfully. 'I've never really thought
about whether it's ugly or beautiful. It's simply home.'

'If depressing. All those miserable grey stone buildings. Narrow
dark streets, scruffy kids. . . . '

'I was one of those scruffy kids once.'

'No you weren't. You've always been beautiful.' He took her
in his arms and kissed her, an oddly chaste and sober kiss after
the passion earlier that afternoon. 'I suppose we should be going
back,' he said as he released her.

'We should.' She picked up another stone and sent it flying
across the water. He reached for his own stone, but when he
threw it it landed in the centre of the pond, creating waves that
travelled outwards in ever-increasing circles until they broke on
the shore. They stood and watched for a moment, lost in their
own thoughts.

She expected him to say something on the walk back. She
wanted to ask him about his plans for the future. A hundred
times over she framed the question that was uppermost in her
mind – 'Are you going to London?' She even pictured the look
on his face as he responded. But try as she might, she couldn't
answer the question for him.

The car was enough to create a stir amongst those residents of
Graig Avenue who either hadn't gone to the fair or had returned
early. A dozen ragged urchins and half a dozen young men clus-

tered around the bonnet before Andrew even had time to open his door.

'Is it safe to leave it here?' he asked Bethan, not entirely humorously, as he looked at the crowd around them.

'Perfectly,' she assured him touchily, deeply regretting the crazy impulse that had caused her to invite him to her home.

'Here, mister, want your car cleaned? I'll do a first-class job. Only a tanner.'

'I'll do it for a joey, mister.'

'Twopence, mister.'

'Clear off, the lot of you,' Bethan said sharply. 'Quick, before I put my hand behind you.'

To Andrew's amazement they all scarpered, reconvening in a tight knot in front of the wall opposite, out of Bethan's reach.

She turned her back on them and climbed the steps to her house, Andrew following, confident and smiling.

'It's only me,' she called out as she opened the door. She walked through to the kitchen without a backward glance. The room was still warm from the stove that had been stoked high earlier that day to cook the main meal, but no washing hung, airing on the rack. It never did on days when Elizabeth expected her uncle to visit.

'Bethan, I wasn't expecting you back early.' Her mother halted on her way from the pantry to the table. Bethan noticed that Elizabeth was wearing her best black frock, and the tray she was carrying was piled high with china that was usually kept in the sideboard in the front parlour. Obviously John Joseph hadn't yet arrived, and Bethan fervently hoped that he wouldn't appear in the next half-hour.

'I've not come back for tea. I've brought someone I'd like you to meet.' She smiled tentatively at her father, who was also wearing his Sunday-best suit and collar. He was sitting bolt upright in his chair in front of the window, reading a book from the lending library. Evan returned her smile, then saw the tall figure of Andrew standing behind her.

'Doctor John, isn't it?' He rose from his chair and extended his rough, calloused hand.

'Please call me Andrew.' For once Andrew bypassed etiquette and shook hands with Bethan's father before her mother.

'Pleasure to meet you, Mr Powell, Mrs Powell.' He touched Elizabeth's cold fingers with his own.

'Pleased to meet you,' Elizabeth said stiffly. 'Will you take a cup of tea with us?'

'Only if you're having one,' Andrew said pleasantly.

'I was just about to make one.' She picked up the kettle and went into the washhouse to fill it.

'Don't make one for me, Mam,' Bethan called, 'I'm going up to change.'

'Change?' Her mother appeared at the washhouse door and looked her up and down.

'I'm going to Andrew's for dinner, and there's a stain on this suit,' she answered defiantly, as she left the room.

'Do sit down, Andrew, please,' Evan offered, hovering in front of his chair.

'Thank you, I will.' Andrew sat on one of the wooden kitchen chairs grouped around the table.

'How long has this been going on then?' Evan enquired, as he resumed his seat. The contrast between Evan's politeness and the bluntness of the question took Andrew aback.

'Do you mean my seeing Bethan?' he asked warily.

'Aye, that's what I mean.'

'We've been spending the odd afternoon together since I came to Pontypridd in January.'

'The odd afternoon?' Evan put down his book and peered at Andrew through narrowed eyes.

'We're friends,' Andrew asserted with more confidence than he felt. There was something in Evan's cool, appraising gaze that made him feel uncomfortable.

'I see,' Evan commented in a tone that clearly said he didn't.

Elizabeth returned with the kettle. She took a pair of tongs, lifted the hotplate cover on the stove and set the kettle to boil and the teapot to warm on the rack above.

'You work in the Central Homes, Doctor John?'

'Please call me Andrew,' he repeated. He found Evan disconcerting, but there was something in Elizabeth's cold eyes that sent a chill down his back. 'Yes, I work in the Central Homes.'

Elizabeth lifted down a tin caddy decorated with scratched and faded pictures of roses and spooned tea into the pot, then she took four of the best cups from the tray on the table, and set them out in front of Andrew. 'Would you like a rock cake or a scone, Doctor John? They're quite fresh. I baked them this afternoon.'

'Thank you,' he replied. He wasn't hungry, but he thought that sampling Elizabeth's cooking might give him the opportunity to compliment her.

While Elizabeth was in the pantry buttering the scones, Maud opened the door and bounced in.

'Have you met my younger daughter, Andrew?' Elizabeth enquired coolly from the pantry door.

'No I haven't had the pleasure, but of course Bethan has told me about all of you,' Andrew said as he rose from his seat.

'She would!' Maud exclaimed pertly. 'I'm Maud.' She looked down at the table. 'Best cups, you are honoured.'

'Fill the milk jug, Maud,' Elizabeth ordered abruptly.

Andrew sat on the edge of his chair, and fervently wished that Bethan would finish whatever it was that she was doing. He looked across the room and saw the book that Evan had laid face down on the hearth and decided to make another attempt at conversation.

'*Crime and Punishment*, Mr Powell, you enjoy Russian literature?'

'I do.' Evan pulled out his pipe and a tin of tobacco, and began to pack the bowl. 'And like most miners I appreciate the socialist ideals of the Soviets.'

'Anyone who lived here would.'

'Do you mean the Graig or Pontypridd?'

'Both. This area has created a great deal of wealth for the nation, but precious little of it has been ploughed back into the Valleys. I don't mean now, in the depression, but earlier,' he said, mindlessly repeating one of his father's favourite observations. As the town's medical officer Dr John senior constantly railed against the housing and living conditions in the town.

'I doubt that the lack of amenities in the town has affected you personally, Andrew,' Evan said pointedly.

'No, not personally, at least not until recently,' Andrew agreed. 'But I grew up watching my father trying to combat illnesses caused by poor living conditions. And now I'm faced with patients who have the same problems. Nothing seems to have changed here in the last thirty years.'

Evan looked at him, a shrewd light in his eyes. 'Let's hope something changes in the next thirty.'

'Your tea, Doctor John.' Maud, a sickly smile on her face, gave him a cup. 'Milk? Sugar?'

'Scones, Andrew?' Elizabeth handed him an empty small plate and a large one laden with buttered scones. 'Jam and cream's on the table.'

'Thank you, a plain one will be fine, and milk and three sugars in my tea please, Maud.' He took a scone and laid it on his plate.

'Is that why you came back to Pontypridd?' Evan pressed. 'To try to do something about the living conditions of the working classes?'

'I don't know about the living conditions,' Andrew mused honestly, 'but I certainly hope to improve the standard of health care.'

'You won't do that until you eradicate poverty,' Evan observed realistically.

'At least we can try,' Andrew replied, manfully struggling with a mouthful of dry scone and blatantly flirtatious looks from Maud at the same time.

'Sorry I took so long.' Bethan bustled into the room wearing a calf-length green silk frock that buttoned modestly to a small collar at the neck. She was carrying a matching blue and green silk jacket, and a blue leather handbag dyed the same colour as her shoes.

'Another new outfit?' her mother commented disapprovingly.

'I bought it from Aunt Megan some time ago,' Bethan lied defensively.

'Seems to me a lot of your wages end up in Megan's pocket. More tea, Andrew?' Elizabeth enquired as Andrew left his seat.

'I'm afraid we haven't time, Mrs Powell. The scone was delicious, but we have to leave. My mother is expecting us.'

'What a shame. My uncle, the minister John Joseph Bull, is coming to take high tea with us. He's bringing his wife. It would have been nice if you could have stayed.'

'Thank you for the invitation, Mrs Powell. Perhaps another time.'

'It's been a pleasure meeting you, Andrew. Hope we see you again soon.' Evan left his chair as Bethan opened the door.

'The pleasure was all mine. Mr Powell, Mrs Powell, Maud.' Andrew smiled at all of them as he left the room.

'Don't be late, Bethan,' her mother admonished, returning to her pantry as they walked out through the door.

'Don't worry, Mrs Powell, she'll be safe enough in my parents' house. And I promise to bring her home before midnight.'

'Your father keeps later hours than us,' Evan remarked loudly.

'I'll be fine, Dad,' Bethan shouted as she ran down the steps.

'That's quite a family you have there,' Andrew said once they were closed into the privacy of his car.

'What's that supposed to mean?' Bethan asked, on the alert for anything that sounded remotely like a sneer.

'What it said. Your sister's going to be a stunner, your father's incredibly astute and intelligent. . . . '

'For a miner?' she broke in nastily.

'For a man,' he replied firmly. 'And your mother . . . ' his voice trailed as he tried to think of a flattering adjective to describe Elizabeth, 'is imposing?' he suggested cautiously, pushing the gearstick into reverse and driving backwards towards Iltyd Street.

'Imposing?'

Glad of an excuse to turn away from her he twisted his head to negotiate the corner. 'She's also a very good cook,' he added blandly.

'Imposing and a very good cook,' she repeated slowly.

He stopped the car to change into first gear.

'Tell me, is your mother imposing and a very good cook as well?' she asked.

Not quite knowing what to expect he looked at her, then he saw mischief in her eyes. Unable to contain himself a moment longer he burst out laughing. She put her hand on his knee.

'I love you, Doctor Andrew John, even if you are an insincere idiot.'

'Quick, someone's looking.' He bent his head to hers without taking his hands off the steering wheel. 'One kiss now and we'll set the whole town talking.'

She leaned across and kissed his lips. He lowered the handbrake and the car began to roll down the hill.

'Release me, woman,' he shouted, hoping that the shocked and startled Mrs Richards would hear him. 'Can't you wait until we get to Shoni's?

'There goes your reputation, Nurse Powell,' he laughed as they turned the corner on to Llantrisant Road.

'And yours, Doctor John.'

'A man doesn't need a reputation. Too much baggage.'

'Is that so?'

'That's so.'

They were both still laughing when he drove under the railway bridge and into the town.

Chapter Thirteen

Andrew's parents lived in a large comfortable villa set in fair-sized private walled gardens, but to Bethan it seemed like a mansion. In fact every aspect of the suburbs on the Common amazed her. The mature trees that shaded the pavements on the wide, well-planned roads and avenues. The nurtured front gardens with their flowering bushes, banks of daffodils and narcissus, and green manicured lawns. The clean, clear aspect over the entire town that sprawled, dirty and untidy, along the valley floor. Distance and sunlight even lent a fairytale enchantment to the bleak slag heaps and grimy colliery on the hillside to the right.

Bethan had only ever walked up to the Common a few times in her life, and then it had been on Armistice days, following her father and the other miners as they trailed behind the Great War veterans who marched to the cenotaph, built high on the hill above Ynysangharad Memorial Park. If she'd seen the neat streets of semi-detached and the walled gardens of the larger villas then, she'd paid no attention. She'd certainly given no more thought to visiting one of them than to the concept of flying to the moon.

Andrew steered the car through the impressive wrought-iron gates that his father had erected to replace those melted down in the war, and into the old coach-house that was now used as a garage.

'Before we go remind me to show you my rooms,' he said as he opened the door for her.

'Your rooms?' She looked quizzically at him.

He pointed to the ceiling. 'We've done up the old stableboy's quarters. Dual purpose – keeps me out of Mother's hair, and gives me privacy.'

She smiled woodenly.

'You'll be just fine,' he whispered, pinching her cheek. 'They'll love you.'

A maid wearing the standard black dress and white starched and frilled cap and apron opened the front door.

'Thank you, Mair,' Andrew handed her his hat.

'Mair?' Bethan looked at the girl's face.

'Wondered if you'd recognise me in this get-up, Beth,' the girl screeched. 'How's Haydn?' she asked, forgetting herself and earning a frown from Andrew.

'Where is everyone?' Andrew asked heavily.

'In the drawing room, sir,' Mair bobbed a curtsy.

Bethan stood bewildered and more than a little lost in the hall. A massive curved staircase swept upwards to the first floor with all the grace and elegance of those she'd seen in the pictures. A few pieces of heavily carved, dark oak Victorian hall furniture stood against the walls between the panelled doors. Stained-glass windows puddled the black-and-white-tiled floor with pools of brilliant crimson and sapphire light. Andrew put his arm protectively around her shoulders and propelled her gently forwards. He passed what seemed like a dozen doors before he finally opened one that led into a room that could have swallowed the front parlour in Graig Avenue four times over and still had space to spare.

'Mother, Father, this is Bethan.' He gave her a small push.

'I'm very pleased to meet you, Mrs John.' Bethan shook Andrew's mother's hand. Small, and surprisingly fair given the dark colouring of her children, Andrew's mother had the figure and disarmingly naive demeanour of a young girl.

'We've been so looking forward to meeting you, Bethan. You've met Doctor John of course?'

Bethan automatically dropped a curtsy to Andrew's father.

'We're not in the hospital now, Bethan,' he laughed. 'You met my daughter and son-in-law earlier, I believe?'

'Hi, Bethan,' Fiona smiled at her from the depths of the sofa where she sat, feet curled beneath her like a kitten.

'I'm so glad you didn't dress,' Andrew's mother observed in a tactless, futile attempt to put Bethan at ease. 'We rarely dress for dinner in the spring or summer, it seems wrong somehow on light evenings.'

Bethan immediately compared her light silk dress with Mrs John's pale blue organza and Fiona's black lace. Hers was undoubtedly cut along simpler lines, but it was passable. Thanks to Megan, her clothes didn't let her down, even in this company.

223

'Jolly nice to see you again,' Alec said enthusiastically before returning to the paper he was reading.

'Shall we all sit down?' Andrew's mother said brightly.

Andrew stood in front of the leather chesterfield alongside Alec, and as his parents had obviously been sitting on the only two single chairs in the room Bethan had no choice but to sit next to Fiona.

'Drink, everyone?' Andrew's father rubbed his hands together as he walked over to a wooden bar in the corner of the room.

'That would be nice,' said Andrew's mother.

'Usual, dear?'

'No, darlings,' Fiona said firmly, uncurling her long legs from beneath her. 'No one drinks sherry in London any more. Only cocktails.'

'Cocktails!' Mrs John demurred. 'I really would prefer a nice sweet sherry.'

'Mother, you're *so* archaic,' Fiona complained petulantly. She joined her father at the bar. 'Now let me see,' she peered short-sightedly at the array of bottles, 'is there any ice?'

'In the ice bucket,' Dr John senior said drily.

'Very witty. Right, I'm going to make a Harvard cocktail.'

'She's been making those since we crossed the pond last year to visit my cousin in New York,' Alec said loudly for Bethan's benefit.

'Would you believe there's no cocktail shaker here?' Fiona looked disapprovingly at her father.

'There's one in the kitchen.' Her mother rang a bell pull that hung close to her chair. Mair appeared a few moments later.

'Mrs Campbell-White needs the cocktail shaker, Mair.'

'Yes ma'am.'

'Right!' Fiona looked along the shelves behind the bar. 'I'll need this.' She lifted a bottle of brandy on to the bar counter.

'Not my Napoleon,' her father groaned.

'Daddy, you're impossible! If cocktails aren't made with first-class ingredients they're practically undrinkable. Now what else . . . ' she mused, biting her bottom lip. 'Oh I know. Angostura bitters and Italian vermouth. . . . '

'Under the bar,' Andrew interrupted, watching the proceedings with an amused grin.

'I was going to add crushed ice.' She took a silver-plated cock-tail shaker from Mair, and dismissed her.

'It should be mushy enough by now,' Andrew commented. 'That ice bucket leaves a lot to be desired.'

'Mushy is not the same as crushed. Is it, darling?' she appealed to her husband.

'Don't ask me, I'm no expert on cocktails.'

'Coward.' She made a face at him. 'Right, here we go.'

'Aren't you supposed to measure the quantities carefully?' Andrew asked as she poured a liberal stream of brandy into the shaker.

'Not Fe, old boy,' Alec said cheerfully. 'Measuring jugs interfere with her creativity. The beauty of her cocktails lies in their element of surprise.'

'That I can believe.' Andrew watched as Fiona tipped in a generous amount of vermouth and filled the shaker with ice.

'Now for the good bit.' She rammed the lid on, held the shaker between her hands and twirled it vigorously from side to side.

'Do you think we're going to survive this experience?' Andrew's mother looked playfully at Dr John senior.

'Oh I think so, dear. Remember she only visits us once or twice a year.'

'Cocktails are served.' Fiona placed half a dozen glasses on the bar, and decanted the mixture evenly between them. Andrew handed them round before sipping his gingerly.

'Well?' his father demanded.

'Not bad, not bad at all. I take my hat off to you, Fanny, you have hidden talents.' He held his glass high. 'Here's to all of us.'

'To us.'

Bethan held her glass up with the others before drinking, but she felt like an interloper not a participant in the scene. Conversations bounced around the room like tennis balls across a court but, too shy to make a contribution, she remained silent. She looked frequently to Andrew hoping to catch his eye, but he always seemed to be engrossed in something his father or Alec was saying. In the end the sound of the doorbell came as a relief, if only because it heralded change. Andrew looked at his mother.

'Someone expected?' he asked.

'Only the Llewellyn-Joneses,' his mother answered. 'We owe them, and it seemed a good night for them to come.'

'Speak of the devil,' his father said cheerfully as Mair opened the drawing-room door. 'Come in, come in.' He shook hands with all three guests, and made the necessary introductions, referring to Bethan as Andrew's friend and prevailing on Fiona to make more cocktails.

Mr Llewellyn-Jones was the manager of Barclays Bank. His wife, a large florid woman, was a well-known charity worker in the town. Bethan had seen her serving dinner to the paupers in the workhouse dining hall on Christmas Day. Their daughter Anthea was an attractive, pleasant girl in a petite, dark-eyed, dark-haired Welsh sort of way, but Bethan couldn't suppress the spiteful thought that her attractions had been bolstered since birth by every advantage that money could buy.

Anthea's hair was expertly waved, back as well as sides. Her white silk dress was styled and tailored to emphasise the good features of her figure, and conceal those that were not so good. She smiled constantly, had a kind or flattering remark, albeit insincere, for everyone in the room, including Bethan. But no amount of kindness could make Bethan like her. From the moment Anthea Llewellyn-Jones walked into the drawing room she couldn't help but compare the warmth of the welcome Anthea received with her own lukewarm reception. But more than that, she knew that someone like Anthea, with all the advantages of money, social position and background, would, in Dr and Mrs Johns' eyes, make a far more suitable wife for Andrew than a mere nobody like herself.

A gong resounded outside the door.

'Dinner, at last,' Dr John beamed at the gathered assembly. They left the drawing room for the gloom of the oak-panelled dining room, furnished with the same type of heavy Victorian furniture as the hall. The enormous rectangular table was covered with a gleaming white damask cloth, on which nine covers of silverware and porcelain had been laid.

'Mrs Llewellyn-Jones, there on the doctor's right.' Andrew's mother began to arrange her guests with the same care she'd devoted to the table decorations. 'Mr Llewellyn-Jones, here, next to me.' She patted the place setting with a coy flirtatious glance at her male guest of honour. 'Fiona darling, I suppose you'd better sit opposite your husband or you'll mope. Bethan, perhaps you'd like to sit next to Alec, Andrew next to Miss Llewellyn-Jones.' She surveyed her handiwork as they took their places. 'Now isn't this cosy?' she beamed.

Bethan sat rigidly on her high-backed chair. Every time she tried to relax the carvings bit painfully into her spine. Dr John said a short grace, hock was poured into one of the four glasses at each place, and a maid Bethan hadn't seen before, handed the hors-d'oeuvres. Bethan looked for Mair and saw her hovering next to the sideboard; evidently she'd been regulated to a secondary serving position. Bethan turned her attention to the array of cutlery before her, and suffered a moment of blind panic before remembering the etiquette books that Laura had devoured during their first months of training in the hope that she'd be swept off her feet by a millionaire patient. 'Start from the outside and work your way in' was sound advice, but 'Watch others and do as they do' was sounder.

She slowly unfolded and settled her linen napkin on her lap, using the time to study everyone's behaviour before copying them, terrified lest she make a mistake, disgrace herself and embarrass Andrew.

'These canapés are delicious, don't you think?' Alec said, as he helped himself to more from a glass plate that had been placed in front of them.

'Yes, delicious,' she echoed inanely, picking at one. She glanced at Andrew, seated further down the other side of the table and deeply engrossed in conversation with Miss Llewellyn-Jones. A moment later Anthea's silvery laughter was joined by Andrew's deeper, more robust tones.

'What do you think, darling,' Mrs John called down the table to her husband, 'Andrew's agreed to escort Anthea to the golf club garden party next week.'

The doctor smiled and carried on talking to Mrs Llewellyn-Jones. A suffocating wave of jealousy rose in Bethan's throat. She choked on a sliver of pastry, turned aside and spat it into her napkin, hoping no one would notice. She needn't have concerned herself. They noticed, but were also too well bred to comment.

The hors-d'oeuvres plates were cleared away by Mair and thick slices of broiled salmon were handed around with a boat of tartare sauce, by the upper maid.

'You always find such good fish, Mrs John,' Mr Llewellyn-Jones complimented. 'This is a truly magnificent specimen.'

'I chose it myself, and the recipe is one of Mother's.'

'My wife always superintends the preparation of the fish herself. Won't trust the cook,' Dr John laughed.

'Most wise,' Mrs Llewellyn-Jones agreed. 'You can't get a good cook these days for love or money. They're simply not bred to it like they used to be. When I was a girl Mother never had any servant problems and now. . . . '

The conversation ebbed and flowed while Bethan played with the salmon on her plate, skinning it, picking out the bones, occasionally ferrying a small forkful of the bland, glutinous flesh to her lips.

'I haven't seen you in town, Miss Powell. Are you from this area?' Miss Llewellyn-Jones enquired politely in a sweet, clear voice.

'Yes,' Bethan replied shortly, colouring at the attention.

'It's strange I haven't seen you before. But then you really *should* join the Ladies' Guild. Absolutely *everyone* belongs to it,' she gushed. 'We meet every Tuesday and Thursday afternoon in one another's homes, and we do such super things. Don't we, Andy?' she appealed familiarly.

'Bethan hasn't time to join you frivolous lot,' Andrew said, gallantly coming to her rescue. 'She works.'

'How marvellous,' Anthea beamed. 'Tell me, what do you *do*, Miss Powell?'

'I'm a nurse.' Bethan laid her knife and fork down on her plate, finally giving up on her fish.

'How *fascinating*. I wish I'd done something as noble as that.'

'You, my darling daughter, would never have stayed the course,' Mr Llewellyn-Jones said dismissively, as he helped himself to a fistful of salted almonds from a bon-bon side dish. 'You haven't the patience to read a cookery book let alone tend to a patient.'

'Mrs John, I appeal to you,' Anthea pleaded. 'I'm an excellent worker aren't I?'

'You most certainly are, my dear,' Mrs John agreed decisively.

'Anthea was a pillar of strength when we organised this year's hospital ball. The committee simply couldn't have managed without her.'

Bethan thought of the tedious hours that she and the other nurses had been forced to put in, either before or after their long shifts, making decorations and garlanding the Coronation ballroom. But she said nothing.

'Fiddling with frills and folderols is very different to nursing, even I know that much,' Mr Llewellyn-Jones said boldly, overriding his wife and Mrs John's objections.

'Daddy!' Anthea protested strongly. 'Decorating the hall was anything but fiddling with frills and folderols. We used a lot of skills absolutely *vital* to nursing. Flower arranging for a start.'

Bethan thought of the bare rooms and corridors of the Graig Hospital and wondered if Anthea had ever been there and taken a good look around. Mair stepped forward and cleared away the remains of the fish course. The first maid replaced the empty hock bottles with bottles of sparkling wine. Bethan hadn't been slow in drinking the hock, but she managed to finish her first glass of wine before the entrée was handed. Chaudfroid of pigeon. She'd never eaten pigeon before and felt sick when she realised what the plump, golden carcass on her plate was.

'Have you ever thought of going to London to nurse?' Alec asked kindly, realising that no one else was making an effort to talk to her.

'No ... no I haven't,' she stammered, trying to hide most of the pigeon under her knife and fork.

'Pay is extremely good, much better than here,' he said heartily. 'And the nursing is more interesting. If you decide on one of the larger hospitals like Charing Cross, where I happen to practise, you'll work with all kinds of specialists. Learn to cope with diseases you never even knew existed.'

'Now that's an offer you can't possibly refuse,' Andrew called down the table, cheering her with the thought that he was paying her some attention after all. 'Bearing in mind that London's a filthy place to live.'

'It is not ... ' his sister began warmly.

'It's cleaner than this valley, old boy,' Alec interrupted. 'And although I haven't worked with this little lady I bet she's a first-class nurse. And we're jolly short of those. She'd really be appreciated on my wards. You wouldn't believe some of the dross we've had to make up to sister level lately.'

'Oh I would. I've only just left the Cross, remember.'

'Stop encouraging him, Andrew, all he ever talks about these days is the lack of trained nurses, and it's *so* boring,' Fiona complained.

Once again the conversation slipped past Bethan without giving her a real opportunity to join in. Mair cleared away the remains of the pigeons and the upper maid set a roast leg of lamb and carving knives before Dr John senior. Dishes containing boiled new potatoes, mint sauce and asparagus *au gratin* were placed in the centre of the table, and a pile of warm clean plates stacked next to the lamb.

Bethan had never seen so much food laid before so few people. There were families of twelve and more on the Graig who didn't consume this quantity, let alone quality, in a week. Dr John cut a choice slice of the lamb for her and she quietly stopped him from cutting more. The maid handed down her plate as Andrew made a joke that she didn't understand, but she joined in the laughter anyway. She helped herself to small portions of asparagus and potatoes from the tureens that the maid handed, and tried to smile at everyone like Anthea Llewellyn-Jones.

After her awkward beginnings it seemed scarcely possible that things could deteriorate, but as the meal progressed she felt increasingly isolated. Perhaps her father was right? The gulf between the Common and the Graig – Andrew and her – was too wide to bridge.

She retreated deeper and deeper into her shell of silence, watching Andrew and Anthea, trying desperately to follow every word of their conversation. Studying the expressions on their faces, she suffered agonies every time Anthea laughed and looked up at him with her adoring, deep brown eyes. On the few occasions when someone troubled to speak to her she said only what was necessary, as succinctly as manners would allow. She ate little and drank a great deal, as the repartee sparkled around the table. There was talk of the theatre. Plays that Alec and Fiona had seen in the West End. Magazines that she had never seen in the shops, let alone read. People she knew only as names in the columns of the Pontypridd *Observer*.

By the time all vestiges of the lamb together with the hock and wine glasses had been cleared away and replaced by champagne and the final sweet and savoury courses of gooseberry fool, fresh cream and cheese ramekins, her head was swimming. Realising that she was rapidly becoming what Haydn called 'sozzled' she made an effort, and managed to eat most of the gooseberry fool that the maid had heaped into her dessert bowl in the hope that it would sober her up. But before she finished the course her champagne glass had been refilled twice, minimising any effects that the food might have had.

'I do so lo-ove champagne, don't you?' Alec whispered in slurred tones that told her his head was in no better condition than hers.

'Right, brandy time I think, my dear, don't you?' Andrew's father stood up and walked a little unsteadily to the sideboard. 'Any ladies care to join the gentlemen in a spot of Napoleon?'

'I think the ladies would prefer a liqueur with their coffee in the drawing room, darling,' his wife said as she left the table. Bethan looked helplessly at Andrew, who merely smiled at her before taking a fat cigar from the silver box that his brother-in-law handed him. She had no option but to follow the back of Anthea Llewellyn-Jones out through the door.

A steaming silver coffee pot and an array of delicate porcelain cups were laid out on a small table in front of the sofa in the drawing room. Andrew's mother began to dispense coffee and sickly sweet cherry brandy liqueurs.

'Nursing must be a fascinating profession,' Anthea Llewellyn-Jones said to Bethan, making a studied, gracious effort to bring her into the conversation.

'It is,' Bethan agreed. 'Particularly the nursing I'm doing now.'

'The new ward and X-ray machine must be an absolute boon to everyone at the Cottage.'

'The Cottage?' Bethan looked at her, confused, before registering what she was talking about. 'I don't work in the Cottage Hospital.'

'Really? Then where?' Anthea asked blankly as if the Cottage was the only hospital in Pontypridd.

'The Graig.'

'The Graig?' Anthea's mother looked vaguely shocked. 'I had no idea. There are so many wards there, and some dreadfully pathetic cases . . . ' She turned crimson. 'Particularly in the workhouse section,' she added as a hasty afterthought.

'I work on the maternity ward.' Bethan suppressed a smile. She knew why Mrs Llewellyn-Jones had blushed. According to the nurses who worked on the venereal disease wards, a good two-thirds of their patients belonged to the crache of the town. 'I'm training to be a midwife.'

'How fascinating,' Fiona drawled. 'Then you'll actually deliver babies.'

'I do that now.'

'How wonderful. Do tell all about it.' Anthea sipped delicately at her cherry brandy and sat, waiting expectantly.

To be entertained by tales of the coarse working classes, Bethan thought contemptuously. She recalled the cold, bare rooms she worked in; the mothers worn down by inadequate food and poverty. The maternity ward in the Graig was as far removed from this overfurnished, gilt-edged drawing room as a shanty was from Buckingham Palace. She could no more discuss the blood, sweat and toil of labour in these surroundings than her father could have expounded his Marxist theories.

'There's not much to it,' she answered evasively. 'We're so short-staffed I not only deliver babies with only a student nurse to call on, I also fill in for the night sister whenever she's sick.'

'Andrew does speak very highly of your ability,' Mrs John said gently.

'I do no more than any of the other qualified nurses who work in the infirmary,' Bethan said quickly, bristling at the patronising tone.

'Well, things have certainly altered since my day,' Mrs Llewellyn-Jones commented. 'Women had no thought of a career then. Outside of a husband and marriage, that is.'

'Oh I don't know.' Mrs John rose unexpectedly to Bethan's defence. 'My sisters worked as VADs during the war, and I myself would probably have done the same if I hadn't had the children to look after.'

'Ah but war times were very different from now.'

232

'Perhaps not so much for women of my class.' Bethan finally reached a breaking point that wouldn't have come without the cocktail, hock, wine, champagne and liqueur.

A deathly silence fell over the room for a moment.

'It is good of Andrew to agree to escort me to the golf club garden party, Mrs John,' Anthea purred, setting her back to Bethan.

'Nonsense. You've had such wonderful times together since you were children. It should be such fun. . . . '

Bethan felt as though someone were twisting a knife in her gut. She looked up at the open doorway. Andrew was standing framed in it. He winked at her.

'Coffee, darling?' his mother offered.

'No thank you, Mother. I'm going to whisk Bethan away if I may. Trevor and Laura are calling into my rooms to discuss their engagement plans. In fact,' he glanced at his watch, 'they should have been there as of ten minutes ago.'

'Engaged. How wonderful,' his mother said despondently with a sideways look at Bethan.

'If you'll excuse us, Mrs Llewellyn-Jones, Anthea, Fanny.'

'You'll pick me up half an hour before the party, Andy?' Anthea asked.

'We may both pick you up if I can persuade Bethan to come.'

'Lovely to meet all of you.' Heart soaring at Andrew's reply, Bethan showed the first signs of animation since she'd entered the house. Smiling at everyone she gathered her handbag and jacket from the arm of her chair. 'And thank you very much for a lovely dinner, Mrs John. You'll say goodbye to Doctor John for me?'

'Of course, dear.'

'We'll go out through the french doors so as not to disturb anyone. Bye, ladies.' Andrew put his hand under Bethan's elbow and pushed her into the garden.

'You see,' he said blithely as they crossed the lawn. 'Not ogres at all.'

'That,' she replied, 'depends entirely on your point of view.'

A path led round the side of the black and white Tudor-styled coach-house to a door in the side wall. Andrew pulled a bunch

233

of keys out of his pocket, and selecting one he fitted it into the lock.

'Are Trevor and Laura really coming?' she asked as he swung open the door.

'His car's already here.' He pointed to a rather battered, shabby vehicle parked close to the gates. 'He brings Laura here most nights when he's not on call. They borrow my spare bedroom.' He grinned at her blushes. 'You're not shocked are you? I assumed you knew all about it.'

'Laura did mention something today,' she admitted reluctantly.

'Today!' He stepped into a small, white-painted brick hallway, switched on a light, pulled her in and closed the door behind them. 'It's been going on for months,' he called back as he ran up the stone stairs two at a time.

'It can't have been,' she protested. 'They only started going out with one another four months ago.'

'Going out?' He raised his eyebrows. 'Is that what you call it?' He opened a door at the top of the stairs. 'Come on, slowcoach. The hall and stairs are not the best place to linger. They're basic to say the least, but there didn't seem much point in doing anything to bare brick. The interesting bit begins here.' He held open the door for her and she walked straight into a living room: a beautiful room with a polished wood floor that was almost covered by a deep blue and cream Persian carpet.

'Welcome to my lair,' he said proudly.

The room was filled with the golden rays of the evening sun. Light and airy, it was dominated by a large mullioned window that overlooked the garden. In front of the window, set sideways to make the most of the view, were two comfortable sofas covered in deep blue tapestry with between them an ultra-modern low table, skilfully crafted in blond wood. A bookcase of the same light wood, crammed to capacity with books and ceramics, filled the back wall. In an alcove behind the door was a sideboard, dining table and four chairs, in the same design as the rest of the furniture. Even the paintings were modernistic – lines and shapes of colour that Bethan couldn't even pretend to understand . . . or like.

'Small, but it has everything I need. Come and see the rest.' He crossed the room and opened a door in the far wall. Bethan found herself in a tiny hallway with four doors opening out from it. 'Bathroom.' He pushed one of the doors and revealed a bath, basin and toilet. The walls were fully tiled in white and trimmed with mahogany. 'Kitchen, at least that's what I call it. It's roughly half the size of my mother's pantry.' He showed her a tiny cupboard-sized room. One wall was filled by a sink set below a window, another held a cupboard topped by an electric hotplate, the third a few shelves on which was stacked an elegant set of plain white china.

He pointed to a door and held his finger to his lips.

'Trevor's universe,' he whispered, 'so I daren't open it, but it's just as well you can't see inside. The suite's dreadful. I inherited it from my grandmother. One of those hybrid things that's too good to throw out and not nearly good enough to put anywhere where it can be seen. So despite the fact that I hate Victorian furniture, Mother decided I should be the one to inherit it. But then I was in no position to argue because I spent every spare penny I had on this.'

He opened the final door in the small hallway. His bedroom was huge: the same size and shape as the living room, with the same mullioned windows that overlooked not only the gardens but the whole of the town spread out like a diorama below. He walked over to the window and knelt on the cushioned ledge. 'I often sit here in the night before I go to bed. When the lamps are lit it's like looking at an illuminated map. And as you can see I have all home comforts to hand.'

'A radio.' She fingered the Bakelite casing on the set that stood on one of the bedside tables. What they would have given at home for a radio, she thought wistfully.

'It's not as powerful as the radiogram in the living room.'

'You have a radiogram as well? I didn't see it.'

'You're not supposed to. I don't like things like that on display. I've hidden it behind one of the couches. But here's different. This room is just for me, and my very special guests. Which is why I had a small bar built into this.' He pulled a box trolley towards him, and opened the lid. 'Gin, brandy, whisky, iced wine?'

'You have ice too?'

'I confess I asked Mair to fill an ice bucket earlier and bring it over.' He took off his jacket and flung it over a chair. His wallet fell to the floor. 'Which reminds me, madam,' he picked it up and opened it, 'I haven't given you your winnings.'

'I didn't give you any betting money.'

'Here,' he handed her nine five-pound notes, 'five pounds at ten to one. Fifty pounds less the five you owe me.'

'I can't take it.'

'Why? I took a lot more than that off the bookie. If you feel at all guilty give it to Eddie. He earned it.'

'I suppose he did.' She took it and pushed it into her handbag.

'Right, now that's done. Drink?'

'I think I had enough earlier.'

'So did I, but that's no reason to stop. It doesn't hurt to let your hair down once in a while.'

'Doctor's diagnosis?'

'Of course.' He opened the wine and poured out two glasses.

She walked around the room looking at everything, trying to commit every detail to memory so she could imagine him here, alone, when they were apart. She rested her cheek against the plain navy-blue silk drapes, touched the bronze figures that held the stained-glass shades of the lamps, rested the palms of her hands on the smooth sweep of the heavy navy and red silk bedspread.

'This is a beautiful room,' she whispered, suddenly aware of how alone they were. Of why he'd brought her here.

'I'm glad you like it. I have a penchant for beautiful things.' He stood up and ran his fingers through her hair. 'All beauty,' he said quietly. 'The exotic, the modern and the artistic.' He pointed to an enormous copy of Manet's *Olympia* that hung, framed by silk drapes above his bed. She stared at the nude, fascinated, yet shocked by its blatant eroticism.

'I don't know how any woman could do that,' she said when she realised he was waiting for her to react.

'Do what?'

'Pose in front of a man without any clothes on.'

'Perhaps she was in love with Manet. From the way he's portrayed her he was obviously in love with her. And you have to admit she is very beautiful.'

Taught from childhood by Elizabeth that nudity was disgusting, she found it difficult to equate beauty with a woman's naked body.

'But my darling,' he bent his head and kissed her, 'she can't hold a candle to you.'

He kicked the door shut with the heel of his shoe.

'Trevor and Laura?' she protested.

'Will lock the door behind them.'

'Your parents?'

'Have no key, and visitors to take care of. Besides they know better than to barge in here without an invitation. I told you. This is my lair.'

He gently removed her hat and handbag from her trembling hands and threw them on to the window-seat. She turned her back on him and looked out of the window.

'Beth, I love you,' he murmured. Standing behind her he wrapped his arms around her, cupping her breasts with his hands. 'Don't you think I've been patient long enough?' he asked softly. 'I could have brought you here instead of taking you to Cardiff that first time we went out alone together.'

'Like Trevor did Laura?'

'We're not Trevor and Laura.'

She turned to face him. Sliding her hands up to his neck she pulled him close and returned his kiss. Still kissing, he drew her down on to the bed. She lay next to him, the wine she'd drunk making the ceiling spin. She tried to think clearly, evaluate the choices open to her. But she couldn't. His presence overwhelmed her senses. The smell of brandy and tobacco on his breath – his cologne – the touch of his fingers burning into the skin on her arm. . . .

He rolled close to her, pinning her down. His hand slid high beneath her jacket, unfastening the buttons on her dress. His tongue darted into her mouth. She lifted her arms to his face, and stroked his cheeks.

'I love you, Bethan Powell,' he mumbled hoarsely. 'More than you can ever begin to know.'

'I love you too, Andrew.' Evading his hands she struggled to sit up on the bed.

'Beth . . . ' he begged.

She removed her jacket and tossed it on to a chair. Then she

237

slid her arms out of the sleeves of her dress and pulled it down to her waist.

Struck dumb, he stared at her, and in that precise moment she felt as though she could see her future mirrored in the depths of his dark eyes.

'Are you sure?' he asked huskily.

She thought of Laura, her friend's amazement at the revelation that she and Andrew had never made love. Of Anthea Llewellyn-Jones waiting in the wings. She loved Andrew, and she knew now that she would do anything . . . anything to keep him.

'I'm sure,' she said decisively, with a tremor in her voice that belied her words.

He reached out and, very slowly, very deliberately pulled her dress down over her legs. She shuddered, afraid that he'd be repelled by her naked body, terrified of what he was about to do to her. Sensing her fear and sensitive to her natural modesty he curbed his mounting passion, left the bed and hung her dress and jacket in his wardrobe.

'I'll be back in a moment,' he murmured, lifting down a thick towelling bathrobe from the back of the bedroom door. 'You're shivering, get into bed before you catch your death of cold.'

She undressed in record time, slipping between the clean, cool linen sheets, so different from the tired, furred, flannelette ones her mother used. She lay, rigid with fear, wondering whether or not to remove her bloomers. He returned before she'd made a decision. Closing the door behind him he locked it and slid between the sheets, still wearing his robe.

She started at the feel of his bare legs touching hers. He rubbed his hands vigorously down her arms.

'You're freezing, woman,' he complained. 'Come closer and I'll warm you.' She inched towards him. 'That wasn't an order,' he murmured. 'Relax. I'm not going to hurt you, darling. Not now. Not ever.'

His mouth closed over hers. He kissed her deeply, thoroughly. His hands moved to her breasts, his fingers teasing, stroking, arousing her nipples just as they'd done the day before. She wrapped her arms around him, running her hand down beneath his robe at the back.

Gently, unhurriedly he caressed her bare skin with the tips of his fingers, sliding his hand down to her waist where it encountered the elastic of her bloomers. He pushed them aside and moved his hand into the valley between her thighs.

She clung to him, burying her head in his robe. It took all the self-control he could muster, but he managed to restrain himself until he succeeded in rousing her passion to the same pitch as his own. Only then did he open his robe and remove the one remaining garment. At that point she no longer cared about anything except Andrew and what he was doing to her.

He eased himself on top of her. She gasped as a sharp, intense pain shot through her.

'Darling,' he smoothed her hair away from her tear-filled eyes, 'I'm sorry,' he murmured, 'so sorry.'

She locked her arms and legs around his body, imprisoning him in a shell of her own making. 'Don't stop,' she pleaded breathlessly. 'Please, Andrew, don't ever stop.'

'You bloody fool,' Haydn shouted as he tripped over a body in the shadows on the steps of the stage entrance to the Town Hall. 'You trying to kill someone or what?'

'Or what,' Eddie mumbled between thick and swollen lips.

'Eddie?' Haydn peered into the battered face of his brother. 'What the hell are you doing here at this hour?'

'Waiting.'

'For what? Not for me, I'll be bound.'

'No.'

'Oh God don't tell me! You got mixed up with one of those girls. Which one was it. Daisy? Doris?'

'Have you seen Daisy?' Eddie asked eagerly. 'She was supposed to meet me here after the show. . . . ' His voice faded as he realised what he was saying, and worse still, who he was saying it to.

'She went off hours ago with the conductor,' Haydn snapped.

'Conductor?'

'Band, not tram, you clot.'

'That's just what I am,' Eddie mourned miserably. 'A bloody clot. No good to anyone. . . . '

'You get drunk earlier?'

'No,' Eddie protested indignantly. 'Why?'

239

'A hangover would explain the self-pity. Look, stay here, I'll finish checking around, give Fred a shout and walk home with you.'

Ten minutes later the two brothers were kicking their way through the litter and debris that the Rattle Fair revellers had left behind in Market Square.

'Pity, it all looks so grubby after the event,' Haydn complained as he peeled a soggy ice-cream wafer from the sole of his shoe.

'What does?' Eddie asked despondently.

'Nothing you'd know about.' Haydn touched his cap to a woman who was pulling down the shutters on a boiled-sweet stall.

The square was quiet. A few fair people and a couple of conscripts from the town were packing away the rides. They moved swiftly, unbolting, unbuckling and folding the metal structures into smaller units that could be easily stacked on the wagons that waited to transport them to the next town.

'Want a pint?' Haydn asked, overcome by a sudden wave of compassion for Eddie.

'It's after stop tap.'

'Not if you're in the know,' Haydn boasted as they walked under the railway bridge and up High Street. When they came to the side door of the Horse and Groom he knocked just once above the latch. The door opened a crack and a woman peeped out.

'Haydn!' she shouted. 'Everyone, it's Haydn! Come in with you. Come in.' She flung the door wide. 'Who's this you've brought?' She eyed Eddie warily.

'My brother, the boxer. Can't you tell from his face?'

'If you're Haydn's brother, you're more than welcome.' She closed the door behind them. 'What's it to be, boys? Pints?'

'He's buying.' Eddie pointed to Haydn.

'After what you won today?'

'I didn't place a bet on myself and get money for nothing like you.'

'Pints will be fine, Bess.' Haydn thrust his hand into his trouser pocket.

'You look smart, Haydn. New suit?' A girl with the most improbable red hair that Eddie had ever seen sidled up to them.

240

'This old thing—' Haydn fingered his lapel— 'only had it today.'

'You're a scream.' She hung on to his arm as they walked through to the back bar. Eddie looked around in amazement. The room was smokier, stuffier and packed with more people than he'd ever seen it during regular hours.

'Haydn, give us a song, boyo?' a man Eddie didn't know shouted as they entered the room. 'Here, quiet everyone, Haydn's here.'

'Come on, Haydn, give us a song and I'll put up pints for you and your friend,' Wilf Horton, rather the worse for drink, shouted from across the room.

'Friend?' Haydn winked at Eddie. 'Pint?'

'Suits me.' Eddie leaned against the wall.

Haydn stood in front of the bar and a hush fell over the crowd. A short fat man pushed his way through to a beer-scarred piano that stood in the corner.

' "Rose of Tralee"?' he asked, supping his pint before setting it down on the top.

Haydn nodded. The man began to play and Haydn came in after the introduction. Eddie had heard his brother sing many times before, in church, in the choir, and around the house, but never a song like 'The Rose of Tralee.' And never in a pub crowded with people none the better for drink. The rapt, expectant silence continued as Haydn carried his voice into a full crescendo, and even when he reached the chorus he attracted no more than a faint humming accompaniment from the more experienced singers amongst the customers.

When the pianist finally played the last soft note the hush continued for a few more seconds, then uproar broke out. Glasses were hammered on tables, feet drummed the floor, someone cried 'again' and the plea was taken up around the bar. For the first time Eddie realised that his brother had talent. Real talent. While he'd sung, he'd held the audience in his hand. He could have done anything he'd wanted with them.

'Hey, less din!' the landlady shouted sharply. The noise ceased and everyone heard a hammering on the outside door.

'I'll deal with this, Bess,' the landlord ordered; he walked down the passageway himself.

'Oh God, it's a copper,' someone shouted as he opened the

door. Eddie pulled his cap down low over his eyes as Megan's brother Huw entered the pub.

'Pint, constable?' Bess asked.

'Pint? I should be booking everyone here.'

'Not on fair night,' Wilf Horton pleaded. 'Give a man a break.'

'Only if that lad sings "I'll Take You Home Again, Kathleen".' Huw Davies' face split into a huge grin at the joke he and the landlord had shared at the customers' expense.

'Well if it's going to keep everyone here out of clink – ' Haydn finished his pint in one draught. Before he had time to dump the empty glass on the bar another three were set before him. He pushed one over to Eddie and resumed his place in front of the crowd.

'I'll Take You Home Again, Kathleen' was followed by 'If I Should Fall in Love Again'. More pints appeared, and after a drinking interval Haydn began the Al Jolson favourite, 'Mammy'.

'Your Haydn's learned a lot about phrasing and timing since he's worked in the Town Hall.' Huw nudged Eddie.

'I didn't know he was this good.'

'Oh he's good all right, lad. But then talent runs in the family. Drink up. I owe you a pint after the way you boxed today. You turned my bob into ten.'

'Cheers.' Eddie'd never had so many free pints in his life. 'Tell me, is it always like this?' He jabbed his finger at the crowd while the landlord pulled two more pints.

'Only on Christmas Eve and Rattle Fair day when the lads have had a chance to earn an extra bob or two helping to put up the stalls and rides. First time here after hours?'

'Yes.'

'Well here's hoping it won't be your last.'

Two songs later Haydn joined them. The perspiration ran down his face as he gulped the first of the line of six pints that were waiting for him.

'At least we've got nothing to get up early for tomorrow,' Haydn said as he took a deep breath. 'No fair, no market, and I've just about given up on the brewery.'

'And no money,' Eddie said glumly.

'You won a fiver.' He took a hard look at Eddie as Huw

242

turned to talk to the landlord. 'You haven't lost it have you?' he challenged.

'Not exactly.'

'What do you mean "not exactly"?' Haydn demanded. 'Damn it all . . . ' An ugly suspicion crossed his mind. 'You bloody fool! You gave it to Daisy didn't you?'

'She'd had her rent money stolen – I snagged her stockings and lost her knick . . . ' Eddie turned the colour of strawberry jam and stared gloomily into his glass.

'She gave you a hard luck story and you gave her a fiver?' Haydn snarled contemptuously.

'Not all of it.' Eddie put his hand in his pocket and pulled out a two-shilling piece.

'That all you got left? Two bob?'

Eddie nodded pathetically.

'Well I hope she bloody well earned every penny?'

'Earned. . . . '

'Don't be thick! You know what I mean. Did she earn it?'

Eddie recalled the afternoon. Daisy lying naked in the long grass. The flies crawling over his naked back as he thrust himself inside her. . . . A large, self-satisfied smirk crossed his face at the memory.

Mollified, Haydn calmed down.

'What can I say except that thanks to you I won enough today to pay for both our suits. Good luck to you, boy.' He pulled another two pints from the stock on the bar towards them. 'Five pounds is steep but Daisy comes expensive. Others have paid more. And when it comes to the things that matter, quality matters more than price. At least that's what Dad always told me.'

Eddie pushed his cap to the back of his head, looked Haydn squarely in the eye and laughed for the first time that day. Haydn was right. When he came to think about it Daisy was quality. What she'd given him was priceless.

Chapter Fourteen

'Has he taken her home yet?' Dr John asked his wife as she switched off the light and drew back the curtains.

'The garage doors are open and his car's gone,' she answered abruptly.

'It's easy to see what you think of that one,' he commented, kicking off his slippers and climbing into bed.

'I never said. . . . '

'That's just it, Isabel,' he observed evenly. 'You never said. You don't have to. After thirty-two years I know you better than to need words.' He patted her arm as she sat beside him on the bed.

'Oh she's a nice enough girl, I suppose,' Isabel added in a tone that said she didn't think so. 'It's just that. . . . '

'She isn't good enough for Andrew?' he interrupted.

'You sound as though you're making fun of me.'

'Don't be so sensitive, darling. I'm agreeing with you.'

He laid his head back on the pillow. The brandy, wine and champagne he'd drunk earlier blurred the fringes of his vision, so he closed his eyes. An image of Bethan came to mind. Dark, slim yet curvaceous – voluptuous . . . yes, that was the word he was looking for . . . voluptuous, with deep smouldering eyes, and a wide, welcoming mouth. He rubbed his hands over his temples. He'd better watch himself, he was beginning to think like the gossip columnist in the *Sunday People*.

'She is a pretty girl,' he chose his words carefully, 'and I'm sure that's all Andrew sees, a pretty girl to help him while away his idle hours. He'll soon tire of her, dear, and then he'll go looking for someone more like himself. Someone he can really talk to. Take my word for it. It will pass.'

'Do you think so?' It was a plea for reassurance.

'I don't know of a doctor who didn't have a fling with a pretty nurse in his youth.'

'Yourself included, I suppose.'

'Present company excepted.' He kissed her hand.

'Liar,' she said fondly.

'Well if it's any consolation I realised early on that despite her medical training she wouldn't make a suitable wife, not for me, or any doctor thinking of career advancement. And given time, and Andrew's ambition to become a fully-fledged surgeon, he'll come to the same conclusion. That's if he hasn't already. Smart move of yours to invite the Llewellyn-Jones girl. They seemed to get on well together.'

'Didn't they?' Isabel gloated. 'But you'll still talk to him?'

'If I have to. But really, dear,' he held back the bedclothes for her to climb into bed, 'I don't think it will come to that. He's a sensible boy. Believe me, he'll soon see the situation for himself.'

The following morning Maud was up early and in Megan's house before eight.

'You told your mother that you're going rag picking with Diana?' Megan asked as she slapped plates down on the table.

'Not exactly,' Maud admitted reluctantly.

'I thought so. Then the pair of you,' Megan looked from Maud to Diana, 'mind that you come straight back here as soon as you've finished to have a bath in the washhouse. You're going to need it after you've been in the rag picker's yard all day,' she warned Maud. 'And remind me to go through your clothes before you go home. Your mother will go spare if she finds a single louse or flea on you. And God knows there's enough of both down Factory Lane.'

'I'll do that. Thanks, Auntie Megan.' Maud took the slice of bread Megan handed her and smeared butter over it.

'We'd best get going,' Diana said impatiently, walking past the table and grabbing a Welsh cake. 'There's always a huge queue on school holidays, and latecomers get sent away.'

'Mind you get Jim Rags to pay you twopence,' Megan called after them, as they went out through the front door. 'He tried to fob Jinny Makey off with only a penny for a full day.'

'We won't take less than twopence, Mam. Promise. See you tonight.'

'It doesn't seem right, lying to everyone,' Maud protested as they

245

ran past the turning to Factory Lane and straight down Llantris-ant Road towards town.

'I told you. Mam wouldn't let us go if we said where we were off to,' Diana snapped impatiently. 'And Mrs Jones will give us a free trip to Cardiff and half a crown each for helping her. That's got to be better than twopence for a whole day sorting rags in the smelly sheds.'

'Why doesn't she take her own kids and save five bob?' Maud asked suspiciously.

'Too young to flutter their eyelashes at floorwalkers and dis-tract them,' Diana informed her as she gave a laudable Mary Pickford impression.

'You girls are late,' Judy Jones complained as they ran breath-less into the ticket office.

'I know. I'm sorry. She. . . . ' Diana pointed to Maud, 'wanted a second breakfast.'

'I've got the tickets,' Betty Morgan called from the front of the queue at the ticket booth.

With the two women humping three large Gladstone bags between them, the four of them ran as fast as they could up the wide flight of steep stone steps, reaching the platform just as the guard was putting the whistle to his mouth.

'Quick.' Betty wrenched open the door to a third-class carriage and they all tumbled in, slamming it just as the whistle blew.

'We'll sort you out in Cardiff.' Judy studied Maud from between narrowed eyes. 'Has Diana told you what we'll be doing?'

'Not really,' Maud answered, a little bewildered by the air of importance and urgency.

'Perhaps it's just as well,' Betty smiled. 'You can't beat true innocence.'

Maud had only ever been on a train to Cardiff twice in her life, both times when her father had been working a five-day week. Lucky enough to have a window seat she made the most of the special trip, sat back and watched the scenery glide past. The smoky, soot-blackened yellow bricks of the backs of terraced houses, the overgrown embankments, wildernesses of scrap iron in the merchants' yards, the stations and the villages rolled past.

Treforest, Taffs Well, Radyr and eventually Cardiff Queen's Street then General.

'Straight to the ladies' waiting room,' Betty barked, gathering her bags together the minute the train stopped. Diana and Maud traipsed behind the women feeling a bit like chicks following two overblown hens.

'Right, you know what to do, Diana. Take Maud into the cubicle with you.' Betty thrust her Gladstone bag into Diana's hand as soon as they entered the toilets. Diana took it, pushed Maud into a cubicle, followed her, locked the door and opened the bag.

'What's in there?' Maud asked.

'Clothes. We can't go like we are. Quick, get your dress off.'

While Maud was undressing Diana pulled out two plain grey cloche hats, two matching grey woollen dresses, cableknit lisle stockings and two pairs of practical lace-up black shoes.

'Daughters of the crache,' she explained in a posh accent.

'I didn't know you could talk like that,' Maud gasped.

'Practice makes perfect,' Diana said airily, very much the experienced tutor to Maud's apprentice. 'And if you can't talk the same you'd best keep your mouth closed. Here, put this coat on, follow me and do whatever I do.'

Betty and Judy were in the ladies' waiting room when they finally emerged. Maud scarcely recognised them. Judy was wearing a thick layer of make-up, flared slacks and a white blouse ornamented by a royal blue and white name tag that sported the name 'Miss Barker'. Underneath the name in smaller letters was the title 'Windowdresser'.

'Howell's,' Diana explained briefly. Judy pulled on a calf-length blue coat that buttoned to the neck, fastened it, and rolled her trouser legs up to her knees exposing flesh-coloured stockings.

'Here, Diana, take this to Left Luggage.' Betty crammed her own, Judy's and the girls' clothes into one of the bags. Then she picked up one of the Gladstones, Judy the other. 'Here we go. Maud, watch Diana, do everything she does, and don't say a word unless you're spoken to, and then only yes or no. I don't have to tell you that you're not to tell a soul about this?'

'Diana warned me.'

'Good. Here's Diana. Hold her hand and walk behind us.'

247

Diana and Maud entered Howell's behind Betty. They'd lost sight of Judy somewhere along the way. Betty made a direct beeline for the ladies' wear department.

'Three floorwalkers, six assistants. The two either side of the shoe department will be going on eleven-fifteen tea break with the tallest of the floorwalkers,' Betty whispered *sotto voce* to Diana.

'Can I help you, madam?' a black-skirted, white-bloused assistant enquired.

'Yes, I want matching dresses for my daughters.' Betty's accent had also undergone a miraculous transformation. 'Something in royal blue?' she said loudly for the benefit of the assistants in the shoe department. 'With matching hats, gloves and shoes of course. It's for a wedding. In London,' she added proudly, if superfluously.

'If madam would care to come this way.' Betty followed her, and the girls followed Betty. By explaining fictitious, trivial details in a loud voice, and by demanding that the dresses be matched exactly to shoes and hats, Betty succeeded in commanding the attention of three of the six assistants. Spot on eleven-fifteen, two of the remaining three and the tallest of the floorwalkers went to tea. One minute after that the last assistant's attention was taken up by another customer.

'This won't do. Won't do at all,' Betty said abrasively. Diana picked up the prearranged cue. Turning abruptly she caught her elbow on the outstretched arm of a plaster tailor's dummy that was modelling an outrageously expensive example of the latest sequinned evening fashions on a central display. The dummy rocked precariously on its perch. Diana screamed, so Maud screamed too. The two floorwalkers rushed to catch it, while Betty apologised to all and sundry. And during those few seconds Judy appeared, coatless, scarf covering her hair, brush and feather duster in one hand, bag in other. She walked behind the counter, opened the panel that led out to the windows and closed it behind her.

The first thing she did was kick off her shoes. Then, trousers flapping around her ankles, she commenced stripping all of the dummies in the window of their clothes, accessories and jewellery, taking the time to fold everything carefully and neatly into her

248

enormous bag. By the time Betty had moved on to looking at cerise gowns as an alternative to blue for her daughters, she'd finished.

It was twenty-nine minutes past eleven. One minute before the end of tea break for those off the floor.

'Hey you!' the senior floorwalker shouted as Judy closed the panel behind her.

'Me?' she asked calmly, valiantly suppressing her initial reaction to run.

'Yes. Can you do something about this model?' he asked, with a backward glance at Diana. 'Customer knocked it over and damaged the sequins on the dress.'

Judy dropped her bag, walked over to the dummy and examined the cloth. Four of the sequins were bent; she succeeded in straightening them with her fingernail.

'If you give me a hand to strip it I'll take it up to repairs,' she said abruptly.

'Can you have it back by this afternoon?'

'Yes. I should think so.'

He lifted down the dummy and between them they peeled off the gown and wrapped the naked plaster body in a sheet, lest it offend the delicate sensibilities of shoppers. Laying the evening gown on top of the clothes bulging out of her bag, Judy walked on into the men's department. Removing a stack of pullovers, shirts and ties from the edge of the counter she tucked them under her arm and proceeded to the lift. The lift attendant helpfully assisted her to stack her load behind the metal safety grille. She got out at the third floor and went into the ladies' cloakroom. Betty and the girls walked in a few minutes later.

While Judy was busy rerolling her trouser legs, untying her scarf and donning her coat in one cubicle, the three of them crammed into another and split Judy's haul between the two bags. Diana took one, pushed the other into Maud's hand and led the way out of the cloakroom, and out of the store.

Maud had never been so frightened in her life. Her mouth was dry, her hands wet and clammy where they gripped the bag. Every murmur of conversation, every glance that came her way from a floorwalker or assistant sent her heart into palpitations.

Smiling at the doorman Diana walked confidently out on to the street. Two minutes later Maud joined her.

'Tea in Lyon's, I think. Shopping is so tiring,' Diana said loudly for the benefit of the doorman in her 'posh' accent.

'Sweets from a baby,' Betty laughed later over a cup of tea in the station buffet. 'Here's your half-crowns, girls.'

'And here's these.' Diana put her hand into her pocket and pulled out a dozen costume rings. Maud stared at them in disbelief. 'Where did you get those?'

'I tried one on,' Diana said indignantly.

'Just one,' Maud repeated dully, 'I know, I saw you.'

'Sweets from a baby.' Diana's laugh joined Betty's.

'And crache clothes for us.' Judy touched her cup to Maud's. 'Congratulations on joining the forties. You're just the type of new blood we need.'

'The forties?' Maud echoed in bewilderment.

'Forty thieves, clot.' Diana put her arm around Maud's shoulders. 'Or should I say forty-one.'

The weeks that followed her first visit to Andrew's rooms were idyllic ones for Bethan. She used some of the money Andrew'd given her to clear her debts with her aunt and loan Eddie a small float to tide him over. Even after a wild spending spree in Megan's she still had thirty-two pounds to hide in the bottom of her jewellery box. Her father seemed happier than he'd been for weeks. And when he took to wearing his best suit, polishing his shoes and stepping out in the evenings via Rhiannon's house, she assumed that he was putting his winnings to good use in the Graig Hotel. She was glad for him. He deserved a few pints after the gloom of a winter spent on short-time work.

Eddie bought himself a new and better pair of gloves and practically moved into the gym at the back of the Ruperra Hotel on Berw Road. No one was more delighted than her when Joey Rees fixed it so Eddie got a job as dogsbody and late-night general cleaner for a bob a night and his gym fees. Elizabeth was quick to point out that six bob a week wasn't enough to keep a baby, let alone a grown man, but Eddie, flush with new-found confidence after winning his fight and laying Daisy, wasn't to be easily put down. Not even by his mother.

He threw his first week's money on the table and told her to keep it. He still had his days free to put up market stalls, work in the brewery and, best of all, run for the bookies who were only too keen to employ him now they knew he could take care of himself, and their cash.

Haydn began leaving for work early in the afternoon. Bethan found out why when she saw him serving in Harry Griffiths' shop beside a proud and blushing Jenny one afternoon. Maud's cough disappeared, just as Andrew had promised it would, and, happy and healthy, she took to spending all her free time with Diana. At weekends they became inseparable, and Maud slept over at Megan's most Friday and Saturday nights with her cousin, chiefly because she enjoyed the relaxed atmosphere but also because the distance made it impossible for her mother to monitor her movements.

Elizabeth continued to moan, but her moans were always easier to bear in the warmer weather when everyone found it simpler to get out of the house.

With her family as happy as they could be, and spring gliding peacefully into a full-blown, warm, beautiful summer, Bethan and Andrew found the time and the passion to create wonderful, exquisite moments that would last both of them a lifetime. They spent every minute when they weren't actually sleeping, or working, together. And occasionally they even managed to contrive to spend some of their working time in one another's arms.

They touched fingers as they passed in the corridor. They stole moments from meal breaks and met in deserted side wards and corridors. Whenever Squeers set Bethan menial duties in the linen cupboards or sluice rooms she ran along quickly with a light step, a delicious sense of expectancy buoying her spirits in the hope that *he'd* be there, waiting to drag her into a secluded corner and steal a kiss. She only had to catch sight of him across the yard or in a corridor for her limbs to grow liquid with longing. And throughout each and every long, hard-working hour there was the prospect of the evening and weekly day off that lay ahead. Glittering golden times that more than compensated for the slights and indignities she suffered at Squeers' hands.

Sometimes Trevor and Laura joined them on their outings but more often than not they were alone, not simply because Laura and Bethan's days off rarely coincided. Each of them valued the moments they spent with their partner too much to share them even with close friends.

Neither Andrew nor Bethan were anxious to repeat the experiment with their respective families. Once or twice a week they went to his rooms, but always late in the evening when he knew his parents would be out, or occupied with visitors. If they had a whole day free they generally drove down to the summer chalet on the Gower; if they had only a few hours or an evening they contented themselves with a walk in the country. Not up Pit Road to Shoni's pond, but further afield. Andrew drove her to the primrose-strewn fields around Creigau, or the picturesque woods above Taffs Well in which nestled the Marquess of Bute's fairytale Castell Coch with its red turrets and grey stone walls. They were magic times. Bethan was too much in love to question anything Andrew did, said or thought. To her, he was always kind, gentle, funny and loving. Very, very loving.

There were moments when she had doubts, particularly when Laura talked about engagement rings, weddings and household linen, but when she was actually with Andrew all uncertainty melted away. He didn't even have to provide excuses for his tardiness. She thought them up for herself – he was considering her nursing ambitions – allowing her time to complete her midwifery certificate. They were happy as they were – what was the point of hurrying? He'd told her he had very little money of his own – he probably wanted to save a deposit large enough to buy a house like his father's . . . she could find a million and one reasons why they shouldn't rush headlong into marriage like Laura and Trevor. And in the mean time she wrung every moment she spent with him dry.

For his part Andrew loved Bethan and told her so – often. If his love was more selfish, less intense than hers, neither of them was sufficiently aware of the difference for it to matter. Once he succeeded in crossing the bounds of courtship and became her lover, sexual obsession took over from romance. He lived for the moments he was alone with her. They made love in his flat, the chalet, secluded areas in the country and – on one glorious, insane occasion – in Squeers' office at three in the morning when Bethan was on night duty and he'd been called into the maternity ward on an emergency.

His parents never said a word in favour of, or against, Bethan. They didn't have to. His father was politeness personified whenever he came across Bethan in the hospital, even going so far as to acknowledge her presence with a nod: an unheard-of courtesy from the senior medical officer to a junior staff nurse. But for all of their forbearance Andrew knew that neither of his parents considered Bethan suitable material for a daughter-in-law. To begin with there was her acquaintance with their under-house-maid. Then there was her strong Welsh accent, her upbringing on the Graig, her chapel connections – the John family had been Anglican for three generations – her miner father and his links with the Communist Party. Dr John senior had taken the trouble to find out what he could about Bethan's family, and he'd lost no time in passing on the information he'd gleaned to his son.

And quite aside from all these things, which were mentioned indirectly and often, whenever he took his meals with his parents there was the memory of the time he'd brought her to dinner. Again it wasn't what his mother said, it was what she left unsaid.

Anthea Llewellyn-Jones had such sparkling wit. She had a word for everyone no matter who they were. She was never tongue-tied or overwhelmed in company. The praise – and the sniping – went on and on, and he was left in no doubt that if it had been Anthea Llewellyn-Jones he was 'stepping out with' his parents wouldn't be pressing him so hard to take up the offer of a short-term placement on the surgical team at Charing Cross. Nor would he have received quite so many offers of late-night whiskies from his father during which the talk inevitably turned to cautionary tales on the dangers of becoming entangled with the wrong kind of girl.

But he was young, he was in love, and it was easy to shrug off his parents' obtuse and not so obtuse hints and advice. Marriage couldn't really come into the equation, not yet, and not for some time. Ambitious and financially dependent on his parents, he had two more years of study in Charing Cross, which he'd have to complete soon if he was going to gain his Fellowship of the Royal

College of Surgeons before his thirtieth birthday, as his father had done before him.

Meanwhile he loved Bethan enough to tarry in Pontypridd and delay his return to London. He'd even toyed vaguely with the idea of asking her to accompany him when he did go. But not as a wife. As a nurse.

As Alec had said, there were plenty of openings for nurses in London. She'd easily get a room in a hostel, and they could live very much as they did here. He loved her, but not enough to lower his standard of living to what she was used to, or Trevor was prepared to accept. Married life in a squalid little house without a bathroom, garden or rooms of the size he was accustomed to wasn't his idea of bliss. So he put the idea of marriage out of his head almost as soon as it entered it. And then again, why even consider it? Bethan hadn't mentioned it. They were both of them extremely happy the way things were. Why change them?

'So you'll come?'

'Andrew, I've never been to a garden party.'

'All the more reason to go to one now.'

'With you and Anthea Llewellyn-Jones?'

'Forget Anthea Llewellyn-Jones.' He crossed over to the desk where she was writing reports and took the pen from her hand. 'Enough, woman, I want you and I want you now.'

'Andrew, the day shift. . . . '

'Won't be on for another hour and a half. It's babies' feeding time, and – ' he kissed the back of her neck – 'I've taken the precaution of locking the door.'

'The reports have to be finished.'

'How much more do you have to do?'

She picked up another pen, inserted a nib and dipped it into the inkwell.

'I have to sign the last one,' she teased.

'Sometimes I think God put women on earth just to torment man,' he sighed in mock exasperation.

'And now that I've signed it I have to check the ward.'

Skilfully avoiding his moves to intercept her, she slipped under his arm and unlocked the door, opening it wide, so if he spoke he'd risk waking the ward. She paused for a few moments for her eyes to become accustomed to the subdued nightlights that burned at either end of the long room, then she trod lightly down the centre aisle checking the occupant of each bed. She stopped to place her hand lightly on the forehead of Mrs Roberts in the end cubicle who was recovering from fever. Her skin was still cool, as it had been since midday when the fever had broken. She left the ward and checked the delivery rooms. Clean, bare, they stank of chloroform and antiseptic. Closing the door she walked back through the ward to the nursery. The trainee was supervising the two ward maids who were feeding the babies bottles of water in the hope that they would eventually stop waking for non-nutritious liquid and sleep through. Not that the ploy worked. It generally meant that the tiny scraps of humanity screamed until six o'clock when they were finally handed to their mothers.

'All quiet, Mills?' she asked the trainee.

'All quiet, Nurse Powell.'

Bethan closed the door and returned to the office. It was empty. Assuming that Andrew had gone to check on his patient who was still in the operating theatre, she sat in the easy chair, rested her feet on the hearth and read through her reports. Satisfied that she'd done all she could, she piled the papers on to the corner of her desk, curled her feet beneath her and closed her eyes.

'Asleep on duty, Nurse Powell?'

She opened her eyes, Andrew was standing in front of her, his face flushed.

'Been outside?' she asked.

'Left something in the car.'

She knew what the 'something' was. He, like Trevor, had begun to raid the stocks of contraceptives in the family planning clinic in Ynysangharad Park.

'Drink?' he asked, producing a hip flask from his back pocket.

'Not before I come off duty. Squeers will have my guts for garters if she smells brandy on my breath during the change-over.'

'What I like most about you, Nurse Powell,' he sat on the edge of the desk close to her, 'is your delicate turn of phrase.' He took a long pull from the flask and rubbed his hand lightly along her

255

neck and shoulders. 'You back for good? Or are you likely to disappear again?' he asked.

'For good unless there's an emergency.'

'Reports finished?'

'Quite finished.' She left her chair, locked the door and leaned against it.

'In that case, let's begin.' He sat on the chair she'd vacated and pulled her down on to his lap. Kissing her, he slid his hand up her skirt. 'Nurse Powell! I'm shocked.'

'Why?' she enquired innocently. 'Wasn't it what you wanted?' She pulled her bloomers out of her pocket and dropped them to the floor.

'Suppose there'd been another doctor on duty.'

'I don't take them off for any other doctor.'

'That's reassuring to know.'

'We haven't much time,' she whispered, tugging at his trouser belt. 'I'll have to check on the ward again in a quarter of an hour.'

'I'll try to make it last that long,' he murmured. She laughed softly as she thrust her hand down inside his underpants, teasing an erection.

'You're a great one for promises, Doctor John.'

'You'll see just how great in a moment.' He wrapped his arms around her. 'What would I do without you, Beth?'

'Install a cold shower in your rooms?' she suggested lightly.

A moment later only the sounds of their breathing and her quiet moans disturbed the night silence of the peaceful office.

Andrew was waiting for her outside the gates when her shift finished.

'We never did decide about the garden party,' he said as they climbed into his car.

'I told you I've never been to one.'

'There's a first time for everything.'

'I've nothing to wear.'

'You can start with this.' He pulled a small leather-covered box out of his pocket.

'What is it?' Her heart was racing. It looked like a jeweller's box. Could it be. . . .

'Why don't you open it and see?'

With fingers that had suddenly grown stiff and clumsy she wrenched it open. Nestling on a bed of satin was the locket she'd helped him choose in Cardiff.

'This is your mother's.'

'No. It was never intended for her. I was going to give it to you on your birthday. But I thought, What the hell, that's not until December. You do like it?' he asked anxiously, studying the strange expression on her face.

'I love it,' she whispered, hugging him, hiding her head in his neck so he wouldn't read the disappointment in her eyes. She'd hoped for a ring that carried the same message of commitment as the one Laura wore on her left hand.

'Here, let me.' He took the locket from her hand and fastened it round her neck.

'No one's ever given me anything as beautiful as this,' she said bravely, fingering it lightly as it hung at her throat.

'Then you'll wear it to the garden party?'

'I still have nothing to go with it.'

'Then go to this famous aunt of yours that you've never allowed me to meet and buy something.'

'Drop me off now and you can meet her.'

'At – ' he flicked open his pocket watch – 'eight on a Sunday morning?'

'You'll never find a better time. She'll have finished work, and be cooking breakfast.'

'Work?'

'She cleans the Graig Hotel.'

'I've never paid a social call at eight on a Sunday morning before.'

'Didn't you just say there's a first time for everything?'

Chapter Fifteen

As Andrew drove into Leyshon Street Bethan directed him to Megan's house and he pulled up outside. The only other vehicle in the street was the milkman's cart. Eddie whistled as he walked towards it, carrying a handful of milk jugs.

'Working?' Bethan asked excitedly.

'Only for a few days.' He interrupted his whistling to answer as he laid the jugs on the back of the cart and pulled the top off a churn. 'Alwyn's sick, so Dai the milk asked me to take over for a week or two. Doctor John,' he acknowledged Andrew reluctantly, as he dipped a ladle into the churn and began to fill the jugs.

'Won any fights lately?' Andrew asked amiably, trying to make conversation.

'Only sparring in the gym, Doctor John.'

'Please call me Andrew.'

'Yes, well, I'd like to stop and chat but I have to get on. I'm late as it is and church people want their milk early on a Sunday. See you later, Bethan.'

Bethan waved goodbye to him and rapped on Megan's door as she walked in. 'Come on,' she said impatiently to Andrew.

'God, I might have known it would be you,' William complained as he walked down the stairs dressed only in a pair of trousers.

'The morning after the night before?' Bethan enquired cheerfully.

'What else?' He opened the kitchen door for her. 'Come in, Doctor John, please.'

Wishing he'd never suggested meeting her aunt, Andrew reluctantly followed Bethan into the kitchen.

'Bethan love.' Megan was frying salt fish on the stove, just as Bethan said she would be. She turned her head, saw Andrew and immediately wiped her hands on her apron. 'And this is your young man?'

'Andrew, Auntie Megan. Doctor Andrew John.'

'Please, call me Andrew.' Andrew was beginning to feel as though that was the only thing he said to members of Bethan's family.

'Well, I asked Bethan to bring you here so we could take a look at you, but I didn't expect her to bring you first thing on a Sunday morning. You'll stay to breakfast of course?'

'I'm afraid I can't, Mrs Powell, I have to call in on a patient on the way home.'

'Both of you been up all night I suppose?' She looked sharply at Bethan.

'Yes, but unlike William we've been working,' Bethan said loudly for William's benefit.

'How do you know I haven't?' he answered as he banged the washhouse door on the way out to the toilet.

'I'm sure your patient isn't going to die in the next half-hour, Andrew, so I'll not take no for an answer. I've more than enough fish and bread and butter for everyone. Pull up a chair and sit yourself down.'

'Auntie, we couldn't. You weren't expecting us.'

'There's plenty of room if that's what you're worried about. Diana and Maud came in so late last night they won't be up for hours. And mind, not a word of that to your mother. I doubt that she was ever young. Not in the same sense as those two, any road.' Megan shook the fish briskly in the pan. 'And the tea's already brewed, so the best thing you can do is keep quiet and pour us all a cup, Beth.'

Deciding that further protest was useless, Andrew sat on one of the kitchen chairs, and watched Bethan as she removed her cloak and moved around the kitchen, laying bread, sugar and milk on the table.

'Well, from what Bethan tells me this has been going on a good while between you two,' Megan said as she took the tea Bethan handed her. 'Serious is it?'

'Auntie . . . ' Bethan protested vigorously.

'I suppose you could say that,' Andrew grinned.

'I hope you're treating her well? That's my favourite niece you've got there you know.'

'My favourite girlfriend too.'

'Mam . . . Mam . . . where the hell are you?' William burst through the washhouse door, his fly unbuttoned, his hair standing on end.

'Language, William,' Megan said sternly. 'We've company and if I've told you once I've told you a hundred times I won't have you tearing around. . . . '

'Mam, there's coppers driving up the Graig hill. Four vans and a car packed with them. Mrs Evans sent young Phillip over the backs to tell us.'

'God help us!' The colour drained from Megan's face as she struggled to think coherently. 'Go next door, Will, and warn Betty and Judy. Now quick. Not that way,' she shouted as William went towards the front door. 'Over the wall at the back. Tell them to dump whatever they've got in the house. Pass it down the street . . . get the kids to carry it up the mountain or over to Shoni's. . . . '

William didn't hang about. He was back out through the door, and leaping one-handed over the wall before Bethan had time to wonder what was happening.

'Oh God, Huw warned me this was coming,' Megan moaned. 'Only yesterday he told me to get rid of everything. I should have listened to him.' She dropped the fish she was frying on to the range to burn. Running to the door she shouted up the stairs. 'Diana, Maud, quick, bring down all my stock. All the specials. Coppers coming.'

Andrew continued to sit in his chair, totally bemused by the bedlam that had broken out around him. Megan dashed back through the kitchen and into the washhouse. She thrust a tin bucket under the tap and began to fill it. Black smoke billowed out from the pan she'd left on the range, and Bethan jumped towards it, picking it up, only to immediately drop it again.

'You've burned your hand.' Andrew leaped out of his chair.

'It's nothing.' She stooped to gather up the fish that were scattered all over the hearth. 'Damn, I've cracked a tile,' she swore as she lifted the pan from where it had fallen, face down. A sound of tin scraping over stone came from the washhouse as Megan heaved the copper boiler close to the sink. Bethan left the pan and the fish on the hearth and went to help. She took the lid off the boiler as Megan emptied the contents of the bucket – floorcloth, scrubbing brush and all – into the boiler.

Diana, wearing a red flannel nightdress, raced through the kitchen into the washhouse and dumped an armful of clothes into the water. 'Maud's throwing them down the stairs, Charlie and I are carrying them through.'

'You know where everything is upstairs. Go back up and I'll help Charlie,' Bethan ordered, bumping into him as she ran out of the washhouse into the kitchen.

A jumble-sale-sized pile of clothes, shoes and hats lay at the foot of the stairs.

'The shoes?' she asked.

'Dump everything in,' Megan shouted as Charlie picked up a second, indiscriminate bundle.

'We all knew it would come to this.' Sam, still buttoning his shirt, bounded out of the front room and scooped up a pile of hats.

'Take the hats over the back,' Megan shouted at him as soon as he walked into the washhouse. 'Dump them somewhere. Get Will to give you a hand.'

'They're all knocked off, aren't they?' Bethan asked Charlie, looking to him to confirm her suspicions.

'Of course they're bloody well knocked off.' It was the first time Bethan had heard him swear. 'How else do you think she manages to sell clothes like these at the prices she's been charging?'

Bethan collected an armful, and following Charlie's example she scrambled into the washhouse and threw them into the tub. Andrew was still standing in front of the range totally mystified by the proceedings. A hammering on the door was followed by a shout.

'Open up. Police!'

'I'll deal with it.' Charlie walked slowly towards the front door; Maud and Diana, clutching their nightdresses, raced along the landing back into Diana's bedroom.

'That's the last of it.' Diana scooped up a tie from the banisters and threw it at Bethan as she disappeared into her room. Bethan opened the stove and tossed the incriminating article on top of

261

the coals. She heard Charlie talking to the police at the door. Red-faced, William appeared in the washhouse.

'Coppers got there same time I did,' he panted. 'They're pulling Betty's house apart. Judy's not faring much better.'

A stranger's voice, loud, official, spoke in the passage.

'We have a warrant, Mr Raschenko. So if you'll kindly step aside?' The sound of hobnailed boots echoed into the kitchen from the passage.

'Mrs Powell, police to see you.' Charlie entered the kitchen and stood aside. A sergeant and two constables pushed past him into the room; two more hovered just outside the door.

'Mrs Powell?'

'Sergeant?' White-faced, Megan looked up, but she continued to stir the soup of cold water and clothes in the boiler with a wooden spoon.

'You recognise the rank, Mrs Powell?'

'I should. I've enough family in the force.'

'Then you know what this is?' He pulled a warrant out of his pocket.

She stepped as far as the washhouse door and glanced at it. 'It appears to be in order.'

'You've no objection to us searching the house then?'

'It would be pretty pointless objecting when you've brought one of those with you,' she retorted tartly.

'Right.' The sergeant turned to his men. He pointed to the two outside the door. 'Upstairs. Search everywhere, and I mean everywhere. Under the beds, in the pillows, bolsters and eiderdowns. Pick up any loose floorboards, go into the attic. Open all the drawers, the wardrobes, pull the furniture away from the wall. You know what we're looking for?'

They nodded acknowledgement before thundering up the stairs.

'May I ask what's going on?' Andrew interrupted.

'That's what we're here to find out. . . . ' The sergeant looked at Andrew for the first time since he'd entered the room, and instantly changed his tone from hectoring to polite. 'Aren't you young Doctor John?' he asked.

'Yes,' Andrew replied shortly, suddenly realising the implications if it became known that he'd been in a house that the police had seen fit to raid.

'May I ask what you're doing here, sir?'

Andrew hesitated, uncertain how to answer.

'I asked him to come and take a look at my sister,' Bethan lied promptly. 'She's recovering from pleurisy, and I'm worried about her.'

'Is that right?' the sergeant asked.

'It is,' Andrew agreed.

'Strange time to make a house call isn't it, sir?' the sergeant pressed.

'Not really,' Andrew replied brusquely, angered by the man's officious tone. 'Nurse Powell here is the duty night nurse on the maternity ward in the Graig Hospital. I was called there early this morning to deal with an emergency, and when she told me of her concern for her sister I offered to examine the girl. I've never heard a doctor's dedication to his patients labelled as strange before, Sergeant. And as for the time, when you've been up most of the night another half-hour is neither here nor there.'

Maud chose that moment to creep down the stairs. She appeared in the doorway of the kitchen, her face flushed from her recent exertions. She began to cough, a rough hacking cough that shook her whole body. Bethan couldn't be sure whether the outburst was real, or skilful acting.

'Maud, what are you thinking of? You've only got a thin nightdress on, and you've no shoes on your feet.' Bethan went to her and put her arm around her shoulders. 'Come on, back up to bed.'

'There's men in our bedroom.' Maud began to cry weakly.

'I'll come with you.' Glad of an excuse to leave the kitchen Bethan steered her gently up the stairs.

'Hadn't you better examine your patient, Doctor John?' the sergeant asked.

'He already has,' Bethan answered for Andrew from the stairs. 'Thank you very much for coming, Doctor John, especially after a night of emergencies. It was very good of you. I'll see that she gets plenty of rest, and I'll get the prescription made up in the hospital pharmacy tomorrow.'

'Don't forget to do that. And it was no trouble to come here, Nurse Powell. Now if you'll excuse me, Sergeant, I have other calls to make.'

'Just a minute, sir, if you don't mind. I won't keep you much longer. You,' he pointed to one of the two constables standing in the room, 'search the front room.'

'That's my lodgers' room,' Megan protested.

'This warrant covers the whole house.'

'There's nothing there.'

'Nothing, Mrs Powell?' The sergeant lifted his eyebrows. 'What kind of nothing?'

'The same kind of nothing that's in this whole house,' she snapped angrily.

'Then you won't mind if we take a look.'

'It's all right, Mrs Powell,' Charlie walked to the door. 'I'll go with him.'

'Same thing,' the sergeant said briskly to the constable. 'Leave nothing unopened, no piece of furniture unmoved.'

'And you–' the sergeant turned to the one remaining constable – 'you start here. Beginning with that dresser.'

The policeman went to the dresser and pulled out the drawers. He tipped them upside down on the floor, checking the backs before rummaging through the contents.

'There's a book here, Sarge.' He held up Megan's exercise book. Megan gripped the wooden spoon so hard her knuckles turned white as the sergeant flicked through the pages.

'Lot of transactions in here, Mrs Powell. Lot of money changing hands. Business good?' The sergeant raised his eyes slowly and stared at Megan.

'I can't grumble. I'm an agent for Leslie's stores.'

'Some of your customers have been seen in model frocks. The kind of clothes you can't buy in Leslie's.'

'My aunt sells clothes that the local dressmakers make up on spec,' Bethan said defensively as she returned from upstairs.

'That so?' The sergeant closed the book and laid it on the table in front of him. 'Now that's not what I heard. But then I hear a lot of funny things. Know what the "forties" are, Nurse?'

'I've no idea,' Bethan said coldly.

'You surprise me. Never heard of Ali Baba and his forty thieves? I thought every kiddy'd either read the book or seen the pantomime. And then again–' He paused for a moment as he opened a box that the constable had lifted out of the dresser. It was Megan's cosmetics box. Crammed full of lipsticks, perfumes and powder. 'You have your very own "forties" here on the Graig. Thieves one and all, and we're well on our way to rounding them up. It's just Ali Baba's cave of goodies that we're looking for.' He picked up a handful of lipsticks and allowed them to run through his fingers back into the box.

'There's nothing stolen in there . . . ' Megan began hotly.

'Did I say there was?' the sergeant continued conversationally. 'Now what was I talking about? Oh yes, these forty thieves. They're good, you know. If not the best.' He walked over to the small window and peered out the back. 'Shop detectives tell us they can get a frock off a display stand in the window of Howell's in Cardiff. Even a twelve-guinea red silk frock. Isn't that right, Mrs Powell?'

Andrew blanched as he recalled the dress that Bethan had worn to the hospital ball.

'They can go into a shop, act pleasantly, even innocently, and walk out with a dozen shirts or blouses tucked into their bags or under their skirts. Coats, costumes, make-up, lipsticks, face powder, perfume. . . . ' He took the box from the table, rattled it, and carried it over to the window. 'All child's play to them. They even manage the odd man's suit, or rug. Nothing's sacred, too hot or too heavy. Isn't that right, Mrs Powell?'

'I don't know what you're talking about.' She picked up a thick bar of green soap from the windowsill above the sink and began to grate it over the water.

The washhouse door banged and William walked in, still barefoot, his hair ruffled.

'And who might you be, young man?' the sergeant asked, stepping over the constable who was still rummaging in the dresser cupboards.

'William Powell. Mr Powell to you,' William asserted full of bravado.

'He's my son,' Megan said defensively.

'Where've you been, lad?'

'Out back. Is it a crime now for a man to visit his own outhouse?' He looked to the ceiling as a loud crash resounded from upstairs.

'That depends on what a man keeps in his outhouse.' The

sergeant nodded to the constable. 'Out there quick. Check the coal shed, the outhouse and anything else in the garden.'

'What right do you have. . . . '

'They've a warrant, William,' Megan warned.

'They've no bloody right to wreck our things.' He picked up the dresser drawers from the kitchen floor.

'Less of that language, young man,' the sergeant warned heavily. 'Or we'll be arresting you for profanity. And for your information we've every right to search any household where we've reason to believe stolen goods are being concealed.'

'You'll find nothing stolen here.'

'That's not what we heard.'

'If you wanted to turn our house over why didn't you ask one of my uncles,' William asked angrily. 'They're all po-faced coppers just like you. . . . '

'William,' Megan admonished.

'Not just like me, lad. They're related to you. That's why we had to draft the Cardiff boys in to do this little job.'

Boots thundered down the stairs. The two constables came in with the entire contents of Megan's wardrobe in their arms. They threw the clothes on top of the box of cosmetics on the table.

'Good-quality clothes, Sarge, just like they showed us.'

'So they are. You have anything to say, Mrs Powell?'

'Those are the only clothes I possess.'

'And?'

'And nothing. Do you expect me to walk around naked?'

'Not naked,' he fingered a silk blouse, 'but not dolled up to the nines either. Where did you buy these?'

'Local dressmakers, mostly. Women on the Graig may not have the money of the crache, but we've eyes in our head. We buy material on Ponty market and copy what's in the shops.'

'Copy?' He took a closer look at the stitching on the blouse.

'Cheap sewing machines can sew as well as expensive ones,' Megan pronounced bitterly.

'Let's get this straight.' He held up the blouse. 'You're saying this was made here, on the Graig?'

'I'm not sure.'

'What do you mean, you're not sure?'

266

'I don't keep books on where I get all my clothes. Some of them are presents. From friends,' she snapped.

'Gentlemen friends?'

'You mind what you're saying to my mother,' William broke in hotly.

The constable barged into the washhouse from the garden.

'Nothing, Sarge. Back's clean,' he announced.

'Sure nothing's been flushed down the toilet?' the sergeant demanded.

'Nothing I can see, Sergeant.'

'Put your hand down, did you?' William enquired snidely.

'No patches of loose earth, no signs of recent burial? Nothing under the coal in the coalhouse?' the sergeant continued, ignoring William's question.

'Nothing, Sarge,' the constable insisted. 'I looked. And there's precious little of anything in the coalhouse. Even coal.'

'Price it is are you surprised?' Megan prodded as many of the clothes under water as she could.

'You two, back upstairs,' the sergeant ordered the two constables who'd carried Megan's clothes into the kitchen. 'And you, back to the dresser.' He pointed to the policeman in the washhouse.

The constable pushed past Megan's washtub. As he did so he looked down.

'My mam never does that,' he criticised abstractedly.

'What, lad?' the sergeant asked.

'Puts dark clothes in with light. She says they run.'

The next thirty minutes crawled past at a snail's pace. Bethan stood, frozen to the wall that separated kitchen and passage, too shocked and too shamed to look Andrew in the eye, as the policemen pulled garment after garment from the boiler. All were dripping wet. Some had shrunk. On some the colours were running, but most were still recognisable as quality clothes. And each and every one matched a description on a long list that the sergeant constantly referred to and checked them off against.

Megan stood still and silent, a pale effigy as they dragged the clothes from the tub. She didn't even object when they heaved the sopping, soaking mess of cloth over the rug and table in the kitchen through the passage and out of the front door. Only when the tub contained nothing but water did the sergeant ask if she had anything to say. She lifted her head, looked at him once before turning to William and Bethan.

'Only that I, and I alone, am responsible for this. No one in this house except myself knew where my stock came from.'

'Your suppliers?'

'I'm not prepared to say any more,' she said sternly, lifting her chin defiantly.

'You won't tell us who did your thieving for you, yet you expect us to believe that your family are innocent? That they lived here, saw you sell these clothes to your cronies day after day, without knowing where they came from?'

'It's the truth,' Megan insisted fervently.

The sergeant studied her. Cool, calm, unflustered, she showed no signs of emotion and he knew he would get no further with her while they remained in the house. He shouted for the constables to finish whatever they were doing in the front room and upstairs. Charlie left the position he'd taken up in the hall while they'd carried out the clothes, and returned to the kitchen. William put his hand on his mother's shoulder.

'Go to Diana, Will,' she said abruptly. 'You'll have to look after her now.'

'Mam. . . . '

'Just do it,' she said harshly. 'Go on, Will,' she added in a softer tone. 'For me.'

He pushed his way past the policemen on to the stairs where Diana and Maud, still wearing their nightdresses, were huddled together. He stepped over them. Sitting one step behind he put his arms around their shoulders.

'Doctor John,' the sergeant addressed Andrew, 'I'm sorry to have kept you here, sir, but it's against regulations for anyone to enter or leave a house during a search. Excepting police officers of course. I hope you understand.'

'I understand,' Andrew said hollowly, looking anywhere but at Bethan.

'You're free to go.'

Andrew walked over the soaking wet linoleum and rug towards the door.

'Aren't you forgetting something, sir?' the sergeant asked as Andrew reached the door.

'Like what, Sergeant?'

'Don't all doctors carry a bag?'

'Only sometimes, Sergeant.'

He turned on his heel, walked out of the house, and straight into a tightly packed crowd of people. The pavement was jammed for a good twenty yards either side, with women, children and men craning their necks, desperate to catch a glimpse of what was going on inside the house. A sudden loud screaming to the left caught everyone's attention. The sea of heads turned as though pivoted on an extension of a single neck. Three large, red-faced, burly policemen were dragging a plump, dishevelled woman from the house next door. She was completely hysterical. A man stood behind her, hemmed in the doorway by another policeman. He was holding a baby in his arms and a toddler by the hand. He shouted something to the woman, but the sound of her cries drowned out his words. Three other children of various ages and sizes tried to keep a grip on the woman's skirt, all of them bawling at the top of their voices. Two of the policemen uncurled their fingers as the third bundled the woman into the van. The door slammed, the engine started and the van careered off up the street. Someone threw a stone. It hit the side of the van and rebounded into the crowd.

'Next one to pull a trick like that gets arrested,' an authoritative voice shouted. 'Man, woman or child, it makes no difference.'

Andrew recognised the imposing figure of Superintendent George Hunt who ran Pontypridd police station with military precision.

'Doctor,' he greeted Andrew. 'I wouldn't stay here if I was you,' he cautioned seriously. 'There might be trouble.'

'I came here on a call,' Andrew explained, perpetuating the fiction Bethan had concocted.

'If we need medical assistance we'll send for the police surgeon,' the superintendent said shortly.

'I was just on my way.' Trying to ignore the angry faces, and angrier talk of the crowd, Andrew fought his way to his car. One or two men blocked his passage, but once they saw who he was they stepped aside, allowing him to open the door and climb in.

All he could think of as he drove down the Graig hill was just how narrow an escape he'd had. Not only his own, but his father's hard-earned reputation would have been on the line if the police had decided to take him down to the station for questioning along with Megan. And Bethan – he was grateful to her for her quick wits – he could never have lied as promptly, or manufactured an excuse as good as the one she had, which enabled him to leave straight after the search. It had been clever of her. But at the same time he was absolutely bloody furious that she'd risked his good name and character by taking him to Megan's in the first place.

It wasn't until later, after he'd shaved, bathed and retired to bed for a couple of hours' sleep, that he thought about the full implications of Megan's arrest from a viewpoint other than his own. If – and from what little he knew, the 'if' was likely to be accomplished fact – if Megan had been charged with selling stolen goods, that made Bethan, Laura and half the women on the Graig guilty of receiving them. A scandal on that scale would rock Pontypridd. He could hear his mother's voice, scathing in its condemnation –

'Did you really expect anything else, dear, from a girl born and brought up on the Graig?'

Chapter Sixteen

Megan's house fell unnaturally silent after she was taken away. Charlie alone seemed capable of logical thought or action. First he saw to the two girls sitting on the stairs with William.

'Hadn't you better get upstairs and dress?' he suggested gruffly in his guttural accent. The sound of his voice roused Bethan. She stared despairingly at the chaos around her. Then she thought of Megan, alone in the police station, no, not alone, they had taken Judy Jones and Betty Morgan, she'd heard their screams. Her tired brain groped with what needed to be done, trying to sort out tasks into order of priority. The house had to be put back together again. But Megan needed help.

'William,' she said urgently. 'Run home and get Daddy.'

'But your mother. . . . '

'Don't speak to my mother. Just tell Daddy we need him. Now, quickly. And while you're there find Haydn. Ask him to run down to Griffiths' shop and tell Jenny – ' she hesitated for a moment, then threw caution and euphemism to the wind. Megan had been arrested. If that wasn't an emergency, she didn't know what was – 'and Harry what's happened. Perhaps if Harry Griffiths comes here he can talk to Daddy. Between them they might know what to do.'

William still sat, shell-shocked, on the stairs.

'Go on, Will, what are you waiting for?' she demanded angrily.

'I think I'd better put a pair of shoes and a shirt on first,' he said wearily.

She looked at him and saw that he was still dressed only in his trousers. 'Sorry. Of course you'd better dress.'

'Diana, Maud,' she called out, after William had left the house. 'As soon as you're dressed see what you can do to tidy the mess upstairs.'

'Bethan, it's awful,' Maud wailed. 'They've torn the pillows and bolsters open. There's feathers everywhere. . . . '

'Find Auntie Megan's sewing kit. Diana will know where it is.

Stuff the feathers back in and sew them up,' Bethan ordered sharply. She bent to the floor and began to gather the contents of the dresser from the floor. 'I'll start in the washhouse.'

She jumped at the sound of Charlie's voice; she'd forgotten he was there. A few minutes later she heard the sound of the boiler being dragged over the flagstones towards the back door, closely followed by the gush of running water as he turned the tap set in the bottom of the boiler on, over the outside drain.

She put the things she'd picked up on to a chair. Then she looked at the floor. It was soaking wet and filthy, heavily marked by the dirt carried in on the hobnailed boots of the constables. She gathered the rag rugs and carried them out the back, then she went to get the scrubbing brush and bucket from under the sink. She found the bucket along with the soap Megan had been grating, but there was no sign of the brush or floorcloth. She looked around, before walking across to the boiler and lifting the lid, but there were only the dregs of dirty water in the bottom.

'Have you seen the scrubbing brush?' she asked Charlie.

'If it was in here they probably took it with the clothes,' he said, heaving the boiler back into position.

Bethan's self-control finally snapped. 'The swines. The absolute swines!' she shouted, wanting to scream something far worse, but unsure what. 'How in hell can we clean up when they haven't even left us a cloth or a brush to do it with!' Venting her anger she kicked the boiler viciously. Then, as abruptly as it had erupted, her fury subsided. She sank weakly against the drum and began to cry.

'Nurse Powell? Bethan?' Charlie's fingers banded around her forearms like metal vices. 'Come on, pull yourself together. You have to be strong,' he hissed quietly. He was close, so close she could see the frown lines etched in his pale forehead. 'William and Diana are good children. But they are just that. Children. They need you.'

'They have you and Sam,' she muttered mutinously.

'No they don't,' he asserted forcefully. 'Sam and I are lodgers. Drifters. Here today, gone tomorrow. No one can rely on us. Do you understand? No one. You have to pull yourself together for their sakes. You and your family are all they've got.'

She looked at him, made a supreme effort and stiffened her

resolve along with her back. 'I'm sorry,' she apologised bleakly. 'That was unforgivable. It won't happen again.'

He released his hold on her, but she could still feel the force of his fingers compressing her flesh. Lifting her arm she wiped the tears from her eyes on her sleeve. Charlie looked at her and nodded briefly, as though he approved of her self-control. 'I'll go up the road and borrow what we need. Then we can start cleaning this mess up.'

A procession of neighbours came to Megan's house that morning. They brought dinner plates piled high with thick wedges of bread pudding and Welsh cakes, pop bottles filled with home-made elderberry, blackberry and nettle wine – and sympathy. They sat on the chairs in Megan's kitchen and spoke in reverential, hushed tones. The only way they knew how to express their feelings for what had happened was by following the pattern that had been set down to cope with a different kind of loss. But it took Diana to voice what was uppermost in everyone's mind.

'Anyone'd think someone had died here,' she said loudly as one group of visitors trooped out and another in.

Haydn came with orders from Evan that Maud should go home at once, and stay there. He told Bethan that their father had decided to walk across town to Bonvilston Road to see if he could find Megan's brother Huw, the one person Bethan hadn't thought of contacting. William was walking down the hill with him as far as Harry Griffiths' shop.

Old Mrs Evans and Annie Jones knocked on the door and followed Haydn into the house. They took one look at the feathers floating down the stairs and set to work with Megan's mending kit. While they repaired the damage Haydn gave Charlie a hand to move the heavier pieces of furniture back into position. With Annie's help Diana and Bethan soon managed to restore order to the bedrooms, and once the repairs were finished and there was only cleaning to be done, Bethan left Diana to it and went to see to the downstairs.

She was scrubbing the constables' dirty footprints from the washhouse floor when William returned with the news that Harry Griffiths had thrown all caution to the wind and was going to the police station in person.

'Are you sure that's what he intends to do?' she asked.

'I'm upset, not stupid, Beth,' he said angrily.

'Does his wife know?' she questioned anxiously.

'She was in church. And as Jenny wasn't too keen on the idea of staying at home to face her mother's return on her own, I brought her back with me.'

'I don't think that was a good idea, William.'

'If you won't make Jenny welcome I know someone who will,' William said irritably, watching Haydn sneak a kiss from Jenny when they thought no one was watching.

Bethan decided Harry Griffiths was a fool to flaunt a relationship that he and Megan had struggled to keep discreet, if not secret, for so long. But not wanting to add to Diana and William's problems she kept her opinion to herself and carried on scrubbing. When the floor was clean enough for her, she washed out the scrubbing brush Charlie had borrowed, tipped the dirty water down the outside drain and rinsed the bucket. Then she took a short breather. Leaning against the outside wall of the house she watched the sunshine as it played over the square of tilled earth where Megan grew a few vegetables. Then she noticed her uniform. Her dress, apron and stockings were filthy. It was just as well that the sun was shining, she thought wearily, because at the risk of offending Mrs Richards and the other chapel-going neighbours, who checked back gardens for evidence with which to confront those who broke the 'no work on the Sabbath' rule, she'd have to wash them before the stains had time to set. Mud was a devil to shift, even when it was fresh.

She picked up the bucket, stowed it under Megan's sink and checked the meat safe that hung high on the pantry ceiling. There were two breasts of lamb in it. While Haydn stoked up the oven with a bucket of coal, she boned and rolled the breasts, leaving Jenny and Diana to prepare the potatoes and cauliflower that she found on the pantry floor. Someone – she wasn't sure if it was Haydn, William or Charlie – opened one of the bottles of home-made wine while the dinner was cooking. Forgetting her sleepless night and the fact that she hadn't eaten since midnight she downed the glassful Haydn handed her in one gulp. It went straight to her head and her limbs. They felt strange, heavy and leaden, but the feeling didn't stop her from drinking a second glass. Or a third. And by the time Evan returned with the news that Huw was going to the police station to see if he could find out anything, the second bottle had been opened.

It seemed ridiculous to stick rigidly to tradition in a household that had been turned upside down during the course of one short morning, but she dished up dinner at one-thirty, as Megan would have done. No one was very hungry, but all the bottles of wine that the neighbours had brought round were drunk. The brews weren't quite up to the standard of the hock or sparkling wine in Dr John senior's cellar, she decided critically when she was well into her third glass of blackberry wine, but they certainly had the desired effect.

'This is good wine, Dad,' Haydn commented as he refilled the tumblers. 'Why don't we ever have home-made wine at home?'

'You know why,' Evan replied tersely.

Bethan kicked Haydn under the table. She was old enough to remember the arguments between Caterina, who'd been an expert wine brewer, and her mother, who wouldn't have a bottle of anything alcoholic kept, let alone drunk or brewed in the house.

'You working tonight, love?' Evan asked her.

'Yes,' she answered, surprised that someone should want to talk about the normal world. In all the trauma of Megan being carted off to jail she'd forgotten about mundane things like hospital and work.

'In that case you'd better go home and get some sleep.'

'I'll clear the dishes first.'

'Diana and I'll wash them,' Jenny offered, 'and Haydn will dry.'

'If you get him to do that, you'll get him to do more than he's ever done at home,' Evan joked.

'I do plenty at home,' Haydn protested.

'I could sleep on one of the beds upstairs,' Bethan interrupted.

'No point, love,' Evan said. 'I'm staying. Tell your mother I'll stop here for as long as I'm needed.'

'I'm nineteen, Uncle Evan,' William said angrily, spoiling for a fight. 'Old enough to look after the house and my sister.'

'No one doubts that, Will, but when your Uncle Huw gets here there'll be decisions to be made on things like solicitors. Three heads will be better than one. And tomorrow morning you may need an extra pair of legs to run errands to the bank, or police station.'

'I suppose you're right,' William conceded grudgingly.

'Go on, girl, off you go,' Evan said to Bethan.

She left the table and took her cloak from the peg behind the door.

'Thanks for staying and doing everything, Beth.' Diana gave her a bear hug and a kiss.

'Yes, thank you, Beth,' William said gratefully. 'See you later?'

'I'll call in on my way to work.' Bethan walked unsteadily to the door. The crowds had dispersed, but there were still puddles on the pavements where the policeman had heaped the wet clothes. Without thinking she turned left at the end of the road and walked up to Rhiannon Pugh's house. Opening the door she went in and bumped into Phyllis in the passage.

'I'm dreadfully sorry.' She hesitated, ashamed and embarrassed at breaking in on Phyllis's privacy unannounced.

'It's all right,' Phyllis said. 'You've come from your aunt's?'

'Yes.'

'We're very sorry, Bethan. It's a terrible thing to have happened.'

'Thank you.' Bethan was amazed that Rhiannon and Phyllis, incarcerated as they were by Phyllis's shame, should have heard the news so soon.

'If there's anything we can do?' Phyllis offered hesitantly.

Bethan struggled to suppress the tide of hysteria that rose in her throat. The thought of the outcast helping the criminal seemed very peculiar. 'There's nothing anyone can do,' she said finally. 'That's why I left.'

'I shouldn't keep you.' Phyllis glanced self-consciously at her stomach.

'Phyllis,' the wine had loosened Bethan's tongue, and she spoke where she normally would have stayed silent, 'if you ever need a nurse who's half a trained midwife I'm only across the road. I'll come over day or night, you do know that.'

'Thank you.' Phyllis flushed crimson. 'I might be grateful for help some time.'

'I'd better get going. I'm whacked. I worked all last night and I'm on again tonight.'

276

'You must be exhausted,' Phyllis agreed. She opened the back door. 'It's been nice talking to you, Bethan. You'll be coming through tonight?'

'If you don't mind.'

'We'll be glad to see you.'

Bethan walked up the steps, opened the door in the back wall and stepped out into Graig Avenue. A crowd of children were playing in the dirt in front of her house. They fell silent when they saw her, a sure sign that the news had already travelled from one end of the Graig to the other. She passed them, climbed up to her front door and opened it. A foul smell of burning cloth greeted her. Panicking at the thought that hot coals had dropped out of the stove on to the hearthrug, she dropped her cloak on the passage floor and ran into the kitchen. Her mother was standing in front of the stove, a knee-deep pile of clothes heaped on the rag rug at her feet. The stove door was open and she was picking up the garments one by one with wooden tongs and stuffing them on top of the coals.

'Stop!' Bethan screamed. She ran across the room and tried to pick up as many of the clothes as she could in an attempt to save them.

'Dad told her to do it, Beth.'

She turned and saw Eddie sitting in the dark corner of the room behind the dresser.

'Chances are they're all nicked, and we can't take the risk of the police coming round and finding them. Not after what's happened to Aunt Megan,' he said despondently. 'Dad said they could have us all up for receiving.'

'I told him,' Elizabeth crowed triumphantly. 'I told your father the first time I clapped eyes on Megan. I said she was trouble, but he wouldn't have it. Oh no. Not him.'

Bethan released her hold on the clothes bundled in her arms. They fell limply to the floor. She stared at them. They were so fine – so beautiful. She could never hope to replace them. Not only the things she'd bought for herself, but the suits and shirts she'd bought for the boys. She looked at her hands. She was still holding one frock – the red silk she'd worn to the hospital ball. She lifted it up, resting it against her cheek for a moment. Then she remembered what the sergeant had said:

'They can even take a twelve-guinea red silk frock out of the display case in Howell's window.'

She allowed it to slide through her fingers. 'I need to wash my uniform,' she said flatly. 'As soon as I've done that I'm going to bed.'

'I washed and ironed your spare dress and apron yesterday. They're hanging in your wardrobe,' Elizabeth replied in a tone that, for her, was gentle.

'Thank you, Mam.'

Bethan dragged her feet as she climbed the stairs. She couldn't remember when she'd last felt so tired. Her bedroom window was wide open, the lace curtains blowing in the breeze. She tipped water from the jug into the bowl on the washstand and washed her hands and face. Afterwards she steeled herself to open her wardrobe door. Pushing Maud's clothes aside she saw her uniform. Behind it hung her grey dressing gown, a plain blue serge skirt, two white cotton blouses, and her ringed black velvet. All the clothes she now possessed. She pulled open her dressing-table drawer. Her everyday plain, serviceable underclothes were stacked neatly in a row. The delicate, frothy lace and silk concoctions Megan had given her had gone. Stripping off her uniform, she emptied the pockets and folded it, ready for the wash. Stretching out on the bed in her underclothes she closed her eyes.

She felt as though she'd only been asleep for a few minutes when a loud hammering on the front door woke her. Pulling the pillow over her head she turned over, hoping that whoever it was would get what they'd come for, and go away. Moments later Eddie clumped noisily up the stairs.

'Bethan,' he shouted. 'Bethan, are you awake?'

'I am now,' she answered crossly.

'Uncle John's sent for you. He says he needs you. It's urgent.'

'He doesn't need anyone,' she answered sleepily.

'Your Auntie Hetty's been taken ill,' her mother said as she walked into the room. 'How soon can you get ready?'

Bethan reluctantly dragged herself out of her bed. She felt hot, sticky and dirty, but she made do with tipping more water on to what was already in the bowl. Sponging as much of herself as she could reach with a wet flannel wrung out in the cold soapy water, she rubbed herself dry and dressed quickly in her clean uniform. She only just remembered to run a comb through her hair before tying on her veil. Her mother and Eddie, hat and cap on, waited in the passage for her. Maud was standing beside them.

'Eddie's coming with us,' Elizabeth said briskly, stumbling over her words from nervousness at the summons. 'We may need him to run errands. Maud's staying behind to mind the house.'

Maud smiled at Bethan. She didn't seem to be disappointed at being left out. But then none of them had ever considered a visit to Uncle John's as a great treat.

'Did Uncle John say what was the matter?' Bethan asked, picking up her cloak which was still on the floor where she'd left it.

'No. He sent Tommy Bridges' boy. There wasn't a note, just a message for you to get there as quick as you could because Auntie Hetty'd been taken ill.'

There wasn't time for any more talking. Elizabeth hurried down the hill looking neither left nor right, leaving Bethan to keep up as best she could. Sensing that his sister was exhausted, Eddie lagged behind so he could walk with her. Every muscle in Bethan's body was aching. She forced herself to go on, though every inch of her was crying out for rest.

'Have you any idea what time it is?' she asked Eddie as they passed the chapel.

'It was five o'clock when we left the house.'

Five o'clock! Only another two and a half hours before she had to go back on duty.

'What I can't understand is why Uncle John sent for you. If Aunt Hetty's that ill he would have been better off sending for the doctor,' Eddie said thoughtfully.

'Pure miserliness,' Bethan whispered in a voice too low to carry to her mother. 'He would have to pay a doctor, and he doesn't have to pay me.'

Elizabeth halted outside the door of a large stone house built a few doors downhill from the chapel. She rapped the door hard and John Joseph Bull opened it himself. His tie was askew, his collar crumpled. Unheard-of, previously unseen phenomena.

'Quick,' he cried out in anguish. Stepping on to the doorstep he heaved Bethan into the house. 'In the scullery. Quick.' 'The

279

scullery?' Strange name for a washhouse Bethan thought in one of those peculiar moments of logical clarity that often accompanies severe shock.

Hetty Bull was lying on the floor in front of the gas stove that John Joseph had bought to save the expense of feeding the kitchen range with coal throughout the summer months. Her feet were curled around the leg of the wash boiler, and the rubber tube that connected the boiler to the gas supply had been removed from the boiler end of the connection and was firmly clamped between Hetty's teeth.

'I sent for you as soon as I found her – you will do something?' It was a plea from the heart.

Elizabeth moaned. Eddie stumbled to the back door and heaved his Sunday dinner up in the yard. Bethan looked around. The windows and doors in the washhouse were wide open but she could still smell gas.

'You have to do something,' John Joseph begged frantically. 'You have to do. . . . ' He wove his fingers together ready for prayer, fell to his knees and sobbed.

One look at Hetty was enough. There was nothing Bethan or anyone else could do to save her. Her face was blue, her lips black. Her eyes, wide open, stared vacantly at the ceiling. Bethan knelt by Hetty's side and gently removed the tube from her mouth. Someone, presumably her uncle, had already turned off the gas. She closed Hetty's eyes and straightened her bent limbs.

'I'm sorry, Uncle John, she's dead. Been dead for some time by the look of her. You'd better send for the undertaker and the doctor.' For the first time in her life she wasn't afraid of him. 'You'll need the doctor to sign the death certificate,' she explained.

'Bethan,' he begged. 'Please, Bethan, send for someone you know. I can't have this – ' he looked down at the gas tubing – 'this . . . on the death certificate. Think of what people will say. The scandal. . . . '

Then she understood why her uncle had sent for her. His wife was dead and he was worried about gossip. He couldn't bear the thought of fingers being pointed, of the ruin a scandal like this would make of his life.

'Eddie?' she called out to her brother. 'Run and get Fred the dead. Tell him what's happened and ask him to come here as quickly as he can. Then go to the hospital and tell them you have to get hold of Doctor Lewis. Remember the name. Doctor Trevor Lewis. Tell them it's an emergency.'

'Wouldn't it be easier if I had a note or something?' Eddie asked. She picked up a pad and pencil that was half lying under her aunt. There was writing on the top page. Without thinking she tore off the first sheet and scribbled a note for Eddie. 'Go on now, quickly,' she ordered brusquely.

Sickened yet fascinated by the sight of the dead body, Eddie couldn't resist taking one last look before rushing out of the door.

'Did Hetty write that note?' her mother asked.

Bethan picked up the piece of paper she'd discarded earlier. She read it before passing it on to Elizabeth.

So sorry. I bought clothes from Megan. I can't live with the sin on my conscience. Forgive me. Hetty.

Bethan watched as her mother read it and passed it on to John Bull. Typical of Hetty, Bethan thought despondently. To apologise and ask for forgiveness. Even for dying.

Chapter Seventeen

The undertaker arrived before Trevor. Bethan made him wait in the front parlour while she stayed in the washhouse with the body. Her mother busied herself making cups of tea for everyone and fussing over John Joseph, who sat slumped in his study, his head in his hands.

'Doctor's here,' her mother announced at last, opening the door and showing Trevor in. She closed the door on them.

'You look done in, Beth,' Trevor said tactlessly as he crouched next to the body.

'I feel done in,' she agreed wearily. 'But as we're into handing out compliments, you don't look much better.'

'I've had a rough afternoon down the police station.' He opened Hetty's eyes, checking her reflexes in the perfunctory manner doctors employ when examining corpses. 'A couple of women went completely hysterical after being arrested for shoplifting. Two constables were injured, not to mention what they did to the cells.'

'The women?' Bethan asked anxiously. 'Are they all right?'

'One of them cracked her knuckles punching a policeman in the eye, apart from that they're fine.'

'You didn't come across a Megan Powell by any chance did you?'

'Your aunt?'

'Yes, my aunt,' she agreed miserably, loath to share her family's disgrace with anyone, even Trevor.

'No, I didn't see her. But then there were a lot of them there, and I only saw the ones who needed calming down.' He took his thumb from Hetty's eyelid and looked at Bethan. 'Your aunt's been arrested?' he asked.

'This morning.'

'Bethan, I'm sorry,' he apologised. 'I wouldn't have said anything if I'd realised. . . . '

'It's all right. Really.' She picked up Hetty's cold, dead hand.

'And this is your aunt too?'

'On my mother's side.'

'And I thought *I* was having a day of it.' He shook his head, opened his case and removed a death certificate.

'You said there was a lot of them. How many?' she demanded.

'I'm not sure. About twenty I think, but the sergeant said they were bringing in more. He was jubilant. Said they'd cracked a well-organised gang that they'd been after for years.'

'The forties,' she murmured.

'Sorry?' Trevor asked, bewildered.

'That's what the sergeant called them. "The forty thieves".'

Trevor straightened Hetty's head as he finished his examination.

'Bethan, I hate having to do this, but I'm going to have to put gas poisoning on the certificate.'

'I know.' She lifted up her aunt's hands and crossed them over her chest.

'That means the coroner will have no choice but to bring in a verdict of suicide.'

'You don't have to explain the situation to me. But my uncle is waiting in his study. I think he'd appreciate a word.'

'How has he taken this – ' Trevor pointed at Hetty with his fountain pen.

'Badly. He's very . . . very upset at the thought of what a verdict of suicide could do to his reputation,' she said hesitantly.

'Eddie was telling me he's a minister.'

'That's right.'

'Then this is going to hit him doubly hard.' He finished writing, and stuffed his pen into the top pocket of his suit. 'You on duty tonight?'

'Yes.'

'I'll take you down to the hospital after I've talked to your uncle.'

'You don't have to,' she said wretchedly.

'I know. But I have to go there anyway.'

'Before you see my uncle, go into the front parlour and ask the undertaker to come in please.'

'I'll do that.'

Bethan helped Fred to wash her aunt and lay her out. While

they cleaned the body, Elizabeth went upstairs and sorted through Hetty's things. She returned with a white shroud, socks and cap that Hetty had stitched in preparation for the eventuality of death. Bethan dressed her aunt with Fred's help. When she'd finished, her mother fastened a plain gold cross around Hetty's neck, and eventually, after a great deal of difficulty, managed to force back on the wedding ring that Hetty had removed before gassing herself.

Fred scooped the body into his arms and carried it into the front parlour, where the coffin stood open and waiting.

'Do you want me to screw the lid down, Mrs Powell?' he asked Elizabeth.

'No . . . yes . . . I don't know.' Elizabeth hesitated. 'Bethan, what do you think we should do?'

Bethan stared at her mother in amazement. She'd never consulted her about anything before.

'Better close it,' she answered decisively. 'But don't screw the lid down. Then if anyone wants to look at her they can.'

'Righto, Nurse. Now, about the arrangements?'

'You're going to have to talk to my uncle about those.' Bethan glanced at the parlour clock. It was a quarter-past seven. 'I have to go to work.'

'I'll see him as soon as he's finished with the doctor.'

He left the room and hovered discreetly in the hall.

'I'd like to stay, Mam, I really would,' she apologised. 'But there's no one else to take over the ward.'

'I understand perfectly, Beth,' her mother said sincerely, without a trace of her usual sarcasm. 'Thank you for what you've already done. I'm not sure I could have coped without you.'

'You would have done fine, Mam. You always do.' Realising how badly shaken her mother'd been by Hetty's death, she hugged her for the first time since childhood. 'See you in the morning.'

She met Trevor in the passage.

'Ready?' he asked.

'Quite ready.'

They walked out into the street, passing a few people who were on their way to evensong.

'I hope my uncle's made other arrangements.'

'If he hasn't one of the deacons will come down and find out what's happened.'

'I suppose you're right.' She climbed into his battered car, so different from Andrew's.

'I thought I'd had a rotten day. But you've had a worse one,' he observed as he sat beside her.

'That's life.' She tried to smile at him, but tears started in her eyes.

'Sunday nights are generally quiet. If you're lucky you might get some sleep.'

'Don't tempt fate.'

He drove in through the main gates and parked the car.

'Thanks for the lift, thanks for coming when I needed you, and thank you for talking to my uncle. I know it couldn't have been easy.' She kissed his cheek.

'Beth?' The doctor in him registered the signs of shock – the pale, strained look on her face; the dark smudges beneath her eyes; the way her hand trembled as she reached for the door handle. 'Your uncle told me about the suicide note. I'm most dreadfully sorry. If there's anything else I can do . . . ' His voice trailed helplessly.

'That's all I seem to be hearing from people. Be different, Trevor. Offer to take me out and get me drunk.'

'Would it help?'

'Probably not. But it would be fun. See you.'

He followed the progress of her tall slim figure as she walked across the women's exercise yard. When she disappeared around the corner of the main kitchen, he looked at his wristwatch. He stared thoughtfully at the grey buildings for a moment, then drove around in a wide circle before manoeuvring back out through the main gates.

When Andrew woke, the muted light that percolated through the thick lace at his bedroom windows was a deep gold. He blinked at his surroundings, then his thoughts turned to the events of the morning. He felt sick as he contemplated facing his parents, but he knew he ought to see them as soon as he was dressed. Better they hear what had happened in Leyshon Street from him first. In a town the size of Pontypridd there'd be no shortage of people wanting to tell them that he'd been caught sitting in a house the police had raided. Enough of their acquaintances had frowned on his relationship with Bethan to want to indulge in that delight.

He threw back the sheets and blankets, stepped naked from his bed and wandered into the bathroom. He put the plug in the bath and turned on the taps. While the water was running he returned to the bedroom to check the time on his pocket watch. Nearly seven o'clock. He'd slept practically the whole day away. Leaving the bedroom he went to check the food situation in his kitchen. Despite the assertions of independence he'd made to Bethan, he still ate most of his meals in his parents' house. The only things in his cupboard were a tea caddy half full of tea, a jar of sugar, a tin of coffee and a tin of shortbread biscuits. Crunching a biscuit he lit the gas and put the kettle on.

Half an hour later, bathed, shaved and dressed casually in white flannels, open-necked shirt and a cream cashmere sweater he walked across the garden to his father's house. The french doors to the drawing room were open. His mother was sitting in a chair in front of them reading the latest copy of *The Lady*.

'Andrew,' his father greeted him from behind the bar. 'Joining us for dinner?'

'If it's all right with you.'

'Of course it's all right, darling. It's only fruit, cheese, cold meat and salads. But there's plenty,' his mother said as she laid the magazine down on a side table.

'That sounds fine,' he murmured absently. 'I've been sleeping all day, so I couldn't face anything heavy. Thank you.' He took the whisky his father poured him and sat on the sofa. Leaning back he stretched out his legs.

'You look tired, Andrew,' his mother observed solicitously.

He tossed off a good half of the whisky and cleared his throat, dreading their reaction to what he was about to say. 'There's something I have to discuss with you,' he said, broaching the subject with difficulty.

'Would it have anything to do with a police raid on a certain house in Leyshon Street early this morning?' his father asked.

'It would.' He sat forward cradling the whisky glass between his hands. 'I take it you already know all about it.'

286

'Did you expect us not to?' his mother said in a brittle voice. His father flashed her a warning look.

'Superintendent Hunt telephoned this morning.' His father carried the whisky bottle over from the bar and topped up Andrew's glass. 'He said he was very concerned to see you there. He didn't say so in actual words, but I got the distinct impression that he didn't entirely believe your story.'

'I sensed that much,' Andrew replied honestly.

'You told him you were there to check on a patient?'

'Bethan did,' Andrew answered sheepishly.

'Whatever,' his father remarked dismissively. 'The long and the short of it is, he's suspicious. He also went out of his way to make sure your presence in the house went unnoticed by the press, which I must say in the circumstances was uncommonly kind of him. He couldn't do anything about the people who were there, of course. But with luck they should have plenty of other gossip to occupy themselves with.'

'You have to admit, Andrew, that you've hardly been discreet about your relationship with that woman,' Mrs John broke in feelingly. 'From what Superintendent Hunt told your father it's common knowledge. A topic of conversation to be discussed in every household on the Graig.'

'What happened in Leyshon Street today is hardly Bethan's fault,' Andrew insisted defensively.

'Do you really expect us to believe that her aunt was one of the ringleaders in a gang of shoplifters, directly involved with selling stolen goods, and Bethan didn't know a thing about it?'

'I'm certain she didn't.'

'What about her clothes?' Mrs John asked pointedly. 'The few times I've seen her she's always been extremely well dressed. Where did she get them from?'

'Her aunt,' he admitted.

'I see.'

'It's not what you think. . . . '

'What we think is of little importance, Andrew,' Dr John said firmly, breaking up the impending argument between mother and son. 'It's what the whole town thinks that concerns me. I've been a physician here all my working life. I have a certain standing in the county of Glamorgan. I, and my family, are expected to

287

behave in the accepted manner. Like Caesar's wife all of us have to be above reproach and suspicion. And if I, and you after me, am to continue to work and live here I don't see how it can be otherwise.'

'I'm sorry to have brought this whole sorry mess to your door,' Andrew apologised contritely.

'Well now you've brought it, the question is what do you intend to do about it?' His mother left her seat and paced to the cold, empty fireplace, screened off by tapestry for the summer.

'I don't know.' Andrew left the sofa, walked over to the bar and poured himself another whisky.

'It's plain enough to me.' A note of hysteria crept into Isabel John's voice. 'You have to break off whatever's going on between you two,' she shouted. 'Immediately. . . . '

'Didn't you say earlier that you had something to check in the kitchen with Cook, dear?' Dr John prompted gently.

'No . . . I. . . . '

'You wanted to tell her which of the cold meats to cut,' he prompted.

'Yes I did.' She squared her shoulders and took a deep breath. 'Thank you.' She looked at her son as she left the room. 'I'm only thinking of you, darling,' she said softly.

Andrew took his glass and walked over to the open window. He preferred his mother's hysteria to her understanding.

'I think the best thing you can do, son, is go away for a while. You obviously need time to think things out for yourself. Why don't you take Alec's father up on his offer? Go up to London for a few months. Work on his surgical team. It will be good experience for you. Stand you in good stead, no matter whether you finally opt for general or hospital practice.'

'I'll think about it,' Andrew said dully, promising nothing as he stared blindly at the garden.

'A short spell in London will enable you to put things in perspective. I'll be able to find a locum to fill your place easily enough, and until I do, Trevor'll double up. He's only too keen to earn extra cash these days. You could go up tomorrow. Stay with Fe and Alec. You know they'd love to have you.'

Andrew continued to gaze blankly at the magnificent display of summer roses that formed the centrepiece of his parents' garden.

'Just how much does this girl mean to you?' his father asked bluntly.

'I don't know.' He wasn't lying. After the events of that morning he genuinely didn't know what he felt for Bethan. His feelings were in turmoil. When he was with her all he wanted to do was undress her and himself and make love. But then again, the sensation wasn't a new one. He'd experienced it before, with other girls. It was just that in London there'd been many other girls. Here in Pontypridd there was only one.

Elated at Andrew's honest revelation Dr John picked up the whisky bottle and joined his son in front of the window.

'I got entangled with a working-class girl once,' he confided as he refilled both their glasses. 'Now your mother's not around I don't mind telling you she was magnificent. Especially between the sheets, if you get my meaning.'

'I get your meaning.' Andrew stared at his father in amazement. Having never considered his father's youth, or the women he'd known before his mother, he was slightly shocked by the revelation.

'You can want to make love to a woman without being in love,' Dr John persisted. 'All sorts of men have found that out. My father told me once that there were two kinds of women. The ones you dally with, and the ones you marry with.'

'Isn't that a little old-fashioned?'

'The war changed many things. But it didn't change people's quality. Take your Bethan for instance. She's certainly pretty enough,' he conceded. 'Curves in all the right places, nice smile, nice enough manners, but a bit quiet, wouldn't you agree?'

'She was when she was here,' Andrew concurred ambiguously.

'What I'm trying to say is that she's probably been careful to show you only her best side. Think about it, Andrew. Can you honestly tell me that you really know her? Hasn't the thought crossed your mind that she's reticent when she's here because she knows that she doesn't fit into our style of life?'

'But she isn't quiet when we're alone together.'

'How many deep, meaningful discussions have you had with her?' Dr John pressed.

'A few,' Andrew retorted sullenly.

'When you both had your clothes on?'

Andrew reddened.

'I'm sorry, that was below the belt, but look at her family, son. What do you know about them? Her father's a miner on short-time working,' he answered for him. 'Her eldest brother earns a pittance in the Town Hall. The other one can't even find a job. And there's a daughter still in school so she can't contribute anything. I've seen enough families like that to know what the temptations are. They see people like ourselves, living well, in a reasonable house with a car; eating the right food, with enough money in our pockets to visit the right places, and they grow envious. They don't see the work we do, only the rewards, and they go out to get what we have the only way they know how. They turn to crime.'

Andrew wanted to tell his father that he was wrong. Very, very wrong. But then he remembered Megan Powell.

'Have they charged Bethan's aunt?' he asked, hoping against hope to find another way out.

'Oh yes. Her and eighteen other women. And from what the superintendent said to me this morning, they're the tip of the iceberg. There's a lot more to come.' He drank some of his whisky and rocked slightly on his heels. 'Bethan's aunt is as guilty as Cain,' he affirmed strongly. 'You know that, don't you?'

Andrew recalled the clothes that Bethan and Charlie had carried through the kitchen and thrown into the wash boiler. Bethan's complicity was something he could hardly bring himself to think about, let alone divulge to his father. But much as he might want to, he couldn't wipe his memory clean. Just how many Powells were as guilty as Cain? 'What will they do to Mrs Powell?' he asked.

'They'll go easier on her than on some of the others because she's already decided to plead guilty. Saves the court a lot of bother, but then – ' his father refilled both their glasses – 'unfortunately she's refusing to talk. The sergeant said her sentence would be a lot lighter if she fully co-operated. Needless to say she won't.' He shook his head and shrugged his shoulders. 'That's these people all over for you. Misguided sense of loyalty. In the end she'll probably get a heavy fine. An order to make some kind of restitution to the injured shopkeepers will be made, that's if she has any assets to speak of. Plus a long sentence and hard labour of course, to deter anyone from picking up where she left off.'

'How long is long?'

'Ten years. Possibly more. Andrew, do try to see this from your mother's and my point of view. Superintendent Hunt warned us that this is just the beginning. There's more to come. Now just suppose for a minute that Bethan's involved. . . . '

'Dad. . . . '

'Hear me out, Andrew,' he barked. 'What if she's arrested for receiving? You can't even begin to imagine what that would do to you. You've been seen with her around the town. You've taken her to decent places, introduced her to decent people. I'm not decrying your motives in doing that. You were going out with the girl, and because you're the kind of person your mother and I have brought you up to be – honest, uncomplicated and straightforward – you went out with her openly. But everywhere you went together she was seen, smart, well dressed and wearing the kind of clothes that a nurse couldn't possibly afford to buy on a hospital board's wages. Particularly when she's practically been supporting her entire family. Let's look on the bright side. Even if she isn't charged, she'll be seen as a thief's accomplice.'

'But. . . . '

'And if you continue to see her – ' his father didn't quite manage to conceal the edge of anger that was lying just beneath the surface of his outwardly reasonable attitude – 'you'll be tainted by the same gossip.'

Andrew sank on to the sofa, his head in his hands.

'Look, I know your mother better than anyone. I know she frequently worries about things that never happen, but in this instance she's right. Go to London, boy. Alec's father will see that you're worked hard, but not so hard that you won't have time for a social life. Meet a few other girls. A month from now you'll be a different man. Take my word for it.'

Mair knocked on the door.

'Dinner?' Dr John asked sharply.

'No sir. It's Doctor Lewis. He says he has to see young Doctor John urgently.'

'Then show him in, Mair.'

291

Trevor walked in. 'I'm sorry to intrude on you like this, sir,' he apologised.

'No intrusion.' Dr John senior was glad of an excuse to break off his talk with Andrew. He had nothing constructive to add. The rest was up to Andrew, and the common sense he fervently hoped would prevail. 'If you haven't a prior engagement, stay to dinner,' he offered hospitably.

'I couldn't possibly.' The slum boy that was never far from the surface invariably made Trevor uneasy in the middle-class atmosphere of Dr John senior's house.

'Nonsense, if you've no other engagement we'd love to have you, wouldn't we, Andrew?'

'What? Oh yes of course, do stay,' Andrew reiterated unconvincingly.

'I need to speak to you, Andrew.'

'And I need to take a trip to the wine cellar. See what I can come up with that will go with cold meat and salad,' said Dr John senior.

'Is this about Bethan?' Andrew asked.

'Yes,' Trevor answered with an embarrassed look at Andrew's father, who was still hovering by the door.

'You may as well say whatever you've got to say in front of my father,' Andrew said with a touch of bitterness. 'If he doesn't already know about it, you can be sure that the superintendent will be on the phone to inform him in the next five minutes.'

'That's unfair, Andrew.'

'At the moment I don't feel very fair.'

'I've just come from Bethan's aunt's house,' Trevor burst out, trying to say what he'd come to say as quickly as possible so he could leave the heavy atmosphere and go to visit Laura. After the events of the day he needed to see her even more than usual.

'Is one of them ill?' Andrew asked anxiously.

'She's dead.'

'Who's dead?' Dr John pressed.

'Bethan's aunt,' Trevor repeated in exasperation.

'But she's in the police station,' Andrew insisted.

'Not Megan Powell. Hetty Bull.'

'The minister's wife!' Andrew exclaimed.

'Yes. She gassed herself. Her husband sent for Bethan as soon

292

as he found her, but there was nothing either of us could do by the time we got there. I saw a note she'd written. Apparently she'd bought some clothes from Megan Powell. Said she couldn't live with herself. I suppose it was impossible for someone as religious as her to come to terms with the idea that she'd worn stolen clothes,' Trevor finished awkwardly.

'The chickens are really coming home to roost on this one,' Dr John murmured, unable to suppress a hint of 'I told you so'.

This second blow, coming so soon after the first, devastated Andrew. He slumped forward on his seat, head in his hands again. The telephone rang and his father went to answer it.

'Bethan looks dreadful,' Trevor ventured. 'She seems to be shouldering a lot of the burden. But she still insisted on going to work tonight.'

'She would,' Andrew said without emotion, inviting no further comment.

'That was the superintendent on the telephone.' Andrew's father stood in the doorway. 'They've arrested two girls. Maud and Diana Powell. Are they related to Bethan?'

'Maud's her younger sister. Diana's her cousin. But they're children. They're only fourteen,' Andrew protested.

'Evidently they're both old enough to steal,' his father pronounced dismissively. 'They wouldn't have been arrested if the police had any doubts about their guilt. And you'd better brace yourself, boy. There's worse.' Dr John took a cigar from the silver box on the bar. A bad sign: Andrew had never seen him smoke before dinner until now. 'Unfortunately for you, and for us as a family, the police suspect there's a connection between you and the nurse they saw in the house this morning.'

'Bethan?' Trevor asked.

Andrew nodded miserably. 'But they haven't arrested her?' It was more a plea than a request for information.

'Not yet they haven't. But in Superintendent Hunt's opinion it's only a matter of time,' his father said firmly, straying well beyond the narrow bounds of the information that Hunt had been prepared to impart. 'Andrew, really, you have no choice. The sooner you're in London the better for everyone concerned. If they arrest her, there's no knowing what she'll say once they get her in the police station. Knowing of our influence with people

293

who matter, she may even send for you. Think of the disgrace.'
When Andrew remained silent he lost his temper.

'Damn it all, boy, if you won't think of yourself, think of me,
of what I've worked for. Of your mother, and Fe. Don't fool
yourself, news of this mess will reach even London, and neither
of them will be able to hold up their heads again. All because
their son and brother got involved with a family of common
thieves. . . . '

Trevor stood up and walked towards the door. 'I have to go.
I'm on duty.'

'You still have to eat, boy, and it's ready. I'll telephone the
hospital to let them know where you are.' Dr John rejected his
excuse out of hand. 'Andrew?' He stood in the doorway, his hand
poised on the doorknob.

Defeated, Andrew looked up at his father. 'You can send a
telegram to Fe and Alec. Tell them I'll be up on the morning
train,' he agreed wretchedly.

'I'll try telephoning them first.' His father left them; a few
moments later they heard him speaking on the telephone in the
hall.

Andrew sat on the sofa staring down into his empty glass. He
wanted to speak to Trevor – to look at him – but he gagged
on the unspoken words. Afraid to say anything in case he saw
something akin to the contempt he felt for himself mirrored in
Trevor's eyes.

The quiet night Trevor had wished for Bethan hadn't materialised.
A mother went into labour. A ward maid, one of only two on
duty, vomited and had to be sent home, making it impossible for
the trainee and the other maid to cope with the normal workload,
let alone the additional strain of looking after a patient in labour.
By two o'clock Bethan felt tired enough to sit on the floor and
cry. But she forced herself to go on. Checking feeding times,
delivering the baby, cutting the cord, washing both mother and
infant, writing reports. There wasn't even time to take a break
until four o'clock in the morning.

When she was finally free she went into the sister's office and
shut the door. The room held so many memories. She only had
to close her eyes to see Andrew standing next to the fireplace,

arms outstretched, ready to embrace her. . . . She opened them again. There was no Andrew. Only two piles of paperwork. And the one that had been completed was by far and away the smaller. Sweeping them both aside she sat down and rested her arms on the desk. For the first time that day she indulged in the luxury of a waking moment to herself. She went over the events of the morning. Saw again the look of horror on Andrew's face as the policemen clumped their way into Megan's house; the shock registering in his eyes when he realised why she and Charlie were running through the house with bundles of clothes in their arms.

Suddenly she remembered that he'd promised to call for her that afternoon. He'd wanted to take her to a garden party. Garden party! They'd discussed it only that morning. It felt like a lifetime ago. So much had happened in the space of a day. She consoled herself with the reflection that even if he'd driven to Graig Avenue she might not have been there. Hetty. . . .

She was tormented by a ghastly, very real image of her aunt the way she'd found her. Lying on the floor of the washhouse, her feet curled around the boiler, dead . . . Dead! As a nurse she'd seen death many times, in many different guises, but apart from her grandmother who'd died peacefully in her sleep, it was the first time she'd witnessed the final tragedy in her own family.

Hot stinging tears of grief and remorse for missed opportunities burned at the corners of her eyes. She hadn't known Aunt Hetty well enough to care about her. Not in the way she cared for Megan. But she'd pitied her. Hetty'd been so small, so fragile – so totally subservient to her overbearing, self-righteous husband. She hadn't had much of a married life – hadn't had much of a life at all. If only she'd made the effort to get to know Hetty better. She might have been able to do something, at least given her a few happy times – hours they could have shared, the way she'd shared part of her life with Megan.

Overwhelmed by grief, misery and sheer loneliness she laid her head on her arms on the desk and allowed her tears to flow, unchecked.

Andrew drove through the town at breakneck speed. On the seat of the car next to him was a letter he'd written to Bethan. He'd penned it after dinner in his father's study while his father and a reluctant, pressganged Trevor had lingered over their coffee and brandy. As soon as he'd finished it he'd returned to the dining room and asked Trevor to deliver it to Bethan after the London train had left. But Trevor had refused. And to his amazement his father had agreed with Trevor.

'You'll have to see her, Andrew,' he declared as he passed the cigars and the brandy bottle round the table a second time. 'Take my word for it. Letters are never final. Not like telling her to her face. A letter will only give her an excuse to see you again and drag the whole thing out. Write to her and you could be enmeshed in the trauma of this for months. Best to see her before you go, even if it means catching a later train. Tell her straight off that it's over. A clean break's what's needed here.'

Neither he nor Trevor had said anything. When they left the table he'd tried to persuade Trevor to join him in his rooms, but Trevor had refused, and left soon afterwards. Trying not to think about the reasons that lay behind Trevor's uncharacteristic reticence, he'd said goodnight to his parents, walked across the garden and packed his bags for London. But all the time he'd been clearing his rooms, shutting away the things he wouldn't need into cupboards, the letter he'd written had lain, like some evil talisman, on the table.

He'd taken a bottle of whisky into the bathroom with him when he bathed, but neither the warm water nor the alcohol soothed him. He'd picked up a new book, one he'd looked forward to reading, from his shelves and carried it to bed, but both sleep and the ability to concentrate on the printed word eluded him. Bethan's image intruded persistently into his mind, colouring whatever he looked at with her presence. He saw her dressed in her uniform, working through the night on the ward. When the half-bottle of whisky was empty and he couldn't stand the screaming silence a moment longer, he left his bed, dressed and went to his car.

He drove into Courthouse Street and parked on the road before walking through the gates into the hospital. The porter called out suspiciously as he passed, then he recognised him and smiled sheepishly.

'Sorry, Doctor John, didn't know there'd been an emergency call.'

'It's all right, Ernie,' Andrew shouted, not wanting to get involved in a discussion about a nonexistent emergency. 'I won't be long.'

'Go ahead, Doctor.'

He walked on through the quiet, deserted yards. The shadows of the tall buildings loomed out to meet him, huge, almost tangible in the indistinct light of the early-morning low moon. He looked up. Lights were burning in the maternity ward, the only lights that burned at full strength in the block. Another birth?

He opened the door slowly, holding it carefully lest it swing back on its hinges and make a noise. Then he climbed the steps, treading lightly, taking them two at a time. A maid and a trainee were settling the last of the babies down after their boiled water feed. He acknowledged them with a brief nod as he walked through to the ward. The glass in the office door shone bright yellow. A light was burning at full strength. That probably meant Bethan was doing her reports. He glanced at his watch. Five o'clock. Not much time before she had to prepare for the morning's change-over. Perhaps it was just as well.

He opened the door without knocking and walked in. She was slumped over the desk. His throat went dry. He thought of Trevor's revelation about her aunt. Had she . . . his heart in his mouth he crept up behind her. Her breath was falling, light, evenly from her parted lips. She was asleep. He leaned against the wall, dizzy with relief. Then he saw her cheeks. They were wet with tears.

He crept to the easy chair next to the fireplace and waited, silently rehearsing what he would say when she woke.

Bethan fell from sleep, landing into consciousness with a start. Her head ached and her limbs were stiff. She opened her eyes, totally disorientated as her mind strove to recognise her surroundings. Then she panicked. She wasn't alone. There was someone in the room with her. She looked around and saw Andrew sitting in one of the chairs next to the gaping black hole in the fireplace. She stared at him, wondering if he were real or a figment of her sleep-numbed imagination.

'You looked so tired I didn't want to wake you,' he said at last.

'I shouldn't have been asleep. If anyone but you had found me

I'd be hauled up before Matron. . . . ' Her hands went to her veil, automatically securing and straightening it. Then she looked at her watch. 'Is that the time? I must check the ward.'

'I'll wait for you.'

She smiled at him as she left, a smile he was unable to return. She walked up and down the aisle between the beds, pausing as she reached the side of the mother who'd just given birth. Then she checked the nursery. She tried not to think of what Andrew wanted. Or why he'd come. She had her suspicions, but until he actually voiced the words they remained just that, suspicions. Eventually she had no reason to tarry longer. She went into the small ward kitchen, washed her hands and face, and made two cups of tea. Then she carried them into the office.

'Tea.' She set the cups on the desk.

'Thank you.' He might have been a stranger she'd just met. She looked at the chair on the other side of the empty fireplace, thought better of it and returned to her seat behind the desk.

'Look, Andrew, about this morning. . . . '

'Beth!' It was as much as he could do to stay where he was. He had to keep reminding himself of what his father had said about two kinds of women. Physical attraction. That's all that lay between them. Nothing more. 'Please don't say anything.' He held up his hand. 'At least not until I've finished. This is going to be hard enough for me as it is.'

She looked down at the pile of reports suspecting, and dreading, what he was about to say.

'I've decided to go to London. At least for a while. Until the scandal . . . until what . . . what happened this morning dies down,' he stammered clumsily. 'I'm taking up Alec's father's offer of a surgical post in Charing Cross,' he explained superfluously.

'Must you?' She spoke so quietly he couldn't be sure afterwards whether he'd heard her or his own conscience.

'I've talked everything over with Father. It's for the best, Beth. I'm sorry about what happened today. Both your aunts. . . . '

'Thank you,' she interposed hollowly.

'But it's not just your family, Beth. You have to realise what the gossip generated by this sort of thing could do to me . . . to my family,' he said, unconsciously reiterating his father's arguments.

She nodded, suffocating on her tears, unable to speak.

'A doctor can't risk any scandal, you of all people should know that.'

'Yes,' she whispered.

'I don't think you quite understand. I'm leaving now, in an hour or so. I don't know when I'll be back. I'm sorry it has to end like this between us, Bethan.' He rose from his chair.

'Andrew, please, take me with you,' she begged, blocking his path. 'Please don't leave me here,' she implored, forgetting all pride and dignity as the spectre of a life without him rose terrifyingly from the depths of her nightmares.

He'd prepared himself for a dignified parting scene. A little cold, unemotional and theatrical perhaps, but he'd pictured himself walking away while she stared silently after him. This was one eventuality he hadn't mentally rehearsed for. She flung her arms around him, entwining her fingers tightly around his neck.

'Please, Andrew, take me with you,' she sobbed. 'I swear I won't be any trouble. You don't even have to live with me. I'll find a job, a room. Just come and visit me when you can – please, Andrew. . . . '

'You don't understand.' He gripped her wrists, forcing her arms away from his body. 'I'll be working, living with Fe and Alec. I won't have time to see anyone.'

'Andrew, I love you,' her voice rose precariously high, 'I couldn't bear to live without you.'

'For pity's sake, Bethan, stop being so melodramatic,' he said harshly, concerned about the noise she was making. 'Of course you can live without me. And it's not as if I'm going to the outer reaches of the Antarctic. I'm only going to London. It's a few hours away on the train. And although we can't . . . can't be what we were to one another, we can still be friends.' He threw her the sop in the hope that it would calm her.

'If you go I know I'll never see you again. Please, Andrew – ' Her voice dropped, until it was barely audible. 'Please.'

He looked at her calmly and dispassionately. Weeping, dishevelled, verging on hysteria. He recalled his mother and Fe's restraint in everything they did. Then he remembered how long it had taken him to rouse Bethan's passions. How she'd behaved in the privacy of his bed. A wave of nausea rose in his throat. He couldn't take any more. Not from her. Not like this.

299

'I have to go,' he said abruptly, disentangling himself from her arms.

'Andrew!' The cry was agonising in its intensity.

He tried to concentrate on what his father had said. It had all made sense in the drawing room at home. Now, none of it made any sense. He only wanted to hold her close. Smother her face with kisses. Console her. Tell her he loved her, that it would all come right. Instead he balled his hands into tight fists. His father had told him to finish it before he left. He remembered her aunts, her sister. The scandal, the gossip. . . . it was her fault. The fault of her family. He didn't want to end their affair. Her family – what she was – had forced his hand. And he was hurting every bit as much as her. He lashed out, said the worst thing that came to mind.

'It's over. I daren't risk demeaning myself or my family any more than I already have by continuing to see you. You've dragged me down as far as I'm prepared to go.'

He heard her cry out his name. The sound echoed at his footsteps every inch of the way as he walked across the yard and into the street where he'd parked his car.

The cry followed him home, and back to the station. He wasn't free of it even when his train pulled into Paddington and he called a taxi to take him to Fe's house.

Chapter Eighteen

The following days passed in a nightmarish haze for Bethan. She rose from her bed after sleepless nights, washed, dressed, walked to the hospital, worked, came home, sat on a chair in the kitchen, played with whatever food her mother put in front of her, stared into space until it was time to return to her room, when she lay down on the bed next to Maud, before beginning the process all over again.

Everywhere she looked, everything she did, brought back memories of the time she and Andrew had shared. And when she found the happiness of the past easier to live with than the cold, comfortless reality of the present she closed her mind to the events of the last night Andrew had visited the ward. She was aware of very little besides Andrew and what she'd felt, and still felt, for him. She walked across the exercise yards in the hospital recalling the times she'd done so with him at her side. She climbed the hill towards home, looking at the streets not as they were, but as they'd appeared from the windows of his car. She went into town, only to see him in shops, in doorways, stepping out of the New Inn – wearing his evening suit – one of his lounge suits – his flannels. She saw his hat on the head of every man she passed. She thought she saw him playing tennis on the courts in the park, caught sight of his even, regular features in the face of every man she met.

She began to live for the times when she was alone and could conjure up images that were far more substantial than anything around her. Hour after hour she lay next to him on her bed. The walls of her room changed, transporting her back to the opulent luxury of his bedroom, or the bohemian comfort of the glassed-in veranda of his parents' chalet.

She was only vaguely aware of events that didn't concern Andrew happening around her, and she had no real recollection of any actual conversations. She was too busy remembering her discussions with Andrew and recreating new exchanges that they might have had if they'd still been together.

Someone, probably Evan, told her that Megan had been sentenced to ten years' hard labour. Maud wandered in and out of their shared bedroom, quiet and subdued after her few hours of hard questioning in the police cells. She hadn't been charged with anything, and was careful not to tell anyone, not even Bethan, of the true extent of her involvement with the gang. She became quieter, more withdrawn as she continued to live in fear of being found out. But Bethan was oblivious to Maud, let alone the changes in her. Unfortunately for everyone Elizabeth wasn't. Lacking any real evidence she ranted and raved at Maud whenever they were in the same room, and Evan had to exert all the authority he could muster to quieten her. There was also a bustle and a fuss about Megan's house that took up a great deal of Evan's time, but Bethan couldn't have said precisely what it was all about.

She knew that her Aunt Hetty's funeral was going to be a private one because that was what she told Matron when asked. She lost all track of time. She no longer cared what she looked like. The only time she glanced in a mirror was to check whether her face was clean and her veil was straight. Days and nights came and went, merging into one. She no longer had the acumen nor the desire to differentiate between the two. She was too busy weaving not Andrew, but his ghost into her life.

On the day of Hetty's funeral she went straight from the night shift to the chapel. Standing between her mother and Maud her thoughts left Andrew for the first time since he'd gone, and centred on the small dark wood coffin that lay on the floor in front of the pulpit. Apart from four deacons and a visiting minister who'd been called in to read the burial service, only John Joseph and her immediate family were present. The shame of Hetty's suicide coming so close after Megan's disgrace was too acute for her uncle to allow outsiders to witness it. Her brothers, her father and John Joseph himself had carried the coffin from the house into the chapel between seven and eight in the morning. The timing was carefully arranged to minimise the risk of curious pedestrians gawping at the cortège. All the colliery shifts began

302

at six-thirty, and the shop assistants, clerks and schoolchildren didn't leave their houses much before eight.

The service lasted a scant five minutes. There were no hymns. Bethan glanced at the empty seat in front of the organ and wondered who would play it now. There wasn't even a sermon, only a short prayer mercifully free of the kind of rhetoric her uncle usually employed, which the visiting minister spoke in soft, soothing tones. As soon as he finished speaking, the deacons picked up the coffin and stowed it in the hearse. Her uncle sat alongside the driver in front of the coffin, leaving her entire family to pile into the second and only other car that he had hired.

They drove slowly down the hill, past the hospital where the paupers leaving after their night's lodging stripped off their caps as a sign of respect, skirted the edge of town, and out along Broadway to the forlorn corner of Glyntaff cemetery reserved for those who were outcasts, even in death. The paupers and the suicides.

They stood silently on the muddy earth alongside the grave as the coffin was lowered in by two workmen in dirty boots and grimy trousers. Her uncle mumbled a few words that made little impression on Bethan. The only thought that entered her head was that they seemed to bear no relation to Hetty or her life.

Afterwards she went home to bed. She was glad she was back on night shift because it meant she could sleep during the day in a bed she didn't have to share with Maud. Those days were the best because she was free from grinding chores – free to think of Andrew. To allow her imagination to run riot, to once again lie alongside him – feel the brush of his skin against hers, the hardness of his muscular back beneath her hands, his lips as they met hers. And so the pattern became established. Work, home, dream – wash, dress, work, home. . . .

Trevor and Laura tried to help. She listened patiently to their plans to include her in their outings, then she fobbed them off with the excuse that she was on night shift for at least another two weeks and they were both on days. She was grateful she was able to do so. She couldn't bear to watch them, to witness their happiness. All she wanted was to be left alone with her routine, her memories and her imaginings.

The days grew shorter and colder. The edges between reality

303

and fantasy blurred to the point when she actually began looking for Andrew. Sometimes she sought him for minutes at a time before she remembered – and with remembrance came the first of the pains. Real, acute physical pains that made her sick in the pit of her stomach, gave her blinding headaches and dizzy spells. She tried to cope with them, and when she couldn't she looked at the painkillers in the drug cabinet on the ward. It would have been simple enough. She was in sole charge in the night. She could have written up doses on record cards for patients who didn't need sleeping draughts. But something, probably fear of Squeers, held her back. Instead she reached for the brandy bottle that was always kept locked in Squeers' desk. It was easier to take a drink from that. She checked the level before she started and was careful to refill it to the same mark with water. But after only two nights she realised she was drinking water. That was when she opened her jewellery box and took out one of the pound notes Andrew'd given her from the bets he'd placed on Eddie. That morning on her way back from work she knocked on the back door of the Horse and Groom and asked for a bottle of brandy. The landlord didn't even question her motives. A nurse asking for brandy was common enough. When that bottle ran out she went to the Morning Star, comforting herself with the thought that there were enough pubs on the Graig to keep her going for months before anyone became in the least suspicious.

Her father and her brothers watched her grow daily thinner, paler and more remote. They noticed that she rarely went out. When Evan plucked up courage to ask after Andrew she simply said he'd gone away. There was no outburst, no tears, only the same blank, dead look in her eyes that had worried him for weeks.

'Eddie, what are you doing here?' Laura asked as she walked out of the hospital gates at the end of her day shift. 'Bethan's on nights you know.'

'I know,' he said awkwardly. 'It's you that I'm waiting to see, not her. Buy you a cup of tea?'

She lifted her cape and pulled out her nurse's watch. Trevor was on duty, but he'd said he'd try to call up her house. On duty days that could mean any time. But just in case he managed it, she wanted to go home and change out of her uniform. 'I'm sorry, Eddie, not tonight. I have to. . . . ' She saw the dejected look on his face and changed her mind. 'All right, one quick cuppa in our café, but I warn you now if it's my love you're after I'm spoken for.'

Eddie blushed at her poor joke and followed her to the café.

Too early for the evening idlers, and too late for most of those finishing work for the day, the place was quiet. There was no sign of Laura's father, only Tina who was serving behind the counter. Eddie bought two teas and carried them over to the table in the corner by the front window.

'Miserable weather,' Laura said, staring at the rain patterning the glass.

'Summer's over.'

'Not entirely I hope. I'm getting married in October and I want the sun shining down on us. You are coming, aren't you? We sent your whole family invitations.'

'If you have I'm sure we'll all be there,' Eddie said.

'Hasn't Bethan said anything?'

'No. Not really,' Eddie admitted reluctantly.

'Typical,' Laura snorted. 'She seems to be in a dream these days.'

'That's what I wanted to see you about,' Eddie said quickly as he spooned four sugars into his tea. 'Haydn and I got talking . . .' he hesitated, not quite sure how to go on. He hadn't wanted to do this but Haydn had insisted that one of them talk to Laura for Bethan's sake. 'He wanted to see you himself, but it's not easy for him with the hours he works. . . . '

'Is there a point to all this?' Laura asked impatiently.

'We're worried sick about Bethan,' Eddie blurted out. 'Have you see her lately?'

'Not really. Not to talk to,' she evaded neatly, as she stirred her tea. It was the truth. Trevor had told her what little he knew about Andrew's break-up from Bethan, but even that little had been tempered by Trevor's sense of delicacy, and she hadn't wanted to press him. She was too happy to want to dwell on other people's misery. Especially that of her best friend. 'Bethan's on nights, I'm on days – ' She shrugged her shoulders. 'We work

305

on the same ward, but not at the same times. I've hardly seen her in weeks.'

'She's not herself,' Eddie continued, repeating Haydn's words. 'She's not eating properly – not sleeping – Laura, do you know what happened between her and that man? He's not around any more, and if he hurt her. . . . ' He curled his hands into fists.

'You mean Andrew I suppose.' She shook her head as she lifted her teacup to her lips. 'I told you, I haven't seen Bethan to talk about anything.'

'But he's gone?' Eddie persisted like a dog worrying a rat.

'He went to London to take up a surgical post,' Laura murmured.

Eddie looked at her blankly.

'He's gone to be a doctor in a London hospital,' she explained irritably.

'And left our Beth high and dry?'

'It might not quite be the way it looks,' Laura said diplomatically. 'They could have wanted to take a break from one another.'

'I don't think so, and neither does our Haydn. She's not herself. Something must have happened. . . . '

'It could have been your aunt getting arrested,' Laura said thoughtlessly.

'What do you mean?' Eddie demanded churlishly.

'He's a doctor, Eddie. He has a position to keep up, and he might feel . . . might feel . . . ' She faltered as she understood the implications of what she was about to say.

'Disgraced?' Eddie suggested bitterly. 'Like my mother. She says she can hardly hold her head up when she walks down the street. Between what Auntie Megan's done and Aunt Hetty. . . . Bloody hell!' he said slowly. 'You're trying to tell me that he thinks our Beth isn't good enough for him!'

'I could be wrong, Eddie.' She stared at him helplessly, frightened by the force of anger she'd unleashed. She wanted to say something that would calm him, but she didn't know what. Eddie wasn't like her brothers or Haydn. He was a much simpler boy who tended to see things in black and white. Perhaps it was the best way for someone who intended to earn his living from his fists.

'That smarmy bastard. . . . '

306

'Language, Eddie!' she warned. 'You don't know the truth of the matter any more than I do. A lot of things can happen between a man and a woman.'

The blood rushed to Eddie's face. Unable to meet Laura's eyes he looked down at his bootlaces, wondering if Laura had heard something about him and Daisy.

'If you want to find out what's really wrong, you're going to have to ask Bethan,' Laura said firmly. 'But if I were you I'd be careful. She might not want to talk about it.'

'Because he dumped her?'

'Or because she dumped him,' Laura said quietly. 'Have you thought of that?'

Evan, Alun and William dragged their feet as they walked up the Graig hill. It was a glorious autumn evening. A huge glowing orange sun sank slowly over the slate-tiled rooftops of the stone houses, bathing the streets in a soft glow that washed the harsh grey, brown and pewter tones of the dirty streets to lighter, kinder shades. If the men had looked to the heavens rather than their feet they might have appreciated just how beautiful the sunset was, but neither its beauty nor the warmth of the evening air on their faces, blackened by a day spent working underground, could lift their spirits. And all of the colliers who walked in front, beside or behind them were the same. Dour, grim and silent.

Evan paused as they reached the entrance to the gully that cut between Llantrisant Road and Leyshon Street. William pushed his knapsack further over his shoulder and looked apprehensively at his uncle. Only the whites of his teeth and eyes showed through the thick layer of coal dust that covered his face.

'What's going to happen, Uncle Evan?' he asked anxiously.

'You heard the man speak, same as me,' Evan replied with unintentional gruffness.

'But I've Diana to consider. Uncle Huw says we may have to sell the house to pay Mam's restitution costs as it is.'

Evan relented. 'We'll sort out something, boy. Don't worry. They can't let us all starve to death. Look, I've got to go home, wash and have tea. I'll come down and see you later. We'll have a talk then.' He would have liked to ask his nephew and niece to come up to his house for tea. But aside from Elizabeth's upset over Megan's disgrace and her vow that she wouldn't let either of Megan's children cross her doorstep again, there was the news he had to tell her. News that could stretch her strained nerves to breaking point. Afterwards he might well have good reason to want to leave the house for Leyshon Street.

He turned his back on William and carried on up the Graig hill with Alun walking close on his heels. As they rounded the vicarage corner they caught up with Viv Richards, Glan's father.

'Fine mess we're in now, Evan,' he commented acidly.

'Aye.'

'Well I'll see myself and my whole family out on the road before I'll go begging for help from anyone. That's all I can say about it.'

'Let's hope it won't come to that, Viv.' Evan watched Viv's short stocky figure as he mounted the steps next door, then found himself measuring the distance between the pavement and the house. Imagining how the front would look covered with furniture when the bailiffs came. Shaking his head in an attempt to free himself from the image, he turned the key in his door and walked through to the kitchen.

Elizabeth was spooning drops of batter on to the hotplate of the stove. A small stack of pikelets piled on a plate on the warming shelf above her testified to her industry.

'I've set up the bath out back,' she greeted him brusquely.

'Thank you, Elizabeth.' Evan sat on the stoop between the washhouse and the kitchen and unlaced his boots. Alun stepped over him and walked out to the sink.

'All the children out?' he asked, wanting to make sure they wouldn't be interrupted for a while.

'Haydn's in that shop again, working for nothing as usual. Bethan's upstairs. Anyone'd think the girl's going into a decline. She's got work in another hour and a half, and if I've called her once I've called her a dozen times. Well, I'll not call her again. It's up to her to get herself to the hospital on time. And Maud and Eddie have gone over the mountain to look for blackberries. I told them there was no point in going. The season's over. There's only the small wormy ones left that the birds don't want.'

She scooped up a pikelet and flicked it over. While it was cooking she stirred a pan of tripe and onions that was simmering in the oven. Evan decided to take the bull by the horns. There wasn't going to be a good time to tell Elizabeth the news he was carrying, and the sooner he began the sooner it would be over with. He kicked off his boots, stood up, and closed the door behind him, shutting Alun into the washhouse.

'You're not going to give the lodger first bath are you?' Elizabeth said in disgust. 'And just look at those socks. You're covering the floor with coal dust. You're undoing all the work I've done today by just standing there. . . . '

'I'm on my way. It's just that there's something you should know, Elizabeth, and it can't wait.'

'What is it now?' She flicked a cooked pikelet on to the pile and spooned another ladleful of batter on the hotplate. 'More bad news about that sister-in-law of yours? Because if it is. . . . '

'It's not about Megan. Manager made an announcement today. The pit's closing at the end of next week.'

Naked fear and panic flashed over her face as she dropped the spoon she was holding on the hearthrug. 'You'll just have to find work in another colliery. You'll have to go up the Albion or down Trehafod. . . . '

'There's no point in going to any colliery. They're all closing. The Maritime, the Albion. . . . '

'Fine! Just fine!' she shouted furiously. 'It's no good talking like that. There has to be work somewhere. All you have to do is go and look for it. If you don't – ' her hand flew to her mouth and she closed her teeth around her fingers in an effort to stop herself from crying – 'we're for the workhouse. Oh God – ' She sank to her knees and picked up the spoon. 'My uncle always said it would come to this if I married you. The means test and the workhouse, and all you can say is there's no point in looking for work. . . . ' She began to sob. Bone weary, sick and terrified what the future might hold, Evan turned his back on her.

'At least if it comes to the workhouse our Beth will be able to look after us.' With that parting shot he unlatched the kitchen door and walked into the washhouse. Alun Jones had stripped down to his trousers and was waiting patiently to use the tub. Evan tore off his shirt, knelt beside the bath and thrust his head under the warm water. He took the soap from its cracked saucer and rubbed it into a lather. Then he realised he'd left his towel and clean clothes on the airing rack above the range where Elizabeth kept them warming.

'Do me a favour, Alun,' he called out, his eyes closed against the soap. 'Fetch me my towel and clothes from the kitchen.'

'Aye.'

He heard Alun walk back and was half tempted to dress outside and go down to Leyshon Street through the back garden. He couldn't face Elizabeth again. Not yet. He needed time to think things out first.

Bethan rose late, washed, dressed and walked downstairs into the doom-laden atmosphere of the kitchen. She scarcely had time to sit down before her mother regaled her with the full story of her father's redundancy. Evan himself didn't say a word. He simply sat in his chair, pushing threads of tripe and onions around his plate. Bethan smiled at him, but he kept his head down and her smile was wasted. She would have liked to reach out and hug him, but her head was swimming and she wasn't sure she'd be able to move without falling over. Her senses were invariably numbed these days. Drinking all day, working all night, and general antipathy had taken a toll, and not only on her looks. She was constantly dizzy and nauseous. She had no appetite and even on occasions like now, when she sat at the table with her family and forced herself to eat, she rarely kept her food down for long.

Life had become one long, grinding chore. The studying that she'd made an effort to keep up with, even when she'd been going out with Andrew, had been abandoned. She'd become obsessed with finding strength enough to get her through her nights of work, so she could spend her days in the comfort and seclusion of her bed with a bottle tucked beneath the pillow. She carried one bottle in the bag she took to work in case she couldn't quite make it through the night, but she was careful to hide a second behind her drawer in the dressing table. Brandy had become a lifeline she could no longer live without. She bought plenty of cheap cologne in Woolworth's and had taken to sprinkling it liberally over her clothes and into her washing water; even going so far as to rinse her mouth out in it when she left her bed at the end of the day, lest any of her family recognised the smell on her breath. And being in charge of the ward during the night had its compensations. If her behaviour seemed a little odd or erratic there was no superior to question it. And by directing others to complete tasks she was wary of doing herself in case she botched them, she managed – by the skin of her teeth sometimes – but she managed, to keep her secret.

But there were times, like now, when she was sitting with her family, when she felt she wasn't actually living life. Merely watching it; like a patient in a tuberculosis ward, forced to stand behind a glass window.

She tried to follow her father's example and concentrated on eating the tripe and onions. She had only swallowed three mouthfuls when she began to retch. She left her chair clumsily and ran out, only just making it to the *ty bach* in time. She lay on the flagstoned floor next to the bench seat in a cold sweat, shaking from head to foot, hoping and praying that her mother wouldn't allow any of the others to go after her. The last thing she wanted was to try to explain the state she was in to Maud.

Her luck held. After five minutes she could sit up. She leaned back against the wooden door, careful to avoid the whitewash on the walls that came off on any surface that brushed against it. A few moments later she was able to struggle to her feet. Holding on to the wall she made it as far as the sink in the washhouse, where she washed her face in cold water and rubbed her teeth with her finger and salt from a block her mother kept next to the washing blue on a high shelf.

'Are you all right?' Elizabeth shouted irritably from the kitchen.

'Fine, Mam,' Bethan called back tremulously.

'We can't have you coming down with anything. Not now when your father's lost his job.'

'For Christ's sake, Elizabeth!' Evan growled with uncharacteristic savagery. 'I've another one and a half weeks to go.'

'And afterwards?' Elizabeth demanded, cold fury glittering in her eyes.

'If you go on like this there won't be an afterwards,' he threatened. Pushing his chair back from the table he picked up his boots from the hearth and lurched towards the front door.

'That's right,' Elizabeth taunted. 'Run away from the problem

311

just as you always do. Well this time you haven't got your precious mother or sister-in-law to rush to. . . . '

Bethan crept upstairs and reached for the bottle in her bag. She put the whole of the neck in her mouth and drank deeply, pausing only when she heard the creak of the top stair. She pushed the bottle back into her bag, only just managing to stopper it as Maud entered the room.

'Beth, what's going to happen to us?' she asked tearfully.

'I don't know.' Bethan heard her voice slurring and realised she was drunker than she'd ever been in the house before. She sat down abruptly on the dressing-table stool and fiddled with her veil. Fortunately Maud was too upset to pay much attention.

'I went to see Mrs Evans today with Diana,' she began tentatively.

'Mrs who?' Bethan tried and failed to focus on her sister.

'Mrs Evans. The deputy headmistress in Maesycoed Seniors.'

'Don't know her.'

'Of course, I forgot you went to the grammar school. Anyway in spite of all . . . all that police business she agreed to write out a reference for Diana. She's applying for a job as a ward maid in Cardiff Infirmary. They need girls to start in September. I'm sure if I asked her she'd write one out for me too. Do you think I should apply?'

'It'll be hard work in Cardiff Infirmary. And not all of it pleasant,' Bethan warned, upset even in her drink-fuddled state at the thought of her sister working as a skivvy in that environment. Maud wasn't strong. She still coughed occasionally, and winter was coming. There had to be something better for her to do, if only they could think of it.

'I don't mind hard work, Beth. You know that. I've been looking around and jobs aren't that easy to come by. I'd rather be a maid in a hospital than in a house, and that's all that seems to be on offer. Besides Dad will be hard put to keep Mam and himself now he's out of work and we can't –'

'Can't what?' Bethan interrupted.

'Haydn says we can't expect you to keep us for ever.'

'Haydn should keep his mouth shut.'

'I was thinking about doing this even before Mam told us about the Maritime closing, honest. You know what it's been

312

like between Mam and me since Diana and I were taken down the police station. I'd rather live away like you did. Of course I'd miss you, and Dad and the boys, but it's not as if I'd be on my own. I'd have Diana,' she said bravely.

Bethan looked hard at her sister. Even with the edges of her slight figure fuzzy, blurred by drink, she looked small, very young and very vulnerable. Bethan grew angry, not with Maud, but with the unfairness of a life where Maud's only way out into the world was through skivvying in a hospital where they'd wring every last ounce of work from her. She wanted to kick someone and there was no one to kick. If she'd been alone she would have picked up the bottle again. Maud reached out, and Bethan opened her arms.

'I miss you already, Beth. It's strange not having you here in the nights to talk to.' Maud gave her a hug that took Bethan's breath away.

'If you're going to be a ward maid you'll have to get used to being by yourself.'

'I suppose I will. You are all right aren't you?' Maud looked keenly at her sister.

'Just tired, that's all.' Bethan extricated herself from Maud's arms, lifted the bottle of cologne from the dressing table and splashed it liberally over herself, soaking the front of her uniform.

'You've drenched yourself,' Maud complained.

'Bottle slipped in my hand,' Bethan lied. She dragged herself to her feet, forced herself to put one foot in front of the other and stood up. Then she knew that she shouldn't have drunk that last mouthful of brandy. 'I've got to go,' she mumbled thickly.

'Can I walk down the hill with you?' Maud pleaded. 'I don't want to stay in the house. Please?'

'Come on then. As long as you're quick.' Bethan wanted to be alone, but she was in no state to argue with Maud. She staggered unsteadily down the stairs. Eddie was sitting on the bottom step lacing up his boots.

'Off out?' Maud asked.

'Down to see Will and Diana. Anywhere's got to be better than here.' He jerked his head towards the kitchen door where Elizabeth was crashing the pots and pans as she cleared away the remains of the meal.

313

Bethan lifted her cape from the hook at the back of the door and they set off together. She was glad when Maud decided to join Eddie in visiting their cousins. The fresh air was making her feel extremely peculiar, and Eddie gave her some very odd looks before he and Maud left her at the foot of the lane that cut between Leyshon Street and Llantrisant Road. By the time she'd walked down the hill and was crossing the yard of the hospital she felt as though she were walking on rubber sheeting that had been stretched to its utmost. Her feet sank further and further down with every step she took. She had great difficulty in picking her legs up in order to place one foot in front of the other. No matter how much effort she put into it, she seemed to make very slow progress.

The staircase that led up to her ward was the worst. The steps were like wedges of sponge. Thick, jelly-like, they soaked up her footfalls and gave her no purchase from which to take the next tread. She kept her eyes fixed on the top and made a superhuman effort. The final step grew in size. It swallowed not only her boot but all of her, and she felt herself falling down and ever downwards into the depths of a huge dune like the ones Andrew had taken her to in Porthcawl. The sand closed over her, soft, warm, comfortingly, blotting the need for effort from her mind.

'I think she's coming round.' Laura's voice echoed towards her from a great distance. She couldn't see Laura. Only hear the sound of her voice as it rolled over a landscape of peaked sand dunes like the ones in the Foreign Legion films.

'I hope you're right.' This time it was a man speaking. 'She gave her head one hell of a mighty crack.' A man? Could it be Andrew? She struggled over the dunes, her feet still slipping, as she searched the horizon frantically for a glimpse of him.

'Bethan? Bethan? Can you hear us?' She ceased to struggle. There was no point. The voice was too coarse, too heavily accented to be Andrew's. It was Trevor's. 'What's Squeers decided to do?'

'She's with Matron now. They've sent a message to one of the sisters who's taking her day off. Matron says that if the sister can't take over she'll cover the ward herself. Trevor, what do you think happened? Did she just trip on the stairs like you told Squeers?'

Trevor knew precisely why Bethan had fallen, but he didn't intend to tell anyone. Even Laura. He could see the reason for Bethan's downfall in her flushed cheeks, her cold, clammy hands, her abnormal heartbeat and the odour of eau de cologne on her breath and on her uniform that didn't quite mask the smell of brandy. He could have kicked himself for allowing it to happen. He should have seen it coming.

'I feel sick,' Bethan moaned pathetically, reluctantly leaving her desert landscape for the antiseptic reality of the hospital bed that Trevor had dumped her in.

'I'm not surprised.' Laura rushed to her side with a kidney bowl. She held Bethan's head between her cool hands, steadying her mouth over the bowl. Bethan went through the motions, but very little came up. She felt absolutely wretched and ashamed. Hating herself for having to rely on Laura to take care of her. But she had enough common sense left to realise that she was too ill to take care of herself.

'Didn't you eat before you came out?' Trevor asked her sharply, as Laura went to empty the bowl.

'Yes,' she mumbled weakly.

'I don't believe you,' he said furiously. 'If you had, you would have brought up something more than bile.'

'I haven't been able to keep any food down for weeks,' she excused herself miserably.

'But you've been able to keep brandy down all right?'

She opened her eyes. He was looking straight at her. She began to deny his accusation, but there was something in his dark eyes that dared her to continue.

'For God's sake, Bethan. You're a nurse. You of all people can't plead ignorance. If you won't think of yourself, think of what you might do to a patient when you're floating around in this condition.'

'I'm sorry, Trevor. It won't happen again,' she apologised abjectly.

'Too bloody royal it won't. The first chance I get I'm going to tell Matron that the strain of night duty is too much for you. And when you switch back to day shifts Squeers will be at your

315

elbow all day long. That should put paid to any secret drinking sessions, at least while you're on the ward. And before you go looking for the bottle in your handbag, I've tipped it away.'

Sudden agonising cramps cut across her abdomen and she curled up on the bed, her face muscles contorting with the effort it cost her to fight the pain.

'I'm not surprised you're in this state,' Trevor lectured heavily. 'Have you been trying to live on a diet of pure brandy for long?' He leaned over her, straightened out her legs and laid his hand on her stomach. His face grew serious as he poked and prodded her.

'Oh God, Beth. I'm sorry, I had no idea. Does Andrew know?'

'Know what?' she gasped as another pain crippled her.

He looked at her closely. 'I know you've been in a stupor since Andrew left, but you must know you're pregnant. Four or five months by my reckoning.'

She closed her eyes and tried to recall when she'd last bled. She couldn't even remember. It had been some time before Andrew left. And that had been a lifetime ago. She went cold with fear. She couldn't have a baby. She simply couldn't. Not now. It wasn't possible.

'Look, I'll go and bring the car round to the entrance,' Trevor said, embarrassed by his earlier anger. 'Then I'll take you home.'

After he left she broke out into a cold sweat as fear beset her. She felt sick again, and there was no sign of Laura. She looked around and saw the depressingly familiar walls of the delivery room. Crawling off the bed she made her way into the corridor, passed the bathrooms and went into the toilet. All she could think of was Trevor's damning diagnosis. She remembered Maisie and the other girls she'd delivered from the 'workhouse' side of the homes.

She collapsed on the floor. That was now her. She'd been a fool. A complete and utter fool. This was one disgrace that no one in her family would be able to take.

Desperate for a solution she cast her mind back to the women who'd been admitted after they'd paid visits to backstreet 'cure-alls'. Old women who operated in their kitchens and washhouses with knitting needles and phials of mercury. She shouldn't have to resort to them. She was a nurse. If only Megan was within reach. She'd know what to do. Then she recalled something one of the women who'd got rid of a child had said when she'd been brought into the ward. All she had to do was go home. Trevor might have poured one bottle of brandy away but there was another full bottle wedged behind her drawer in the dressing table. Her mother had used the stove that day, so that meant there had to be hot water. If she waited until everyone went to bed, ran a hot bath and drank the brandy while she was sitting in it she wouldn't have any more problems.

It would soon be over. And she promised herself that the bottle at the back of her drawer would be the last bottle of brandy she would ever drink. A few more hours – that's all it would take to straighten everything out, and put her life back on course. If it worked, if everything came right, she vowed to God that she'd devote her life to nursing, and never, *never* commit a sin again.

Chapter Nineteen

Bethan lay awake in her bed and listened to the sounds of the house closing down for the night. Maud was the first to walk out into the yard. She heard the distant murmur of voices as her sister returned to the kitchen and spoke to her mother. The kitchen door opened and closed. The stairs creaked and Maud stole into the bedroom and switched the light on.

She strained to keep her eyes closed and her breathing soft, regular. Feigning sleep she heard a splash as Maud tipped water into the bowl and washed. That was followed by the thud of flannel petticoats hitting the lino. The light went off. Moments later the bedsprings dipped and creaked as her sister climbed in beside her.

'Beth, you awake?' Maud whispered anxiously.

She remained still, loglike. Maud turned over. She stayed silent, locked into her own misery, reliving the awful moment when Trevor had brought her home. Seeing again the look of shock and fear on Maud's face as Trevor and Laura had carried her up the steps and through the front door with the news that she'd had a bad fall. There'd been such a fuss – her mother scolding her and everyone else within earshot; Eddie asking questions which Trevor and Laura pretended not to hear; her father mouthing platitudes that soothed no one, least of all himself. And none of them had even guessed at the extent of her true disgrace. That knowledge still remained her and Trevor's secret. But for how long?

How could she have done it? Allowed herself to be taken in by Andrew, to fall in love with him and bring dishonour on her entire family. She tried to hate him, to blame him for her drinking – for the shameful state she was in – but a cold logical voice of reason rose unbidden from the back of her mind, telling her that if he was guilty of anything, then so was she. He might have made the first move, but he'd never forced himself on her, and it hadn't taken her long to become every bit as willing and ardent

318

as him. The truth was that Laura had excited her curiosity, and she'd wanted to wear Andrew's ring, as Laura did Trevor's. If she'd been trapped, it was by her own desire to become Andrew's wife.

Her biggest mistake had been in believing that the easiest route to marriage was via the bedroom. Andrew'd never lied to her. Never promised her anything other than outings and picnics. She'd simply set her sights too high. When he told her he loved her she'd been the one to equate love with marriage, not him. And now, after what had happened to Megan, it was totally ridiculous of her to imagine that an educated, respectable doctor would involve himself with a family of criminals.

Wallowing in the luxury of self-pity, tears fell thick and fast from her eyes on to the pillow. A cramping pain shot through her foot. She moved it involuntarily and Maud stirred sleepily beside her. She had to remain still. She had to! At least until everyone was asleep. She tried to concentrate on the sounds downstairs.

She heard her mother raking the ashes out from underneath the fire in the oven. There was the dull slam of iron on iron as she damped down the flames with small coal, and closed the flue door. Just as well it wasn't the one night in the week when her mother allowed the fire to burn out so she could give the stove a good cleaning. Six nights a week her mother banked the fire, on the seventh she raked the coals and doused the embers. If tonight had been that night it wouldn't have suited her purpose at all.

Elizabeth went out the back before climbing the stairs. Bethan sensed her mother pausing for a moment outside their bedroom. She breathed in deeply, exhaling loudly in a parody of sleep. Moments later Elizabeth opened her own bedroom door and closed it. The sound of curtain rings grating over the pole echoed through the dividing wall closely followed by the screech of china sliding over the marble surface of the washstand. The floorboards protested as Elizabeth moved around the room while she undressed. Bethan waited patiently until she heard the final moan of the bedsprings on her parents' bed. All she had to do now was wait for her father, the lodger and her brothers.

Footsteps resounded in the street outside. She heard Haydn,

Alun and Eddie shout goodnight to Glan. Eddie must have left Leyshon Street and walked down to the Town Hall to pick Haydn up. From there they must have gone to the pub, because that was where Glan and Alun spent most of their evenings. Eddie laughed, a wild, high-pitched giggle as the front door opened. He only ever laughed like that after he'd been out with Haydn. She didn't need to see them, or smell the beer on their breath. They'd had a few. She wondered where they'd got the money from.

She continued to listen, tense and nervous, waiting for the familiar sequence of events. The latch went on the kitchen door as they took it in turns to go out the back. She picked up her nurse's watch from the bedside table and tried to read its hands but the plush curtains were firmly drawn and it was too dark. She tried to guess the time. Her mother always went to bed at ten. It could have been half an hour, or an hour since.

The latch went on the downstairs room directly below. Alun was going to bed. Soon afterwards the boys with much 'hushing and shushing' climbed the stairs and went into their own bedroom. A loud crash rocked the house. Eddie began to laugh again, and Elizabeth's voice cut, harsh and reprimanding, from her bedroom. Silence reigned once more. There was only her father to come.

The boys were both snoring when the key turned in the lock of the front door again. The heavy tread of her father's boots clumped down the passage and out the back. He must have lingered over a pipe in the back kitchen, because it was a long while before he came upstairs. The bed sighed as he climbed in beside her mother. She listened for the sound of their voices. Neither spoke. But that didn't mean that they slept. Her mother had been so angry earlier in the evening she could be playing doggo, just as Bethan was.

There was a steady tramp of feet as a late-night reveller, or worker, walked beneath her window up the Avenue. Then more silence. Later a dog barked in Phillips Street below them. Someone shouted at it. A cat screeched. And still she waited. Holding her breath, rehearsing a hundred times the moment when she'd finally put a foot out of bed. She just had to be sure that no one would be awake.

When she could stand the suspense no longer she rolled over

to the very edge of the bed. Slipping her feet out first she slid on to the floor. She crouched on the lino and eased open her dressing-table drawer. It gave a few inches. Then it stuck. She pushed her arm into the small gap, bruising the inside of her elbow as she fumbled around. She couldn't reach the bottle. The drawer wasn't pulled out far enough. She tugged at it again. This time it came out with a jerk that sent her reeling backwards, but even as she fell her hand closed over the bottle she'd secreted behind it. Not daring to feel beneath the bed for her slippers or rummage in her wardrobe for her dressing gown, she crawled towards the door, lifted the latch and, keeping her fingers on the metal bar, slowly drew it open. Resting her hands on the banisters and the wall she hopped over the stairs that creaked. She dared not put on the light when she reached the bottom step. Instead she fumbled along the narrow passageway. No longer familiar it took on terrifying twists and turns. Walls stood where there were none in daylight. The edges of the rag rugs curled, waiting to trip her up. Her heart felt as though it was pounding in her mouth when she finally made it into the back kitchen. She closed the door, leaned back against it and switched on the light, very conscious that she was directly below her parents' bedroom.

She had intended to carry the bath in from the back yard, fill it with boiling water from the oven, and sit in it to drink her bottle of brandy. Now she'd actually made it as far as the kitchen she realised how impossible that would be. The sound of the washhouse door opening would, in all probability, be enough to wake her mother, who was a light sleeper at the best of times. There was no way she could lift the bath from the garden wall, which was very close to her parents' open window, without making a noise. And then she would have to refill the boiler once she'd drained it, a noisy operation even in daytime. And aside from her parents above her, there was the lodger sleeping in the next room.

She sank down on one of the kitchen chairs and tried to collect her thoughts. She had to get rid of her problem. Of that much she was certain. She regarded her pregnancy as a problem, not a child. No images of babies crossed her mind. The likes of Baby Davies tucked up in her cot in the nursery of the Graig Hospital, all curly hair, sweet mouth and peaceful closed eyes above a small round lump of nappy, was as far divorced from the predicament she was in as the Graig mountain from the Common.

All she could think of was destitution She only had two pounds left of the forty-five Andrew had given her. It was barely enough to rent a room for herself for a month, and that was without taking food into consideration. With Megan in prison there was no saviour on her horizon to support her in the same way Rhiannon Pugh was supporting Phyllis. Once Elizabeth became aware of the baby's existence, daughter or not she'd throw her out on the street. Left to his own devices her father might have taken a more charitable view, but it was her mother not her father who laid down the rules of the house.

Her Uncle John Bull would see that she was never accepted in his or any other chapel again. She'd be shunned, perhaps even stoned like Phyllis. Her only recourse would be the unmarrieds ward in the workhouse, where she'd have to wear the grey flannel workhouse dress. She wouldn't even be allowed to keep or wear her own underwear. She'd be forced to scrub floors and yards for her keep until her child was born – and afterwards she'd have to live in the homes until someone either adopted it or took pity on her and gave her a job as a live-in maid. Even then she'd have to hand over whatever she earned for her own and her baby's keep. That would be her life. She'd have no opportunity to save anything for a better one. There wouldn't even be any hope. She'd be like Maisie Crockett. . . .

She shook herself free from the bleak picture she'd painted of her future and looked at the clock. The hands pointed to three. Her mother always rose at five. Two hours. That was all the time she had. Tomorrow Trevor would return. He could slip up, say something untoward. Her mother might guess. She daren't risk putting off what had to be done for another day. Cradling the bottle of brandy on her lap, she considered the alternatives to a hot bath. Epsom salts . . . placing her feet in a bowl of scalding water . . . knitting needles – she caught sight of her mother's steel pins crammed into an empty jam jar on the windowsill, and shuddered. The hands on the clock pointed to ten minutes past three. Steam rose gently from the water boiler in the stove. If she was going to do something she'd have to do it now. But not here. Anyone passing through on their way to the back yard would see

322

her and if Alun and her brothers had been drinking that could be in the next few moments.

There was only one room in the house that was shut off, the front parlour. She tiptoed back down the passage. A full moon shone in through the lace curtains that hung at the bay window, creating a beautiful pattern of shadows on the floor. She rolled the rug back lest she soil it, and stood the bottle of brandy on the linoleum next to the couch. Returning to the kitchen she fetched one of the old sheets from the back of the washhouse that her mother kept to use as dust sheets when she was spring-cleaning. She had to risk the sound of running water, but not a bathful. A bucketful would have to be enough. She rinsed out the enamel bucket from under the sink and filled it with boiling water from the stove. It came out bubbling. It took two trips to refill the boiler with her mother's enamel jug. Switching off the light and closing all the doors she carried the steaming bucket into the parlour and set it, and herself, down on the dust sheet. She skimmed her fingers across the surface of the water and only just stopped herself from screaming. It was scalding hot. She touched everything she'd gathered around her. The dust sheet, hot water, brandy – what if she passed out with the pain, or was sick? Deciding she couldn't risk either, she sat on the Rexine-covered sofa and pulled the dust sheet up beneath her nightgown. Then closing her mouth around the brandy bottle she began to drink. She didn't find the courage to lower her feet into the water until the bottle was half empty.

Elizabeth rose before five as she did every day. She liked to blacklead and clean the oven and boil the water for tea before Evan and Alun rose at half-past. She dressed in her bedroom, putting on a grubby house overall, only stopping to wash her hands and face and brush her hair. She would have a good wash later, when all the dirty household chores had been completed and she had the house to herself.

The first thing she did on entering the kitchen was check the stove. She poked up the fire, breaking the crust of small coal she'd laid the night before. Then she raked the ashes out on to the hearth. Fetching the ash bucket from the washhouse she shovelled the residue on top of yesterday's, picking out any bits that weren't burnt to dust to put back on the fire. When the grey dirt had been swept up and deposited in the bucket, she built up the fire with fresh coal and sticks from the scuttle that Evan had refilled before going to bed. Recollecting the events of yesterday evening she was even more parsimonious than usual, resolutely replacing five lumps of coal and a handful of sticks from her normal morning's allowance. Soon even Evan's reduced coal allowance would be gone. And she couldn't begin to think how they would afford twenty-five shillings for a load of coal with no man's wages coming into the house.

She went to the washhouse to fetch the bucket. She spent five minutes hunting high and low for it before eventually making do with the bowl she kept for soaking Evan's pit clothes. By five-thirty she'd washed the hearth and cleaned and blackleaded the top of the stove. While the kettle boiled she scrubbed her hands and arms under the cold tap in the washhouse. When she'd finished the water had boiled, and steam was just beginning to rise from the porridge oats she'd mixed with water in her mother's old fish kettle and set on the range. She laid the table, cut bread and carried the butter and jam in from the pantry.

Punctually, at five-thirty, Evan and the boys came down the stairs, and Alun walked in from his room. They fought over the tap in the washhouse, ate the breakfast laid out on the table and left, Alun and Evan to the pit, the boys to the market. It was Haydn's day to work for Wilf Horton, and Eddie had decided to go down to Market Square with him in the hope of picking up some casual work.

Left once more in sole possession of her domain, Elizabeth cleared the dishes, stacked them in the washhouse and relaid the table for Maud. She wondered what to do about Bethan. Perhaps she should take her breakfast up to her bedroom? It was probably best to wait until Maud had left. Bethan had certainly looked ghastly last night when young Dr Lewis had brought her home. But she hadn't entirely believed his and Laura's story that Bethan had slipped on the stairs in the homes and fallen. However, Bethan herself hadn't said much. Refusing even Maud's offer of help, she'd put herself to bed. But young Dr Lewis must be worried about her to say he'd call again today. She hoped the stupid girl hadn't done herself a serious injury. Without Bethan's contribution to the household budget she'd be hard put to buy food, let alone pay the mortgage next week.

She poured herself a cup of tea from the cold dregs in the pot and looked at the clock. It was past seven, time to call Maud. She left the kitchen and shouted from the foot of the stairs. Then, and only then, did she lift the hotplate cover and put the kettle back on to boil. She only ever brewed fresh tea if someone else in the house wanted a cup, considering it a selfish extravagance to do so just for herself.

Ten minutes later, washed, dressed, hair neatly combed back and tied at the nape of her neck, Maud appeared. She sat at the table and ate the porridge Elizabeth put in front of her in silence. When she finished she carried the plate through to the washhouse, returning to drink the tea that her mother had poured for her.

'Bethan was well enough to go to work then?' she asked innocently.

'Not likely, young lady,' Elizabeth said sharply. 'Not after that fall she took last night.'

'Then where is she?' Maud asked, looking around the kitchen.

'Where you'd expect her to be. In bed.'

'She wasn't there when I got up,' Maud asserted.

'Did you disturb her in the night?'

'Not that I know of, Mam. She was sleeping when I went to bed.'

Elizabeth left the kitchen and ran upstairs. She crashed open Maud and Bethan's bedroom door. The bed was neatly turned back, the curtains pulled, the sash window left open six inches at the top, just as she liked Maud to leave it. She darted into the boys' bedroom. She couldn't imagine why, but she thought it might just be possible that Bethan had gone in there. The bed was rumpled untidily, the wardrobe door left ajar, the window and curtains still closed. It was messy, but empty. In her own room the blankets were turned back and the window open, just as Evan had left it. She stepped across the landing to the box room and pushed open the door. It shuddered protestingly across the bare floorboards. The cardboard boxes in which she'd stored the wooden bricks, fort and doll's house that Evan had made for the children when they were small were piled neatly along the wall on the left-hand side of the room. She looked behind the door. Her college textbooks were stacked where she'd left them, under a thick layer of dust. No one had been in here.

Fear slimed, sick and leprous from the base of her spine. If Bethan had left her bed to go to the toilet she would have seen her pass through the kitchen. She remembered Andrew. His sudden departure from Pontypridd. It was as if Bethan's disappearance had turned over a stone in her mind, uncovering a seething nest of fears she'd been terrified of for years. All she could think of was Hetty.

She almost fell down the stairs in her haste to return to the kitchen. On the way she opened the door to Alun's room. The air was stale, musty. The single bed was made, the sash in the centre of the bay open a scant half inch at the top. But it was tidy, his clothes hung away on the rail Evan had hammered across the alcove. She called out Bethan's name. Quietly at first, then louder, not really knowing why she did so when it was plain to see that Bethan wasn't in the room.

She closed the door and entered the back kitchen, checking the pantry, the washhouse and the back yard while a bewildered Maud looked on. She climbed the garden steps, looked in the coalhouse – the dog run – the shed where Evan kept his tools –

'Beth is all right, isn't she, Mam?' Maud demanded pathetically, seeking reassurance.

'I don't know,' Elizabeth replied tersely. She closed all the outside doors and ran back down the passage. Perhaps Bethan was in the street – she wrenched open the front door, looked up and down. . . .

'Nice morning, Mrs Powell,' Glan's mother called from next door where she was scrubbing her doorstep. 'How's your Bethan? Heard she took a bad fall last night.'

'She's going to be fine, thank you, Mrs Richards.' Elizabeth shut the door on the street. The parlour . . . she tried to open the door and failed to move it more than a few inches. Something was behind it. She pushed with all the strength she could muster and stumbled over the body of her daughter.

Bethan, wearing only a nightdress, lay on the floor, an empty bottle of brandy in her hand. Her feet were in the bucket, which had fallen on its side. The water it had held had flooded the linoleum, damming up against her rolled-up, best handstitched tapestry rug. Elizabeth knelt down and placed her hand on Bethan's forehead. It was burning. She moved the bucket and Bethan's feet fell out into the puddle of water. She thrust her hand into her mouth to prevent herself from crying out. The skin hung in long white threads from the red, raw mass of Bethan's feet. Someone screamed. It wasn't until Maud called to her from the passage that she realised she was making the noise herself.

'Mam. Mam!'

'Stay there, Maud,' Elizabeth commanded. Years of discipline paid off. Maud remained exactly where she was. Elizabeth thought rapidly. The bucket – the brandy bottle – she knew exactly what Bethan had done. She'd tried the same trick herself years ago. It hadn't worked then, and judging by the spotless state of Bethan's nightdress it hadn't worked now. If it had worked for her . . . if . . . She heaved the thought from her mind. 'Bethan's ill,' she said quickly. She studied her daughter's mutilated feet. She didn't want to send for help, but this was way beyond her nursing capabilities. 'Run down the hill as fast as you can to Uncle John's. Tell him . . . tell him that we need Doctor Lewis quick. Tell him to send messages to the hospital and anywhere else he might be.' She stared at Maud's face, white, strained. 'Do it!' she shouted. 'Now!'

Maud sprang to life. Not waiting to exchange her slippers for her boots, she wrenched open the front door and fled down the steps.

Elizabeth put her arms around Bethan's shoulders and lifted her out of the pool of water. She had dreaded something like this since the day Bethan was born. Now that it had actually happened she didn't feel any of the emotions she thought she would. She wasn't angry. She didn't want to punish Bethan – in fact one glance at Bethan's feet told her that there'd been punishment enough, and to excess. Instead of wanting to cast Bethan out, she held her close. Her heart reached for Bethan's as it had never done before. This was one problem they would face together, as mother and daughter.

Bethan's eyes flickered open, as Elizabeth stroked the hair away from her face. 'It's all right,' she murmured softly, laying Bethan's head down on her lap. 'I've sent for Doctor Lewis. He'll know what to do. It's going to be all right.'

Bethan looked down, plucked at her nightdress, checking the damp patches. Seeing only clean water she began to cry. She pressed her hand against her stomach. 'Mam. I'm sorry,' she whispered. 'I . . . ' She faltered. She had no apology. No defence to offer.

'It's all right. Try not to talk. You need to conserve your strength.'

'Mam, please, don't throw me out,' she pleaded feverishly. 'I have nowhere to go, I. . . . '

'Bethan, it's going to be all right,' Elizabeth said in the strong voice Bethan hadn't dared disobey from childhood. 'I know you're going to have a baby.'

Bethan stared at her mother, wide-eyed, disbelieving. Her mother knew what she'd done, and she was caressing and petting her? She had no memory of her mother ever doing that before.

'Don't worry, Bethan, I won't let you go on the streets or into the workhouse.' Elizabeth voiced her own fears of twenty-one years before. 'First we nurse you back to health, then we'll sort out your problems.' She looked hard at her daughter. 'Just promise me one thing?'

'Yes, Mam,' Bethan murmured. At that moment she would have promised her mother anything.

'No more tricks like this.' Elizabeth threw the bottle into the bucket with a crash. 'They don't work. All you'll succeed in doing is killing yourself. Now here, put your arms round my neck, let's see if we can lift you out of this puddle on to the couch.'

In one single blinding, screaming moment Bethan's feet came to life. She couldn't have moved them to save herself from death. If anyone had offered to amputate, she would have allowed them to do so, and gladly. Clinging tightly to her mother she sobbed as she hadn't done since childhood. Elizabeth's tears mingled with her own as they fell into the puddles on the floor. For the first time in her life Bethan actually felt close to the woman who had borne her.

'Andy, Anthea, is that you?' Fiona called out as she heard the maid open the front door.

'It is.' Andrew dropped his doctor's bag on to the hall floor, divested Anthea of her coat and hat, and handed them to the maid.

'Dwinkie?' Fe waved a cocktail glass in front of their noses as she peeped around the drawing-room door.

'I'd love one,' Anthea cooed.

'What is it?' Andrew demanded suspiciously, eyeing the peculiar colour of the liquid in her glass.

'Champagne cocktail, with some of my added, my-ster-ious ingredients,' Fiona purred.

'I think I'd prefer a small whisky, thank you.'

'You're worse than Father.' She made a face at him. 'Be adventurous for once in your life.'

'I value my stomach too much to take a chance.' He followed Anthea into the drawing room, and slumped down into a chair next to the drinks tray. 'Alec home yet?' he asked.

'Hours ago,' she drawled. 'He's speaking to Daddy on the telephone.'

'Daddy – ' He left his chair, 'I'd like to talk to him.'

'Daddy England, not Daddy Wales,' Fiona said irritably. 'There's some men-only thing on tonight, and they're both going. I don't suppose you two would like to take me out, would you? I hate staying in when Alec's out having fun. We could go to the cinema, or a show?'

'Fine,' Andrew agreed enthusiastically, ignoring the tight-lipped expression of annoyance on Anthea's face.

Anthea had written to Fe soon after his arrival in London. Pleading boredom, an empty wardrobe and a desperate need for an urgent London shopping trip she'd ask Fe if she could visit. Ever accommodating, and only too glad to have someone to stay to help amuse and lighten her lonely days, Fe had welcomed her with open arms, but Andrew had seen the heavy hand of his mother's interference in the scheme. And five days and nights spent under the same roof as Anthea had done nothing to dispel the unpleasant notion.

Anthea rose early so she could breakfast with him and, worse still, chatter about trivial nothings when all he wanted to do was eat, drink and read the paper in silence. She rooted out the small café where he and the doctors lunched when they could get away from the hospital, and turned up there with Fe in tow, feigning

329

amazement at his presence. She 'happened to be making her way back to Fe's', or 'passing' in the evenings when he was returning to Fe's after finishing work in the hospital for the day, a stroll he'd always regarded as a pleasant one until she joined him. And whenever they were alone together she prattled on about how wonderful life in London was; what a marvellous doctor's wife his mother made; and how well she got on with his entire family. Rather obvious topics that did nothing to endear her presence to him.

'Right, where shall we go?' Fiona asked as she handed Anthea a cocktail and Andrew a whisky.

'Cinema,' he suggested, thinking that at least he wouldn't have to talk to either of them while the film was on.

'I'll have a look at what's showing,' Anthea volunteered, cheering herself with the thought that Fe might go to bed early when they got back, leaving her alone with Andrew.

'Thank you,' Fiona smiled as she handed Anthea the paper. 'You've no idea how much I was dreading this evening.'

Andrew sipped his whisky slowly. He could understand his sister's reluctance to spend an evening by herself. He hadn't been comfortable in his own company since he'd left Pontypridd. The problem was, he often felt lonelier, more solitary and miserable when he was with someone else. Particularly Anthea. Outings with her had, if anything, sharpened his longing for Bethan. He missed her with a pain that became more acute with each passing day.

'Dinner won't be long.' Fiona freshened up his and Anthea's glasses. 'Oh, I almost forgot, there's a letter for you, Andy.' She picked up an envelope off the tray and waved it in front of his nose with a sly glance at Anthea. 'It's from Pontypridd,' she said, lifting her eyebrows suggestively. 'And it's not from Daddy or Mummy.' She sniffed the paper. 'There's no perfume. Your little nurse may belong to a den of thieves, but I'm afraid she isn't in the least bit romantic, dear brother,' she teased.

'Give me that, Fanny,' Andrew said irritably.

'My my, we are a crosspatch aren't we? What's the matter, Andy? Finding it difficult to get rid of her? Won't she take no for an answer?'

'Some women just don't know when to let go,' Anthea said,

allowing her acid thoughts to reach her tongue for the first time in Andrew's presence.

Andrew wasn't proud of the way he'd left Pontypridd and sought refuge in London, and every time he recalled how he'd taken leave of Bethan his blood ran cold. But Fiona's constant carping about her was driving him to distraction. He grasped hold of her wrist, making her cry out, then he tore the letter from her hand.

'That hurt,' she complained petulantly, rubbing her wrist.

'It was meant to.'

'Is it a love letter?' She tried to sit on the arm of his chair and look over his shoulder at the same time.

'It's from Trevor Lewis,' he snapped, flicking through the pages.

'Oh how disappointing.' Her face fell as she checked the signature. 'I suppose I should go into the kitchen and chase Cook up about dinner.'

'That might be an idea. I'm starving.'

'Do you want to come, Anthea?' she asked. 'If we leave grumpy to himself he might change his mood.'

Rebuffed, glasses in hand Fiona and Anthea wandered off. Andrew read and reread his letter. There wasn't a word about Bethan from beginning to end. Most of it concerned the wedding that was scheduled for the end of October, and there was a reminder in the final paragraph that he'd promised to act as best man, but if he couldn't make it for any reason they would understand and ask Trevor's brother to take his place.

The sheet of paper fell from his hand as he refilled his glass. Bethan would undoubtedly be there. Laura had always said that she'd wanted her to be bridesmaid. A vivid image of Bethan came to mind, reminding him just how much he loved and wanted – no, needed – her.

He swallowed the whisky and poured another. His father wasn't always right. Perhaps there was a way for him and Bethan after all. London was a cosmopolitan place. Cosmopolitan enough even to swallow a disgraced Welsh nurse and her husband. The idea appealed to him. He could go home, see her at the wedding, and ask her to return with him. Accommodation wasn't a problem. Half of London was up for rent, and if they started off modestly like Trevor and Laura – what the hell. They'd make it through. Thousands of other couples did. He didn't stop to consider that his thinking was a complete turnaround from that of only a few short weeks ago.

He'd been a fool not to have asked her to marry him when he'd had the chance. And if his parents kicked up a fuss, so what? He was qualified. So was Bethan. They could both get work. They'd survive without any help. His parents would have to come to terms with his choice of wife. Bethan was the only one who mattered. They didn't even have to marry in Pontypridd, they could marry here. He would carry on working at the Cross – go home to her every night instead of to Fe and Alec. Her aunts' transgressions were of no interest to anyone in London. No one would give a toss about anything that had occurred in Pontypridd. Most people didn't even know where it was. And in time she wouldn't be known by the name of Powell any more. Not even in Wales.

He finished his whisky and reached for the bottle again. He checked the date of Trevor's wedding on the letter. It wasn't that far away, another five weeks. He frowned as he lifted his glass. He couldn't wait that long; not after the way he'd treated her. He had to write. Tell her he was sorry. That he loved her. That he hadn't been thinking straight the last time he'd seen her.

A smile crossed his face for the first time since he'd been in London. His future stretched out before him, cosy with domesticity, glittering with the rewards of career achievement. A future that included love, Bethan, surgical duties in the Cross and a small but comfortable apartment to return to in the evenings. It didn't once enter his mind that perhaps he'd damaged his relationship with Bethan beyond repair.

Chapter Twenty

'You sure you'll be all right?'

'I've been fine every day so far, Mam.' Bethan sat in her father's easy chair in the kitchen with her feet propped up on a stool Haydn had made. There was a cup of tea at her elbow and a book from Pontypridd lending library that Maud had got for her on her lap. Two walking sticks leaned against the frame of the kitchen stove next to her. Her feet had healed enough to allow her to hobble out to the yard and back. She was grateful for small mercies; the pain of the walk was infinitely preferable to using the chamber pot her father had brought down from upstairs.

Elizabeth fixed her hat on firmly with the jet-headed pin that had been her mother's and checked her image in the mirror that hung above the stove. Her grey coat was close on twenty years old and it showed in the threadbare lines around the collar. The black felt hat was even older. Her dress was newer; bought at the market it was a cheap one that had shrunk in the wash. Its narrow lines skimmed even her thin figure too closely.

The woman who glared back at her from the glass was wrinkled, lined, old before her time, the result of trying to subsist for too long on air that was heavier on coal dust than oxygen, and on food bought with an eye to cost rather than nourishment. Cheap food, cheap housing, cheap clothes, she thought disparagingly, thinking not for the first time since Bethan's 'accident' of the clothes she'd be wearing if she'd managed to succeed where Bethan had failed.

But even then, unlike Bethan she'd had to struggle through all the physical and mental agonies of a failed abortion attempt with no one to help her, no woman to confide in. No one brought her cups of tea to soothe away her hurt. She'd been left to work through throbbing, pain-filled days. Her only comfort, if it could be called by that name, had been Evan's reluctant, martyred, declaration: 'I'm responsible for your condition, and I'll do what's right by you, never fear.'

She'd felt that she had no choice but to accept his sacrifice. She held him to his promise, married him knowing that he loved Phyllis Harry. That if he and Phyllis hadn't had a stupid row that fateful night, he'd have been with her still. He never would have got drunk, made a pass at her after choir practice. A pass that had flattered her into forgetting herself for the first and hopefully last time in her life. If she hadn't given in, been stronger, if . . . if . . . Bethan would never have been conceived. . . .

'You all right, Mam?' Bethan asked concerned.

'Fine.' She picked up her handbag from the chair next to the range. She really had to stop thinking in terms of 'what if twenty years ago'. She wasn't doing anyone, least of all herself, any favours. 'I won't be long.'

'Give Uncle Bull my regards,' Bethan muttered from behind her book.

'I will.' Elizabeth pulled on her shabby cotton gloves and left.

As she walked down the hill she considered the immediate problems that faced her. Bethan! There was only one way out of that situation. She hadn't discussed it with anyone, and didn't want to. Gossip spread like wildfire on the Graig. One whisper to a neighbour could spread scandal over the entire hill, but sooner or later she'd have to trust one other person. And it wouldn't be her uncle. He was too wrapped up in the traumas of his own problems to spare time for the troubles of others. John Joseph Bull wasn't the same minister who'd ruled his wife and his parish with a rod of iron a few weeks before. He was a broken man, totally reliant on the daily trips she made down the hill to clean his house and prepare his food. Without her, he would have been sitting in squalor in front of an empty table.

She knocked on his door. John Joseph's door, along with the doors of the Leyshons' large house and that of the vicarage, were the only ones on the Graig that didn't have keys protruding from the locks. He opened it himself, and preceded her into the kitchen without a greeting. She noticed that his shoulders were rounded. Hetty's passing had pitched him from the prime of life into stumbling old age, a transformation she wouldn't have believed possible in such a short space of time if she hadn't witnessed it herself.

She'd never seen him stoop before, and when he turned to face her, running his fingers through his uncombed hair in an attempt to make himself more presentable, she noticed that the grey hairs at his temples had multiplied. Even his face had altered. It was thinner, more haggard.

'Elizabeth, you don't have to watch me as though I'm a child,' he said irritably. 'The cawl you made yesterday is still good.'

'You haven't eaten much of it,' she commented, lifting the lid on the pot and stirring it. She replaced the lid, lifted the pot off the shelf above the stove and put it on the hotplate. Only then did she put down her bag, take off her gloves and hat and hang her coat on a peg at the back of the kitchen door. 'I may as well check on your stove as I'm here.' She pulled open the door. 'Look at that,' she complained, opening it wide so he could see the dying embers. 'It's almost out.'

The coal scuttle hadn't been touched since she'd filled it the day before. She picked up the tongs, and fed the fire with large lumps of coal and a smattering of small coal from the bucket kept next to the scuttle. John Joseph sat in a chair by the table and watched her as she worked.

'Would you like some tea?' she asked, suspecting from the absence of dirty dishes that he hadn't eaten since she'd left the house the day before.

'I'll have a cup if you're making one.'

She allowed the remark to pass without comment. She filled the kettle and set it on the range. 'You promised to watch the fire,' she reprimanded. 'Did you put a match to the one I laid in your study?'

'No. The weather's not cold enough for fires yet. Besides I went out yesterday.'

'Where?'

'The chapel. Just for a look around,' he qualified.

Elizabeth saw the admission as progress. He'd avoided entering the chapel or seeing any of his deacons or parishioners since the day of the funeral. A lay preacher had taken the service every Sunday since Hetty had died.

'I talked to the chapel committee yesterday,' he volunteered. 'I think it might be a good idea for me to move. There's a chapel in Ton Pentre in the Rhondda, or rather two that have no minis-

335

ter. Too poor to afford one. But I won't need much money now that Hetty's gone.'

'What did they say to the idea of you leaving?'

'It was decided that I should discuss the matter more fully with the deacons.'

She took down the old cracked blue and white cups and saucers from Hetty's dresser and made the tea, bringing in sugar and milk from the pantry.

'Uncle, it won't be as easy for me to visit you in Ton Pentre,' she warned.

'I know that. And I thank you for what you've done out of charity for me, Elizabeth, but it's time I moved on,' he said harshly, his voice cracking with strain. 'You've enough troubles in your own house without coming here to take on mine. Has Evan finished in the pit yet?'

'Tomorrow's his last day,' she answered curtly.

'How are you going to manage?'

'I don't know.' She poured the tea, rammed a handknitted cosy on the pot, and sat stiffly across the table from him.

'How's Bethan?'

'Still unable to work. Doctor says she could be off as long as two months.' She couldn't look him in the eye when she spoke about Bethan.

'Stupid thing to do,' he commented. 'Knock a bucket of boiling water over when you're drawing it from the boiler. I don't understand. . . . '

'I told you, it was easily done. I was there,' she lied.

'Yes . . . yes of course, you said,' he continued impatiently. 'But if the bucket was balancing on a piece of coal you'd think the girl would have noticed.'

'She didn't, and there's no point in talking about it.'

'At least you've got Haydn in work.'

'He doesn't bring in enough to keep himself.'

'Then that husband of yours will have to do something.'

'Easier said than done with all the pits closing.' She lifted the cosy from the pot, and poured out two more cups of tea, pushing the sugar and milk towards him.

'I've something here that may help. It's not a solution, but you may find it useful.' He rose unsteadily to his feet and walked over to the cupboard set in the alcove to the right of the stove. He lifted down an old chipped jug. Pushing his fingers inside he pulled out a roll of notes held together with an elastic band. 'I found a bank book amongst the things in Hetty's drawer when I was clearing it out. Didn't even know she had money of her own. Probably her father gave it to her when she married. She certainly hadn't put any into the account for years.' He thrust the bundle at Elizabeth. 'I couldn't use it. Not Hetty's money. You were always kind to her, Elizabeth. She would have wanted you to have it. Particularly now with Evan unemployed.'

'I couldn't . . . ' Elizabeth began half-heartedly. Money would solve so many problems. Especially now.

'Take it.' He pushed the roll into her hand as he sat down. 'I feel it's tainted,' he declared, negating any notions she might have had about his generosity. 'It brought no happiness to Hetty. And it's not enough to bring you happiness either. I think you'll need a great deal more than the seventy pounds in that roll for that. But it's enough to pay something off your mortgage.'

Elizabeth stared at the bundle of five-pound notes in her hands. She hadn't touched a five-pound note since she'd given up teaching.

'I suppose I could use it to pay some bills.' She walked over to the chair where she'd left her handbag, opened the clasp and secreted the roll in the bottom.

'Of course if you'd prefer to open a post office account for each of the children and put something in it for them to remember their aunt by, that will be all right by me too. Only don't tell them it's there. Otherwise they'll spend it before they really need it. Especially Bethan and Haydn. Those two dress far too smart for my taste.'

'I won't tell them, Uncle.' She looked at the notes one last time before closing her handbag. Her mind worked feverishly. Hetty's money could be used to buy Bethan respectability. She could think of no better use for it than that.

'Mam, no!' Bethan protested tearfully.

'You have no real choice in the matter, girl,' Elizabeth pronounced firmly. 'As I see it there's only three roads open to you. Either you go into the homes like Maisie Crockett, become a pariah and outcast like Phyllis, or marry. And I can think of no other man who'll take you with the doctor's bastard growing bigger inside you every day.' Elizabeth painted the options as bluntly and as crudely as she was capable of, hoping to shock Bethan into submission.

'But I hardly know him. I don't even like him. He's old . . . he has bad teeth . . . he drinks. . . . '

'He's only thirty-five, and he's a good, God-fearing, Christian, chapel-going man. And if he does take a drink I'm sure it's not more than your father does from time to time,' Elizabeth added acidly.

Bethan remembered something her Aunt Megan had said one morning after she'd finished working in the Graig Hotel.

'Damned North Walian. Swept him and that widow of his out with the slops again this morning. There's more than a touch of your uncle's hellfire and damnation about that one, only he isn't even honest about it. All chapel on Sunday, and boozing when he thinks no one is looking. This is not the first morning I've put him out of the Graig Hotel when your mother thought he was staying with friends. Give me my heathen lodgers any day of the week.'

She shuddered.

'Have you anyone else in mind?' Elizabeth asked nastily.

'No,' Bethan admitted.

'Then we have no choice. Just for once in your selfish life think of someone other than yourself. This would kill your father if he got to know about it. Eddie and Haydn would feel duty bound to tackle the man, and to what end? To one of them getting hurt. Killed even, knowing what Eddie's like when he's roused to a temper. And what about Maud? Have you considered what her reputation would be when this little lot becomes the property of every rumour-monger and gossip on the Graig? She'd be known as the sister of a whore.' Elizabeth spat out the final word.

The speech had the desired effect. Bethan's raw nerve had always been her brothers and Maud. She'd spent her life playing the role of the protective older sister; she couldn't abandon it now. She stared down at her bandaged feet, resting on the stool

'Do what you think best, Mam. You always do in the end,' she added bitterly. But the bitterness was lost on Elizabeth.

338

Elizabeth picked her time. After the evening meal Evan helped Bethan upstairs to her bedroom then left for a union meeting. Maud went to jazz band practice with the Dan-y-Lan Coons, and Eddie walked down the hill to the gym. She hadn't seen Haydn since midday when he'd gone to Griffiths' shop. By now he'd be working.

She cleared away the dishes quickly, and glanced at the kitchen clock. It was nearly seven. Maud was expected home first and she wouldn't be in the house until half-past eight at the earliest. Drying her hands on her overalls, she took them off and hung them on the back of the door. Straightening her blouse, she walked to Alun's door.

'Mr Jones, may I have a word with you?'

He opened the door. 'If it's about the rent, Mrs Powell, it's not due until Saturday and I am good for it.'

'I don't doubt that you are, Mr Jones. It's not about the rent.'

'Please come in. Sit down.' He pointed to the only chair in his room. An old upright kitchen chair. She sat on it.

'I wanted to ask you what you intend doing now?'

'Now that the pit's closed you mean?'

She nodded.

'I'll be honest with you, Mrs Powell. I don't know.'

'When you first came here you said that you were trying to save enough money to open a lodging house?'

'That's right.' It was a sore point with Alun. After a childhood and adolescence spent working fourteen-hour days on the hill farms and in the slate quarries of North Wales he'd promised himself an easier life. The rumours that reached North Wales from the south said there was good money to be earned in the Rhondda pits: five years' hard graft was all that was needed for a man to earn enough to set himself up for life. But here he was ten years later with only twenty pounds to his name, no job and still no sight of that good life ahead.

'Have you managed to save enough money towards that lodging house of yours?' Elizabeth prompted, breaking into his reverie.

'No. I haven't managed to save a penny since we were put on short time, and now ... ' he shrugged his shoulders, 'I have

339

twenty pounds put away. That's not enough to secure a house, and furnish it.'

'How much more do you need?'

His eyes gleamed hopefully. Could Mrs Powell be looking for an investment? He knew about her uncle the minister. And by all accounts her father had been a minister too. Chapel people were notorious misers. If she had her own money she could be looking to hide it from the parish relief investigating officers before Evan went on the dole.

'I could probably go ahead if I had another fifty,' he said carefully, watching her face for signs that he'd gone either too high, or too low. 'If I had that much I'd be able to buy all the furniture I wanted and put a deposit down on one of the four-storeyed houses on Broadway. There's one that I've had my eye on for months. The bank evicted the owners and foreclosed on the mortgage. They're asking two hundred pounds, but now that the pits are closed they might drop to a hundred and eighty, perhaps even lower. But whatever the final figure they'll still be looking for a deposit of fifty. It's in a bit of a state, been empty for a while, but there's nothing wrong there that I couldn't put right.'

'The mortgage would be a good ten to fifteen shillings a week,' Elizabeth warned.

'I'd have the rents to pay it with. There's a three-roomed basement that could be let out as a separate flat. Two rooms and a kitchen above the basement, and six bedrooms and a box room above that on two floors. I intend to let out the flat for seven and six a week . . .' He looked at her. 'You don't think that's too much do you?' he asked seriously. 'It's half a crown less than the houses in Leyshon Street.'

'It would be worth about that if it's got its own entrance,' Elizabeth observed practically.

'It's got that all right, back and front. I thought I'd live in the two rooms on the same floor as the kitchen and let out the rest. Seven shillings and sixpence a week for a single, and six and six each for those sharing a double. For that I'd have to give them breakfast and tea of course, but given enough beds – that's why I need the extra money,' he explained, 'to buy the beds. I could get at least ten men into those six rooms. With the rent from the basement that would make over three pounds ten shillings a week coming into the house. Even allowing for food and a woman to come in and do the cooking and cleaning, I reckon on clearing at least one pound ten shillings a week. If I paid that off the mortgage the house would be mine in no time.' He smiled, happy that he'd found someone prepared to listen to his scheme.

'I can see that you've got it all worked out, Mr Jones.'

'I've had nothing else to think about. It's been pretty obvious which way the pits have been going for a long time. Things would be a lot different if I had that fifty pounds, I can tell you, Mrs Powell,' he added craftily. 'First one house, then who knows, another maybe. Perhaps even a third if I could find the right people to run them for me,' he said unsubtly. 'Lack of money has never stopped me from dreaming.'

'If I gave you fifty pounds. Gave . . . ' Elizabeth repeated. She saw the greed in his eyes and knew she'd marked the North Walian right.

'What could I do for you that's worth that much, Mrs Powell?' he asked cautiously.

'A favour,' she said carefully. 'And before I tell you what it is you have to promise never to repeat what I'm about to say to anyone. Not now or in the future. If you say no to my proposition we'll both just forget I asked. If you say yes, that will be a very different matter. What do you say, Mr Jones?'

'That I agree to your conditions, Mrs Powell. What exactly is this favour?'

'Marry my daughter, Mr Jones. And quickly.'

Elizabeth led the way upstairs. She knocked on the girls' bedroom door and opened it. Bethan was lying in semi-darkness staring at the vista of rooftops and skyline framed within the narrow confines of the sash window.

'Mr Jones wants a word with you, Bethan.' She switched on the lamp, killing the soft, pleasant, twilight glow with a cruel blast of yellow light. 'I'll be in my bedroom if you need me. All you have to do is call out.'

'Yes, Mam.'

Alun Jones hovered uneasily in the open doorway of the room.

He waited until Elizabeth had closed her bedroom door before speaking.

'Won't you sit down?' Bethan asked, indicating the dressing-table stool. She felt calm, flat; the tears and emotion of earlier completely spent.

'I'll just say what I've come to say, then I'll go if you don't mind.' Intimidated by Elizabeth's presence in the room next door and seeing Bethan in the intimacy of her bedroom, he shifted his weight uneasily from one foot to the other.

'Suit yourself,' Bethan said ungraciously, steeling herself.

'I've saved some money, Nurse Powell, it's not much but it's enough to put a down payment on a house and there's one going on Broadway. It's got six bedrooms and a basement flat. I intend to take in lodgers. With the pit finishing I have to think of other ways of making a living. If you'll be kind enough to marry me, we could build up a tidy business between us. I'm not saying it will be easy. There'll be a lot of cooking, cleaning, washing and so on, but as I wouldn't be working I could help out.'

'Thank you for the offer.' The inane phrase was all Bethan could manage. She might have lived under the same roof as Alun Jones for three years but she knew absolutely nothing about the man. Nor had she ever felt the urge to find out anything. Given her indifference she felt that his proposal was ludicrous. Totally and utterly ludicrous.

'I know about – about – your condition,' he stammered, pulling his earlobe and biting his lower lip in confusion. 'And. . . . ' He took the bull by the horns and blurted out what he'd really come to say. 'And I'm prepared to accept the child in return for your help in my business. Of course it will take me a week or two to sort out a mortgage for the house, perhaps longer. But if you're agreeable I could make arrangements for us to get married in the Registry Office in Courthouse Street. It wouldn't be the same as a chapel wedding of course. But I hope you'll agree that it's what comes after the ceremony that's important. And I already know of one married couple and four men who are looking for decent lodgings.'

Bethan turned away from him and stared disconsolately at one of the Rossetti prints on the wall. It had been a favourite since childhood: the wedding of St George and Princess Sabra. She couldn't even begin to count the hours she'd stared at it as a child, dreaming of the day when she'd grow up and fall in love with her very own knight. Imagining the beauty and romance of the wedding that would follow.

'May I go to the Registry Office tomorrow, Nurse Powell?'

The question intruded into her lifelong daydream, shattering it utterly. Completely and for ever. She put all thoughts of romance aside and remembered her shame, her family, and her duty in that order.

'You may.'

She couldn't even bring herself to ask him to call her Bethan.

Four weeks later Trevor pronounced Bethan fit enough to return to work. They'd argued dreadfully during her convalescence. He'd wanted to write to Andrew about her condition. By dint of lies and a fair amount of acting she'd managed to convince him that the baby was the main reason why Andrew had left Pontypridd for London. Eventually, after a great deal of soul-searching during which she'd continually reminded him that she had the full and knowing support of her mother, he'd finally agreed not to inter-fere.

Armed with Trevor's medical certificate and terrified of receiv-ing a refusal she requested that she be returned to night duty. To her amazement Matron agreed. She failed to find out whether she'd been given the shift because the hospital was short of night staff, or because Trevor had balked at carrying out his threat to ask that she be transferred to days. But once she knew she was being returned to her old shift she didn't care about the reason. She was simply grateful that she was being allowed to work with a skeleton staff, away from Laura's concerned and prying eyes.

All she could think of was holding out. Keeping the child within her a secret, from everyone except her mother and Trevor, the only two people acquainted with her shame. And maintaining her distance from Laura, her father, brothers, Maud – everyone who was likely to ask questions she didn't want to answer. It was easier to do that when she worked nights and slept during the day. The evenings were the only dangerous times, and she even managed to cut down on those by staying in bed until an hour before she was due on the ward.

At the end of Bethan's first week in work, Elizabeth made breakfast, saw Evan and the boys off down the hill, but, instead of settling down to do the housework she broke with her normal routine and went straight back upstairs to wash and change. When she came down a letter was lying on the doormat, just inside the door. She picked it up and turned it over in her hand. It was addressed to Bethan and bore a London postmark. The third to come in as many weeks. Why couldn't the man leave Bethan alone! She clutched it tightly, wanting to destroy it or open it, but lacked the courage. She'd sorted Bethan's problems out beautifully without help from anyone, except perhaps poor dead Hetty. She didn't need this. A few hours from now Bethan would be Mrs Alun Jones; a respectably married housewife with a lodging house and a husband to take care of, and a nice steady income flowing in to keep the wolf from the door. That is unless . . . unless she suspected . . . .

Elizabeth stuffed the envelope into her pocket, consoling herself with the thought that she might be reading more into the letters than they contained. Perhaps the man merely wanted Bethan to return something he'd given her. Perhaps he was warning her not to press a paternity suit. Yes, that was it. His parents had heard rumours, perhaps from Trevor Lewis, and he wanted to make sure that Bethan didn't implicate him in any way. After all, he hadn't ever really cared for Bethan. If he had, he'd have stayed in Pontypridd to look after her.

'Mam, I didn't see you, did I knock you?' Bethan asked as she walked in from work, drenched to the skin by the early morning autumn rains.

'No. No you didn't.' Elizabeth hastily laid her hand over her pocket, crunching the paper. 'Letter from the bank manager,' she explained. 'No doubt he's wondering, like I am, how exactly your father intends to pay the mortgage. You look soaked,' she said to Bethan, sounding positively garrulous for once.

'It's filthy out there.' Bethan went into the kitchen, hung her dripping cloak and uniform dress on the airing rack, and tied the dressing gown that her mother had ready around herself.

'No one's home except Alun,' Elizabeth volunteered as she laid bread and jam out on the table. Bethan knew that Maud would be in school. She didn't ask where her father and brothers were.

If they hadn't planned anything, her mother would have found some pretext to send them out. And then again they never needed much persuasion to leave the house. Her mother hadn't created much of a home to linger in, she thought miserably, closing her eyes to the dingy kitchen.

'And there's no time for sleeping either,' Elizabeth said abruptly. 'The ceremony's set for ten sharp.'

'I know,' Bethan agreed wearily. 'I'll go up and change now.'

'I'll bring your washing water up.'

'Thank you.' Bethan knew why her mother was being nice and resented her for it. Nevertheless she dragged her feet and went upstairs.

As soon as she was alone Elizabeth pulled the letter out of her pocket again. She looked at it one last time then she opened the dresser drawer, and thrust it next to the others, beneath a pile of tea towels. Only then did she fill the jug and take it up to Bethan.

Bethan washed and dressed mechanically, putting on her blue serge skirt and a white blouse. She packed her spare underclothes, uniform, slippers and dressing gown into the cardboard suitcase her mother had left lying on the bed. She'd already slept her last night, or rather day, in Graig Avenue. She took one final wistful look at the double bed she'd shared with Maud for so many years and went downstairs.

Half an hour later she walked back down the hill in company with her mother and Alun. He carried her suitcase; he'd taken his own to the house on Broadway the night before. She wore her old, shabby black coat which soaked up the rain like a sponge despite the umbrella Elizabeth held over both their heads.

They sat in the damp ante-room to the Registry Office and waited. There were puddles of dirty water on the mock-mosaic floor, and the brown paint on the woodwork was cracked and peeling. Bethan felt strange, remote. As if she wasn't really in the room at all, but watching from the outside. She started to weave a pretence that she was in the White Palace, seeing a film about someone sitting in a doctor's waiting room waiting for news of their loved one. Then Alun offered to help her off with her coat, and she returned bleakly to the world of reality.

She noticed that he was wearing a black suit, shiny with age and frayed at the cuffs. Not wanting to meet his eyes she looked away and saw a huge patch of damp that had spread across the whole of one corner, staining both walls and ceiling. She wove a fantasy, imagining it was a map, and when she was in the middle of populating it with towns and villages the registrar called their names. They left their uncomfortable seats and walked into a second room, smaller than the first. There were two rows of schoolroom chairs, a large wooden desk that held a book that had already been opened out, and a vase of dusty wax flowers. The registrar murmured something to Alun then left the room for a few moments, returning with a woman Bethan had never seen before.

'We need a second witness,' Alun explained.

The ceremony, such as it was, began. Afterwards Bethan remembered little of it. Mainly the absence of what should have been. There were no flowers, no music, no choir, no relatives, no friends, no laughter, no joy and no good wishes. Only the cold, damp brown and cream room, the rain beating on the window, the long silences whenever the registrar ceased speaking, and the strange woman and her mother standing behind her, blocking her only exit.

She must have said 'yes' when the important question was asked, because Alun pushed a ring on to her finger. She recognised it: a heavy gold band, dark with age and engraved in the centre with a single cross. It had been her mother's mother's. As a child she'd never been allowed to touch it. It had lain in pride of place in Elizabeth's half-empty jewellery box. She found it peculiar that a ring she hadn't been allowed to touch then, now bound her to a man she didn't know – or love.

'You may kiss the bride.'

She stared at the registrar then at Alun and panicked. She stepped back, stumbling over her own feet. Alun put out his hand and caught her before she fell. The registrar laughed.

'All brides are shy in company, Mr Jones,' he joked. 'But don't worry, you'll soon be alone with Mrs Jones.'

'Mrs Jones.' She looked around, confused for a moment. Then the enormity of what she'd done hit home. She was Mrs Jones.

Chapter Twenty-One

After the ceremony Elizabeth led the way back into the waiting room. The registrar and the witness said goodbye, and the communicating door between office and ante-room closed behind them.

'Well . . . ' Elizabeth looked at Bethan and Alun, and gave them a tight little smile, which neither returned. She debated whether or not to break into a pound of the twenty she had left of Hetty's money and offer to buy them a meal in Ronconis' café, but on reflection she thought better of the idea. After all, it was Alun who was sitting on the lion's share of the money, not her.

'We'd better be going,' Alun said, picking up his and Bethan's coats. 'I think the house is ready to sleep in but Bethan may have other ideas.'

'I'll see you soon, Bethan.' Elizabeth walked over to Bethan, pecked her cheek and left the building. She paused in the doorway for a moment to put up her umbrella, then began the long, lonely walk back up the hill.

She'd done it! She'd bought Bethan respectability, but her elation was tempered by the knowledge that the worst was to come. She had yet to break the news to Evan.

'This is it.' Alun turned the key in the lock and pushed open the glass-panelled door. The wood, swollen by damp, scraped grudgingly over the tiled floor of the porch, and Bethan found herself facing an inner door, glass-panelled again, this time in ornate etched glass. She turned the knob and stepped into a dark, damp, musty-smelling passage.

'It needs a lot doing to it, but I've got everything in hand. A few months and you won't recognise the place, I promise you. And you're seeing the worst bit,' he gabbled, afraid that her silence meant disapproval. 'The kitchen should be nice and warm.' He walked ahead of her to the end of the passage and opened a door. 'I paid the woman next door to lay a fire ready for us and clean up the place a bit. She's been at it all week. I won't be able to afford to pay her again of course, but seeing as how you worked last night and had a week's wages coming to cover the cost I decided it would be worth it.'

'That was thoughtful of you.'

He failed to detect the irony in her voice.

'You carry on and have a good look round while I put your case in the bedroom.'

He stepped past her and she walked on into the kitchen alone. It was a large square room, built one storey up from the garden. A range was set into the centre of the wall to her right. Clean, newly blackleaded, it radiated a little warmth into the chilly atmosphere, but the air was still several degrees colder than in her mother's kitchen at home. Shivering in the draught she went to close the door just as Alun came in.

'Sink in the kitchen,' he said proudly, pointing to a stone sink complete with wooden draining-board fixed under the window with a tap high on the wall above it. 'You won't have to carry water far for cooking or washing.'

'So I see. Did you buy the furniture?'

'Most of it came with the house,' he admitted. 'I know it's old, but it's solid.' He kicked the leg of the pine Victorian table to demonstrate its strength. The six matching upright chairs, two easy chairs and dresser were of the same wood. Chipped, stained, yellowed with age – the best that could be said about them was that they were still strong. The covers on the easy chairs were threadbare but clean; obviously the 'woman next door' had done some washing as well as cleaning. The shelves of the dresser were crammed with china, but when she went to examine it she tripped over the lino. She glanced down and saw that the floor covering was torn as well as stained.

'It needs a lot doing,' he repeated. The phrase was beginning to irritate her. Like the refrain on a cracked record.

'Is this the way down to the back?' Treading carefully, she opened a door in the far wall. It led into the washhouse. Glass-roofed and half walled in cracked, dusty glass, it was built out over the back yard. Another door led to a flight of rickety wooden steps down to the garden below.

'At least the kitchen's reasonably clean,' she commented, trying

348

hard to find something complimentary to say, as she returned to the kitchen.

'Told you I paid the woman next door to give the house a good going through,' he said, brightening at her show of interest. 'I know the walls could do with a lick of paint, but we'll soon have that done.'

She looked at the peeling paint, the damp patches above the sink and around the windows and thought it needed a lot more than a 'lick of paint' but she didn't contradict him.

'Come on, I'll show you the parlour.' He led the way into the front, bay-windowed room. A deal table-desk and chair were set on the bare floorboards, which had been swept, and a fire was laid in the cast-iron grate, but there were no curtains at the window and no shade over the naked bulb. 'I bought the desk off the second-hand stall on the market. I would have got more, but as this is going to be your room as well, I thought you might like to choose something yourself. When the money comes in to pay for it, of course.'

She stared at the peeling wallpaper and scarred surfaces of the skirting boards and windowsill.

'It needs decorating first.'

'I'll give you a hand to do that.'

He shut the door and led the way into the middle room. Dark and dingy, it was lit only by a single tiny window sandwiched between the protruding kitchen wall on one side and the house next door on the other.

'I'd thought we'd sleep in here. You can't hear the traffic like you can in the front.'

She looked around. As in the front room, the wallpaper was hanging loose off the walls. But this room was fully furnished. A large double bed, gentleman's and lady's wardrobes, a tallboy, dressing table, washstand and bedside cabinets all in the same clumsily carved heavy dark wood were crammed into its narrow confines. There was barely room to stand between one item of furniture and the next. The smell of beeswax polish hung suffocatingly in the still, stale air.

'All the bedding is new,' he said proudly, patting the dark green candlewick bedspread. 'The woman next door bought it in Leslie's. The furniture was the best in the house so I brought it down here. Would you like me to light the fire?' He pointed to the grate where a fire was laid, but unlit.

'It might be an idea. The whole house seems a bit damp to me.' She shuddered as much at the sight of the bed as from the chill in the air. It was ridiculous, particularly in view of the condition that had forced her to marry Alun in the first place, but until that moment she hadn't really considered that sharing a bed with him was part of the bargain.

'That could be because your coat's soaking wet. Come on, hang it up in the kitchen next to the oven so it can dry, and then I'll show you the upstairs.'

Taking her coat off and hanging it up was the first small act that brought home to her that this was the house she was going to live in from now on. Until then she'd felt like a visitor; someone who'd been invited to look over a friend's new house.

He gave her a conducted tour of every room except those in the basement; he'd already let them for six shillings a week.

'Not as much as I hoped for,' he apologised as if she'd been expecting more. 'But then letting it go unfurnished saves me the expense of buying beds and tables, and they don't come cheap.'

He'd furnished every bedroom. Three had double beds, two had twin single beds, the rest only one. He'd even managed to squeeze a short put-you-up into the box room.

'Could come in handy,' he explained. 'Even if I only charge four shillings a week for sleeping here, I'll soon recover the price of the put-you-up.'

'It must have cost a lot?' she observed, wondering where he'd got the money from. 'All this furniture as well as the down payment to buy this place.'

'I've a mortgage of a hundred and fifty pounds,' he offered defensively. 'And until the rent starts coming in we'll have to manage on your wages and savings and the five pounds which is all I've got left from my pit money and savings. It may have to last us as long as a month, and I warn you now the mortgage is seventeen shillings and sixpence a week. I also thought I might waive the first week's rent for anyone who's prepared to decorate their own room.'

'That might be an idea. The woman next door must have worked hard, but you can't clean dirty wallpaper.'

'We are in the worst room.'

They were standing in the bay-windowed bedroom built over the parlour. Like all the other rooms, it contained beds, complete with old but clean sheets and clean blankets. No bedspreads. A chest of drawers, a washstand, toiletware and a wardrobe. Nothing else. Not even a picture or an ornament.

'The first four lodgers are moving in on Sunday. If they're not agreeable about the decorating I'll give you a hand to do it when they're out during the day.'

There it was again, the 'I'll give you a hand'. This time she couldn't let it pass. 'I've never decorated a room in my life,' she countered.

'Didn't your mother teach you? I watched her when she did out your kitchen two years ago. She's a dab hand.'

'That's my mother, not me. Besides, I may have to work for a while yet. They'll not be able to replace me on the ward that easily.'

'I thought . . . I thought with the baby coming and everything you'd have to give up working in the hospital,' he said awkwardly.

'I don't intend to tell anyone that I'm pregnant just yet,' she snapped back tartly.

'That suits me,' he agreed. 'And if you're happy to carry on working it might be just as well if you do earn a wage for a few weeks longer. Just until all the rooms are full. That way we might even stretch to paying for someone to do the wallpapering.'

'I think that would be better than expecting me to do it.'

A crushing silence fell between them, accentuated all the more by the sound of the cries of the rag and bone man passing by on his cart. Alun sensed that somehow they'd got off on the wrong foot. He'd expected her to show more pleasure in the house; to be grateful to him for allowing the child to use his name, and for the roof he was providing for both of them. After all, there weren't many men prepared to marry a woman who was carrying another man's bastard. He'd even gone out of his way to make things easy for her. He hadn't had to employ Ada Richards to set the house to rights, but he'd done it. He'd given Bethan a lot better start than most wives had. Now it was time for her to pull her weight and show willing. Every woman knew what a wife had to do. And every husband had the right to demand that a wife do everything necessary to turn a house into a home. But instead of displaying the humble appreciation he'd expected, Bethan faced him unbowed, and unrepentant. Refusing to even try her hand at wallpapering, when everyone knew that the woman, not the man of the house, saw to things like that.

'I'll have to go into work early tonight before the day shift finishes,' she informed him briskly. 'I have to make an appointment to see Matron in the morning, to tell her I'm married.'

'Yes, of course. Are you hungry?' he asked as an afterthought. 'Because if you are, there should be food in the cupboard. I asked. . . . '

'I know, you asked the woman next door to buy some.'

He looked at her with such a peculiar, hurt expression that she couldn't help but smile. 'No, I'm not hungry, Alun, but I am tired,' she admitted, suddenly realising why she was so irritable. It was a strain just to stand and face him, let alone think about the future. 'I've been up all night, and if I'm to see Matron I have to leave before six tonight.'

'That early?'

'Yes,' she said firmly, knowing full well what was on his mind.

'Bethan, we haven't really sorted anything out, but then if you're tired, now's probably not the time.'

'No it isn't. I'm going straight to bed.'

'Would you like me to come and keep you warm? Just for a bit?' he asked suggestively.

'Not now if you don't mind, Alun,' she said stiffly. 'I really am tired.'

He reached out and squeezed her left breast hard. 'You don't know what you're turning down,' he leered, trying to unbutton her blouse.

'I said I'm tired,' she repeated, pulling her blouse together and backing away from him.

'Just one quick look.'

'I said not now,' she snapped, on the verge of hysteria.

'Tomorrow morning then.' He rubbed his hands together. 'First thing.' He might have been talking about a milk delivery. 'The *ty bach* is out the back. It's a bit of a climb up and down the steps. It's not right next to the house, that's the coal shed. It's along a bit.'

'I'll find it.'

Shaken and repelled by Alun's crude advances she ran downstairs, opened up her suitcase, took out her damp uniform and hung it over the airing rack next to her coat. Returning to the bedroom she sank wearily down on the bed and looked around at the signs of masculine occupancy. She should unpack, but she couldn't bear the thought of lifting her clothes out and putting them away. Not here, not in this room that she'd have to share with Alun.

Eventually she closed her case and lifted it, clothes and all, on top of the tallboy. Steeling herself to pass him, she walked through the kitchen and into the outhouse. The steps down to the back were rotten in places and slippery with rainwater. The garden, if you could call it that, was a wilderness of waist-high weeds and discarded rubbish. She made out the rusting shapes of old cooking pots, pram or 'bogey' wheels, and a hill built up of old tin cans. When she finally climbed back up the steps she saw Alun sitting at the table eating a slice of cold pork pie smothered in mustard.

'Sure you won't change your mind about the food?' he asked.

She looked at the pie, thick with congealed fat, and almost retched.

'I'm sure, thank you. Will you call me at five?'

'It's twelve now.'

'That can't be helped. I'll try to make up for lost sleep tomorrow.'

'As you like.'

She went into the bedroom. The ancient cotton curtains were so rotten they fell apart in her hands when she tried to pull them. Hooking the ragged ends over the rail in an attempt to give herself a little privacy she checked the jug on the washstand. It was empty so she returned to the kitchen to fill it. Alun was at the sink rinsing his plate. He took the jug from her hand and put it under the tap.

'I've always been fond of you, Bethan,' he said clumsily, rubbing himself against her. 'You do know that don't you? That's why I agreed to marry you when your mother asked.'

She walked to the stove, ostensibly to warm herself, glad to be out of his reach. Then she looked at him, really looked at him for the first time in her life. Not that many years separated him from her father. And like her father he was broad built, although a good deal shorter, only about the same height as herself. There was nothing obnoxious about him. In fact the worst she could have said about his looks was that they were nondescript. Instantly forgettable.

His face was plump, circular, his skin pock-marked, his features regular, even. His round, dark brown eyes had the same appeal as those of her father's lurcher. But despite his not unattractive appearance and his bungling attempts at kindness she could not bring herself to respond to his brutish attempts to caress her.

'I need time, Alun,' she emphasised, as he carried the jug towards her.

'Not too long. After all, it's not as if you're not used to it.' He lifted her skirt and she pulled it down.

'Once more and I'm going home,' she hissed.

'This is your home, bach,' he said flatly.

She backed towards the door. Catching it with her hip she inadvertently closed it. Exhausted and frightened, she fumbled for the handle. He slammed his free hand above her head, holding it shut behind her.

'I'll take the water before I go,' she said bravely, holding out her hand.

'Bethan . . . ' He tried to fondle her. Instinctively she lashed out, kicking his shin and pushing him away from her at the same time. He tipped the water, soaking the front of her skirt and blouse.

'Serves you right,' he said angrily, 'for getting me going like that.'

'Getting you going?' she shouted frenziedly. 'I told you I was tired. That I'd been up all night.'

He turned to put the empty jug on the table. Taking advantage of his movement away from her, she wrenched open the door, ran out into the passage and into the bedroom, slamming the door behind her. Fortunately it had a lock. Not a very strong one, but still a lock. She turned the key and walked to the far side of the bed. Heaving with all her might she pushed it against the door for extra security. Just as she'd finished, the doorbell

354

rang. She heard the murmur of voices as Alun answered it. He walked back down the passage, tried the doorknob, and when it wouldn't give, called out to her.

'That was the woman downstairs. Appears there's a problem with water coming up through the basement floor. I have to go and look at it. I'll see you later, but don't worry, I won't try and touch you again. Not today,' he said acidly. 'I can wait until tomorrow morning. After all, we've our whole lives ahead of us.'

It was with that thought in mind that, still fully dressed in her soaking wet clothes, Bethan finally cried herself to sleep between the freezing, damp sheets on the bed.

'You've done *what*, woman?' Evan thundered.

Elizabeth backed away trembling. She'd made Evan angry many times before. But she'd never seen this cold, savage temper burn in his eyes before.

'I saw our Bethan married to Alun Jones this morning . . . ' She looked past his shoulder and fell silent. Evan turned and glimpsed Eddie and Haydn, white-faced and dumbstruck, standing behind him in the passage.

'I want to speak to your mother, boys. Alone!' he ordered. Eddie retreated but Haydn stood firm.

'I have as much right as you, Dad, to know why our Bethan married the lodger without saying a word to any of us about it.' He folded his arms and stood his ground.

'She left me no choice,' Elizabeth said defensively. 'I had to arrange it. She brought disgrace on all of us. Would you have rather she'd brought a bastard into this house?' she asked belligerently.

'She wouldn't have been the first Powell to roll with a man before she was married,' Evan countered aggressively.

'At least I was able to marry the father of my bastard in chapel,' she shouted. 'Which is more than your precious Bethan could have done.'

It was the first time Elizabeth had raised her voice in anger. That, as much as what she'd said, sent Haydn and Eddie scuttling back down the hall and out on to the front doorstep.

'That's always been your problem, hasn't it, Elizabeth?' Evan ranted. 'You never could truck our Bethan being more beautiful and clever than you ever were. . . . '

'What good's beauty or brains to a woman,' Elizabeth hissed, 'when men use a woman for one thing and one thing only? You weren't concerned with what I thought, or my looks, when you walked me home by Shoni's pond that night after choir practice.'

'You didn't exactly fight me off. You damn well enjoyed it every bit as much as I did.'

'If I enjoyed it, I've paid for it every day of my life since. Putting up with your groping night after night. Bearing your children. Living amongst common worthless people who insult me every time I show my face in the street. Hearing whispers about you or your low, criminal family behind my back every time I walk into a shop. One slip. Just one slip. . . . '

'I wouldn't have touched you that night if you hadn't led me on, and if I hadn't quarrelled with. . . . '

'Go on, say it,' Elizabeth taunted. 'If you hadn't quarrelled with the great love of your life.'

'You knew damn well then and you know now that I wouldn't have touched you if I hadn't been drunk. All you had to do was push me away. Tell me to stop. But not you . . . you. . . . '

'Don't go trying to blame me for that night, Evan Powell. If it hadn't been me it would have been some other girl. Any other girl. You were like a dog looking for a bitch, and any bitch would have done.'

'I found my bitch,' he thundered violently. 'A bitch on heat. On the one and only night in your life you behaved like a female of any species. I wish to God I had gone with someone else,' he uttered fervently. 'Almost anyone would have done, because I don't think any other woman would have brought as much misery to this house, my children, or me as you have.'

'How dare you! You . . . you. . . . ' Lost for words Elizabeth lashed out with her fists. Evan caught her arm before she had a chance to hit him. Instinctively, without thinking of the consequences, he slammed her full in the face with his open hand. The blow sent her reeling to the hearthrug, bleeding from a cut on her mouth. Too stunned even to cry.

'Swine!' Eddie exclaimed feelingly as he sat on the doorstep.

'Who?' Haydn asked blankly, too stunned to think coherently.
'That smarmy bloody doctor, who else?' Eddie demanded viciously. 'Well if this is what I think it is, he can look out,' he threatened. 'If he ever sets foot in Pontypridd again, he can look out.'

Evan walked out of the house just after four. He'd left Elizabeth nursing a swollen face, split lip and black eye. The knowledge that he'd hit a woman for the first time in his life left a sour, rancid taste in his mouth, but it didn't stop him from hating Elizabeth with every fibre in his body. This time she'd gone too far. He'd never forgive her for what she'd done to Bethan. He'd worked with Alun Jones for ten years, long enough to know that the man didn't do any favours for anyone unless money was involved. He couldn't begin to imagine how Elizabeth had paid him. She of course had hotly denied that she had, speaking only of Alun's regard for Bethan. Regard! Pah! He spat in the gutter. He had to see Bethan so he could hear the truth for himself. But he didn't know her address. Elizabeth had said that Alun Jones had bought a house on Broadway. She hadn't even bothered to find out the number. And that was another thing – Alun Jones had talked about opening a lodging house for years. But he was too fond of the drink to save anything like the kind of money needed to put a down payment on a house the size of the ones on Broadway. There were far too many unanswered questions in this 'marriage' for his liking.

He clenched his fists tightly at the thought of Bethan being handed over to the man like a parcel of unwanted goods. As a lodger and fellow miner Alun Jones was one of the boys. But the idea of him as a son-in-law, sleeping every night in the same bed as Bethan, incensed him. Elizabeth had said she thought he'd make a good husband. What the hell did Elizabeth know about the darker side of a man's nature? The bloody woman had never taken her nightdress off once in all the time they'd been married, and more fool him, he'd never made her. When Bethan had been conceived . . . he thrust the image swiftly from his mind and concentrated on the bitter, frigid years that they'd shared a bedroom. The years when she'd used every excuse she could think up to repulse his advances. And he'd never pushed her, or forced her once, no matter how much he'd burned and ached for a sensual touch.

He tried to recall all the rumours he'd heard about Alun. There'd been a widow in Zoar Street who'd sported a black eye that gossip attributed to Alun's doing. And he'd seen the man himself going off with tarts in the pubs in town. Drink and women – that's where Alun Jones' wages had gone. Some life in store for his favourite daughter.

Inwardly seething, he slowed down when he reached the foot of the Graig hill. He strolled over to the group of idlers standing on the Tumble, and watched the traffic. People trudged past with shopping bags full of windfall apples and potatoes. Children carried newspaper cones that the bakers had filled with a shilling's worth of stale ends. Some of the toddlers already had the white pinched look of hunger about their faces that he remembered from the strikes of the twenties. His own children along with many others from the Graig had been fed then in the soup kitchens set up by the Salvation Army. And the *Observer* had reported that the Salvationists, ever ready to help in any crisis, were reopening the Jubilee Hall kitchens on the Graig again for the children of the unemployed. Charity stuck in his craw. But at least in the twenties the miners had the option of going back to work, albeit for less money. *They* had taken that option away this time, and he trembled not only for the bleak, hungry future of his own family, but for that of every other miner in the town. He damned the government, and the system, that had brought a whole class of workers to this misery.

Slowly, gradually the stream of pedestrians and carts dwindled to a trickle. The painted ladies of the town began to leave the two foot nine and join him on the station square.

'Out of work, love?' asked one small, improbable blonde who lisped badly because her front teeth were missing.

He nodded, not wanting to get into conversation.

'Come on then, sunshine, I'll give you one for free. For luck.'

He shook his head. There was something familiar about the woman. Something. . . . 'Dottie?' he asked tentatively. 'Dottie Miles?'

'Evan Powell?'

'It's a long way from Graig infants' school, Dottie.'

'That it is.'

'I thought you married Bill Moss.'

'I did. He died four years ago. Pit accident. Got to feed the kids somehow so I'm here,' she said, clearly ashamed that he'd recognised her.

'Do you remember when me and Richie Richards fought over you in the playground and Mr Lewis caught us and gave us ten whacks each?' he laughed.

'That I do,' she smiled, holding her hand in front of her mouth so he couldn't see the full extent of the damage to her teeth.

'Here, Dottie, take this.' Evan fumbled in his pocket.

'I'll not take handouts, Evan Powell. From you or no man. I earn my corner. Now if you should want to take a walk with me, it'd be a different thing.'

'I would if I could,' Evan refused gently. 'But I'm waiting for my daughter.'

'Didn't know you had one.'

'I have two, and two sons. The one I'm waiting for is a nurse.'

'That must be nice. Well can't stay around here all night talking to you. See you, Evan.'

'Bye, Dottie.'

She walked off down the station yard. The Cardiff train had just come in and she hovered at the foot of the steps eyeing the men as they ran down them.

At last Evan saw a tall slim figure dressed in nurse's uniform striding across the road from the slaughterhouse.

'Bethan love?' He intercepted her as she stepped on to the pavement in front of the station.

'Dad, I . . . ' she faltered. The nerves that had been blissfully numbed and deadened since Elizabeth had begun to make all her decisions for her jangled agonisingly back to life when she saw the pain in her father's eyes.

'Look, can you spare a minute? I have to talk to you,' he pleaded.

She opened her cloak and glanced at her watch. It was no more than a formality; she'd left the house a whole hour and a half before she needed to, simply to get away from Alun. She'd woken up, forgone any thought of washing, rubbed herself over with cologne and dressed in the bedroom, stuck her head around the

359

kitchen door and said goodbye. She wouldn't even eat tea with him, telling him that she always ate in the hospital.

'We could go to Ronconis' café,' Evan said persuasively.

'All right, Dad,' she agreed reluctantly.

He went to the counter and ordered two teas while she found a table.

'You look a bit peaky, love. Do you want anything to eat?' he asked solicitously.

'The pies are good today. Fresh in,' Tina shouted from behind the counter.

'Then I'll have one please.' She wasn't hungry but she suddenly realised that she hadn't eaten all day. Still refusing to think about the baby's needs, only her own, she decided that if she was to survive the night shift she ought to put something in her stomach.

'Take the teas, Mr Powell, and go and sit down, I'll bring the pie over when it's ready,' Tina said as she pushed one into the steamer.

'Mam told you?' Bethan asked as her father sat across the table from her.

'She did.' His mouth set in a grim line. 'Beth, why didn't you come to me?' he rebuked.

'You had enough on your plate. Losing your job and everything. Mam said – '

'I don't want to hear a bloody word that your mam said,' he cursed savagely, slamming his fist into the table. Heads turned as the other customers gawped in their direction.

'Dad, please.' Embarrassed, she stared down at the table.

'Just tell me one thing. Was it your idea to marry him or your mother's?'

'Does it matter?'

'Yes?'

'He asked me. It was the only offer I had, and the way things are – '

'What about your young man?' he demanded angrily. 'Your Doctor John. He seemed a nice enough fellow. Surely if he knew the circumstances he'd come running.'

'He wouldn't, Dad,' she asserted bitterly.

Tina interrupted them, bringing over the pie and a knife and fork. She smiled at Bethan.

360

'How are things on the night shift?' she asked cheerfully.

'Fine,' Bethan replied mechanically.

The smile died on Tina's lips as Bethan turned away. She remembered the pit closures. It must be difficult for Bethan and her father, with only Bethan's wages coming into the house now. Just enough money to stop the family getting dole. She resumed her place behind the counter without another word.

Picking up the knife and fork, Bethan prodded the pie. She couldn't see what she was doing. Tears blinded her, as she remembered the last time she'd seen Andrew. The foul, cruel words he'd flung at her: 'You've dragged me down as far as I'm prepared to go.'

'He left me, Dad,' she mumbled. 'It's the old, old story. I should have known better. I'm sorry. I was such a stupid fool.' Tears fell on the surface of her tea.

He put his hand over hers. 'I didn't come looking for you to make you cry, love.' He had to struggle to keep his voice level. 'I wanted to tell you that you can come home. You don't have to stay with Alun.'

'But Mam . . . ' she began.

'Your mam's got no say in the matter,' he snapped. 'Come home, love. Where you belong. I promise I'll look after you. . . .' His voice trailed pathetically as the same thought crossed both their minds. How could he look after her when he wasn't bringing a penny into the house?

Bethan pulled a handkerchief out of her sleeve and blew her nose, wiping her eyes at the same time in the hope that no one else in the café had seen her tears. 'Alun's bought a house on Broadway,' she prattled in a forced, bright manner. 'It's been empty for a while, so it's in a bit of a state, but he intends to do it up. Turn it into a lodging house. He needs someone to cook and clean. . . . '

'So you're his bloody skivvy?'

'I'm his wife,' she contradicted with a firmness that amazed herself. 'He's promised to give my baby his name.'

'But at what price? Oh God, I wish you'd come to me with this instead of your mother.'

'Don't be too hard on her, Dad,' she whispered, remembering how kind her mother had been when she'd found her in the

361

parlour. 'She picked up the pieces when I tried to get rid of it.' She looked up. Evan was staring at her, horrified. 'I know, it was a stupid thing to do. Particularly when you think I'm half a trained midwife. But I was desperate. And when she found me, Mam didn't say one unkind word. Whatever she did, Dad, she did because she thought it was best.'

'Then you intend to stay with him?'

'I knew what I was doing when I married him. I'm not a child any more,' she declared vigorously.

He'd never been prouder, or pitied her more than he did at that moment. 'I know you're not, darling.' He spooned sugar into his rapidly cooling tea and stirred it. 'But please, Beth love, listen to me. We all make mistakes. God alone knows I've made enough in my time. But if there's one thing I've learned in nearly fifty years, it's this. There's no mistake so bad that you can't walk away from it.'

'Auntie Megan can't walk away from hers,' she blurted out unthinkingly.

'I wasn't talking about stupidity. Megan's made her bed, she's going to have to lie on it. What I'm trying to tell you, snookems, is that you only have one life. It's no good making a mess of it and sticking with the mess simply because you think it's the right thing to do. No one's going to pat you on the back or give you a putty medal for being noble. If you can't live out your life to make yourself happy, what chance have you got of bringing happiness to anyone else?'

He sat back and stared out of the window, embarrassed by the depth of feeling he'd put into his speech. It was fine enough. Pity he hadn't thought to take some of his own advice years ago.

'I know what you're trying to tell me, Dad. And I'm grateful. I really am.' She pushed the virtually untouched pie aside. 'But I married Alun because I couldn't see any other way out. And I still can't. I work in the homes. I see what happens to the unmarrieds.'

'That would never happen to you.'

'Dad, I'm beginning to think we're all one short step away from the workhouse. Alun was kind enough to take me on, and he's found a way for both of us to make a living. I owe him for that.'

'But. . . . '

'Look, I have to go. I have to make an appointment to see Matron in the morning.' She left the table, then turned back. 'Do the boys and Maud know I'm married?'

'They know.'

'Give them my love and tell them I'll see them soon.'

'I will.'

He pushed back his chair and left the café with her. 'The next few weeks aren't going to be easy for you,' he warned. 'Another day or so and the ins and outs of your wedding will be all over the Graig.'

'The sooner the better,' she said with more bravado than conviction. 'There's no going back. But thank you for offering to stand by me, Dad.'

She turned the corner, amazed at her own resolution. Perhaps she'd needed to talk to her father to sort out things in her own mind. She owed Alun for the use of his name and the respectability he'd lent to her condition. At that moment she resolved that it was her duty to pay him back in any and every way she could. Tomorrow she'd share his bed. If she closed her eyes and gritted her teeth, it wouldn't be that bad. After all, the thought of facing unpleasantness was always worse than living through the reality.

Chapter Twenty-Two

Evan waited until it was dark before he slipped out of the back door of the Graig Hotel and up the road. He looked around as he reached Phillips Street. When he was sure no one was about he climbed the steps stealthily and turned the key in the lock.

'Oh it's you, Evan Powell.'

'Good evening, Rhiannon.' He closed the front door and stepped through into the passage. 'Phyllis around?' he asked.

'Upstairs resting,' Rhiannon said tersely.

'May I go up?'

'You most certainly may not. I'll call her. Go and wait in the front parlour. And make sure you pull the curtains before you turn the light on. I don't mind telling you, Evan Powell, you're only welcome in this house because Phyllis won't allow me to make it any different.'

'Thank you, Rhiannon.' Evan closed the curtains and switched on a small table lamp in the parlour. Then he sat on the edge of the cold, hard *chaise-longue* and waited. A large, oak-framed studio photograph of Rhiannon's husband stared down at him. Below it, on the mantelpiece, stood a smaller one of a group of people crowding in front of a charabanc. He walked over to it and picked it up. The picture had been taken outside the chapel just before an outing. He studied the faces and recognised himself, his brother William, Rhiannon's son Albert, Elizabeth, Phyllis and John Joseph amongst the revellers. He, Phyllis and Elizabeth all looked so young, no older than his children were now. It had been taken the year before he'd married. Half a lifetime ago. They'd been on their way to Roath Park in Cardiff.

'Evan.' Phyllis came in moving with the slow awkward gait of a woman who's almost at full term. 'It's lovely to see you,' she murmured shyly.

'And you.' He kissed her sleep-flushed cheek, and smoothed her tousled hair away from her face.

'Sit down, won't you?'

'If Rhiannon will let me. To be honest, every time I come here half expect her to put me outside the door.'

'She wouldn't do that. She's only worried that someone will watch the back and front of the house at the same time to see who stays.'

'I know she worries about you. I won't stay long. But look ove, I've been thinking. . . . '

'So have I.' She smiled. Completely captivated, Evan watched er. She was beautiful when she smiled. Happiness softened the nes around her mouth and eyes, and lent her face a gentle adiance that never failed to warm his heart.

'Phyllis, please listen for a minute.' He took her hands into his wn. 'You know I haven't got anything.'

'No one can say I went after you for your money, boyo,' she aughed.

'Let's go away together,' he suggested recklessly.

'I can't go very far at the moment.' She patted her stomach.

'Have you still got the money I gave you from the bet I put on ddie?'

'Evan, it's only five pounds.'

'It's enough to get us away from Pontypridd.'

'To where?' she probed gently.

'Does it matter?' Anywhere, as long as it's away from here.'

'It will matter when the five pounds runs out. And while we're unning what will Elizabeth and the children do?'

'Elizabeth and the children don't need me any more. Not even Maud. She's going to work in a hospital next month. Bethan's narried. . . . '

'Bethan!' Phyllis exclaimed. Then she sensed the pain within im and fell silent.

'The boys can take care of themselves,' he continued quickly, gitatedly. 'Haydn's got a steady job and will see Eddie all right.'

'And Elizabeth?' she enquired softly.

'I couldn't give a damn about Elizabeth,' he said harshly.

'Evan, I want us to be together more than anything else in the vorld, but not like this. Not because you're angry with Elizabeth. 'hat would be for all the wrong reasons.'

'What about this little one – ' He curved his strong calloused

365

hands with their blackened, broken nails tenderly around her stomach. 'Isn't he reason enough for us to be together?'

'Not when you have other duties and other calls on you, Evan. I never intended to trap you or make you unhappy.'

'And you haven't.'

He left his chair and knelt at her feet.

'Phyllis, if I talk to Elizabeth. If I square it up with her, will you come away with me?'

'Please, sweetheart, don't make it harder for me than it already is. You know I'd like to say yes, but I'm not sure I can. Rhiannon's been good to me. I can't leave her.'

'We'll find someone else to look after Rhiannon.'

'Even if we did, running away from our problems won't solve them. Nor will five pounds keep us for very long,' she said practically.

He sank back on his heels. 'There has to be something I can do,' he said, raging at his own impotence.

She cupped her hands round his face. 'Keep on coming to see me from time to time. Like this.'

'And if I leave Elizabeth?'

'Please don't. Not on my account. We both have responsibilities. Me to Rhiannon. You to Elizabeth.'

'Then we'll never live together,' he said bitterly.

'I didn't say that.'

'Yes you did.'

The grandmother clock ticked deafeningly into the silence. He buried his head in her lap. She ran her fingers through his thick black hair, noticing many grey strands that hadn't been there a year ago.

'If we could sit like this, *Sion a Sian* in front of a fireplace most nights, Evan Powell, I'd be happy,' she murmured. 'Even if the whole world shunned me in the day, and I didn't have a penny to buy a lump of coal for the fire, or a slice of bread for the table.'

He lifted his head and looked at her. 'Do you mean that, Phyllis Harry?'

She kissed the tip of his nose, and smiled into his black eyes. 'I mean it, cariad.'

366

'Then I'll try to find a way for us to be together. I promise you I'll try.'

'The only promise I want you to make is to call in and see me whenever you can,' Phyllis replied. More realistic than Evan, she'd long since learned to be content with the cards that the fates had dealt her.

Bethan was still writing out the patients' reports when Laura walked into the office at five-thirty in the morning.

'You're early,' Bethan said, closing one of the files.

'I saw your Haydn yesterday. Beth, how could you do it? How could you marry Alun Jones without saying a word to anyone? What about Andrew?'

'He went to London.'

'Beth, did you ever look into his face when he looked at you? Even that first night when he and Trevor took us to the theatre, and I wanted him for myself. I tried every trick in the book and a few more, but he wouldn't take his eyes off you. If that wasn't love I don't know what is. The man clearly adores you.'

'It was that belief that got me into the condition I'm in,' Bethan retorted crudely.

Laura's hand flew to her mouth. 'Oh Holy Mother of God! Haydn didn't say. . . . '

'He was probably too embarrassed.' Bethan put down her pen and leaned back in her chair. She was finding it a lot easier to talk about her situation than she'd expected.

'Why didn't you tell me?' Laura demanded when she managed to speak again.

'So you could do what?' Bethan asked coolly.

'I don't know,' Laura said in exasperation. 'It's just that I thought I was your best friend.'

'You are.' Bethan smiled. A grim, wintry smile that failed to touch her eyes. 'Look on the bright side. I'm a lot better off than the Maisie Crocketts of this workhouse.'

But what about Andrew? Does he know you've married Alun?'

'No, and I doubt that he'd care.'

'Of course he'd care. He loves you. And if he knew there was a baby. . . . '

'He'd do sweet nothing. I really don't want to talk about

367

Andrew,' Bethan said petulantly. 'He left me, not the other way round. I have to think of myself.'

'So you married Alun Jones?'

'The child needs a name, Alun was kind enough to offer. No one else came forward.'

'But you and Andrew were like Trevor and me,' Laura persisted stubbornly. 'You had something special. . . . '

'He had something special all right,' Bethan said harshly. 'He had a girl who was stupid enough to open her legs when he said he loved her.'

Laura sat down abruptly. She'd come in early to give Bethan a piece of her mind, believing that Bethan had married Alun Jones on the rebound purely to spite Andrew because they'd had a silly row. Now she didn't know what to think.

'Is there anything that I can do?' she asked finally.

'You could congratulate me,' Bethan suggested flatly.

'But Beth,' Laura ventured tentatively. 'Is this what you want?'

'Whether I want it or not, this is what I've got.'

'Oh Bethan.' Laura shook her head miserably. She felt suddenly guilty for having a wedding and Trevor to look forward to.

'Please, no pity. Not from you, I couldn't stand it. It's friendship I need. Now more than ever.'

'You've got it.' Laura crushed her in an enormous hug. 'You'll always have it. I promise you.'

'Even when you're a doctor's wife and live on the Common?' Bethan tried to smile but tears fell despite her efforts. She rubbed her eyes with her sleeve. 'I'm sorry, all I seem to do these days is cry.'

'That's all right, the starch in my uniform could do with softening. And yes, I'll be your friend even when I'm a doctor's wife. That's if you'll come to my wedding?'

'Laura, I don't know,' she answered uneasily.

'Please, you agreed to be bridesmaid.'

'Not like this.' Bethan laid her hand across her abdomen.

'I'm getting married in six days not six months.'

'In six days I will be almost six months.'

'You don't look it. Are you sure?'

'You're asking a nurse who almost made it to midwife.'

'All right, I'll let you off being my bridesmaid,' Laura compromised, 'on condition you come to the wedding as an honoured guest. I hope you realise this means that I'm going to have to put up with all five of my sisters trotting up the aisle after me in their Whitsun dresses, because if I choose one the others won't speak to me for months, if ever again.'

'Please, Laura, I'd really rather not come if you don't mind,' Bethan begged.

'I do mind.'

'I couldn't face him.' Bethan didn't have to say who 'him' was. They both knew.

'I don't think he'll come,' Laura said hesitatingly. 'I made Trevor write to him. . . . '

'To tell him what?' Bethan interrupted anxiously.

'Nothing about you, I swear,' Laura reassured quickly. 'I told Trevor I didn't want him there. Not if you two weren't speaking. After all, you're my best friend and Andrew's. . . . '

'What?' Bethan broke in quickly.

'Only a friend of Trevor's. And that puts him way down in the pecking order of importance when it comes to *my* wedding.'

'Oh Laura!' A peculiar expression, half pain, half tenderness, crossed Bethan's face.

'Then you'll come?'

'I'll see.'

It wasn't the assurance Laura wanted, but she knew that for the moment it was all she was going to get.

The pride that had sustained Bethan in her encounters with her father and Laura left her, and she felt weak, tired and sick when she finally left the hospital after seeing Matron at the end of her shift. Without thinking she turned right instead of left in High Street and began to walk up the Graig hill towards Graig Avenue. She reached Temple Chapel before she realised she was going the wrong way. Feeling extremely foolish she turned and began the walk down the hill and out along Broadway. Another two weeks . . . that's all she had left in the hospital before she'd be spending every minute of every day in Alun's company.

The interview with Matron hadn't gone as smoothly as she'd hoped. Astute, and experienced in life, particularly in Pontypridd life, Matron had taken one look at her, asked if she was pregnant, and dared her to say no. Bethan had to admit it. There was generally only one reason for marriages as quick and secretive as hers and Alun's, and when she recalled the gossip she and Andrew had generated in the hospital – gossip that Matron was undoubtedly aware of – she blanched in embarrassment.

'To be honest, I'll be sorry to lose you, Nurse Powell,' Matron announced briskly. 'Good nurses who are responsible, reliable and prepared to work nights are few and far between.' Bethan wondered if there really had been a flicker in Matron's eye when she'd said the words 'responsible and reliable', or if it had been her imagination. 'But as you no doubt appreciate, I cannot have a pregnant nurse working on the wards,' she continued practically. 'Particularly the maternity ward where there's so much heavy lifting to be done.'

'I'll be sorry to leave,' Bethan apologised.

'Well at least I know why you've neglected your studies of late.'

'I'm sorry, Matron,' Bethan repeated dully.

'I suppose it's perfectly understandable, if disappointing given the circumstances. Young girls will marry. But don't allow that brain of yours to atrophy, Nurse Powell. You're an intelligent woman. Don't forget it. And should you ever want to return to nursing, please come and see me first, before applying to any other hospital.'

'I will, Matron. Thank you.'

She'd walked away, trying not to think of her shattered career – of Alun waiting for her in the dingy house on Broadway. She shuddered at the thought of what lay ahead of her that morning. The imminent prospect of sharing Alun's bed, of his sweaty, hairy body lying next to hers, of him touching her as Andrew had. Kissing her, sharing the most intimate moments of her life.

She almost turned back when she reached the slaughterhouse at the town end of the road. Then she remembered she had nowhere else to go. She thought of Hetty, and something akin to envy stirred within her. Oblivion seemed a preferable alternative to the life that stretched before her in that damp, bleak, run-down house.

She walked on along the shining, waterlogged grey pavement,

370

glancing up at the other houses in the terrace. Some were bright, clean, gleaming with new paint and freshly washed lace curtains at the windows. If it had been the old Andrew of the spring and early summer who'd been waiting for her further down the road instead of Alun, she'd be running towards him, not dragging her feet. Making plans to transform the house into a comfortable and cosy haven from the world.

She had to force herself to recall that Andrew had rejected her. That he despised her. Never wanted to see her again. It was Alun not him who was waiting. . . .

'Can't go in there, Nurse,' a young constable barked officiously as he rocked on his heels in the doorway, full of self-importance at the task that had been entrusted to him.

'I live here,' Bethan protested mildly.

'Do you now?'

'She does.' Megan's brother Huw interrupted from the porch behind him. He looked down at Bethan. 'You'd better come in, love,' he said gently. 'I think we've got some news for you.'

The young constable stepped aside. She followed Huw down the passage, squeezing past two policemen who were standing outside the open bedroom door watching Alun dress. One of them stepped inside and closed the door as she passed.

'What's going on?' she demanded of Huw. The sight of so many men milling around in uniform took her back to that fateful Sunday morning in Megan's. And all the foul, disastrous repercussions of that awful day.

'Is it all right if I tell her, Sarge?' Huw asked the same sergeant who'd supervised the ransacking of the houses in Leyshon Street.

'Go ahead.' The sergeant squinted at Bethan as he left the back kitchen. 'Haven't I seen you before, Nurse?'

'Yes,' she answered briefly, not about to volunteer information as to where.

Huw guided her into the kitchen where the kettle was just beginning to boil on the stove. Without stopping to take off her cloak, she walked over to the range, lifted it off the hotplate and picked up the hook to replace the cover.

'Don't do that, love,' Huw stopped her. 'I'll make us both a cup of tea. You look as though you could do with one. It's a long cold walk from the hospital to here in the rain.'

371

'It is,' she agreed, taking off her cloak and sitting in one of the easy chairs.

The tea caddy, sugar basin, milk jug and cups were already laid out on the table. Huw put the kettle back on to boil while he warmed the pot and spooned in the tea.

'You got married yesterday then?' he asked.

'Yes,' she answered flatly.

'Bit sudden, wasn't it?'

'No doubt you've guessed the reason why,' she retorted sullenly, resenting his prying.

'We were afraid of that.'

'We?' She looked questioningly at him as he spooned three sugars into both of the teas without asking her what she took.

'Me and my sergeant.' He handed her a cup.

'Who I marry is none of your, or your sergeant's, concern.'

'If it's Alun Jones it could be,' he said mysteriously. 'And then again from what Megan told me I never reckoned on you marrying Alun. I thought you were going out with that doctor fellow.'

'I was.'

'Tell me,' he eased his bulk into the small rickety chair opposite her, 'do you love Alun?'

'Why do you ask?'

'It could be important.'

'No,' she answered honestly, taking a sip of the strong, bittersweet tea. 'Why? Has he done something terrible?'

'To you, love, yes. Mary Bennett came down the station last night. Know her?'

'I'm afraid I don't.'

'I thought you might at least have known the name. Alun's had his feet under her table for years, if you take my meaning.'

'Is she the widow who lives down the bottom of the Graig hill?' she asked, recalling something Megan had said.

'That's the one. She heard the gossip about you and Alun yesterday, and came to see us. Appears he told her years ago that he wanted to marry her, but couldn't because he wasn't free.' He took Bethan's cup from her fingers, and enveloped her freezing hands in his great calloused paws. 'He's already married, love. Left a wife and two children in North Wales ten years ago. Never sent them a word or a penny in all that time. Not even a present

372

for the kiddies at Christmas or on their birthdays. We telegraphed Wrexham last night. There's no doubt that it's him. He even admitted it when we tackled him about it this morning. He thought he could get away with it. And knowing you, love, I'm not surprised he tried. You would make any man a wife to be proud of. I'm only sorry that I have to be the one to tell you.'

She stared at him, dumbfounded.

'It's not that you've done anything wrong,' Huw tried to reassure her, putting his huge tree-trunk of an arm round her shoulders. 'But you've still got to come down the station. Just to make a statement. There's nothing to worry about, I promise you. I'll stay with you all the time if you want me to. And afterwards I'll ask the sergeant if I can borrow a police car and driver to take you home.'

'Home?' She stared at him blankly.

'Graig Avenue,' he suggested gently.

'Alun's already married?' she repeated dully, trying to digest the enormity of what he was telling her.

'Yes.'

'Then the ceremony yesterday . . . ?'

'Doesn't mean anything, love.'

'The wedding certificate?'

'Isn't worth the paper it's printed on.'

She began to laugh. A high-pitched giggle that bordered on hysteria.

'Please, love, don't take on so.'

She bent her head and kissed Huw's bristly cheek. 'I'm not married?'

'No,' he replied, bewildered by her reaction.

'Uncle Huw, you're a wonderful, wonderful man. Don't look at me like that,' she commanded between gales of laughter. 'Can't you see how hilarious this all is!'

True to his word, Huw took charge of everything. He suggested that she pack all her belongings before they left the house, and carried her case out to the waiting police car. Alun, he assured her, had gone ahead in a police van. He steered her thoughtfully through the procedure at the station, oiling the formalities with several cups of sickly sweet, strong tea. He sat with her while she made her statement, explaining every detail in simple terms that could be easily understood, even by her, in her shocked state. He parried the sergeant's suggestion that she should see Alun, allowing her to make her own response.

It was swift, and decisive.

'If I never see Alun Jones again it will be too soon.'

The policemen who overheard her shook their heads knowingly. They saw a beautiful, wronged woman smarting from hurt pride. Not one of them realised she genuinely felt indifferent towards Alun and his fate. But she didn't see, care for or solicit their sympathy. All she could think of was that she was in possession of her own life again. She had her freedom. Penniless, pregnant, it danced ahead of her, a glittering spectre that brightened her future. At that moment she failed to see the other ghosts crowding in the wings. The shades of hunger, shame and destitution.

'Dad, please, do the rights and wrongs matter?' Bethan pleaded wearily. 'What's done is done. Can I or can I not come home?'

'Of course you can, Beth,' Evan said, ashamed of himself for keeping her and Huw talking in the passage when by the look of her all she needed was her bed. 'Look, I'll carry your case upstairs.'

'Will you take a cup of tea with us, Constable Griffiths?' Elizabeth asked as Evan left the room, struggling to remember her manners after suffering the trauma of having Bethan walk through the door with a policeman in tow, who told tales of Alun Jones and bigamy.

'I won't if you don't mind, Mrs Powell,' Huw refused, trying not to show too much interest in the cuts and bruises on Elizabeth's face. 'I've got to get back to the station. We'll probably need you in court, Bethan. You know that. But it won't be for a few weeks yet.'

Bethan sank wearily on to a kitchen chair and nodded. 'Thank you for bringing me home, Uncle Huw.'

'That's all right, love. Mrs Powell. Evan.' He passed Evan in the passage on his way out.

'Uncle Huw!' Bethan ran after him.

'Yes, love?'

374

'Have you seen Auntie Megan?'

'Yes. Last week.'

'How is she?'

'As well as can be expected,' he said uneasily, conscious of Elizabeth's disapproving eye in the background.

'She is still in Cardiff prison, isn't she? They're not going to move her?'

'Not as far as I know.'

'Next time you see her, tell her I'll be in to see her as soon as I can,' Bethan said, not even considering Elizabeth's wishes. For the first time in her life she was thinking only of herself. Of how much she wanted to talk over what had happened to her with someone who would understand. She knew of no one who would understand better than Megan.

'We'll both go and see her,' Evan echoed. 'I'll see you out, Huw.'

'Just one more thing, Uncle Huw,' Bethan smiled. 'Thank Mrs Bennett for me.'

'Who's Mrs Bennett?' Evan asked mystified.

'Perhaps you'd like to tell him, Uncle Huw,' Bethan said as she returned to the kitchen.

Elizabeth was standing in front of the tiny window staring blankly at the Richards' garden wall.

'I'm sorry, Mam,' she apologised, closing the door behind her.

'What for?' Elizabeth asked coldly. 'This has all worked out to your advantage. You never wanted to marry Alun Jones in the first place.'

'No I didn't. But if he hadn't already had a wife, you would have gained what you wanted most of all. A respectably married daughter.'

'Would that have been so terrible?' Elizabeth demanded, turning to face her. 'Tell me, what are we going to do now? No money coming into the house. You having to give up work with a bastard to keep. . . . '

'I'll tell you what we're going to do, Elizabeth,' Evan said harshly as he opened the kitchen door. 'We're going to survive. It's high time I carried the responsibilities for this family. I'm going back to work, and I'm going to bring in a living wage.'

'You – ' Elizabeth began to sneer, then a gleam in Evan's eye stopped her in her tracks. Her face was still smarting from the blow he'd given her the night before; she didn't want to risk pushing him into giving her another.

'I'm going into business,' Evan announced bluntly.

'Doing what, Dad?' Bethan ventured.

'Tatting.'

'Rag and bone man!' Elizabeth's blood ran cold at the thought of her husband shouting in the streets for people's rubbish.

'It's a perfectly legal and respectable occupation.'

'I'll never be able to hold my head up again.'

'That's as may be,' Evan said unconcernedly. 'But while you're staring in the gutter you'll be looking over a full belly.'

'And that's all that matters to you?'

'At this moment, woman, I can't think of anything that matters more.' He turned his back on his wife and looked to Bethan. 'It's good to have you home, snookems,' he said feelingly.

'It's good to be home.' She hugged her father and went to her mother. Elizabeth stood grim-faced and rigid, ready to repulse any show of emotion. Bethan pecked her withered cheek, opened the door and left the room.

'Where are you going to get the money from, Dad?' Haydn asked Evan a few days later as everyone except Elizabeth sat huddled around the range, trying to siphon off some of the warmth it radiated into their chilled bodies.

'Charlie's offered to lend me a fiver,' Evan said. 'He's a good mate.'

'Will you need as much as that, Dad?' Bethan asked, afraid that her father was plunging into more debt than he could afford on her account.

'I hope not.' Evan stretched out his legs and put his pipe into his mouth. He hadn't bought any tobacco since the pit had closed, but old habits died hard, and he stilled pulled it and his empty pouch out of his pocket every time he sat in front of the fire. 'I've taken ten bob off him to start with, that should see us right for a week. It's only sixpence a day to hire a shire horse and cart down Factory Lane. So tomorrow morning bright and early, Eddie and me will be down there picking out the best they have to offer.'

'So many people have tried tatting, Dad,' Bethan ventured prudently.

'Not where Dad and I are going to try, Beth,' Eddie said enthusiastically. 'We're not going round here. We're going where the crache live. They're the ones who can afford to throw out old for new.'

'And if we can't find any saleable junk tatting, we'll offer to cart garden rubbish away,' Evan suggested.

'Or move furniture,' Eddie chipped in.

'Powell and Sons, no carting job too big,' Haydn murmured.

'Or too small,' Evan said philosophically.

'Don't forget, Beth, I'm still working on Wilf Horton's stall as well as the Town Hall.'

'And you've got a week's money to come, Beth,' her father smiled.

'And we haven't got Maud to worry about any more,' Haydn added, thinking back to the tearful scene that morning when he and William had put Maud and Diana on the Cardiff train.

'If she sticks it in the Royal Infirmary,' Bethan commented.

'She'll stick it,' Haydn said firmly. 'She's like you. Stubborn little thing.'

'Charming.'

'So you see, Miss Pessimist, there's no problem. The finances of the Powell family are all worked out, and you and my grandson are going to want for nothing,' Evan said firmly.

'We've also got money coming in from our new lodgers.' Haydn left his chair and began to stack the dirty plates on the table.

'Mam let that room out quick,' Bethan commented.

'Mam didn't. I did.' Evan leaned forward in his chair. 'Will's had to give up Megan's house. Now the pit's closed Sam's moving on, but Charlie's staying. He and Will are going to share the front room.'

'What is Mam going to say about that?' Bethan looked from Haydn to her father.

'The same she said about my tatting,' Evan said carelessly. 'Nothing. Right, it's nearly six. I'm off out.'

'To see a man about a dog?' Eddie winked at Haydn.

'Something like that. Who's going to clear up before your mother gets back from Uncle Joe's?' Evan asked.

'Not me, I have to get to work.' Haydn reached for the mug holding the toothbrushes.

'So do I.' Bethan picked up her veil from the back of her chair.

'And I have to get to the gym,' Eddie protested.

'That settles it. You can do with one less sparring match. We lose our jobs if we're late,' Haydn pointed out logically.

'That's not fair,' Eddie complained.

'I can see we're going to miss Maud more than we thought,' Evan mused. 'You did say you were giving up work at the end of next week, Beth?'

Bethan looked at her father. She was grateful for the sentiment, but miserably conscious of her forthcoming dependence on her already overburdened family. 'I'm not sure, I went to see Matron about staying on for a bit this morning.'

'I hope she said no,' Evan countered sternly. 'You're soon going to have your work cut out for you, love.' He laid his hand on her shoulder as he left his chair. 'So if I were you I'd get all the rest you can, while you can.'

'She said I could do relief work on the unmarrieds ward starting next week. It's not strenuous. . . . '

'I'd rather you didn't.'

'It'll only be for another two weeks at the most, Dad.'

He glanced at the kitchen clock. 'I've got to go. We'll talk about it tomorrow night. And you,' he pointed to Eddie, 'no staying on down that gym too late. We've got work early in the morning,' he warned.

'Work! Tatting is only a stopgap, Dad. I'll make my money boxing.'

'Not this week you won't. Table, boy. Don't forget.'

378

Chapter Twenty-Three

'You're not worried about money are you, Sis?' Haydn asked as they left the house. 'You heard Dad. We'll all take care of you.'

'You shouldn't have to.'

'After all the months you took care of us? Come on.'

'I've made a right pig's ear of my life, haven't I?'

'There's some who would say that.' He looked at her and they both laughed. 'Hello, Glan,' he greeted him as he walked around the vicarage corner towards them.

'Haydn,' Glan said abruptly.

'Is it my imagination or did he cut you?' Haydn demanded, temper flaring in his nostrils as he turned his head to look back at Glan.

'It doesn't matter.' Bethan hooked her arm into her brother's and pulled him around the corner.

'Beth. . . . '

'It really doesn't matter,' she repeated warmly.

'How much of that has gone on?'

'Enough for me to find out who my friends are.'

'I'll kill the bastard. . . . '

'Haydn, he's not worth bothering with. Please. You can't kill half of Pontypridd.'

'Half? Beth, I had no idea. Honestly.'

'And some of the other half aren't quite sure whether to cut me because I'm pregnant and have no husband. Or because I'm pregnant and was a party to bigamy. Or because I went around with a doctor who dumped me.'

'It's that bad?'

'I lied to Dad earlier. Matron didn't find me that job on the unmarrieds ward as an extra. She moved me there last night because the women in the ward complained about having to be nursed by me. And even with Matron's protection I'm only there now because they're desperately short-staffed. The minute they find a replacement I'll be out.'

379

'Is that why you won't go to the wedding on Saturday?'

'That's part of it,' she admitted reluctantly.

'And the other part is Doctor Andrew John?' He barely managed to speak Andrew's name.

'Laura doesn't think he's coming. But whether he is or he isn't, I'd really rather go to bed. I'll need the sleep after a week on nights.'

'Laura'll miss you.'

'She'll have you and Eddie to make up for it.'

They walked on down Llantrisant Road, towards Griffiths' shop. Jenny was on the pavement outside, handing a large box to the delivery boy. She turned and waved to them.

'Jenny!' The upstairs window of the shop banged open, and her mother stuck her head out of the window. 'Jenny, I want you. Inside this house now.'

'In a minute, Mam.' Refusing to look up at her mother, Jenny smiled at Haydn, mischief glowing in her pale blue eyes. 'Haydn and Bethan are walking down the hill and I want to have a word with them.'

'Jenny Griffiths, you get back here this minute,' her mother shrieked.

'I will, Mam, after I've talked to them,' she shouted defiantly, walking away from the shop and up the hill to meet them.

'Hello, Bethan,' she said quietly, as she slipped her hand into Haydn's.

'You're still going out with this brother of mine then, I see.' Bethan's voice came out sharper than she'd intended. It was a struggle to hold in check the emotion Jenny's friendly greeting elicited.

'He just can't seem to stop following me around,' Jenny answered quickly, with a possessive glance at Haydn.

Bethan saw that the Jenny standing next to Haydn had come a long way from the shy girl who'd sat on the edge of her seat in the New Inn and answered Andrew's questions in monosyllables. 'Well I've got to get down to the hospital,' she said briskly, wanting to get away from them and their obvious loving happiness. The sight of it hurt more acutely than she would have believed possible, in her present emotionally battered state.

'Hang on a minute, I'm coming, Beth.' Haydn pulled away from Jenny.

'You've still got a few moments, and I really do have to go,' Bethan insisted. 'See you in the morning,' she called over her shoulder.

'She's a big girl, Haydn,' Jenny prompted, holding him back. 'Let her have a little time to herself.'

'I don't like her walking down the hill alone.'

'She has to, sooner or later. You can't protect her for ever.'

'I can try.'

'Haydn, she's not going to want you around for the rest of her life,' Jenny said in exasperation. 'Not like me,' she murmured in a softer voice.

He read the message in her eyes. 'Will I see you tonight?' he asked, forgetting Bethan for a moment.

'I could leave the store-room door open for you after the show,' she teased.

'Does that mean you will?'

'Perhaps, if you promise to be nice to me.'

'Will it be safe?' he asked anxiously.

'Mam'll be snoring by the time you walk up the hill. And Dad sleeps soundly enough now he's taken to going to the Morning Star every night to drown his misery at losing Megan.'

'Then I'll see you about eleven.' He squeezed her hand.

'I'll hold my breath.'

'Not too hard I hope,' he smiled, winking as he left.

Bethan walked down to the hospital along Albert Road, a side street that ran parallel to and behind Llantrisant Road. She knew she was being cowardly. But she'd rather not face people until she had to, and Albert Road was never as busy as the main thoroughfare at this time of night.

She felt strange, peculiar, as though something was missing. Then it came to her. She was alone, albeit in the street, for the first time since she'd returned home. She hadn't realised until that moment just what a protective shell her father and her brothers had woven around her. Haydn escorted her down to the hospital every night, and Eddie had been waiting for her at the main gates every morning, with the excuse that he'd come down early to try to get work in the brewery and there'd been none going. She'd been suspicious, and in view of the number of people who suddenly seemed unable to see her, or hear her simple greetings, grateful. Too grateful to resent their mollycoddling.

She paused for a moment and stared at the rows of terraced houses clinging to the hillside as it swept down to the Barry sub railway station and the Maritime colliery. The chill of winter was in the air, but precious few chimneys smoked. It seemed madness: people going cold and hungry for want of coal and the food that wages could buy when the colliery buildings lay, blackened, deserted and lifeless like the husk of a plundered coconut, discarded, useless, with nothing more to give. She went on slowly, thinking about the future that waited in store for the Graig, her family and herself.

For the first time she considered the needs of the child that was growing all too rapidly within her. Her father was, in his own clumsy way, trying to make things easier for her with his frequent and proud references to his coming grandson. But in so doing he was forcing her to do the very thing she least wanted to: making her see the child as an accomplished fact, a being in its own right who in the space of a few short months would take over and totally disrupt her life.

She hadn't been so afraid since the night she'd tried to abort it. She felt as though she were losing everything she'd worked for, everything she valued and had striven so hard to gain. Her career. Her prospects of qualifying as a midwife. Andrew . . .

Andrew. She pictured him laughing next to her in the Empire Theatre. Driving in shirt-sleeves through warm, green, sun-dappled countryside. And then as he'd been that last time in the hospital. Well dressed in his blue suit, white collar and tie; smelling of cologne and soap, his chin smooth, freshly shaved. Incredibly handsome, but for a contemptuous sneer that contorted his full and sensuous lips. She was sure that at that moment he'd hated her. Everything that had passed between them, all the experiences and loving they'd shared had meant nothing to him. Nothing at all.

He'd seen her as an embarrassment. Something dirty to be washed from his life, his mind . . . and his bed. Yet even now, after everything that had happened her senses responded alarmingly to the remembrance of their lovemaking. She gripped her fingers together. If she must think of Andrew at all, she had to think of the way he'd looked when he told her that she'd dragged him down as far as he was prepared to go. If she didn't . . . if she didn't, then what?

She'd told her father and Laura the truth. Andrew and her – it was the old, old story. Probably the oldest in the world. She had to thank her lucky stars that her family were prepared to keep her. And as for Andrew – she looked back and saw cold calculation in everything he'd done. Seduction behind every kindness he'd offered her. Lust, not love, in his caresses.

She walked on as her battered emotions groped their way painfully back to awareness. Only this time it was hatred not love that bore her forward on the crest of life.

It was nearly midnight when Andrew left the illuminated platform of Pontypridd station and walked down the steps to street level. The porter who struggled behind him shouldering his trunk groaned as he finally dumped the box at the foot of the steps.

'There's no taxis, sir,' he crowed, stating the obvious.

'So I see.' Andrew looked around the dimly lit, deserted yard and wished he'd telephoned his father from Cardiff. But then he'd been wary of disturbing his mother. She could well be alone if his father'd had to go out on a night call. And no one was expecting him to arrive until tomorrow.

Not for the first time that day he cursed the impulse that had led him to take a half-day holiday from the hospital and run off to Paddington station. Impulse, or image of Bethan? Her face came vividly to mind, just as it did at least a dozen times a day. It haunted him.

'You want to put your trunk in the stationmaster's office, sir?' the porter suggested.

'Would it be possible to use the telephone?' he asked, hoping to catch Trevor in his lodgings.

'I'm not allowed to let the public near the telephone, sir,' the porter said officiously. 'Besides, it's all locked up and I haven't got the key.'

'Looks like I've no choice but to leave my trunk in the stationmaster's office,' Andrew replied resignedly.

'Righto then, sir. I'll put it away for you.'

Andrew watched as the man heaved the trunk into the ticket office on the ground floor and locked the door behind him. Afterwards he pulled the compacted steel trellis across the wide doorway and secured it with a padlock.

'Safe as houses until five-thirty tomorrow, sir.'

'And then?' Andrew enquired wryly.

'It's got your name on the label, sir, Doctor John. They're not likely to hand it over to anyone else.'

Andrew tipped him sixpence.

'Thank you, sir. If there's nothing else, I'll be off. I'm on early shift again tomorrow.'

'Thank you for your help. Goodnight.'

'Goodnight, sir.'

Andrew picked up his doctor's bag. Even that was heavy. Too heavy to lug all the way up to the Common, he thought as he took the first step forward. The Tumble, so alive with people during the day, was devoid of life. The lamps flickered over grey, vacant pavements and the shuttered façades of Ronconis' café and the New Theatre. There was nothing for it but to keep going.

The air was freezing, so he thrust his free hand into his pocket. He paused for a moment outside the station and looked up the Graig hill, wondering if Bethan was working nights. He was sorely tempted to walk up to the homes. But then what if she wasn't on the ward? How could he possibly explain his presence there when he hadn't worked in Pontypridd for weeks?

Turning his back on the Graig hill he faced downtown, and forced himself forwards.

Eddie had lingered late in the gym built behind the Ruperra Hotel. Much later than usual. Joey Rees had arranged a sparring match for him with Bolshie Drummond. Bolshie had been a first-class boxer, and unlike most of the old-timers in the gym, not that long ago. The match had gone on for hours. They'd all lost track of time. Especially him, and he should have known better, because ever since Joey had trusted him enough to clean up and lock up after everyone left he rarely got home much before twelve. Tonight it would be nearer one o'clock. And that was bound to set Mam off.

384

He quite enjoyed staying on in the gym by himself. He liked walking around the ring imagining himself winning bouts. He liked being able to look at the photographs of past champions without being disturbed, but most of all he liked having his gym subs waived and the five shillings a week Joey slipped into his pocket. It was worth handing it over to his mother intact to cut down on her continual nagging about money.

He ran as far as the fountain in the centre of town then, hands on knees, paused to breathe in deeply. He heard someone walking towards him. He looked up expecting to see Megan's brother Huw, or one of the other policemen. Instead . . . instead . . . his heart thundered, and his mouth went dry.

A man was walking towards him, no ordinary man. Even under the shadowy lights of the street lamps he could see that he was wearing an expensive overcoat. One he knew was made of cashmere wool. He was carrying a small case in his hand and his hat was pulled low over his forehead.

'Doctor John?' he ventured.

Andrew stopped. 'Yes.' He squinted into the darkness. 'Do I know you?'

'Too bloody royal you do.'

The first punch caught Andrew unawares and sent him reeling backwards. He dropped his case and cried out as the back of his head connected painfully with the pavement. Eddie allowed him no time to recover. He jumped on top of Andrew. Hauling him up from the pavement, Eddie smashed into Andrew's jaw with his clenched fist.

'In God's name,' Andrew mumbled through loosened teeth, as he desperately attempted to defend himself. It was useless, the attack had been too quick, too sudden. His opponent had all the advantage. A boot connected with his ribs.

'You bastard. You smarmy bastard. That's for what you did to my sister.' Eddie was sobbing and oblivious to the fact. 'She's in one hell of a state and you . . . ' Eddie thrust forward. His toe connected with the soft part of Andrew's stomach.

'I love Bethan,' Andrew protested through a haze of pain. 'I've come back to marry her,' he mumbled, lost in a red and black fog of anguish. 'Please, please . . . I want Bethan. . . . '

A whistle blew. The blows ceased. He heard the sound of feet running away. But all he was capable of doing was lying where he'd fallen on the spittle and dog-fouled pavement, curled in excruciating torment.

Chapter Twenty-Four

Elizabeth was woken by a hammering on the door. She put out her hand and touched Evan as he left the bed.

'It's all right, I'll see to it.' He reached down to the floor for his trousers. 'It's probably one of the boys. Had too much to drink.'

'They'd keep quiet, not make a racket if they were drunk,' Elizabeth said, unable to conceal her fear. Bethan could have had an accident at the hospital. Eddie could have been hurt in a fight. Haydn – oh God, not Haydn! She shivered at the thought of anything happening to her favourite.

'They wouldn't keep quiet if they were too drunk to find the key in the door,' Evan said baldly. 'Stay there, girl, I'll be back in a minute.'

He flicked on the light and checked the time on the battered alarm clock on the bedside table. The hands pointed to three-thirty. When he opened the bedroom door, the hammering began again. Haydn stepped out on to the landing.

'Do you want me to see to it, Dad?'

'No, I will. Is Eddie in his bed?' Evan asked as an afterthought as he was half-way down the stairs.

'I didn't look,' Haydn replied truthfully. 'I'll check now.'

'Who's there?' Evan demanded irately, and somewhat ridiculously considering that the door had its key protruding from the lock.

'Huw Davies.'

Evan opened the door, shivering in the blast of cold air that rushed into the passage. 'What's wrong?' he asked, staring at Huw's uniform. 'Official visit, is it?'

'I'd rather talk in your kitchen if you don't mind,' Huw said, glancing up at Haydn who stood white-faced on the stairs.

'He's not there, Dad.'

'You'd better come in, Huw.'

Huw lifted off his helmet and stroked his bald head nervously.

Pulling the edges of her dressing gown close together Elizabeth left her bedroom.

'What's wrong?' she demanded.

'In the kitchen, Elizabeth,' Evan said, leading the way. He switched on the light and walked over to the stove. Opening the door he poked life into the coals. 'Tea, Huw?'

'When I've done perhaps.'

'Well, sit yourself down, man.'

Huw took the easy chair Evan pointed to. Elizabeth and Haydn entered. Sitting quietly on the hard, wooden kitchen chairs, they turned their faces expectantly to his.

'They brought your Eddie into the station an hour ago,' Huw explained bluntly, without embellishment. 'He attacked a man.'

'Is he hurt?' Evan demanded.

'Not your Eddie. He's fine. The one he had a go at is a mess. We had to call the police doctor out to see to him. By rights he should be in hospital. But he wouldn't go. Leastways he wouldn't when I left an hour ago.'

'Who did he attack?' Haydn asked shrewdly.

'Doctor John. Doctor Andrew John.'

Evan gripped tightly at the poker in his hand.

'Your Eddie,' Huw continued, 'he could go down for a long time on this one.'

'Can we see him?' Evan demanded.

'In the morning. He's already been charged, Evan. He's going to need a solicitor.'

'We've no money for one of those,' Elizabeth retorted quickly.

'Quiet, woman,' Evan hissed, holding his head in his hands. He tried desperately to think.

'You going back to the station now, Huw?' he asked.

'Yes.'

'I'm coming with you.'

'Me too,' Haydn said, jumping up.

'You're staying,' Evan said firmly. 'Bethan will need fetching in a few hours. And someone has to stay here with your mother.'

'Why me?' Haydn replied without thinking.

'Because you're the only one here,' Evan said harshly. 'Go on, boy, back up to bed. As soon as there's any news I'll get word to you. You'd best go on up too, Elizabeth,' he said in a gentler

388

tone, remembering that Eddie was every bit as much her son as his.

'I'll just make Huw a cup of tea while you dress, Evan,' she said stoically, adopting the role she'd had most practice in. That of martyr.

'I warn you now, they'll not let him go without setting a bail too high for you or anyone around here to pay,' Superintendent Hunt insisted dogmatically as he faced Evan from behind his desk. He'd had a bad night. Hauled out of his warm, comfortable bed just after he'd fallen into a deep sleep by a panic-stricken telephone call from the station. Dr John's son had finally had his head cracked by the brother of the pretty nurse he'd courted and abandoned to the tender mercies of a bigamist. His emotions were divided between pity for the pathetic, duped girl, admiration for Eddie for giving Andrew John what he deserved, and a desire to punish the lad at the same time for setting on the doctor in the middle of the night and disturbing his rest.

'How much will it be?' Evan pressed tentatively.

'The amount's for the magistrate to set in the morning.'

'Can I see Eddie?'

Instead of answering, the superintendent glared eagle-eyed at Huw who was hovering close to the door. 'You've had quite a lot of favours between one thing and another with your family lately,' he cautioned bluntly. 'Go — Davies,' he jerked his head towards the door. 'Take him down to the cells to see his son. But no more than five minutes. And you stay in the cell the whole time. The last thing I need is an attempted cell break. As it is, my neck's stuck out so far it's likely to drop off with the next change of wind.'

Eddie didn't look up from the floor as the door to his cell opened. He sat, stiff, immobile on the edge of the bare planks of the wooden bunk. The temperature in the basement was uncomfortably low; but seemingly oblivious to the cold, Eddie hadn't attempted to make use of the blanket folded on the boards next to him. His jacket, belt, braces and shoelaces had been taken and he was dressed only in a thin, collarless cotton shirt and summer trousers. His laceless shoes and the turn-ups of his well-worn

389

trousers were spattered with blood, his knuckles red from burgeoning bruises.

'Are you all right, son?' Evan sat down on the bunk next to him.

'They shouldn't have dragged you down here. Not at this time of night,' Eddie said truculently.

'If you're in trouble I want to help.'

'I'm not sorry for what I did.' Eddie lifted his face, clearly unbowed and unrepentant. 'If they'd let me get near the bastard, I'd do it again. I only wish I'd done it last spring when he first started messing with our Bethan.'

Huw stepped inside the cell and pulled the door to, lest anyone overhear them. 'That's not the line to take, Eddie,' he warned seriously. 'Not when you're seeing the magistrate first thing in the morning. You gave that doctor a good going over. Cracked ribs, cracked skull, he's in a right mess. And the way they'll see it is that he's crache, and you're as good as a professional boxer.'

'I couldn't give a damn what they see,' Eddie retorted defiantly.

'If you tell them about Bethan,' Huw began doubtfully, 'they might go a bit softer on you.'

'No,' Eddie interrupted quickly. 'She's been through enough.'

'You don't seem to understand. You could go to jail. For a long time,' Huw advised bluntly.

'I'd be happy to swing for the bloody swine. And I would be swinging if I'd had enough time to put him where I wanted to. In a box.'

'Eddie, please, this kind of talk isn't going to help you or Bethan.' Evan put his arm round his son's shoulders. Eddie was cold. Cold as ice.

'I mean it, Dad.' Tears rolled down Eddie's face. 'I mean it,' he repeated, raising his arm and wiping his nose and eyes on the sleeve of his shirt. 'I'm not sorry.'

'Time to go, Evan.' Huw opened the cell door.

Unlike Eddie, Evan had many regrets. But his biggest one when he left Eddie alone in the cell was that he hadn't chanced upon Andrew John before his son.

'Bethan?' Sister Thomas walked into the ward and called her into the office.

390

'You're early.' Bethan hung the patients' duty sheets back on to a nail hammered into the wall and followed her. 'I'm not quite ready for the change-over.'

'There's no time for the change-over.' She hung her cape on the back of the door. 'Matron wants to see you in her office. Now.'

'I'll come back afterwards, shall I?' Bethan asked as she lifted down her own cape.

'I think Matron has other plans for you. She told me to make sure you took everything with you. Your cape, your bag. She could be moving you back on to maternity,' Sister Thomas smiled. 'If she is, good luck, and thanks for the help.'

Bethan gathered her things together and left the building. The grey light of early dawn was just beginning to streak across the sky. It promised to be a fine, dry autumn morning, if a little cold. She hoped that the weather would hold until Sunday for Laura's wedding. Shivering, she walked quickly across the yard. The door to the office was open and Matron was already behind her desk. Bethan checked her watch. It was seven o'clock; a full half-hour before the day shift officially started.

'Come in, Nurse Powell, and close the door behind you.'

Bethan did as she was asked and sat on the same hard chair that she'd occupied when she'd last been called to see Matron. The day she found out she'd qualified as a nurse.

She looked back on the thoughts that had occupied her mind then. Ideas of advancing her career – getting enough money together to buy Haydn and Eddie suits, ways to avoid dancing with Glan at the hospital ball. So many changes. So much had happened in the space of two short seasons. She felt like an old, old woman when she recalled the girl she had been. And all the changes including the ageing process had stemmed from Andrew, who'd been waiting for Squeers to allocate him a second nurse. She wondered if her life would be any different now if she'd been working on the men's ward instead of maternity.

'I'm sorry, Nurse Powell,' Matron said briskly, facing an unpleasant situation the only way she knew how, 'but I'm going to have to let you go.'

'Let me go,' Bethan echoed in amazement. 'But I'm leaving at the end of next week.'

'You *were* leaving at the end of next week,' Matron contradicted. 'I had a telephone call last night from the chairman of the Hospital Board. They've found a replacement for you. You may go immediately. Here,' she opened her desk drawer and withdrew an envelope, 'this is for you. Payment for services rendered to date and a little extra.'

'But yesterday you said. . . . '

'I think this is for the best, Nurse Powell,' Matron said kindly. 'After all you really should be resting more at this stage.'

'And after the baby's born,' Bethan pressed. 'You said that I might be able to come back.'

'Get in touch with me by all means.' Matron evaded the question. 'But I'm not sure there'll be a vacancy. Goodbye and good luck.' She rose majestically, shook Bethan's hand and ushered her through the door, closing her out into the corridor.

Hugging the envelope to her, Bethan walked away in bewilderment. Something must have changed since she'd last talked to Matron. But what?

When she saw Haydn's tall, fair figure lounging against the gatehouse she ran to him, too wrapped up in her own affairs to notice the expression on his pale, tired face.

'Haydn, they've laid me off. I haven't a job any more. . . . '

He put his arms round her and told her as gently as he knew how to what Eddie had done to Andrew John. Bewildered no longer, she understood everything. Only too clearly. There'd been no Hospital Board appointment of a replacement nurse. Just one short quick telephone call to Matron from Dr John senior. She ripped open the envelope Matron had given her. Inside were two five-pound notes. Haydn only just stopped her from tearing them up. He was anything but proud of the way he did it.

'We may need them for our Eddie's defence,' he muttered practically.

'There you are, darling.' Isabel John removed the lunch tray that the maid had brought up earlier, and gently smoothed the satin coverlet over the guest bed that Andrew was lying in. 'You should feel a little better by tonight,' she murmured soothingly.

'For goodness' sake, Mother,' he snapped irritably. 'It's only a mild concussion.'

'And cracked ribs,' she emphasised.

'Cracked rib,' Andrew corrected bad-temperedly.

'Dreadful.' His mother shook her head briskly as she fussed with the trunk that Dr John senior had arranged to have brought up from the station. 'I don't know what the world's coming to when a man can't walk down the main street of his home town in safety.'

'I do,' Andrew said shortly. 'I had it coming to me. I didn't exactly treat his sister very well.'

'If I remember rightly you treated her extremely well,' Isabel protested indignantly, watching him carefully out of the corner of her eye. 'Took her to nice places. Introduced her to all the right people.'

'And left her high and dry, knowing that she loved me.' He couldn't look his mother in the eye. Love between a man and a woman was something they'd never discussed in a personal context.

'Loved you? Really, Andrew, you're deluding yourself. The girl barely waited for you to leave town before getting married.'

'Married? Bethan? Come on, Mother, don't try that one on me. I don't believe it.' He rejected the news contemptuously.

'Well, perhaps it wasn't quite that soon after you left. I think it happened two or three weeks ago. Mrs Llewellyn-Jones told me all about it.'

'She would,' Andrew commented scathingly. 'And who exactly is Bethan supposed to have married?'

'Apparently a man who was lodging with her family. At least that's what Mrs Llewellyn-Jones heard. A miner like her father.' She slowed her speech, conscious of saying too much, too fast. She wanted to get the revelations just right, so he wouldn't ask any questions of anyone else while he was in Pontypridd. He'd told her he only had four days' leave. Trevor was getting married tomorrow so he wouldn't see him. And really there wasn't anyone else. At least not anyone who'd talk about Bethan Powell. 'Anyway they've opened a lodging house down Broadway,' she concluded briskly. 'So please, darling, don't go upsetting yourself over a girl like that. She simply isn't worth it.' She picked up the tray from the floor. 'Will you be all right with the maids if I go out? Normally I wouldn't dream of leaving you, but the Reverend

Price has called an emergency committee meeting of the Distress Fund. . . . '

'Go ahead please, I really would like a long sleep.'

'Well, if you're sure, darling. I'll be as quick as I can. An hour or two at the most.' She stroked the hair back, away from his bandaged forehead.

'I intend to sleep longer than that.'

'I'll see you later. Arrange a nice dinner to be brought up.'

'I'll get up for dinner.'

'We'll see what your father has to say about that. Sleep well, darling.'

Andrew lay back on the pillows and stared at the whitewashed ceiling listening to his mother's footsteps as she descended the stairs. He couldn't believe it! He didn't want to believe it. And he didn't. But he found it equally difficult to believe that his mother was lying. He knew she'd never liked Bethan. He just didn't realise that the dislike ran deep enough for her to fabricate an entire story. Lowering the standards of behaviour and integrity she'd adhered to all her life.

The last thing Eddie had shouted at him before he'd lost consciousness had been that Bethan was in a hell of a state . . . 'One hell of a state'.

Confused, needing to know more, he fought his instinct to rest. He waited until the front door opened and closed. The Distress Fund committee meeting would well and truly buzz with gossip this afternoon, he reflected sourly. A few minutes later he rang the bell.

'You wanted something, sir?' Mair knocked on the door and opened it a crack as though he were a wild animal that would bite.

'Yes, Mair.' It didn't occur to him to ask Mair whether Bethan was married or not. His mother had brought him up too well to see servants as people with lives and minds of their own. 'Would you make a telephone call for me to Doctor Lewis. You do know how to use the telephone?' he added as an afterthought.

'Of course, sir,' she said, offended.

'Tell him I need to see him as soon as possible. It's very urgent. Can you remember that?'

Trevor was packing in his rooms when the call came. Another five minutes and he would have left for the house that he and Laura had rented in Graig Street, opposite St John's church. It wouldn't have a telephone for another two weeks and three days – all the honeymoon that he'd managed to squeeze out of Andrew's father.

'It's good of you to come. I know you must have things to do for the wedding tomorrow.'

'I was in the middle of moving out of my digs into the new house,' Trevor said ungraciously.

'Are you and Laura going away?'

'To London for a week. She's never been there.'

'You should have told me, I could have arranged a hotel. . . . '

'All done. I knew of a good place close to Marble Arch.'

'Hope you have a good time.' Smarting at Trevor's dismissal of his offer of help, Andrew waved a bandaged hand at the surroundings. 'I'd rather be in my own rooms,' he said, changing the subject. 'But Father insisted on putting me in here, so he and Mother could keep an eye on me.' He realised Trevor was watching him with a professional eye. For all of his efforts to appear normal, he knew his speech was slurred, like that of a drunk. And quite apart from his throbbing head, his bandaged ribcage stabbed into his chest every time he drew breath.

'I saw your father briefly in the hospital this morning. He said you've got concussion and a cracked rib. Considering Eddie's talents, you're lucky.'

'Very,' Andrew agreed drily. 'I think he was out to kill me.'

'That's hardly surprising,' Trevor commented coolly.

'Look, won't you sit down?' Andrew asked as he struggled to sit up.

'I can't stay long.'

'I know. It was good of you to come.' He fumbled on the bedside table for his cigarettes, holding out the case to Trevor. 'It hurts having to ask this, especially when it's a question that I of all people should be able to answer, but I didn't know who else to get in touch with.'

'If I were you I'd lie down. You're not making much sense.'

Trevor took two cigarettes. He lit them with a lighter Laura's father had given him and handed one back to Andrew.

'I need to know how she is. I don't need you to tell me I don't deserve to. I treated her abominably that last night.' Andrew puffed nervously at his cigarette, avoiding Trevor's eyes. 'I wrote to her. Three letters. She didn't answer one of them. I don't blame her, not really, not after what I said. . . . '

'You wrote to her and she didn't reply?'

'Not a word. That's why I came back a day early. I hoped to straighten things out between us before your wedding tomorrow. I behaved like a bloody fool.' He drew hard on the cigarette and tapped the ash out into a tray on the floor. 'I should never have left for London the way I did. But my father said – ' he looked up at Trevor – 'no!' he said vehemently. 'No, that really would be the easy way out wouldn't it? Blame him. Blame everyone except the person most at fault. Me. The simple truth of the matter is I went away thinking I'd soon get over her. But I didn't realise what I had,' he murmured softly. 'Not then. Not until weeks later. You could say I didn't really appreciate her until I'd lost her. I thought I'd find another girl to take her place.' He laughed derisively. 'I found plenty all right. But not a one to touch her. There wasn't anyone who could come anywhere near her.'

'And now, after everything you've done, you've come back to carry on where you left off?' There was incredulity as well as contempt in Trevor's voice.

'I hoped to,' Andrew said defensively. 'I thought I had a chance. She'd told me she loved me. I still love her. . . . '

'My God.' Trevor turned on his heel, opened the window and threw his cigarette outside.

'Trevor, what's wrong?' Andrew pleaded. 'I know something's happened, but no one will tell me anything. Mother gave me some cock and bull story about Bethan getting married. . . . '

'It's true.'

'It can't be!' Andrew protested. 'She loved me. She cared for me. . . . '

'Oh she cared for you all right. That was the bloody trouble.'

'She really is married?' Even Andrew's lips were white, bloodless.

'You bastard!' The vehemence in Trevor's voice hit Andrew with a greater force than Eddie's blows. 'You walked away leaving her destitute, and now you've got the gall to lie there and ask me questions about her marriage.'

'Destitute? She had her job. . . . '

'For Christ's sake, man. Do I have to spell it out for you? She tried to keep it a secret from everyone, but I found out when she fell down the stairs in the hospital . . . ' He faltered, remembering the reason for her fall. 'Afterwards she told me the truth. That you went to London to get away from her and the baby.'

'The baby?' Andrew stared at him dumbfounded.

'The baby. Your damned baby. Why else do you think she'd marry a man like Alun Jones? She wanted to give it a name.'

'My God.' Andrew felt as though the room was spinning around him. 'Do you think I'd have left her if I'd known there was a baby?'

Trevor stared at him. 'Didn't you know?'

'No.'

It was such a flat, blunt denial Trevor couldn't help but believe him. 'She said she'd told you. That you'd gone to London to get away,' he finished slowly.

Andrew lay back stiffly on the pillows. 'Do you really think so little of me?'

'You must admit you couldn't wait to go. You even asked me to take her a letter and say goodbye for you.'

'I did, didn't I?' he murmured as if he was talking about someone else not himself. 'God, how she must hate me. Not to have said a single word . . . Trevor, how is she?' he pleaded.

'As well as can be expected. I haven't seen her for two days. But I do know that she was given her cards and her pay at the hospital this morning. It's not done for a nurse to have a brother who beats up the Senior Medical Officer's son.' He couldn't resist the gibe.

'Then she's still working?'

'Until this morning.'

'What about . . . about her husband?' he asked, choking on the word.

'Alun Jones? He's in jail,' Trevor admitted sheepishly, regretting the impulse that had made him want to see Andrew squirm.

'He was arrested the morning after the wedding. Apparently he had a wife already in North Wales.'

'Then she's not married?' Andrew stared at him keenly.

'Not legally, no.'

'Did she love . . . did she. . . . '

'I've told you all I know,' Trevor said finally, as he moved restlessly towards the door. 'She doesn't confide in me. After Alun was arrested, the family closed ranks around her. You know what they're like.'

'I can imagine.' He lifted the bedclothes back. 'She's living with them now?' He sat up and swung his legs out of bed.

'You don't think for one minute she'll see you?'

'Eddie will when I go to the police station to drop the charges against him. I just hope he'll listen to me. And take her a message.'

'I doubt it,' Trevor observed realistically. 'You'd be better off lying there until you can think straight and talk coherently.'

'Do me a favour?' Andrew said grimly, wincing as he opened the wardrobe door and reached for a shirt.

'What?'

'It's nothing too dreadful.' Andrew stripped off his pyjama jacket. 'Go downstairs and call me a taxi.'

'The police station is on my way back to the Graig. If you're set on going there anyway, I suppose I could drive you down seeing as how you're incapable.' He smiled at Andrew for the first time.

'That would be good of you. Just one more thing?'

'What?'

'Do up my shoelaces, there's a good chap. My head hurts like hell when I bend down.'

'This is most irregular, sir,' the duty sergeant protested.

'Not at all,' Andrew said evenly. 'Don't you understand? There was no fight.'

'But. . . . '

'No "buts" either, Sergeant.' Andrew smiled wanly as he leaned against the high desk in the reception room. 'I fell over and hit my head. The boy was trying to help me.'

'But he ran off when our man came.'

'Very possibly to avoid the type of accusation he's facing now.'

398

'You expect me to believe this fairy story?' the sergeant demanded aggressively.

'I was there, Sergeant,' Andrew pointed out calmly. 'You weren't.'

'And this gentleman?' Sergeant Thomas looked at Trevor.

'Offered to bring me down here. I have a concussion.' Andrew pointed to the bandage on his head. 'I didn't think it safe to drive myself.'

'And you're sure you want to do this, sir?'

'How many times do I have to tell you? I'm absolutely sure that there are no charges for the man to answer to. If I'd been fully conscious last night they wouldn't have been made in the first place.'

'If you'll take a seat, sir,' the sergeant moved out from behind his high desk, 'I'll get the paperwork.'

The 'paperwork' turned out to be half a dozen forms of interminable length, each of which seemed to require at least three signatures to a page.

'He will be released straight away?' Andrew asked as he signed the last one.

'As soon as we can bring him up from the cells,' the sergeant replied suspiciously. He wondered if the doctor had some sort of private revenge lined up for young Powell once he left the security of the police station.

'I'd like to see him if I may,' Andrew said, reading the sergeant's thoughts. 'I'd like to thank him.'

'Thank him, sir?'

'For coming to my assistance.'

'I'll ask if he wants to see you. If he does I'll bring him here.'

Trevor waited until the sergeant left before speaking out. 'Wouldn't it be better to wait until you can be sure he's calmed down? Eddie's always been a hothead, from what Laura's told me.'

'I have to see Bethan, and the quickest way to her is through Eddie. Trevor. . . . '

The door opened and Eddie, jacket slung over one shoulder, stood framed in the doorway.

'Come back for more, John?' he threatened viciously, raising his fist. 'I'd like to kill you here and now. . . . '

'No fight?' Sergeant Thomas queried disbelievingly, pushing his bulk between Andrew and Eddie.

'No fight, Sergeant,' Andrew said flatly. 'Mr Powell has clearly been upset by spending a night in the cells. A natural enough reaction from an innocent man. I'd like to apologise, Eddie. For everything,' he emphasised warmly. 'If I'd known what was happening last night you wouldn't have been put in the cells.'

'You. . . . '

The sergeant pushed Eddie into a corner so Trevor and Andrew could walk past. 'You'll have to sign for your things,' he told Eddie sharply.

'Come near me again if you dare, John,' Eddie called out savagely. 'Five minutes. That's all I need. Five minutes and you're dead.'

'Now what?' Trevor asked as they walked into the car park, which was bounded by low grey walls built of the same stone as the police station.

'Drop me off at the railway station, and I'll get a taxi.'

'Home?' Trevor asked hopefully. When Andrew didn't answer, he said, 'You're going up there aren't you? To Graig Avenue?'

'I have to see her.'

'I doubt you'll manage that. The rest of her family are likely to be as friendly as Eddie.'

'I have to at least try.'

'Get in. If you're hell bent on killing yourself you'll need a doctor along with you.'

Andrew sat slumped in the front seat as Trevor drove slowly up the Graig hill. He pulled his hat down low, to hide his battered face and avoid recognition. The streets were teeming with people: women and children hauling heavy bags of vegetables and offal up from the market; boys hanging around the outside of shops, barefoot, bare-headed, hoping to earn an extra penny or two running errands for the shopkeepers; groups of men congregating around lamp-posts, hands in pockets, caps pulled down over their eyes; idlers who didn't want to be idle; miners with no money in their pockets and no prospect of earning any.

'If I park in Graig Avenue you'll have every neighbour in the street nosing at the car,' Trevor commented. 'This really isn't a good idea.'

'Drop me off at the vicarage.'

'I've a better idea. Why don't I ask Laura to go down there and see her for you?'

'Would she?'

'I don't know,' Trevor replied honestly. 'But I think Laura's a better bet than trying to get past her brothers or her father.'

He stopped the car outside Laura's house in Danycoedcae Road. Even when he was standing on the pavement he could hear feminine giggles and raised voices of excitement. 'I think there's a crowd of women in there. I'll go by myself and ask her.'

'So Laura hates me too?'

'Afraid so,' Trevor said honestly.

'Well that's understandable. I don't like myself very much at the moment either,' Andrew said philosophically, unable to keep a trace of self-pity from his voice.

Trevor closed the car door, walked up the steps to Laura's house, turned the key and stepped inside the front door.

'Mamma mia!' Laura's mother, bulk quivering, came down the passage to greet him, blocking his path with her ample figure. 'Don't you know it's unlucky for the groom to see the bride the day before the wedding?'

'That's the morning of the wedding, not the day before, Mama,' Laura walked out of the back kitchen. She looked quizzically at Trevor. 'Hello, sweetheart, you haven't come to tell me that you've changed your mind have you?'

'Nothing like that,' Trevor smiled, kissing the top of her head and wanting to kiss a whole lot more. 'Is there anywhere we can talk?'

'In this house?' She stared at him in astonishment. 'There's the y bach.' Grinning at his uncomfortable look, she relented. 'I was joking.' She stuck her head round the door of the front parlour. 'Gina, Tina, out for five minutes,' she barked.

'What's the matter, Laura? Can't wait until you're alone with him tomorrow night?' Gina giggled at the blush that was spreading over Trevor's cheeks.

'Less of your cheek, madam.' She pushed them out of the room and pulled Trevor in. 'Can't close the door I'm afraid,' she

401

apologised. 'Not even with the wedding tomorrow, Mama and Papa wouldn't stand for it.'

'I've got Andrew outside in the car,' he blurted out.

'You've got *what*?'

'Ssh, not so loud. He's just been to the police station to drop charges against Eddie.'

'Least he could do,' Laura said unforgivingly.

'He wants to see Bethan.'

'What for? So he can insult her and leave her all over again?'

'Laura, he says he didn't know about the baby, and I believe him.'

'Yes, well, that's the difference between us, Trevor. You're gullible. I'm not.'

'And if he's telling the truth?'

'Even if he is, which I don't believe for a minute, Bethan's got her head screwed on the right way. She knows when she's well off. She won't want to see him again, take my word for it.'

'Can't you persuade her?'

'Why should I try?' she demanded indignantly.

'She loved him once. He wants to marry her.'

Laura snorted sceptically.

'Won't you at least go and see her?' Trevor coaxed.

'There's no point. When I left her half an hour ago she was going to bed. And Haydn and her mother are standing guard. They'll never let me wake her.'

'Laura, it's his baby.'

'He should have thought of that when he left her.'

'I think he's really sorry.'

'I'll believe that when I see it.'

'Then you will see him?'

Caught in a snare of her own making she went to the window and looked out. 'Where is he?'

'In the car.'

'Oh no he isn't.'

Trevor joined her and looked through the bay. 'Damn him,' he muttered. 'He wouldn't bloody well wait.'

Chapter Twenty-Five

Andrew pulled the collar of his coat up until it met the brim of his hat and knocked on the Powells' front door. He had to knock three times before he heard the sound of footsteps echoing over the flagstones in the passage.

'The key's in the door,' a voice shouted in exasperation. When he didn't turn it the door was wrenched open. Haydn stared at him in total disbelief. 'You've got a bloody nerve coming here!' he exclaimed when he recovered from the shock.

'I would like to talk to Bethan,' Andrew ventured, summoning up all his courage.

'Well she doesn't want to talk to you,' Haydn retorted belligerently.

'Then your father. It's really important.'

'Who is it, Haydn?' Elizabeth called out from the kitchen.

'Nobody.'

'It's Andrew John, Mrs Powell. May I see you for a moment?'

The silence that greeted his request closed around him and Haydn, immuring them in a tense world of red shadows and threatening, imminent violence.

'Now can you see that you're not wanted here? And if you try setting foot on this doorstep again I'll finish what my brother began last night.' Not trusting himself to remain within striking distance of Andrew a moment longer, Haydn slammed the door in his face. He leaned back against it, breathing heavily.

'Haydn?' Bethan stood at the top of the stairs, her long night-gown flowing round her ankles, her hair ruffled from the pillows, her eyes puffy from crying. 'Was that who I think it was?'

'Go back to bed, Bethan.' Haydn went to the foot of the stairs.

'Was it?' she repeated.

'Yes, and he's got a bloody cheek coming round here. But don't worry, Sis, I sent him packing. He won't be round again.'

Bethan returned to her bedroom, but she didn't climb back into bed. Instead she pulled the curtains aside and looked down

403

at the street. Andrew was standing in the middle of the unmade road in front of the house. She withdrew quickly, a host of conflicting emotions surging within her. She'd seen enough to know that Eddie'd done some damage. She'd noticed the bandage on Andrew's hand and beneath his hat; his pale face and bloodless lips. But she consoled herself with the thought that he must be all right to be walking around – better than Eddie who was still in jail.

Why did he want to see her? Why? After what he'd said to her the last time they'd spoken she had nothing to say to him. Nothing at all.

Andrew saw the curtains in the bedroom twitch and guessed that it had been Bethan who had moved them. He lowered his head and looked up and down the street, uncertain what to do next. As he was deliberating, the door in the garden wall opposite opened and Evan Powell emerged on to the street.

'Mr Powell,' he said eagerly.

Evan stared at him blankly for a moment. Then anger dawned as he recognised Andrew. 'You're the last person I expected to see standing outside my house,' he said heatedly.

Refusing to be intimidated or put off, Andrew pressed his unexpected advantage. 'I'd like to talk to you for a few moments if I may, Mr Powell.'

'Why?'

'Please, I know what you must think of me but it's important. Not to me, to Bethan.' He waited patiently for Evan's reply.

'All right, boy, I'll talk to you,' Evan relented gruffly. 'But not here. In the Graig Hotel around the corner. I'll be down in five minutes. The back bar.'

'Thank you, sir. I'm very grateful.'

Despite his thumping headache Andrew almost ran down the street. He entered the hotel through the double doors at the front, and looked down the dark central passageway that divided the building into two. Bars opened out either side of him, typical valley pub bars that gleamed with polished mahogany, shining brasswork and highly coloured, leaded light windows. He glanced into both: one was a men's bar, the other a lounge. He knew there was a jug and bottle that opened from a side entrance. But he could see no sign of a back room.

'Can I help you, sir?' the landlord asked, through a serving hatch cut into the passage wall.

'I've arranged to meet someone in the back bar, but I can't seem to find it.'

'Through there.' The landlord pointed past the stairs.

'Thank you.' Andrew had been wondering if Evan had deliberately led him astray. 'Could I have two pints of beer please?'

'If you pay now, I'll bring them through.'

Andrew counted out the correct money from the loose change in his pocket, and walked on.

The room was empty as Evan knew it would be. Dark and gloomy, it was lit by one small, high window that was overshadowed by the garden wall of Danygraig House. The dark brown paintwork and the wallpaper of pinkish chintz were overlaid with a thick nicotine-stained patina from the smokers who congregated in the room most nights. Andrew sat on an uncomfortable, overstuffed horsehair chair, pulling it close to an iron-legged, marble-topped table.

It was ten minutes, not five, before Evan arrived and he came carrying his own pint.

'I bought you one, sir,' Andrew said, rising as Evan walked into the room.

'I'd rather drink my own,' Evan said bluntly. 'Well, say what you want to, and quickly. This place will be closing for the afternoon in a quarter of an hour.'

'I've dropped all the charges against Eddie. He should be home soon.'

'Do you expect me to be grateful to you for that?'

'No. Not at all,' Andrew stammered, realising what he must have sounded like. 'I just thought you'd like to know. You must be worried about him.'

When Evan didn't say anything, he stumbled on, tripping over his words, wishing he could think clearly, that his head didn't hurt quite so much. 'I know I treated Bethan badly. . . . '

'You don't have to state the obvious,' Evan said briefly.

'I was sorry as soon as I left. I wrote to her, three times. When she didn't answer my letters I didn't know what to think. I came

405

home yesterday hoping to see her before Laura and Trevor's wedding. I intended to ask her to marry me. . . . '

'Bit bloody late.'

'Mr Powell, I take full responsibility for what I did to Bethan, but I swear to you I would never have left her if I'd known about the baby. I didn't find out until this afternoon when Trevor told me. Please, Mr Powell, all I want is to see her. Explain why I left if I can – and try and straighten all this out between us.'

'You're not short of guts, Andrew John. I'll give you that,' Evan said grudgingly before he drained his pint.

'Please, Mr Powell. I know I'm not welcome in your house. But I'll be in the New Inn tonight between six o'clock and eight. I'll wait for any message she might want to send me. Would you please just tell her that?'

'Aye, I will.'

'There's just one more thing,' he said wretchedly. 'Tell her . . . tell her that I love her,' he said simply. 'That I never stopped loving her. Not for one minute.'

'He said he wrote to me?' Bethan looked at her father through dark-rimmed eyes.

'Three letters.' Evan pushed his feet out on to the hearthrug, accidentally kicking Haydn and Eddie.

'I never got any letters.' She looked at Elizabeth, who was stirring a pot on the range. 'Mam, did any letters come for me?' she asked. 'Mam?' she asked again when Elizabeth failed to answer.

'Yes. But they came too late,' Elizabeth replied without turning around. 'You'd already married Alun.'

'You could have given them to me afterwards, when I came home,' Bethan reproached.

'I could have, if I'd remembered them.'

'Can I have them now?'

Elizabeth went to the dresser drawer. Pushing aside a neat pile of clean, ironed and darned tea towels she extracted three envelopes and handed them to Bethan. Bethan stared at them for a moment, turning them over in her hand, reading the address on the other side. Then she looked at the postmarks. The first

406

had come two weeks before she'd married Alun. The second a week later, the third had been posted the day before her wedding.

'I kept them from you because I believed it was for the best, Bethan,' Elizabeth said coolly. 'I thought you had a respectable married life ahead of you with Alun. This one's crache. And they don't marry girls like you.'

'He's offering, Elizabeth,' Evan contradicted angrily.

'Mam's right for once,' Eddie said unexpectedly. 'He's a marmy sod.'

'Language,' Evan reprimanded strongly. 'And after the scrape you've just got out of, you'd better keep your mouth closed and your fists for the ring.'

'Yes, Dad,' Eddie said meekly, elated because it was the first time that his father had recognised boxing as an essential part of his life.

'You don't intend to take up with him again do you, Beth?' Haydn demanded warily.

'No,' she said shortly, rising from her chair. She went to her mother and kissed her withered cheek. 'I know you did what you thought best, Mam, and I'm grateful for it,' she said kindly. 'I understand. I really do. I might even have done the same thing myself if I'd had a chance to.'

She left the room, carried the letters upstairs, lay on her bed and opened the first one.

Dear Bethan,

I'm sorry. Those two pathetic words are totally inadequate. They don't express a millionth part of the remorse I'm feeling right this minute. I love you, I miss you, and I want you, here in this cold miserable room of mine right now. Then I could tell you to your face that I didn't mean any of those things I said in the hospital that last night. Please, Bethan, can you forgive me?

If you came here, to London, we could rent rooms around the corner from the hospital. You'd like London. There's so many things to do and see, parks to walk in, fine buildings to look at, so much I could show you, museums, art galleries . . . we'd have to visit those because they're free and we wouldn't have much money. It will take me a few years

407

to get my career to a stage where we'd be comfortable but I could put up with a little discomfort as long as it was with you. I know now that the only thing that matters to me is you. Bethan, if you want to just sneak away from Ponty- pridd, write to me and I'll send you a train ticket. Just say the word . . . .

The letters danced before her on the page, especially the final line –

Bethan, I love you.

I love you – The words seared into her mind as she opened the other two letters. They were in the same vein, except for questions as to why she'd ignored the first one. She could see Andrew's hand penning them, read the selfishness behind the sentiments. Selfishness that she'd refused to recognise when they'd been together. He would have liked nothing better than for her to sneak away unnoticed from Pontypridd, and join him in London. And if he was talking marriage now, it was only since he'd found out about the baby. There was mention of rooms that they could share in the letter, but no marriage. She left the papers on the bed and went to the window, half expecting to see him still standing in the street. But it was empty, the thickly gathering twilight casting shadows on to the stone-strewn roadway.

Weak, selfish, pampered, spoilt, sensual, kind – loving . . . all those adjectives and more could be applied to him. She felt she knew him better than he knew himself. And for all his arrogance, all his faults, she knew now that she loved him. Would always love him.

She closed the curtains, switched on the light, opened her dress- ing-table drawer and took out the chocolate box. Lifting the lid she resisted the temptation to explore the treasures it contained and laid the letters on top. After she closed it, she pulled down an old ribbon of Maud's that was hanging over the mirror and tied it round the box. Taking her time, she fashioned the end into a neat bow before stowing it away again. Memories and memory box. She felt as though she were physically consigning Andrew John to her past.

'Bethan?' Her father knocked on the bedroom door.

'Come in,' she called out as she closed the drawer.

Evan didn't enter the room. He opened the door and remained on the landing. 'I forgot to tell you. He told me to say that he'd be in the New Inn tonight between six and eight if you wanted to send a message.'

'Thank you, Dad.'

'You've no intention of seeing him?'

'No.'

'You know your own mind best.'

'He left me,' she said bitterly, 'not the other way round.' She tensed herself, forcing the tears back that hovered behind her eyes. 'He hurt me. He hurt me. . . . '

'And now you're afraid to see him in case he does it again. Is that it?'

'Something like that.'

'Bethan love.' He went up to her and put his arm round her shoulders. 'I told you the night you married Alun that you only have one life. The best advice I can give to you is live it. Do whatever you want to do without being afraid of anything or anybody. Even failure.'

'You think I should see him, don't you?'

'I think you have to make your own mind up about that.'

'You must have an opinion,' she pressed.

'He's one unhappy young man who was brave enough to face me, Eddie and Haydn today in an attempt to get a message through to you. His last words to me in the pub were "Tell Bethan that I love her. That I never stopped loving her." '

'Then I'll go.'

'Not for me, love. You don't get out of it that way. Your own decisions and your own mistakes, remember. Besides I've only met him twice. I don't know him well enough to tell when he's lying. If you go and see him, end up marrying him and make a pig's ear out of your life you could come back to me and say "I took your advice, Dad, and look at the mess I'm in." I'm not taking responsibility for a decision like that.'

'Oh Dad,' she laughed as she buried her head in his shoulder. 'What would I do without you?'

'I hope you won't have to, girl. Look, Bethan, we all love you, and we'll take care of you, never fear. Only you can know if you want this chap or not. It appears he's there for the taking, but so is what you've got here. Suit yourself, girl, and make at least one person happy. Yourself.'

He looked over her head to the lights that burned behind Rhiannon Pugh's wall. He knew then that he'd never take his own advice. Caught between two women he'd live out his life as they dictated and as he lived it now. Facing Elizabeth's daily disappointments and bitterness, and handing out crumbs of comfort to Phyllis because that was all she was prepared to accept from him. Any more would upset the safe little world she had cocooned herself and Rhiannon in.

'We all love you, snookems, but in the end you have to do what's right for you,' he murmured. 'If you don't you'll make a dog's dinner of your life like your mother has. And,' he closed his eyes to Rhiannon's light, 'and like I have,' he whispered softly. So softly she failed to hear him.

It was deserted in the New Inn at six o'clock when Trevor walked in with Andrew.

'She won't come, you know,' he said bluntly.

'I know. But anywhere's better than home. I couldn't have sat with my parents for another minute.'

'Trouble?' Trevor raised his eyebrows. 'They didn't approve of you dropping the charges against Eddie?'

'That and the few home truths I told them about getting Bethan pushed out of the Graig Hospital this morning.'

'I see. Happy families.'

'Take note. It could be you one day.'

'Not me, I'm going to be the perfect father.' He faltered as Andrew paled. 'I'll get the drinks. What do you want? Whisky?'

'With concussion?'

'Should go nicely.'

'I'll stick to a small beer.'

Trevor went to the bar and carried the beer and a whisky over to the unobtrusive corner table that Andrew had chosen.

'Some bachelor party. I'm sorry,' Andrew apologised.

'I'm meeting Laura's brothers at seven in the Vic. If you want to come you can.'

'Would I be welcome?'

'With Laura's brothers? I don't know,' Trevor replied honestly. 'Feelings run pretty high in that family, and they're all fond of Bethan. You know what Graig people are like about one of their own.'

'I'm beginning to find out.'

'I invited Evan Powell, Haydn, William, Charlie and Eddie as well. Haydn can't come until later because he's working, but it's a fair bet the others will. Can you see yourself drinking round the same table as them?'

'Not really. Well here's to you and yours.' Andrew raised his glass, and pushed a small package across the table.

'What's this?'

'Wedding present. Sorry I won't be able to make it tomorrow but I'm catching the early train to London.'

'I thought you had four days off.'

'I have. I want to spend a couple of them looking for a new place. It's time I moved on from Fe and Alec's house.'

Trevor tore open the brown paper package and stared at the notebook it contained. He looked quizzically at Andrew.

'I've booked dinners and tickets to seven shows in London. The venues, dates and times are all there. Do turn up, I've already paid for them. I telephoned a chap who works in my bank this afternoon to arrange it all.'

'I don't know what to say.'

'Laura deserves a decent honeymoon. And we all know that your idea of an evening's entertainment is a newspaper full of fish and chips and an evening's stroll.'

'Not my idea. My pocket's.'

'Enjoy yourself. On me. Time for one more?' he asked, picking up the glasses.

'Quick one.'

She walked in when he was at the bar. Her old black coat hid her figure, but she was thinner in the face, paler than he remembered.

'I'll see you, Andrew.' Trevor walked into the next room, where Ronnie and William were sitting, full pints in front of them.

'You brought bodyguards?' Andrew said caustically. 'For pity's sake what did you think I was going to do to you in here of all

411

places?' He could have kicked himself. He hadn't meant to open on this tack.

'Ronnie brought me down, and he's taking me back. Eddie and Haydn guessed where I was going and they wouldn't let me come on my own. Not on a Saturday night, and after what happened yesterday I wouldn't let either of them come with me. This is a compromise.'

'Can I get you something?'

'No thank you,' she said politely. 'I can't stay very long. Ronnie wants to go back in a few minutes. Big night, Trevor's bachelor party.' She shrugged her shoulders. 'And I promised to spend the evening with Laura.'

'A coffee then?'

'No really, nothing thank you.'

'It appears I can't buy any Powell a drink,' he commented lightly, remembering her father and the pint he'd refused that afternoon.

Their conversation might have been one spoken by total strangers. But the quick, nervous movements of her hands and his eyes betrayed their emotions. She sat in the chair Trevor had vacated. 'You wanted to see me?' she asked.

'I'm sorry. . . . '

'I know. I read your letters. I didn't get them until today.'

'I meant what I said in them. I know it's late to ask, but will you marry me?' he said quietly, with dignity.

'Because I'm carrying your child?'

'No. Because I love you. God, when I think of what you've gone through . . . marrying Alun Jones – '

'He didn't touch me,' she snapped defensively. 'Not in the way you did.'

'Beth, you don't have to explain what happened. Not to me. I blame myself for all those dreadful things I said. Please, can't we put it behind us? Won't you come to London with me tomorrow? We'll get married there as soon as I can arrange it.'

'You think it's that simple? Do you realise you're asking me to uproot myself from everything I know? My friends. My family. . . . '

'I know I'm asking a lot.'

'You're asking for too much,' she said firmly. 'My brothers

hate you. My father's desperately trying to be fair, but he doesn't like you, not really. . . . '

'Beth, that's your family,' he protested. 'Not you.'

'Your family despise me. It's good of you to ask, Andrew. Particularly given my background. . . . '

'Bethan!'

'Please let me finish. It wouldn't work, Andrew. We're from different worlds.'

'We could live in the same one in London.'

'Even in London there's bread and dripping and melba toast and caviare. I'm one, you're the other.'

'You don't love me any more?'

'I don't trust you any more, and London's a long way from help and my family.'

'I'd look after you, Beth. And you could come back whenever you wanted to. It's only a day away by train.'

He wanted to change her heart and mind so much he had to restrain himself from reaching out and physically carrying her off there and then. He racked his memory, trying to remember eloquent phrases. Words with which to convince her that he was sincere.

'When you left, my family were wonderful,' she said quietly. 'I realised then how lucky I was to have them. I know them. I trust them, and my father and brothers have promised to look after me and the baby after it's born. With their support I can build a life for both of us. A good life. I hope to go back to nursing if I can. My mother will take care of the baby.'

'You're shutting me out,' he said despairingly.

'No. I'm choosing the safe option. One I know will work. One I'm familiar with.'

'You'll let me pay maintenance or whatever it is?'

'For the baby when it comes.'

'I could give you some money now.'

'I'd rather you asked your father to influence the Hospital Board to look kindly on any future job applications I make.'

'Beth, I'm sorry, I had nothing to do with that.'

'I know.' She rose from her chair. 'Goodbye, Andrew, I really do have to go.'

'You sure you won't reconsider? I'm leaving on the eight

413

o'clock train tomorrow. If I thought there was a chance that you'd change your mind. . . . '

'There's no chance.' She held out her hand. He took it, but instead of shaking it he held it tight.

'Beth, does it have to end like this?'

'Goodbye, Andrew,' she said loudly. William and Ronnie left their seats. Moving close to Bethan they stood behind her, waiting.

'Goodbye, Bethan,' he whispered forlornly, as he watched her leave.

'Drink?' Trevor held out a fresh half-pint.

'No thank you. I have packing to do.' He smiled. 'Have a good wedding tomorrow.'

'I'll try,' Trevor replied, feeling utterly helpless as he watched Andrew walk out.

'You didn't have to wait up for us, love,' Evan said as he walked into the house with the boys and Charlie.

'I couldn't sleep. Never can after a stint on nights. And judging by the state of you, it's just as well I've made some tea. You could all do with something to water it down with.'

'Water nothing down,' Haydn grumbled. 'I've only had two pints.'

'You're the only one who did,' she said, watching Charlie prop William up as he tripped over the step up to the washhouse.

'If you think we're bad,' William slurred, 'you should see Trevor.'

'Oh God, what have you done to him?'

'Nothing Laura won't be able to fix tomorrow,' William laughed maliciously.

'Quiet,' Bethan commanded, 'or you'll wake Mam up and then we'll all be for it.'

It took the combined efforts of Evan, Charlie and her to get the three boys to bed. But she didn't feel tired, not even after she cleared up the dishes they'd left.

'You saw him then?' Evan sat in his chair pulling on his empty pipe, watching Beth as she moved around the room.

'Yes.'

'And?'

'And nothing, Dad. After what he did I just don't trust him any more.'

'I see. Just answer me one thing, love,' he said slowly. 'Do you love him?'

'I thought I did,' she answered sharply.

'And now?'

'I don't know,' she said wearily, sitting on her mother's chair.

'You've sent him packing?' She nodded her head. 'I hope you're not making a mistake, Beth. It's just that the way you spoke to the boys just now, you put me in mind of your mother.'

Bethan knew he would never have made such a damning comparison if he'd been sober.

'Don't grow old and bitter before your time.' He tapped his empty pipe from force of habit against the range as he left his chair. 'It blights lives.'

He could have added 'like ours have been blighted by your mother', but didn't. The inference hung unspoken in the air, like smoke from damp coals smouldering on a fire.

Andrew paid the porter to carry his trunk and case up from the car to the train. The platform was cold and windswept, the rain snarling in great sheets under the overhanging roof, soaking his socks and the legs of his trousers.

'Pity about the weather,' he said as he huddled into his coat. 'Trevor and Laura deserve a better day.'

'I wish you wouldn't rush back this way,' his father fussed.

'I want to get back.'

'But you're not one hundred per cent, and there's no real hurry. You said so yourself. You can hardly work with that head of yours.'

'I'm well enough. And I want to use the next couple of days to look for an apartment. I can't live with Fe and Alec for ever.'

'You've upset your mother. She's very disappointed.'

'I'm sorry she's disappointed. But the time has come for me to make my own decisions, and run my own life.'

'So I see.'

'Dad, there's really no point in discussing this any more.'

'If all this nonsense had been about a decent girl I might have understood it. But about the daughter of a miner . . . . '

415

'Here's my train.' Andrew breathed a sigh of relief, shook his father's hand and followed the porter to the first-class carriages behind the engine.

'We'll see you soon,' his father called out as Andrew stepped on board.

'I'll write,' he replied briefly.

Goodbyes said, he settled down in a compartment that was mercifully empty. His trunk safely stowed above him, he stretched out and opened his small doctor's case, extracting the newspaper he'd bought from the boy outside the station. Underneath it he saw a book, the same book he'd tried and failed to read the night he'd gone to the hospital to tell Bethan it was over between them. He'd never read it, and he didn't want to start now. Next to it he'd packed her photograph. He picked it up and unwrapped it from the scarf he'd wound around the glass to protect it. The whistle blew. The train moved slowly out of the station. Disconsolately he stared out of the window – at the blackened brick walls that led out of the station; the dirty moss-green and bracken-spattered hillsides; the tips, slag heaps, smoking chimneys of the terraced houses . . . everything reminded him of her. He was leaving Bethan behind and he felt as though his heart was being wrenched out of his body.

The stations passed and his newspaper remained unread. Treforest . . . Taffs Well . . . .

'I only had enough money for third class so if you want to sit with me you're going to have to come down in the world, Doctor John.' Bethan stood in front of him in her shapeless black coat. A cardboard suitcase in her hand. A ridiculous cloche hat on her head. 'I'll be honest with you. I'm not at all sure that I'm doing the right thing. I've a feeling that I've just made the biggest mistake of my life. I meant every word that I said to you last night. . . . '

He rose to his feet and silenced her by placing his mouth over hers. She dropped the suitcase as he gathered her into his arms.

'I love you, Bethan Powell,' he murmured after he'd kissed her. 'More than you'll ever know.'

She clung to him, burying herself in the old familiar sensations:

416

the warmth of his body close to hers, the smell of his tobacco mixed with his cologne, the feel of his fingers stroking her neck.

'I love you too, Andrew John, but is love enough?' she asked seriously. 'We're different beings from different worlds, you and I. We've nothing in common. I'll never be a lady like your mother and you'll never be a collier like my father.'

'We could try being ourselves.' He pressed his cheek against hers.

'I mean it,' she murmured, reeling from the hunger he aroused within her. 'You should know what you're taking on. All I own in the world is in that suitcase, and the whole lot isn't worth much more than a pound. I'm six months pregnant, and practically penniless. . . . '

'Tickets!' the conductor called as he walked down the corridor towards them.

'I have to go,' she said. 'Back to third class where I belong.'

'I could pay the difference.' He swung her down on to the seat beside him.

'You could, but you still won't make a silk purse out of a sow's ear,' she smiled.

'Then how about we split the difference, my love, and move down to second class?'

She laughed softly as he swung her into his arms.

'Is this where married life begins; with you demoting me to second class?' he asked.

She looked at him with her enormous dark eyes, and held out her hand. 'Yes please, Doctor John,' she murmured quietly. 'Shall we go?'